# THE
# LIMERICK CITY LIBRAR

Phone: 407510
Website:
www.limerickcity.ie/library
Email: citylib@limerickcity.ie

**This book is issued subject to the Rules of the L**
**e Book must be returne' not later then the last**
star

## HERE

# THE
# THINGS
# THAT
# KEEP US
# HERE

CARLA BUCKLEY

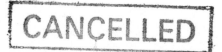

First published in Great Britain in 2010 by Orion Books,
an imprint of The Orion Publishing Group Ltd
Orion House, 5 Upper Saint Martin's Lane
London WC2H 9EA

An Hachette UK Company

1 3 5 7 9 10 8 6 4 2

A CIP catalogue record for this book is
available from the British Library.

ISBN (Hardback) 978 1 4091 1307 2
ISBN (Trade Paperback) 978 1 4091 1308 9

Printed and bound in the UK by CPI Mackays,Chatham ME5 8TD

The Orion Publishing Group's policy is to use papers that are natural,
renewable and recyclable products and made from wood grown in sustainable
forests. The logging and manufacturing processes are expected to
conform to the environmental regulations of the country of origin.

www.orionbooks.co.uk

*For my sister, Liese*

# THE
# THINGS
# THAT
# KEEP US
# HERE

## BIOLOGICAL SCIENCES (BIO)
## ACTIVE FUNDING
## OPPORTUNITIES

---

The National Science Foundation (NSF) is urgently seeking research proposals related to the surveillance of avian influenza virus H5N1 among U.S. migratory birds. NSF is expediting solicitation, review, and funding, and will accept abbreviated proposals. Please consult the website for submission guidelines.

*National Science Foundation*

# PROLOGUE

*I*T WAS QUIET COMING HOME FROM THE FUNERAL. TOO QUIET. Ann wished Peter would say something, but there was just the soft patter of rain and the wipers squeaking back and forth across the windshield. Even the radio was mute, reception having sizzled into static miles before.

As they crossed into Ohio, Ann turned around to see why Maddie hadn't called it, and saw her seven-year-old had fallen asleep, her head tipped back and her lips parted, her book slipped halfway from her grasp. The first hour of their trip had been punctuated by Maddie asking every five minutes, "Mom, what does this spell?" Ann leaned back and teased the opened book from her daughter's fingers, closed it, and put it on the seat beside Maddie. Kate hunched in the opposite corner, a tangle of brown hair falling over her face and obscuring her features, the twin wires of her iPod coiling past her shoulders and into her lap.

Ann turned back around. "The girls are asleep."

Peter nodded.

"Even Kate. I don't know how she can possibly sleep with her music going."

He made no reply.

"Do you know I caught her trying to sneak her iPod into the

church? I don't think giving her that was such a great idea." When Peter remained silent, she went on. "It's just one more way for her to tune everyone out."

He shrugged. "She's twelve. That's what twelve-year-olds do."

"I think it's more than that, Peter."

He said nothing, simply glanced into the rearview mirror and flicked on the turn signal, glided the minivan around the slower-moving vehicle in front of them.

It was an old argument, and he wasn't engaging. Still, there was something else lurking beneath his silence. She read it in his narrow focus on the highway and along the tightness of his jaw. "You all right?" Of course he wasn't.

"Just tired. It was a long weekend."

A long, horrible weekend. All those relatives crammed together in that small clapboard house, no air-conditioning, Peter's mother wandering around, plaintively asking everyone where Jerry was. "I'm glad your brother made it."

"Yep."

Not *yes*, or *yeah*. *Yep*. He never talked like that. He was throwing up warning signs, telling her to back off. But fourteen years of marriage made her plow straight through anyway. "Everything okay between you two?"

"Sure."

So he wasn't going to tell her. "Bonni said she saw you and Mike arguing."

He glanced at her. So handsome her breath snagged for a moment—the strong, tanned planes of his face and the beautiful blue-green of his eyes that Kate had inherited. Now he looked drawn and older than his forty years. He returned his attention to the road. She wanted to cup her hand to his cheek, but he was sending out those keep-away signals.

She crossed her arms. "Mike doesn't think it was an accident."

"Mike doesn't know what he's talking about."

"He has a point, though. It *is* strange your father wasn't wearing blaze orange."

"What are you suggesting, Ann? Suicide by hunter? Give me a break."

She should have, but she couldn't let it go. The questions piled up inside her, three days' worth of strangers whispering, three days of Peter's mother tugging at Ann's sleeve. "Things have gotten so bad with your mom, Peter. I had no idea. This morning, she told Maddie that her parents must be looking for her and that she'd better run along home. You should have seen the hurt look on Maddie's face." Ann shook her head. "It just breaks my heart. We can't leave her like this."

"Bonni will check in on her."

"Checking in's not enough. She needs round-the-clock care."

The rain had stopped. A watery sunshine glinted through the clouds. Peter switched off the wipers. "I don't want to talk about it. Especially with the girls in the car."

"You mean the girls who are sound asleep?"

"Ann."

Maybe she *was* pushing too hard. She leaned her forehead against the window and watched a hawk spin circles high above. "You sure you need to go into the field tomorrow? Maybe one of your students can go in your place."

"I've got no choice. Hunters are nervous enough right now without me sending in some twenty-year-old."

"Because of the bird flu?"

"Exactly."

"Do you think you'll find anything?"

He shifted position. "Probably. But it's not an isolated case that's a problem."

"It's a cluster of cases."

"Right."

The hawk grew smaller and smaller, a smudged dot that eventually disappeared, no doubt to perch on a branch somewhere and watch for prey. "I forgot to tell you, things were so rushed Friday, but that interview came through."

"At Maddie's school?"

She nodded. "I go in next week to meet with the principal. I keep thinking, what if I don't get the job? Then I think, what if I do?"

"You'll be fine."

"I haven't worked in, God, twelve years."

"How hard can it be?"

She flashed him an irritated look, but he was staring straight ahead. "It's not finger painting and Popsicle sticks, Peter."

"I just meant I know you can do it."

"It's theory and history, too. What if I teach above their heads? What if they're bored? What if Maddie hates me being her art teacher?"

"There must be some part of you that's looking forward to it."

Did she want to talk about this? "It's the whole . . . thing. I'm not sure I can do it."

"You mean art in general?"

"Exactly."

He heaved a sigh. She heard the impatience in it. "It's been a long time," he said.

Nine years. An eternity. A blink.

"Maybe you're ready, Ann."

"In other words, I *should* be ready."

He lifted his hands briefly from the steering wheel. *I give up.* "Whatever."

The hills undulated by, the woods fiery red and burnt orange. She caught glimpses of barns and houses set high and solitary. She wondered about the people who lived there, if they were lonely.

"It'd be good for you to go back to work," Peter said. "A fresh start."

She nodded, distracted. They needed the second income, what with two college tuitions coming up. And everything had gotten so frighteningly expensive, especially gas. It was costing as much to fill up the minivan as it was to take everyone out to dinner and the movies.

"Actually." He cleared his throat. "We could both use a fresh start."

She turned to him, worried by the strangeness in his voice. "Okay."

"Not okay, Ann. It hasn't been okay for a long time."

"What does that mean? What are you talking about?" But she

knew. This quiet autumn day had suddenly become strange, queered by intensity and the feeling that something terrible was about to happen.

"I think we need some time apart."

She stared at his profile, speechless, feeling her heartbeat accelerate. He was suddenly a stranger to her. The seatbelt slid down her arm, she was skewed so sideways. "You don't mean that."

"I have to."

"I thought we were doing okay. Not good but . . . better." Maybe this weekend had been the last straw. Was it just his father's death? Or had he been thinking about this for a while? How could she not have known? How foolish she'd been, taking things for granted, being her clumsy, pushy self. She'd been too harsh about his father's death. Maybe she should have been kinder, but she'd never really liked the man.

"Dad was sixty-two. Sixty-two." Peter gripped the steering wheel, his knuckles white. "There were so many things he never got to do. So many things he put off. Going to Gettysburg. Seeing the Vietnam Memorial. Finishing that tree house for our girls. I stood there and watched them put his coffin into the ground." He leaned back and let out a breath. "I don't want to be that man. I don't want to live like he did."

She put her hand on his arm, felt the warmth of his skin. "But . . . you're not."

He shook his head. "I'm just like him, living in suspended animation, watching everything go past."

"Is this some kind of midlife crisis?"

He glanced at her. "I wish it were, sweetheart." His eyes were gentle. "Ever since the baby died—"

"Don't," she said, hearing her voice sharpen, and took her hand away. She'd never forget walking into the nursery. Seeing William silent and unmoving in his crib.

"We can't even talk about it."

"This isn't talking about it. This is telling me to get over it." She twisted to look back at the girls, saw that they were still fast asleep. He didn't want to discuss his mother with them sleeping back there, but it was okay to talk about the one thing they struggled every day to get past? She felt a spark of anger at his indifference. "Which is all you've ever done."

"That's not fair. You won't let me in to do anything else. It's like you slammed all the doors shut and threw away the keys."

"I've tried."

"I know you have." There was that horrible kind voice again. "I've tried, too. Don't you think it's time we both stopped trying, and started loving one another the way we used to?"

She stared at him. "But we can't," she said, helpless. "We're not the same people." They couldn't be that man and that woman who fell in love at that insanely crowded party; they couldn't be that naive twosome who thought finding each other was the hard part. She tried again. "We *do* love each other."

"I know."

He sounded so sad. She hated this. Couldn't he understand she was doing the best she could? Couldn't he be happy with the way things were now?

He slowed to take the exit toward Columbus. They passed a cluster of gas stations, then a series of strip malls.

"But Thanksgiving's next week." A stupid thing to say. Who cared about that? She clenched her fists in her lap. It wasn't about Thanksgiving. It was deciding whether to go with his mom's traditional stuffing or her mom's walnut-apple. It was picking out the Christmas tree, loading the dishwasher, and bringing in the mail. It was waking up in the middle of the night, hearing the person breathing next to you. About knowing you weren't alone.

"We both need to move on," he said. "We can't live like this, two people afraid to be real with one another. I love you. I'll always love you." His voice was low but relentless. "I'm just not in love with you anymore."

She didn't want to hear this. She sat back and stared numbly through the glass. This was one of those hideous things that happened to other people. The fabric of her life shredded just like that, all the truths she'd clung to now melted into nothing. Everything she was or thought she was, everything she thought they were, had vanished as though they'd never been.

Another house appeared, tucked among the golden trees by the roadside. Someone was there, crouched and working in a garden. A woman. Ann watched as she straightened, lifted a hand to shade her eyes to watch them shoot past, the four of them entombed in a blue minivan and hurtling toward the unknown.

ONE YEAR LATER

## AVIAN INFLUENZA—
## SITUATION IN SOUTH KOREA

---

Five more people have been hospitalized this morning in Seoul with avian influenza. Early tests confirm it as the same strain that killed two people in Singapore earlier this week. Health officials have been unable to determine how and where these people may have contracted the disease. To date, a total of 670 cases of human avian influenza have been confirmed worldwide, resulting in 328 deaths.

*World Health Organization*
*Epidemic and Pandemic Alert and Response*

# ONE

—

PETER HEARD THE LOW MUTTER OF A MOTORBOAT somewhere out there in the cold fog. He rolled down his truck window and listened. The sound swelled into a grumble, someone evidently headed in to shore. Already? The sun wasn't even up yet. He fitted his cup into the holder, reached for his toolbox, and climbed out of his truck.

A muffled hiccup as the engine cut off. Water lapped the wooden piles and unsettled the pebbles along the shore. The squeak of fiberglass against rope. Fog rolled back across the water, revealing the frosted grass beneath Peter's boots, a section of pier stretching before him, patches of dark water, the thin, gray sky. Now he could see the motorboat and the two figures working within it.

One of them looked up as Peter approached. Broad face, small mouth, a curl of pale hair beneath a dark cap. The other man turned and revealed himself to be a younger version of the first, possessing the same mouth and squint but with brown hair instead of white. Father and son. They wore heavy brown camouflage jackets, rubber waders, thick gloves with the fingers snipped off. Peter had met so many people these past few weeks that they more or less merged into one wary, jostling group, but he remembered this pair.

He'd examined their chocolate Lab, a big, slow-moving dog with white on his muzzle and tail, and a spreading rash across his ribs.

"You again," the son said. He tossed a rope over a pile and tied a knot. "The vet."

More university researcher than veterinarian, but Peter didn't correct him. "Any luck?"

"Not much," the father replied. "Couldn't flush any out."

The son gave the rope a vicious tug. "The ones we did were crappy."

The father rested his hand on the side of the boat and looked at Peter. "I suppose you want to see for yourself."

Peter waited. He had no jurisdiction here. The NSF grant paid for lab work and his graduate student, but that was all. Hunters didn't have to comply with his requests.

The man shrugged. He reached into the center of the boat, lifted out a bundle of feathers, and set it onto the pier. Peter crouched to have a closer look.

Four small ducks, all of them brown-and-cream with a telltale blue patch along the wing. The white crescent around the eye revealed three of them to be male. It was uncommon to find blue-winged teal in Ohio in mid-November. Usually by now they'd taken themselves down the Mississippi to South America or across the Great Lakes to the Chesapeake Bay for the winter.

Their presence here was odd, and so was their appearance. Where were the sleek, domed chests? These birds looked deflated, their wings overlarge for their shrunken torsos. He opened his toolbox. "How were they flying?"

"Low and slow." The father looped rope over a second pile and pulled the boat up against the pier. "Like they were drunk. Hardly any challenge."

Teal normally flew fast and erratically. Peter snapped on a pair of gloves, picked up the first teal, and cradled it in his hand.

"Got to be global warming." The son stepped onto the pier and squatted beside Peter.

"Looks poisoned to me." The father was watching Peter. "What do you think?"

"Could be," Peter said.

Botulism would account for the birds' labored flying. Peter lifted tail feathers to check for signs of diarrhea and found none. He turned to the small tucked head and gently palpated. Here was a worry. Facial edema and, yes, petechial hemorrhage inside the eyelids. He laid the bird down, picked up another male. The edema was more pronounced in this one. He reached for his penlight from the tray of his toolbox. Prying open the duck's bill and tilting back its head, he shone the beam of light down its throat. Blossoms of red against the pale membrane.

"What?" the father said as Peter put the bird down and reached for another.

The eyes of this one were almost swollen shut. Peter couldn't imagine how he'd been able to fly at all. The female showed less swelling about her face, but when Peter checked the inside of one eyelid, he saw bright red. These birds had suffered. He ran a gloved finger along the female's wing. The speckled brown-and-cream feathers were dull, as if they'd lost hope.

"It's either a viral infection or exposure to an environmental contaminant," Peter said. "I'll have to run some tests."

"That's what you're here for, isn't it?" the son said.

True, but he hadn't thought it would be necessary. Naturally, he'd hoped for the opposite. Peter unscrewed a test tube. He peeled the paper back from a sterile swab.

"We can't eat them if they're poisoned," the father said. "Can we?"

"I'm telling you, Dad—"

"You think everything's global warming." The father leaned back and put his hand on the gunwale. "You find anything the other times you been out?"

He was talking to Peter.

"No." Peter dropped the swab into the test tube and twisted on the lid. No one had, not that he knew of. But it was still early days yet. Duck season was just gearing up.

"Poison." Turning, the father spat into the water. "We should've left them where we found them."

"Mind showing me where that was?" Peter said.

Father and son exchanged a glance.

Duck hunters were a unique breed, willing to endure freezing temperatures, sleet, snow, and bitter wind, and secretive as hell about their prime hunting spots. These two were worried he was going to steal their spot, though there was no threat of that. He didn't hunt. Not anymore.

"I need to take water samples." Peter made his voice mild and nonthreatening, the sound of the professor, not the hunter.

The son scowled at the horizon. The rising sun was beginning to thin the fog and cast a general yellow glow over the marsh. The father busied himself in the boat.

"We don't find the cause, the whole season could be like this." Peter indicated the ducks lying on the pier.

A quick glance from the father.

"You try that ointment I recommended?" Peter said. "For Gus?" He hoped he'd remembered the Lab's name.

The son said, "Yeah. His rash is getting better."

Peter nodded. "He should be able to get in the water in another week."

Father and son looked at each other. The father rubbed his chin and then shrugged. "Come on, then. It's a piss-poor spot, anyway."

THEY MOTORED THROUGH THE REEDY WATER. PETER SAT IN the middle, the father at the stern, steering. The son knelt in the prow. Once they were out on open water, the father revved the engine and they bounced across the polished silver surface.

Cold wind buffeted Peter's hair. Spray whipped across his face. The shoreline opened up on both sides, lined by sycamores and red maples blooming gold and crimson and reflected between sky and water. Spangles of sunlight below, bright sky and a wisp of cloud above. Flapping geese lifted themselves from hiding, sounding mournful echoing honks. It was nice to be out here. Uncomplicated.

The son shouted something to his father, stretched out his arm and pointed. The father yelled something unintelligible back.

Peter turned his head and saw a distant dark shape. Another

boat trolling these same hunting grounds. The father made a wide loop, watching the other boat as it chopped past, then opened up and headed north.

After a while the engine shifted into a lower gear, and their boat, turning, cut through the waves, rolling in its own wake. The engine slowed even further, thrummed. Around another curve, and there was the duck blind. Wooden poles rose from the water, their tops shrouded with branches, to form an unlikely tree house in the middle of the lake. The two men had taken care constructing it, weaving the branches in a dense mesh, leaving a space high enough to allow them to slide their boat inside.

They slowly circled the structure.

"See?" the son said. "Nothing."

Peter unstoppered a tube and leaned over the side to dip it into the icy water.

"How's it look?" the father said.

"I won't know anything until I get back to the lab." But the tea-colored water appeared clean enough. No scum or creeping algae that would indicate bacterial overgrowth, no white froth or oily bubbles that would suggest a chemical spill. Peter pressed the stopper on top, looked around. It was a peaceful, beautiful morning. Despite it, he felt a growing unease. "Where were the ducks when you found them?"

The son turned around in his seat. "Over there." He pointed to where the shoreline bulged out into the water.

"Waited for two hours," the father said. "And then those four showed."

"Let's take a look," Peter said.

"It's all the same lake," the father said.

"There could be something over there, though, that's not over here."

"Like a dead animal?"

Peter shook his head. "Teal don't feed on carrion, but maybe it's a localized contamination, someone dumping something where they shouldn't." That'd be a welcome sight—a big old rusted barrel sticking out of the water and disrupting the delicate harmony between bird and environment. Even a discarded paint can would do.

The father brought the boat around and sliced through the marshy water.

"Fish look okay," the son said, staring down into the water. "There'd be floaters otherwise, right?"

"Some things can affect one species and do nothing to another," Peter answered. "There are plenty of diseases that are fatal to birds that pass right through fish. And vice versa."

"Where again?" the father said.

"Around there," the son said. "Careful. Water's getting shallow."

The engine dropped to a slow chug. Another tight turn. The engine stuttered, then stopped. All three men stared at the sight before them.

On the clear water, surrounded by golden reeds, bobbed a legion of blue-winged teal, hundreds of them, mottled brown and cream, every one of them silent and turned the wrong way up.

# TWO

————

THE BIRD TUMBLED IN FREE FALL, ITS WINGS OUT-stretched, its yellow beak gaping wide. A cat waited below, a wide grin splitting its whiskered face.

Ann tilted the painting toward her. "Wow, Hannah. This is some story."

"Her kitten caught a bird yesterday," Maddie said. She and Hannah sat close together, their chairs practically touching. "And *killed* it." She shuddered.

Hannah nodded, a little ruefully, Ann thought. "My mom says Furball is a real hunter."

Across the table, Jodi sniggered. Her sheet of paper lay before her, untouched. "With a name like that, he'd better be."

"You're just jealous," Maddie said. "You just wish *you* had a new kitten."

So did Maddie. But that would never happen.

"It looks like you're having trouble getting started, Jodi," Ann said. "Why don't you go through the book on my desk for ideas?"

"I *know* what I want to do." Jodi narrowed her eyes and stuck out her lip. "I *want* to make a story about an airplane, but *you* said the Aborigines don't have planes."

So Jodi had been paying attention. Good for her. Sometimes

Ann wondered if Jodi had some sort of attention disorder. Next time she saw Jodi's mom at the mailbox, she'd find a polite way to ask. Ann barely knew Sue Guarnieri, so no telling how she'd react, even if Ann was the child's teacher. "Well, this is your story, Jodi, not an Aborigine's. You can paint an airplane if you like. Maybe you could paint a story about a trip you're planning on taking with your parents."

The corners of Jodi's mouth turned down. "My mom and dad don't take me on their trips. They say I'm too young. They make me stay home with Nana and Poppa. And Nana makes me wear stupid dresses and Poppa won't let me drink pop at dinner."

Until she started teaching, Ann had no idea how much personal stuff children revealed in the classroom. She could just imagine what Kate and Maddie had been saying this past year. "Well, you can make a picture about the trips you'd like to take when you're old enough."

A heavy sigh, then Jodi dragged the paper toward herself. "I guess."

Beside Jodi, Heyjin worked on, seemingly oblivious to the chatter around her. Maybe she couldn't follow it. The principal had assured her that Heyjin spoke English, but the girl had hardly spoken a word since appearing in Ann's class two weeks ago. Instead, she usually just sat and nibbled on her fingernails, watching everyone out of the corners of her eyes.

But today she was really digging in. Perhaps Heyjin had finally caught on. Or maybe there was something about this particular art style that spoke to her.

"Heyjin?" Ann said. "How's your painting coming?"

At the sound of her name, the little girl glanced up, her dark eyes sober behind the round lenses of her glasses, her black hair parted precisely down the middle and tied into tight pigtails. She lowered her head and went back to work.

So maybe she didn't understand English.

Ann observed the child for a moment. Heyjin certainly seemed to have grasped the process. She dipped the cotton swab into the paint and coated the tip with just the right amount of paint, exactly as Ann had demonstrated, before carefully carrying it to the paper and pressing firmly to form a tidy dot. But when Ann looked to the paper itself, she realized that the concept might have eluded Heyjin: the entire sheet was peppered with uniform brown dots, every one of them barely perceptible against the black surface. No story there at all.

Ann could suggest that Heyjin try a different color. But the girl seemed so content. Ann decided to let her be. Art was all about self-expression. Heyjin certainly seemed to be expressing something. Ann just didn't know what it was.

She glanced up and found Maddie watching her. "What's your story about, honey?"

Maddie curled her arm protectively around her work. "Don't look until I'm done."

But Ann had already glimpsed enough to guess: happy family. The symbols for father, mother, and two children marched down the middle of the page. A big arc soared over their heads. Was that what Maddie imagined would happen to them, that after the storms of this past year, a rainbow would climb into the sky? But not every story had a happy ending.

"Mrs. Brooks?" Jimmy had his hand up. "I forgot what you do for a campfire."

Ann forced down the knot of sadness lodged in her throat and turned to her class. "Does anyone else remember?"

Hannah waved her arm. "It's a circle with a dot in the middle."

"Very good, Hannah." Walking to the board, Ann picked up a stick of chalk and drew the dashes for rain, the wavy lines for river, the oblong man and semicircular woman. "Don't forget how important color is. The Aborigines use color to express mood." Now she made the honey ant and the kangaroo. "Red for happy—"

A siren shrieked, shattering the calm. Puzzled, Ann turned from the board. A fire drill wasn't on the schedule, not so far as she knew.

A few children were standing and scraping their chairs back. Others groaned and pretended not to hear, still bent over their drawings.

"Come on, everybody." Ann clapped her hands. "Who's my line leader?"

Steven waved. "Me!"

"You come right here and stand by the door. Everyone line up behind Steven."

"But I'm not done," Jodi said.

"Just leave it, honey. Come on."

"I only have to do this one part."

"It's okay. Come on. Let's go."

Jodi pushed back her chair and dragged herself over to where the other children lined up by the door. But Heyjin was still in her seat, looking around with wide eyes. Had she any idea what was going on?

"It's all right, Heyjin. It's the fire alarm." Ann held out her hand. Even if the child didn't understand the language, she could follow gestures. "We have to go."

Heyjin allowed herself to be pulled to her feet.

"Follow Maddie, okay?" Ann guided her into line. She strode to the front of the room. "All right, Steven. Let's go."

They burst through the heavy door onto the playground. Groups of children stood clustered here and there, chattering excitedly as more children streamed from the building. A little girl stumbled, and Ann helped her up, leading her class to a spot by the swings.

"It's freezing," Jodi said. "I need my coat."

Which was back in her homeroom, hanging from its hook. "Stamp your feet," Ann said. "Think warm thoughts." She went down the straggly line of shivering children, counting.

Another teacher was going down her line. "It's the real thing," she said in a low voice.

Ann glanced at her. "What happened?"

The woman rolled her eyes. "One of the parents was showing the fourth-graders how a volcano works and blew up the science lab."

"Omigod," Jodi wailed. "We're going to be out here *forever*."

"Oh, it won't be that long." Ann absently patted Jodi's shoulder. She'd counted nineteen children. That wasn't right. There were twenty in Maddie's class. She began counting again.

"I want to go back inside."

"Can I play on the playground while we wait?"

*Maddie, Hannah, Jodi . . .*

"Is that smoke?"

"No way."

"Yeah, right there. See? Coming out of that window."

*Kristen, Michael, Foster, Stephanie . . .* Wait a minute. Where was Heyjin? Ann spun in a circle, scanning the playground for a petite child in a bright red sweatshirt. "Does anybody see Heyjin?"

Maddie shook her head as Jodi said, "She's inside."

That couldn't be. Ann herself had placed her in line.

Jodi shrugged. "She doesn't *ever* go outside."

"It's true, Mom," Maddie said. "Heyjin doesn't like the playground."

Ann stared at Maddie, then wheeled around to the other teacher. "Would you keep an eye on my class?"

No way back into the building but through the main entrance, the black double doors standing wide open. The unrelenting alarm wailed as red warning lights pulsed along the ceiling. No one stood in the hall. The front-office staff was gone, and classroom after classroom stood empty.

A gray haze drifted down the far corridor. Ann wheeled in the opposite direction, almost running toward the art room, and yanked open the door. Everything was as they'd left it, papers strewn across the tables, chairs akimbo. No sign of Heyjin anywhere. Could Jodi have been mistaken? No. Maddie had nodded in agreement.

The supply closet. There Heyjin crouched, her arms around her bent knees, a pigtail undone and hanging in glossy tendrils.

Relief rushed through Ann, cold and filling. "Oh, thank God, Heyjin!" She held out her hand. "Come on. We have to go."

Heyjin shook her head hard enough to dislodge another plait of her hair.

A fire truck wailed in the distance. "I'll carry you."

The girl pressed herself deeper into the corner. "I not going."

So she did speak English. The siren grew louder. Colored lights sliced across the ceiling. She bent and gripped the child beneath her armpits, pulled her out of her hiding place.

Heyjin wriggled and twisted, trying to get free. "No, no."

"It's okay, honey. It's okay." Ann pressed her to her shoulder and ran down the smoky hall, Heyjin's small hands flat against her and pushing.

Maddie would be panicked, seeing the emergency vehicles and knowing her mother was still inside.

The doors were just ahead. The siren shrieked overhead in great pulsing bursts, and Heyjin writhed in Ann's arms. The bulky shapes of the firefighters appeared in the doorway, dragging the long fire hose. Their masked faces turned toward her as she pushed past them.

Outside, she sank, sweating and breathless, onto a bench. Heyjin scrambled out of her arms and onto the bench beside her. Ann wanted to shake the child. What on earth had prompted her to behave in such a way? "Heyjin, what *is* the matter?"

Heyjin looked around at the people massing on the grassy slope, and the fire trucks lining the curb. She shrank back, turning her head and burying her face against Ann's shoulder. She grew almost limp. Ann slid an arm around her and drew her close. She felt the hard beating of the child's racing heart, the dampness of the little girl's tears seeping through her blouse. "Heyjin?"

"My daddy die. My daddy did." The words came out muffled.

Ann held her breath. She'd had no idea. Why wasn't this in the child's file? Why on earth hadn't anyone told her about Heyjin's problems? "Sweetheart, I'm so sorry."

Heyjin lifted her chin and looked at Ann. Her cheeks were pink and the lenses of her glasses smeared with tears. She held her gaze for a long moment. It was as though she was searching for something. Then she spoke. "First the chickens get sick. Then Daddy did."

There were no poultry farms in this school district. Then Ann understood. "In Korea?"

Heyjin nodded.

Korea was dangerous. There had been several barely contained flu outbreaks there. Millions of chickens had been slaughtered. A hundred people had died. One of them must have been this child's father. Ann pulled the child into her embrace. "You're safe now, honey. I promise. You're safe."

After a moment, she felt the girl's arms come up and circle her neck. Ann held her close, the child's hair soft against her cheek, and rocked her. She couldn't imagine what Heyjin had witnessed back in Korea. It was a miracle she'd escaped unharmed.

It was a miracle they'd let her into the country.

Heyjin cuddled closer and spoke softly into Ann's ear. Ann had to bend to hear the child's whispered words. "It coming here."

# THREE

PETER LIFTED A HAND TO LEWIS AS HE HURRIED DOWN the corridor. He owed the guy a draft of the grant they were working on, but it'd have to wait.

He sliced his keycard through the reader. The lock sprang open and he stepped into the carpeted veterinary science suite of labs and offices. Pushing open the door to his lab, he saw Shazia working at the bench along one side of the room. Another student worked the microcentrifuge beside her.

Peter frowned at him. "You chewing gum?"

"Sorry." The boy shot upright and looked around.

Peter pointed to the trash can. The kid had probably been chewing it when he'd entered the room. A common mistake but one that needed correcting. With all the pathogens in here, they could never relax their guard.

Shazia scraped back her stool. "Peter?"

"Hold on." Peter reached for the phone on the counter. "Dan," he said when the fellow answered. "I'm going to put you on speaker."

"What's up?" echoed Dan's voice.

Peter set down his cooler. "We've got a die-off."

A rustle of paper over the phone. "Where?"

"Sparrow Lake. Northwest tip."

"How bad?"

"Two, three hundred. All of them teal."

"What do you think it is?"

"Looks viral to me."

"Shit." A pause. "You think we've got Qinghai Lake on our hands?"

"I don't know." Peter had pored over the photographs from that massive die-off in China a number of years before, when avian influenza had killed more than five thousand migratory birds. It was too early to know what was going on here, but Dan had given voice to Peter's greatest fear. What if H5N1 had landed here, right in Peter's backyard?

"When will you get back to me?"

Dan knew as well as anyone that running the initial tests was a full-day process. It was impossible to make it go any faster. "First thing in the morning. Tomorrow afternoon at the latest."

Shazia had come up to stand beside Peter. She was shaking her head at him. He held up a finger. *Hold on.*

"Call me on my cell when you know something," Dan told him.

Peter disconnected. "What?"

"Professor Alfonso's secretary stopped by to ask if you could fill in for him today. He's stuck at the airport in Madrid."

The undergraduate epidemiology class Peter had agreed to guest lecture the following week. He didn't have anything prepared. Lord knew where his old slides were. Probably stuffed into one of the filing cabinets that lined the hall outside his office. Maybe still at the house.

"I could do it, if you want." Shazia stood close, looking up at him.

It was a generous offer. It'd be good for her to gain the teaching experience, but was it fair to the undergraduates who really needed to master this material? Shazia verged on the shy side, and when she was anxious, her voice dipped to a whisper. Peter looked down at the test tubes nestled among the ice packs in his cooler. He glanced at the wall clock. One-ten. Classes started at one-thirty. By the time he got out of the lecture hall, it'd be going on three. But Alfonso had helped him out of a bind once before.

Oh, hell. "That's all right. Why don't you get started on these?"

She nodded, clearly relieved.

It was a routine procedure, and she was a smart girl. She wouldn't make any mistakes.

PETER LOOKED AROUND AT THE STUDENTS THAT FILLED THE hall. A number of them looked back. "Good afternoon. My name is Peter Brooks. I'm a professor over in the School of Veterinary Medicine. Professor Alfonso couldn't be here this afternoon. He asked me to come and talk to you about zoonotic disease."

A few yawns. Some low-level chatter along the back rows.

He set his briefcase by the podium and loosened his tie. "Let me ask you guys something. How many of you have gotten your flu shot?"

Some kids straightened in their seats. A couple of hands went up.

"Let me guess. Your parents made you."

Laughter. More students were sitting up.

"Not my mom," one called out. "She says the flu shot doesn't work."

A common misperception. "Well, in a sense, she's right. It only protects against the strains that scientists predict will be circulating in a given year. We'll get to that in more detail shortly. Anyone want to take a stab at how many Americans die each year from influenza?"

Another straggle of waving hands. Peter pointed to a girl in the second row with blunt black hair and a gold hoop hooked through her eyebrow.

"Ten thousand?" she said.

"Try thirty to forty thousand."

There was a murmur and a general shifting of position.

"That's slightly more than one percent of the U.S. population. Not terribly significant . . . unless you happen to be one of those thirty to forty thousand."

A few students scrawled notes. Good. That sort of statistic would definitely be on the final exam.

"So, you might say that influenza is nothing to sneeze at."

A few smiles.

"Anyone know how many influenza variants there are?"

"Two?"

"Close. There are three. Influenza C is a mild respiratory ailment, usually referred to as the common cold. Influenza B is the human variant and can lead to epidemics. That's generally the one that the flu vaccine addresses. And then there's A, the avian variant, also known as bird flu. It also happens to be the only one that can result in pandemics."

Peter looked to a T-shirted boy with long sideburns sprawled in his chair. "You might want to jot that down."

Hastily, the boy righted himself and flipped open his binder.

Peter slid a fresh sheet of acetate onto the projector and lifted his pen. After so many years of using PowerPoint, it was nice to return to the old-fashioned, hands-on way of teaching. "Pandemic." He underlined the first syllable. "*Pan*, a prefix that means *all*. In 1918, a pandemic swept across the entire globe and killed fifty to one hundred million people."

The smiles faded.

"Let's look at how influenza A can develop into pandemic flu." He drew a line parallel to the bottom of the screen. "Imagine that H3N1 is the current influenza A virus. It's going along infecting people." The line sloped up. "Those people who survive develop immunity. At the same time, we develop a vaccine, which we use to inoculate key players, such as day-care providers, emergency room doctors." He turned and wiggled his eyebrows at the class. "University professors."

Laughter.

He turned back to the board. "And so on."

The line flattened out.

"Now we've got two populations that can't pass the virus on. We call this 'community immunity.' As a result, the virus now produces fewer and fewer human infections and may eventually have to move to wildlife. That specific virus is out of the picture, at least temporarily."

The line dwindled to a series of dots.

"But wait. All of a sudden, it alters the form of its protein receptors so that our vaccines are no longer effective."

Now the line rose up in a second gentle slope.

"Once again we have to build up a new sort of immunity. Which we eventually do."

A second flattening out. The line resembled a series of rounded steps climbing across the board.

"This is antigenic drift." He wrote the term in capital letters and underscored it. "This is what the World Health Organization is working hard to monitor and control. Anyone have any idea how?"

A flurry of raised hands. He pointed to a fair-haired boy in the back.

"By tracking the virus in poultry. And killing it when they find it."

"Exactly. Now, antigenic *drift* is no small thing. But antigenic *shift* is Freddy Krueger, Dracula, and Hannibal Lecter rolled into one."

Now every head was up. They should be. He wasn't exaggerating.

"Antigenic shift occurs when two viruses, one avian and one human, mix together within a single host." He sketched two blobs with antennae. "The pig is ideally suited for this role, because it's susceptible to both avian and human influenza viruses. So let's say these two viruses meet and mingle within a pig. Out pops a new virus, one that carries avian code but has human protein receptors. Now we have humans getting infected with an avian virus." An alien-looking thing with protruding nodules. "What's the significance of this?" He scanned the class and nodded to a boy in a front seat.

"Um, we don't have any immunity against it?"

"Worse than that. We don't have any community immunity against it, and we have no quick way of attaining it. By the time science catches up, this little guy will have ripped through the entire human population"—another series of circles—"and utterly devastated it." Peter slashed his pen through every circle.

A hushed silence, then someone said, "That's what's happening with H5N1."

"That's what we're *worried* can happen with H5," Peter corrected. "That's why WHO has issued alerts, why our health departments are stockpiling latex gloves, and why I'm freezing my butt off beside Sparrow Lake at five in the morning."

A ripple of laughter.

Someone called out, "Do you think we're going to have a pandemic?"

Peter regarded the young faces turned toward him. He thought of all those mute bobbing birds, felled by the same sharp blow. "What does the science tell us?"

Silence. They were thinking about this.

"Put yourself in the virus's place. If you had a good thing going, hooking up with everybody in town, would you move on?"

Nervous laughter.

"Of course you wouldn't. You'd hang around as long as possible."

"So that means yes?"

"That means . . ." Peter reached over and shut off the projector. He faced the room. Every head was lifted, every pen stilled. "It's inevitable. Maybe not in my lifetime. Maybe not in yours or even your children's lifetimes. But sometime."

He didn't say the last part. That the world's population was greater than ever. That when the pandemic did arrive, it was going to result in the most devastating loss of life mankind had ever seen, many times worse than what had happened almost a century before. That science was helpless to stop it.

These were kids, after all. No need to terrify them.

"Doctors refuse to give the condition of the six people admitted to a Barcelona hospital this evening, but sources reveal they are two men and four women, all in their twenties and thirties, and all suffering from what seems to be avian influenza. One man had recently entered the country from South Korea. Anyone who has visited that country should be watchful for signs of disease. The onset is rapid, beginning with a severe headache or fever. Individuals experiencing these symptoms are advised to consult a physician immediately."

CNN Headline News

# FOUR

*I* HATE, HATE, *HATE* TENNIS." KATE DUMPED HER RACKET
into the footwell and reached for her seatbelt. Her hair looped
over her shoulder in a shining ponytail, her green eyes carefully out-
lined in black. Tiny pink earrings twinkled in her earlobes. Ann
thought she looked adorable. "I have the absolute *worst* backhand
of everyone. I don't know why you're forcing me to play."

So it was going to be one of those days. Ann pulled the minivan
away from the curb and decided to go for a light approach. "You
know, Kate, you never went through the terrible twos. Maybe you
were saving it all up for the terrifying thirteens."

Maddie giggled from the backseat.

Kate frowned. "I'm serious. You *always* make me do things I
don't want to."

"Well, I'm not forcing you to play. Your father and I have talked
to you about this." Ann pulled to a stop at the red light and looked
over at Kate. "You were the one who signed up for the team. It's important to keep the commitments you make. We don't want you to
be a quitter."

"Oh, you mean like *you*?"

Ann winced. This separation was hard on all of them. Kate

lifted her chin and glared back at Ann. But beneath that arch defiance, Ann saw her unhappy little girl looking back, longing for reassurance. "Oh, honey." She put her hand on her daughter's forearm. "It's not like that at all."

The corners of Kate's mouth turned down. She looked utterly bereft. Ann tightened her grip on her daughter's arm. If only she could take this from her child.

Then Kate's features smoothed out again. She wrenched her arm away and turned to the window. "Whatever."

Maddie piped up from the backseat. "We had a fire at school today."

"Yeah, right." Kate lifted a hip to tug her cell phone from her jeans pocket.

"No, we really did. Ask Mommy. The firefighters came and everything."

Kate glanced at her.

Ann nodded. "It's true. We really did have a fire. Fortunately, it was just a small one."

Kate looked over the seat at Maddie. "So the entire school building didn't burn down?"

Ann glanced in the rearview mirror. Maddie had been bouncing a little in her seat, and now she stopped and looked apprehensive. "No."

"And you still have to go to school tomorrow?"

"Well . . . yeah."

"Sucks for you."

Maddie crossed both arms over her chest. "You used to like school."

It was true, Ann thought sadly. Kate used to bring home perfect report cards. She never talked back to her teachers. Ann never got a phone call from the guidance counselor asking her to come in and discuss why Kate wasn't handing in assignments. *Is there something going on at home that's upset Kate?* the woman had asked.

"Listen, guys." Ann braked to allow a couple of teenagers to dart across the street. "I'm thinking of pulling you out of school next Wednesday. I thought maybe we could head to Grandma and Grandpa's a day early."

Maddie squealed and clapped her hands. "Can we?"

"Don't you have to work?" Kate said.

Said with some bite to it. Ann understood. Her going back to work was yet another thing that Kate had had no control over. "I've already talked to your homeroom teacher, and you don't have any tests or projects due that day." The teens reached the curb and Ann accelerated. "So I think we can do it."

There was a sudden jangle of music. Kate flipped open her cell phone and began pressing buttons.

"Daddy's not coming with us, is he?" Maddie wanted to know.

Ann sighed. "No, honey. Daddy isn't coming." It had been a year, long enough for any new routines to start feeling like old ones, but Maddie still kept asking things like that. Did she really not understand? Or was she simply hoping? "Kate, who are you texting?"

Kate's thumbs flew over her phone's tiny keypad. "Michele. We're trying for the longest text-messaging record."

"Well, stop it. We can't afford that."

"It's okay." Kate smirked. "Dad upped my limit."

Was that true? He'd never said a word to her about it. "Since when?"

Kate shrugged. "I don't know. Last month?"

This was one of those things she and Peter should have discussed. Letting Kate text even more than she already did might affect her schoolwork, and Ann would have said no. That was why Peter hadn't said anything. He hated conflict.

"I forgot to tell you, Mom," Maddie said. "Hannah can't play today. She's starting piano lessons."

"Really? But Hannah's mom and I talked about you two taking lessons together."

"Then I guess we're not."

Ann heard the disappointment in her daughter's voice. She felt it, too. "I'm sorry, honey. I should have let Rachel know we were still interested."

Maddie's voice was small. "It's all right."

"Maybe it's not too late. I can call her as soon as we get home and—"

"It's okay. Just forget it."

"Well, we can at least see if Hannah can play tomorrow."

"Tomorrow she's got karate."

Yet another thing she and Rachel had discussed the girls doing together. But maybe Rachel had forgotten. "I'll figure something out."

Ann turned the car into their neighborhood.

Mr. Finn was out walking his dog again. He'd stopped by the evening before, petition in hand, and Ann had shooed him away by telling him it was dinnertime. He'd promised to come by earlier tonight. Maybe this time she'd plead a migraine or something. She braked to let the white sedan in front of her turn in to a driveway. An elderly woman stood on the front porch, waving as Ann passed by. Sue's mother, taking care of Jodi again, Ann thought, returning the wave.

"Kate?" Maddie said.

"What."

"Would you rather step on a slug in your bare feet or—"

"Just say it."

"—or play bingo with old people?" Maddie said, all in a rush.

Kate considered as another trill of music burst into the car. She frowned at the phone display and thumbed a quick reply. "How old?"

"Grandma old."

"Slug. Definitely."

Ann steered the car into the garage and switched off the ignition. "All right, you two. Get started on your homework. No more texting, Kate."

"Mom. Come on. We're already up to ninety-seven messages. And that's only since sixth period."

"You were texting in class? And your teacher didn't confiscate your phone?"

Kate shrugged. "We had a substitute."

"Listen, honey. You really have to start pulling up your grades. When you get to high school—"

"Fine. Got it." Kate pointedly held out her cell phone and pressed the Off button.

Ann walked out to the curb. The mailbox yawned open, its contents threatening to spill onto the sidewalk. It had been days since Ann had thought to bring it in. She worked the bulk of paper free and pressed the mailbox door closed.

"Hey, lady."

Libby bore down on her, stroller bumping along the sidewalk in front of her. Jacob lay nestled inside, his head tipped to one side, his eyelids at half-mast, tiny blue-mittened hands curled over the satin trim of the yellow blanket tucked around him.

For one heart-stopping moment, there he was. Her own sweet William, with just the barest glint of golden hair on his bald little head, his lips pursed as though he were blowing bubbles, his cheeks rosy with sleep. She ached to scoop him up and press him to her shoulder, feel his butterfly breaths once more against her neck and the steady rise and fall of his sturdy back beneath the flat of her hand. But of course he wasn't William. He was Jacob, her best friend's son. Her own baby boy was long gone from her.

"Don't you look at him like that. He's no angel." Libby swiped a sleeve across her forehead and stood there, jogging up and down. "He screamed all day at the sitter's."

"Still working on that tooth, huh?" A gust of cold air swept past and Ann tugged her sweater tight about her.

"It's going to come in sometime, right? Tell me it's going to come in."

"It's going to come in. Before he goes to college, for sure."

"Funny." Libby reached for the bottle of water from the cup holder strapped to the stroller handle. "Did you hear H5N1's in Spain now?"

It wasn't just the flu anymore. That term was too benign, summoning up all those years where the flu was just something most people didn't think of unless they came down with it. Now it was H5N1. "It's just a small outbreak."

"Yeah, but it's the third one this month." Libby tilted back her head and drank.

"Well, at this time of year, we are going to see outbreaks from time to time."

"And our being in Phase Four doesn't freak you out?" Libby ran a hand below her mouth, catching a drip.

It had, at first. Ann had run out with everyone else and loaded up on the essentials. She'd taken the girls in for flu shots. But things had gradually quieted. Doctors overseas were containing the isolated cases that popped up. Scientists around the world were working on a vaccine. Little by little, other events started to take over the headlines. Terrorist activity in Japan. Two missing tourists. An *E. coli* outbreak. Life, such as it was, had returned to normal.

"Not really. It's not until we start seeing major, simultaneous outbreaks that we should be concerned."

Libby grimaced. "You sound like Peter." As soon as she said it, a horrified look crossed her face.

INSIDE, THE PHONE WAS RINGING. "ANYONE GETTING THAT?" Ann called.

"I will," Maddie called back.

Ann shut the door behind her and kicked off her shoes. Padding down the hall, she paged through the mail, stopping at the thick envelope with her attorney's name printed in the corner. "Hi, Grandma," she heard Maddie say.

It was an unusual time for her mother to call. Maybe she had news. Ann hurried into the kitchen and found Maddie holding the cordless phone as she wandered around the kitchen while Kate sat at the table, textbook opened before her.

"It was a real fire," Maddie was saying. "Mom saved Heyjin's life." Pause. "Heyjin's a new girl in my class. She's from Korea." She listened. "No, but one of the bulletin boards in the science room melted."

Ann held out her hand.

Maddie said, "Mom's here. Love you, Grandma. See you soon."

Ann took the phone. "Mom? Is Dad okay?"

"Oh, he's fine. Well, he had some trouble breathing yesterday, but the doctor said that was to be expected. He fit us in right away. Wasn't that nice of him?"

There her mother went, sounding like a ditz so as not to worry anyone.

Maddie sat down at the kitchen table across from Kate and picked up her pencil.

"Very nice," Ann said. "So everything's okay?"

"Oh, yes. Sounds like you're the one who had all the excitement today."

"Only for an hour. Then everything went back to normal."

"Maddie said something about you having to rescue one of the children?"

"Yes." Ann realized Maddie was listening intently, head tilted, pencil slack. She stepped outside, the pavers cold beneath her stockinged feet, and closed the sliding glass door behind her. The aluminum chairs still ringed the patio table. This year, putting them away would be her job. She dragged one out and sat, setting the bundle of mail on the table in front of her. She tucked her feet beneath her. "A little girl from Korea. She has a phobia about being outside. She's afraid she's going to get bird flu like her father."

"Bird flu! Here?"

"No, no. Back in Korea."

"Oh, the poor little thing. It's gotten worse over there, you know. Has Peter said anything about it?"

"Not to me. We haven't spoken in weeks."

"I thought he was supposed to take the girls every Saturday."

An informal arrangement. "The last few visits haven't worked out."

"Why not? The girls need to be with their father."

"I know, Mom. Of course they do. But this is his busiest time of year. Plus, the girls have had things going on, too. Maddie was invited to a birthday party. Kate had a tennis tournament."

"Couldn't he have gone to that?"

"Kate didn't want him to." Ann glanced to the kitchen and saw her oldest daughter leaning back in her chair, fitting the earbuds of her iPod into her ears. "She's going through such a tough time, Mom."

"I know. And Peter's leaving hasn't made things any better for her." Her mother sighed. "She was always his little girl."

Ann stared out at the birch tree in the corner of the yard. "Tell me she'll be okay."

"Of course she will. She's a levelheaded girl. She'll work things through. Besides, she has you." Her mother gave a soft laugh. "She reminds me so much of you."

"Well, whatever you do, don't tell *her* that." Ann pulled the pile of mail toward her and tugged out the lawyer's letter. She slid her finger beneath the flap and removed the thick sheaf of papers. Heavy paper stock, lots of tiny type.

"This has got to be so hard on Peter, too. Do you think maybe . . . ?"

Ann stared down at the pages. "No, I don't think he's changed his mind."

"I just can't understand that. I know he loves you and the girls."

He'd promised to love her forever, but it had turned out to be much shorter than that. "He loves the girls, but . . . there's nothing between us anymore."

There was another silence, longer this time. "Maybe if you—"

Not another suggestion to go for counseling. "I'd better go, Mom. I have to get dinner started. Give my love to Dad."

"All right, honey. I'll call you tomorrow."

"All right. Love you."

Ann set down the phone and paged through the papers. Post-it notes poked out from the margins like little pink flags. SIGN HERE. INITIAL HERE. Proof that Peter was gone.

But she was still stuck in that hot, bright hospital room ten years ago with the social worker, trying to answer her questions. Someone had given Ann a pill, and the woman kept swimming in and out of focus. She wore brown shoes and a blue suit. Her blouse gaped in the middle. Little Kate sat in Peter's lap, hiccuping in her sleep, her small face blotchy from crying. The social worker's voice was unceasing, a syrupy flow of southern accent. The way she kept saying "baby," wrapping up the hard vowels in soft fluff. *Bay-bee, bay-bee.* Then she'd stood and reached for Kate. Ann had come hastily to her feet. She couldn't possibly let this person, this stranger who couldn't even button her clothes properly, carry off her child.

But Peter had handed Kate over. "We don't have a choice, Ann." Even then, he'd taken that first step away.

Pulling a pen from her pocket, she flattened each page on the hard glass of the table, and pressing the nib down hard enough to leave an imprint on the next page, she signed her name beside every bubblegum-colored sticky arrow. Every last one.

Peter had moved on.

She knew she never would.

". . . following confirmation that several people hospitalized do indeed have the H5N1 influenza virus, airlines have canceled all incoming and outgoing flights from Heathrow and Gatwick, stranding thousands of travelers. Lodging's filling up. Some hotels are turning away international guests. A manager at a large city hotel confided that he's directed his staff to refuse anyone with a passport from the affected countries."

*NBC Breaking News Report*

# FIVE

$P$ETER SAT UP, WINCING AT THE SUDDEN SPASM OF PAIN across his shoulders. He glanced at his bedside clock. Five a.m. He'd slept right through the alarm.

Later, as he drove along the quiet, blue-washed streets, he rubbed the back of his neck. He'd have to remember to call Ann and arrange to see the girls over the weekend, before they headed east to visit Ann's family. He'd be alone for Thanksgiving. He'd treat it like any other workday. Probably get more done. No phones ringing, no people stopping by.

He unlocked the door to his lab and went around turning on lights. Long fluorescent tubes flickered, then sprang to life. He sat down at the laptop and opened to the gray grid covered with tiny printing. It was always a relief to find results waiting for him. He was old enough to remember the days when nothing got done unless you were there doing it.

Rows of colored graphs popped up across the computer screen as he clicked through each square. He studied them, one by one, and frowned. Something must have gone wrong. Maybe the test had failed or the samples been somehow contaminated. He returned to the first graph and checked it again. The curving blue line verified that the PCR had worked. He scanned the temperature spike of the green band. Okay, so the first sample was positive. He moved to the second reading, then the third. One by one, he proceeded through each square.

He sat back, stunned. Out of thirty-two samples, twenty-nine were positive. That meant that ninety percent of the dead teal had the virus in their systems. Ninety percent. An unbelievable rate.

Viruses jumped quickly from migratory birds to poultry. It was only a matter of time, maybe even just a few short hours, before every farm within miles of Sparrow Lake was at risk. Millions of dollars were at stake, an entire industry.

He checked the time and picked up the phone. But Dan didn't answer. Peter tapped his fingers on the counter and waited for the beep. "It's Peter. Call me."

The door behind him opened with a pneumatic sigh.

"Morning," Shazia said.

Peter swiveled in his chair to look at her. "You were careful yesterday, weren't you? No spills, nothing like that?"

"Why?" She came over to stand behind him and bent to stare at the screen. Her hair brushed his cheek. He scrolled through the graphs so she could see for herself. She sucked in her breath. "Influenza?"

He stood. "I'll get the aliquots." Shazia had assumed the risk yesterday. "You prepare the red blood cells."

She stepped back, watching worriedly. He couldn't blame her. Those teal had suffered. This didn't look like a virus either of them would want to battle.

He pulled on gloves and his lab coat. Opening the freezer, he selected some of the samples and carried them over to the hood. Thirty minutes at room temperature should be ample time to defrost them. Now he brought over fresh pipettes and plates and set them alongside the aliquots.

"Which antisera are you going to run?" Shazia asked.

"Let's do H1, H2, H5, and H7." They'd test for the most common subtypes first, move on to the others if those didn't show up. He pulled down the small glass bottles and settled himself on the stool. They were going to be working fast. They wouldn't have time to neutralize the virus's infectivity. He'd just have to be careful.

Reaching beneath the clear plastic faceplate of the hood, he drew out four thin, flexible plates filled with cylindrical depressions. Labeling them, he lined them up before him. He pipetted one hundred milliliters of raw sample into each of thirty-two wells on the first tray and repeated this for the remaining three trays. He changed pipette tips as he went, covering each tray as he finished it and moving it aside.

No need, really, for him to be holding his breath. After all, the hood was working. He was gloved, and his hands had been steady. He hadn't knocked a tube or spilled anything. Nevertheless, he felt a rush of relief when he finished with this step.

Now he dripped one hundred milliliters of H1 antiserum into every well across the first tray. He covered the tray and reached for the second. This one would test for H2. When he finally completed the fourth and final tray, he sat back. It would take an hour for the antibodies to recognize the antigens. He had to be patient. Whatever was going on inside those tiny depressions filled with fluid was invisible to the human eye, but it was critical. Exactly which strain of avian influenza were they talking about?

He rolled his head. How long had he been sitting hunched over like this? He glanced at the clock on the wall. He was shocked to see it was going on noon.

The phone rang and Shazia answered it. She extended the receiver to Peter. "It's Dan."

Peter cradled the receiver between shoulder and ear as he washed his hands in the industrial sink. "We've got avian influenza. The way it ran through those teal makes me think it's high-path." Maybe he'd try that experimental RT-PCR technique he'd heard about. "I'm subtyping it now." Silence. "Dan?"

"Yeah, I'm here. Feel like taking a drive?" Dan said.

*Uh, no.* "You kidding?" But Dan didn't make casual requests. "Why?"

"I just got a report of another die-off."

That couldn't be. Peter had never heard of two die-offs occurring back-to-back. "Where?"

"Thirty miles north of Sparrow. A lodge owner just called it in."

Forget his afternoon class. Shazia could finish the lab work. "I'll be there by one. Give me the address and I'll MapQuest it."

"Great. And Peter? Better bring your gear."

PETER BUMPED HIS PICKUP DOWN THE GRAVEL ROAD. RADIO static assailed him.

"... *current* ... *passages* ... *its inability* ..."

The few words breaking through the clutter were spoken with a kind of urgency. What was the announcer worked up about, another congressional bill up for debate? Maybe interest rates were taking a hike.

He reached over and pressed buttons, skipped past bleats of music and talk, settling at last on an old Eagles song.

Yellow fields opened up on both sides. Pine trees fringed the horizon. The aroma of grass and manure seeped through his opened window. When he rounded the curve, he saw big heavy Angus dotting the farmland on his right. A cow ambled to the fence to watch him pass by, her udders swaying with her deliberate steps.

Here was the turnoff, a dirt road cut into the tall grass. He slowed and came to the next opening. No sign to mark the narrow entry. His rear tires spun and spat out pebbles before catching.

A muffled chirp made him glance at the seat beside him. It came from his leather jacket. Patting around, he located his cell phone and flipped it open. Shazia.

"What's up?"

"—ter? ... finished with ..."

"Hold on. I didn't get that."

He swooped around a curve, and now her voice came through clearly, her excitement plain. *"It's H5."*

Okay. So now they know which hemagglutinin they were talking about. But they were only halfway there. "Start the neuraminidase subtyping."

"Should I get things ready to send off to NVSL?"

Was it premature at this point to involve the national lab? The minute they did that, all sorts of official wheels would be set in motion. Peter didn't say so, but he intended to run some additional tests of his own. He flashed back to the lake filled with bobbing teal. And now he was on his way to another kill. "Go ahead," he told Shazia. "Doesn't hurt to be prepared."

Peter bumped up onto the shoulder and pulled in behind two FSW vehicles and an unmarked truck. Two men in khaki stood there, talking. The shorter one turned as Peter approached.

"Hey, Brooks." He extended his hand. "Glad you could make it." Peter shook his hand. "You bring in reinforcements?"

"You'll see why." Dan indicated the man beside him. "This is Special Agent Monroe. Mike, this is Peter Brooks, one of our veterinary medicine experts. We go way back."

The other man leaned forward to shake Peter's hand. "I hear you came across another die-off yesterday."

"We just learned it's H5," Peter said. "You think that's what we've got here?"

"Rapid screening shows it's flu. We don't want to jump to conclusions, but Jesus." Dan rubbed the back of his neck, grimacing. "What else could take down ducks like this? Come on, I'll show you."

The path cut into the woods. The smell of pine was heavy, the trees tall and lacy with sunlight. "Beautiful," Peter said.

"Yeah. This is one of our most popular fishing areas." Dan stopped. "We'd better put on our stuff."

Peter set down his toolbox. Another pair of gloves from the box, a fresh mask, and his old plastic goggles, bleary from years of use.

"I've called around." Dan fit goggles onto his face. "No one else is reporting anything unusual."

Good news. "What about the poultry farmers?"

"I've notified everyone within thirty miles, just to be on the safe side." Dan snapped on a pair of gloves.

Peter couldn't imagine the financial stakes involved. Had to be millions, easy. He'd been as surprised as anyone to learn America was the world's largest poultry producer.

"Any of the farmers mention seeing signs of disease?" They

shuffled out from the woods onto sandy soil, the world now reduced to muffled sight and smell, their shoes digging into the soft, slippery surface. "They know what . . ."

His words fell away. He stopped and stared at the scene spread out before him.

Thousands upon thousands of birds lay heaped along the shore. He'd never seen so many birds packed so close together before, and so utterly silent. It couldn't be. It couldn't be, but it was. The horror of Qinghai replicated right here in central Ohio.

The only sound was the irregular rasp of his breathing.

He began walking blindly toward the water. Dan was saying something, but Peter wasn't listening. He stopped and looked down. Matted clumped feathers, opened bills, little feet moving in the motion of the water.

There were green and blue teal, mallard, northern shoveler, pintail, all of them piled together regardless of species. A red-breasted merganser lay half in, half out of the water. The spirited spray of feathers at the back of its head, the long, pointy beak in comical contrast to the large webbed feet. Peter crouched. Mergansers were the first ducks he'd been able to identify as a boy.

"You call this in?" he asked Dan. He heard the wobble in his voice and cleared his throat.

"All the way up the chain of command."

He stood. "I'm surprised the media's not here."

"They will be," Dan said grimly.

Off to one side, two men suited up in white protective clothing knelt in the sand. They worked in a determined sort of rhythm. Pick up a bird, reach for a swab, set down a test tube. "How many are you doing?"

"A minimum of three per species. Nasal and cloacal."

"I'll start running them through as soon as I get back." He'd pull his students from their other projects. Hell, he'd contact all his colleagues and have them pitch in.

A shout sounded from behind them. "Dan!"

They looked over. A figure was running from the woods behind them. It was Mike Monroe, stumbling in his haste to get to them.

# SIX

A NN GLANCED AT HER WATCH AND HURRIED DOWN THE
corridor. She had barely thirty minutes before she was due
back, enough time if the lines weren't too long. Rounding the corner, she saw Rachel standing in the front office, bent over the sign-
out book.

Ann pushed open the glass door. "Hey, stranger."

Rachel straightened. Tall, her blond hair clipped into a perfect
pageboy, she had a confident way of holding herself that made her
stand out in a crowd. Ann had noticed that Hannah had inherited
the same trait.

"Well, if it isn't the school hero." Rachel cocked a sculpted eyebrow. "Hannah told me you ran into a burning building and rescued one of her classmates."

"Some hero. The only things burning were my ears after the fire
chief chewed me out."

"And what would he have done if you'd just left her there?"
Rachel waved at the secretary, who had the telephone pressed to
her ear and was listening to whoever was speaking on the other
end. She didn't respond. Rachel shrugged. She turned to Ann. "You
coming in or going out?"

"Out. I'm squeezing in a quick trip to the post office before I sic the fifth-graders on Georgia O'Keeffe. You?"

"I'm on my way home. I'm done volunteering for the day."

They used to volunteer together, coordinating their schedules so they could squeeze in a quick lunch afterward or a trip to the mall before they had to race back to pick up their kids. But that had all changed this year. Now Ann was the one phoning around for parent volunteers and Rachel was the one answering. Or not.

The secretary stood. She knocked on the principal's door and went in without waiting for a response.

"I'm glad I ran into you." Out in the hall, Ann leaned on the front door and held it open for Rachel. They stepped into a swirl of leaves and cold air. "I called you last night."

Rachel nodded, fastening the buttons on her black coat. "I got your message. Sorry I didn't call back. It's been crazy with Rich out of town. You know, just me and the kids." Rachel made a face. "I guess you'd know how that is."

Ann supposed she did. She didn't like to think of herself as a single parent, but of course she was. Peter was there in a big-picture way, but it was up to Ann to shepherd their daughters through the day and oversee all the small events that made up their lives. "I hear Hannah started piano yesterday."

"Yes. A space opened up and I nabbed it." Rachel tugged on her gloves. "I know we talked about the girls taking lessons together, but that was before you went back to work."

"I know. My schedule's been awful. Maybe Hannah could play after school."

"Today? I'm sorry, but she's already got plans."

Right. Maddie had said Hannah had karate this afternoon. "What does your weekend look like?"

"Pretty packed, I'm afraid. Cheerleading practice, haircuts. And Rich is still stuck in Belgium. His plane's delayed for some reason, so he's no help. I'll let you know."

Rachel had said pretty much the same thing last week, a vague response about checking her calendar and promising to get back to her. And she never had. "How about after we come back from

Thanksgiving break? Aren't Mondays your yoga night? Hannah can come home with us after school."

"I don't think that's going to work."

Ann stopped on the sidewalk. "Rachel, is everything okay? We used to have Hannah over all the time, and now—"

"Oh, it's no big deal. I just think the girls need to make some other friends."

Rachel said it so lightly. What had happened to make her feel this way? The two girls got along so well. They'd been inseparable since preschool. Ann looked at Rachel, but Rachel wouldn't meet her eyes. She knew Maddie didn't have any other friends. She knew that Maddie was the kind of person who made one true friend, and that friend was Hannah. Maddie wasn't like Kate, who had lots of friends, the better to hide among.

"I see," Ann said, although she didn't.

Rachel slid her hands into the pockets of her coat. "It's just that Hannah doesn't understand why Maddie can't come over to play. She thinks it's something she did."

Ann frowned. "Of course it isn't. She must know that."

"Hannah's only eight. It doesn't matter how much we reassure her. All she knows is that her best friend can't come and play at her house anymore."

"Maddie misses playing at your house, too." It was such a small thing, couldn't they move past it?

"You know she's welcome anytime."

Ann couldn't believe it. Rachel knew as well as anyone that Maddie could never come over, not as long as Hannah still had her kitten.

Rachel had phoned her in the middle of the night, waking her from a deep sleep. "Is Maddie allergic to anything?" she'd demanded without preamble.

"No," Ann had replied, already pulling on her clothes, instantly frantic at the urgency in Rachel's voice. "At least not that I know of."

"Her lung collapsed," Ann reminded Rachel now. "She spent two nights in the hospital."

"I know," Rachel said. "It was awful. But you told me the doctor said medication would help."

"He said it *might* help."

"You won't know unless you try."

Rachel couldn't possibly be serious. She'd been there. She'd raced Maddie to the emergency room that night, begging her to hold on. "You know I can't do that."

The wind lifted Rachel's hair from her face and pressed the collar of her coat against her throat. "Ann, don't you think you're being a little overprotective?"

Was she? Maybe. But the memory of her child, eyes swollen shut, panting for breath, was enough to make Ann feel her own throat close up.

Rachel sighed. "I'm sorry. I shouldn't have said that. I guess I'd feel the same way if I were you."

*If I were you.* Something about the questioning way Rachel said that warned Ann they were on the precipice of something new. "What do you mean?"

The words were out before Ann could stop herself. She didn't want to know. She didn't want to go there.

Rachel looked away. "You never said anything. I kept waiting for you to tell me."

Ann had the dizzying sensation of standing on the edge of a cliff and looking down at the jagged rocks. She needed to step back. She needed them both to move to safer ground. "Rachel—" she began, but Rachel pushed on.

"I'm sorry. I know I shouldn't say anything. But if we were really friends, you would have told me. You would have at least mentioned it to me."

Her tone was accusing. Suddenly they weren't talking about Hannah and Maddie anymore. How had this happened? How did Rachel *know*?

Rachel crossed her arms. "The last time Maddie was over, she told Hannah. When Hannah told me later, I thought at first Maddie had been making it up. Because if it were true, you would have told me. When I had that miscarriage five years ago, you would have told me then."

"It wasn't the same thing," Ann whispered.

"Are you sure?" Rachel shot back.

They stood there on the sidewalk, the brick school building beside them, the flag whipping above them on its metal pole. Cars drove past, a thumping burst of music. Children called to one another on the nearby playground.

"What did Maddie tell Hannah?"

Rachel slid her hands into her coat pockets. "She said there was a baby brother who never woke up from his nap."

So simple.

"Is it true?" Rachel said.

Maddie, her sweet, uncomplicated child, painting rainbows. Maddie, whom Ann had thought was safe, whom Ann had wanted so much to believe was untouched by all the sadness around her that she'd refused to see the truth for what it was. Something inside her daughter had at last spoken up, some tiny little questioning voice yearning to be heard, yearning to be answered. *How do you help a child when you can't even help yourself?*

THE POST OFFICE WAS CLOSED WHEN SHE ARRIVED. ANN shifted the bulky envelope under one arm and tried both doors, but they were securely locked. The times posted on the window said it should be open for another four hours. She rapped on the glass. Wasn't that someone moving around inside? She rattled the door handle and waved, but no one came. She glanced at her watch. *Drat.* No time to try another branch. She'd have to wait until after school let out. A few more hours wouldn't make any difference.

The front office was empty when she entered the building. Ann walked down the hall, her footsteps ringing in the quiet. No one was in the nurse's office. The cafeteria was empty. So was the library. Where was everyone? A voice echoed down the hall, a man speaking into a microphone. She pushed open the gymnasium door and saw the room filled with children sitting cross-legged on the floor. The faculty and staff lined the walls. Maddie was toward the front, hunched beside Hannah, the two of them sitting closely together, one blond head and one brown, engrossed in some covert clapping game, completely unaware that the clock had already started ticking on their friendship.

The principal stood at the podium in the front of the room.

". . . by the Ohio Department of Health that school will be closing." He lifted his hand to hush the cheer that went up from the children.

School was closing? Some horrible infection must have gotten loose, like hepatitis or bacterial meningitis. But no one was coughing. No one looked sick. Maybe it was an environmental contaminant, like lead in the water or asbestos coming loose from around the pipes. With a pinch of fear, Ann wondered how many times Maddie drank from the water fountain.

"Your teachers will be handing out a note for you to take home to your parents. When you go back to your classrooms, you'll need to empty your desks and cubbies. If you need a plastic bag to carry items, let your teacher know. The announcement's being made on the radio and television, so car riders, your parents should start arriving soon. They'll have to sign you out first. Listen for your name over the loudspeaker. Bus riders will wait in their classrooms until their buses arrive. For those whose parents are delayed, we'll be setting up tables in the cafeteria. Now, I want everyone to stand up and, in a quiet, orderly fashion, return to your classrooms. We'll start with kindergarten first."

The noise level soared as everyone stirred into motion. Ann looked for Maddie and spotted her in the stream of chattering, laughing children flowing toward the doors. Ann waved.

Maddie pushed closer. She looked excited. "Did you hear, Mom? We don't have to go to school anymore."

"I heard." Ann kept her voice light. What on earth had happened that would prompt the Department of Health to shut down the school?

Hannah pushed Maddie along. "Go."

Maddie turned and called back to Ann. "You're coming to get me, right, Mom?"

"I'll be right there, honey."

Maddie's teacher brought up the rear of the line, her face grim. She had Heyjin by one hand and held a sheaf of blue papers in the other. "If you're not doing anything, Mrs. Brooks, I could use your help getting the children ready."

"Of course." It wouldn't take long to seal up the art room. Ann had already begun putting things away in preparation for the upcoming Thanksgiving holiday. "What's going on? Why are they closing the school?"

"Not just this one. All of the schools."

"What?"

The woman peeled off the top page from the stack she held. "Here."

Ann read the sheet and slowed. Sudden coldness flooded her body. Kids swarmed around her, but she didn't feel them bumping into her. The words on the page swam before her. She saw them clearly printed there, but she had to read them twice before the meaning sank in. "We're in Phase Five now?"

"That's right."

Ann stared at her. So the clusters of flu cases had multiplied to the extent that they were threatening to sweep across entire communities. That meant H5N1 had mutated again, cleverly adapting itself to jump more easily from human to human. She had the sensation of standing on a cliff again, looking down into an eternal unknown. "When did this happen?"

"An hour ago." She clasped Heyjin's hand again, looked down at her, and shook her head. "Ironic, isn't it? She traveled all that way to get here, but in the end, it didn't matter a damn."

Heyjin glanced up at her teacher and then looked to Ann. The triumph in the child's eyes was unmistakable.

*TEXT OF SPEECH GIVEN BY*
*DR. NIGEL ATWANA,*
*WHO DIRECTOR-GENERAL,*
*WHO HEADQUARTERS,*
*GENEVA, SWITZERLAND*

---

Good evening, ladies and gentlemen.

For several years, the world has been in Phase Three of alertness with regard to avian influenza. Phase Three means that there have been few human cases of avian influenza. In September, clusters appeared in several Asian countries and we moved into Phase Four, a situation in which the virus can be more easily transmitted among humans.

Today, in response to reports of large, multiple outbreaks in Europe and Africa, we announce an entry into Phase Five of alertness. We caution the public not to panic. Phase Five just means increased protective measures in the affected countries, appropriate to the situation. These measures are:

People with confirmed or suspected cases will be quarantined.
All schools and universities will be closed until further notice.
All indoor concerts and public events will be canceled. This
    includes gatherings for religious purposes.
International and domestic travel will be curtailed.

Please be reassured that a pandemic is by no means inevitable. If we work together, we can contain and halt the spread of the influenza virus.

# SEVEN

$P$ETER STOOD IN THE DOORWAY OF HIS LAB, CELL PHONE
pressed to his ear. Ann still wasn't answering her phone.

People rushed past in the corridor carrying folders, books,
boxes. They nodded at one another, barely stopping. He wondered
how many of them would be alive next month, next year. The air
was filled with abbreviated conversations.

"Did you get . . . ?"

"They're in there. . . ."

Behind him, Shazia was wiping surfaces and turning off equipment. She'd managed to get through the neuraminidase testing.
She'd greeted him with the news—the teal influenza had been
H5N1. He'd greeted her with his own announcement. She'd been
sequestered all afternoon behind the hood and hadn't heard. Somehow the bird and human variations had simultaneously picked up
speed. Both viruses were busy tearing through their respective host
populations.

Peter tried the home number, but the answering machine
picked up. He hung up without leaving a message. He'd call again
shortly. Ann would have heard the news. She'd be out getting the
girls. "You put everything in the freezer?"

Shazia shut the cabinet. "Yes." Her navy wool coat was folded over the back of a chair. Her briefcase leaned against the rungs. Black-bound manuals sat stacked on the desk. She saw him looking. "I hope it's okay that I borrow those."

"It's a good idea." He eyed them, crossed to the shelf, and pulled down several more. "You'll need these, too."

In his office, he began fitting books into one box, papers into another. He'd take his laptop, of course. And his tape recorder.

"You get the rough draft I sent you?"

He looked up and saw Lewis leaning in. His curly blond hair was more vertical than usual, giving him an alarmed look. "I'll work on it at home and email it back to you."

"Fair enough. We can submit it online."

A voice boomed from down the hall. "Let's go, people."

Lewis swore softly and pushed himself away from the doorjamb. "See you, Peter."

Now a series of knocks, getting louder. "Locking up in five minutes."

Peter slid his laptop into the case and zipped it up. Where was the folder with Liederman's notes in it?

"You too, Dr. Brooks."

Peter looked over. Hank filled the doorway, a tank of a man.

"Sure," Pete said. "Just give me a minute. I need to find something."

"No can do. I was supposed to have secured the building fifteen minutes ago."

"All right, all right." He shuffled through the papers on his desk. Here were the minutes from last week's preparedness meeting. How ironic. Here was an invitation to the division holiday party. His secretary was always despairing of the condition of his office, always warning him that she was going to sneak in one day and clear everything out. Now Peter wished she'd gotten to the mess before she'd gone on maternity leave.

"Dr. Brooks." Hank had his jacket open now, showing the gun holstered at his hip. A subconscious move on Hank's part, or was he making a point? Peter looked into the security guard's small eyes. The man was afraid. Fear could make people do stupid things.

"Fine." Peter picked up the entire pile and shoved it into his briefcase. The weathered leather bulged with the effort of containing it all.

Hank moved aside to let him out, reached back and drew the door shut. A jangle of keys and the door was firmly locked.

Struggling under the weight of two boxes and the overstuffed briefcase on top, he made his way down the corridor. Shazia stood waiting for him, under the weight of her own box and papers. They came to a stop by the elevator. She frowned at the numbers above them, watching them glow in sequence.

"You should call your family as soon as you get settled."

"Yes." She shifted the box in her arms. "Do you think the H5 we've been working with made the jump to human form?"

"Unlikely. But even if it had, I wouldn't be concerned. We took precautions."

"Right."

There was something in her tone. "Shazia."

She looked at him.

"You were careful, weren't you?"

The elevator door wheezed open, and she stepped inside. "Yes," she said. "Of course."

"Can you tell our listeners why the scientific community is particularly worried about what's going on?"

"Certainly. What I think has everyone concerned is the apparent emergence of a virus that seems to have made the genetic leap from avian to human form. Of course, this may be a short-lived phenomenon. H5N1 is constantly mutating, and this may be one brief stage in its life span. It could change once again and evolve into a virus that is no longer as harmful to humans."

"But you don't think so."

"I think a more likely scenario would be that the virus becomes so successful at propagating that it settles into this more deadly version for a long time."

"Resulting in more human casualties."

"Unfortunately, yes. The fatality rate of this virus is much greater than the one we saw in 1918 that killed twenty percent of the people it afflicted. We are currently seeing fatality rates approaching fifty percent."

"That's hard to imagine."

"Yes. A couple of factors play into this. First, H5 bypasses nasal passages in favor of digging deep into the human lung, where it can inflict more damage."

"Which explains the increased incidence of pneumonia."

"Partially. And then there's the length of illness. Even though the period of contagion before onset of symptoms is shrinking to twenty-four hours, H5 is living an average of eight days in its human host. This is a significant length of time. The longer the virus can keep its host alive, the more time it has to propagate and infect another host. And then there's the speed at which it's traveling. H5 is beginning to spread with the same rapidity that hallmarked the 1918 virus."

"Which circled the globe in months."

"Yes. Although in today's world, I think a more accurate estimate might be more like weeks. Conventional wisdom says the virus could reach the United States in the length of time it takes a plane to cross the Atlantic."

"So we're talking hours?"

"That's right. Six hours. The virus could already be here."

The Frank Sherman Hour,
*WBBS*

# EIGHT

"MICHELE SAYS THEY'VE CANCELED THE WINTER Dance." Kate sat at the kitchen table with her laptop opened in front of her. She frowned down at her cell phone.

"They'll reschedule it." *Though probably not until the following year.* Ann slid her arms through the sleeves of her coat. This was just the beginning. What about report cards, birthday parties, dental appointments?

"Get ice cream," Maddie said. "And goldfish crackers."

"I will."

A car horn sounded. The television in the family room showed long lines of people standing in an airport, waiting to have their temperature taken. Ann lifted the remote and turned off the television.

"Mom," Maddie said.

"Just while I'm gone, honey." Who knew what they'd see in her absence? "Kate, lock the door behind me."

Kate moved her thumb across the mouse pad. "Okay."

Ann checked her purse for her wallet and her cell phone. Here was Maddie's medicine. That shouldn't come with her. "If anyone rings the doorbell, don't answer."

"Not even for Libby?" Maddie said.

"Libby will be with me. Mr. Finn might come by for me to sign another of his petitions. You can call through the door, but don't open it."

Maddie shook her head. "He'll be mad."

"That's all right. Kate?"

Her daughter was focused on the laptop screen, her hands typing busily.

"Kate!"

She glanced up. "What?"

"What did I just tell you?"

"Something about the door and Mr. Finn."

Ann looked at her with exasperation. "You need to stop fooling around with your laptop and watch your sister."

Kate pushed herself away from the table and stood. "Why don't you just take Maddie with you if you don't think she'll be safe with me?"

"That's not—"

But Kate was stomping up the stairs.

Libby's SUV waited in the driveway. "Thanks for coming," she said as Ann opened the car door.

"No problem. It makes sense to go together." Ann climbed in and glanced back. Jacob sat nestled in his car seat behind her, bundled in navy corduroy and wearing a scarlet cap. He saw her and pumped his legs, his cheeks bunching around his pacifier. He was grinning.

"You little sweetie," she said, smiling back at him before turning around to pull the seatbelt across her lap.

"I hope you don't mind me bringing him. Smith's not home yet."

"Of course not. He can help us choose cereal."

Libby swung the steering wheel and they bumped onto the street. "I don't get it. Why are they closing school for three whole months? The flu's not even here."

"It's in the state preparedness plans. A lot of things are going to start happening because we're in Phase Five." The announcement had been so sudden. Ann still couldn't believe it. She'd thought there would be some indication, but maybe she'd been so preoccupied that she'd missed the warning signs. The Health Department would start closing everything, including Peter's university. She wondered how he was doing. She wondered if he'd seen this coming. No. He'd have said something. Despite everything, he'd have wanted her and the girls to be prepared.

Libby honked at the car waiting to make a turn in front of her. "How am I going to get any work done? I have a major deadline coming up."

"Maybe your boss will let you work from home." All the lights were on at the bank and the lot was filled. Cars stood in line for the ATM. How much cash did she have? As a rule, she didn't keep much on hand. So, maybe twenty bucks.

"Yeah, sure. That'll happen. He about had a heart attack when I took maternity leave. He must've called ten times, asking when I was coming back." Libby gripped the steering wheel. "Maybe my mom can come and stay with us for a while."

"There you go." Ann's parents hadn't answered the phone. Of course, they didn't have a cell. They had to be out, doing just what Ann was doing. Getting groceries, stocking up on cash. She'd try them again as soon as she got home.

Libby glanced over. "What about you? Do you even have a job anymore?"

"I don't know." Another worry. "We'd better stop at an ATM on the way home."

"Good idea." Libby turned into the shopping center and braked hard at the sight of cars packed into the sprawling space, lined up against the curbs and across the grassy median. Still more cars prowled around, headlights shining, exhaust puffing behind them in weary streams. "Jesus."

Ann pointed. "There's a car pulling out over there."

Libby slid the SUV into the spot and turned off the engine. She lifted the car seat from the backseat.

Ann slammed the door and, glancing around, spotted an abandoned cart nearby. She dragged it over and helped Libby fit the car seat on top. Another cart stood at the curb. She grabbed it. "You take the baby. I'll start in the bread section."

The doors glided open. Libby wheeled her cart to the right while Ann swept left.

Shoppers clogged the front of the store. Ann pushed through them to reach the bread aisle and stopped, staring in disbelief down the long, empty space. The shelves were completely bare. Not a single loaf or package of buns in sight. She'd never seen anything like this, not even after Phase Four had been announced. Maybe there was some in the back—

A man in a white windbreaker strode past, a name tag pinned to his chest.

"Excuse me," Ann said. "When will you be restocking the bread?"

"You gotta be kidding." He walked away.

All right. So there wasn't bread here. But sometimes there was bread at the deli counter. She swung her cart around.

Sure enough, two racks stood by the swinging doors beside the shining glass deli cases. People were pawing through the shelves. Ann waded in among them and reached to grasp the necks of plastic bags. She didn't know what she had until she brought them to the cart. English muffins. Cinnamon-raisin. She removed her coat and tossed it on top of the bread and went back in for more. Rye. Wheat. Everyone was pushing now and using their elbows.

"Hey." A loud voice from nearby.

"You can't stop me." Another voice, just as loud. "Long as I pay for it, I can take as much as I want. This is America!"

Ann took some loaves from the bottom racks. She stepped back out of jostling range with relief. Stuffing the bread beneath her coat, she turned. Forget taking a ticket for the deli counter. One look at the long lines there convinced her—any lunchmeat she wanted would have to come from the refrigerated section.

Milk.

The meat section was on the way, and she reached in among the other shoppers for chicken breasts and ground beef. Not stopping to sheathe them in plastic first, she dumped packages in the cart and moved the bread up to the top. How much was enough? A glance to one side showed a woman stepping back, balancing a tower of Styrofoam packages in her arms. Ann took armloads of everything. She'd split them with Libby.

People thronged the dairy section. She jogged her cart as close as she could and tried to peer around people's shoulders and heads. Was she too late? She couldn't get close enough to see anything.

"There's a line, you know," a woman snapped.

*All right.* That was good. Some sort of order had been imposed here. Ann got in line and waited her turn. Slowly she inched closer, bringing her cart with her. At last she glimpsed the rounded shapes of milk cartons. From behind the shelves, a hand was pushing containers of milk through the plastic flaps. Gallon after gallon thudded into place, just as swiftly grabbed away.

She took a gallon in each hand and heaved them into her cart. She turned for another two. The girls drank a lot of milk. Six wasn't too much.

"That's it," the guy behind her said.

Oh. So there was a limit. Ann nodded. "I'm getting some for my neighbor." She took four more. She was beginning to sweat. She removed her sweatshirt and tied it around her waist.

She steered her cart along the back of the store, piling stuff in as she went. Yogurt. Cheese. Juice. What was she forgetting? She'd circled the perimeter of the store and now she began to try and push her way into each packed aisle. When she reached the cereal section, she couldn't even get two steps into the aisle. Down the crowd of people, she saw Libby's blond head, heard her voice. "You push that cart into me one more time—"

"Lady," a voice said behind Ann, and she swung around to see a store employee wheeling a tall stack of boxes toward her. The dolly nudged the back of her heel. "You the one looking for Merry Berries?"

"They're mine!" A short woman with a pixie haircut waved her arm. "I'm the one who asked for them. I'm the one who should get them first."

"Libby," Ann called. "Get me cornflakes."

"Got it."

The frozen-food section was welcomingly wide. Shoppers stood two abreast. Ann was reckless in her choices, tugging each glass door open and pulling something out. Pizza, toaster waffles, ravioli. She stood with a bag of peas in her hand. No place to put it. She had things wedged in everywhere and piled along the bottom of her cart.

When she reached the front of the store, she came to a stop at the end of a line that snaked into the aisle. She looked at her cart. It looked foreign to her, someone else's shopping cart filled with things she would never buy. Marshmallow Fluff, cocktail wienies, diet milkshakes, candy-flavored vitamins. Raisins, though the girls hated them. She dialed her cell phone.

"Hey," Libby said.

Over the phone, Ann heard voices raised in anger. "Everything okay?"

"A fight over batteries."

"Grab as many as you can. I'm in line for register"—Ann peered over the heads in front of her—"twelve."

"I'll be there in a minute. Sit tight."

A male clerk slid cases of bottled water onto an endcap. Water. That should have been her first stop. She looked to her cart. It was hopeless. She couldn't fit in a single bottle.

The clerk was now heaving cases of water directly into people's carts. They formed a protective barrier around him.

"I'm with her," she heard a familiar voice say, and turned to see Libby push past a skinny woman in a miniskirt. "We're together," she informed the man behind Ann. She was breathless, and her cart was just as full as Ann's. She gripped a twenty-four-pack of toilet paper. Jacob looked as though he was riding a haystack of paper towels, sucking furiously on his pacifier.

"I forgot water. Watch my cart." Ann pushed through the people to where the clerk was working.

"That's mine," a woman said.

"I've been here longer," someone else said.

The clerk straightened. "Sorry, folks. That's it."

The man in front of Ann said, "You bringing out another load?"

The clerk shook his head. "The truck comes Sunday."

Sunday. Four days away.

Libby had been watching. "No luck, huh?"

"I'll be right back."

An empty cart sat in the middle of an aisle, people streaming around it. Ann grabbed the handle and headed to the health food section. It was quieter here. Juices were in a middle aisle. Colorful, bright, unusual flavors, and yes, farther down, a gleaming row of specialty waters.

In the detergent aisle she grabbed distilled water, big jugs of it that she levered into her cart.

The neon video store sign glowed in one corner. No one was there, not even a clerk. She worked her way from cold case to cold case, opening the doors and reaching past the sodas for the chilled bottles of water.

Pushing her cart was hard work now. She gripped the handle with both hands and leaned into it. Without warning, a man stepped in front of her. She came to an abrupt halt, the front of her cart swinging to one side. He grabbed the cart with a hand. He was young and clean-shaven, wearing a football jersey and jeans, and he wasn't letting go of her cart. He didn't look crazy.

"Excuse me," Ann said, trying to move around him.

But he had both hands on the wire basket. And she had a firm grip on the handle. They pulled in opposite directions.

"Let go," Ann told him. "Are you insane?"

"Joan!" he yelled.

This was a deserted part of the store. No one was rushing over here to stock up on video rentals. He was younger and stronger, and he was slowly but surely pulling the handle from her grasp.

"Joan! C'mere!"

"Stop that!"

Thank goodness. Someone was coming to her aid. A woman ran down the aisle toward them, shopping cart racing along in front of her. Long bleached hair, black leather, heels clacking on the linoleum.

Ann smiled at her.

The woman glared back, her heavily penciled eyebrows drawn down with annoyance. "Good job, Kenny." She reached into Ann's cart, pulled out a jug of water, and set it rolling into her cart. "The bread's gone," she told him.

"So's the milk."

Ann was frozen with disbelief. Without thinking, she slapped the woman's hand away from a jug of water. "What is *wrong* with you people? Go get your own."

The woman slapped back. "You haven't bought it yet. It's not yours." She yanked Ann's cart toward her.

"There's more back there." Ann grabbed the cart and shoved it behind her.

"We're not going back there," Joan snapped. She took a step forward.

Ann blocked her. They glared at each other.

"Get out of my way, bitch." The woman shoved Ann.

Ann shoved back. Then Joan leaned back and punched Ann in the chest.

Gasping, Ann stumbled back. Her hands curled into fists. Then she caught herself. Water. This was about water.

From behind her, Kenny said, "We're done here. Let's hit the frozen-food aisle."

Ann wheeled around. Her cart was empty. Kenny had taken it all.

He grabbed his cart, now loaded with bottles of water. Joan reached around and gave Ann's empty cart a vicious shove. It cracked against Ann's shin.

The world blinked white.

Then Ann saw Kenny and Joan farther down the aisle, reaching in and helping themselves to a stack of toilet paper from another person's cart. The single woman pushing that was no match for the two of them, either.

Ann never thought she'd have to shop in teams for safety.

# NINE

P ETER FOLLOWED SHAZIA DOWN THE OVERLY BRIGHT DORMI-
tory corridor filled with people and stepped aside to let an
older man carrying a big carton pass by.

"You got everything?" he was saying to the skinny brunette
walking half a step behind him.

"I got my laptop, Dad. That's all I need."

Shazia paused in front of a door. A piece of paper was taped
there, and she pulled it down, unfolded it, and scanned its contents.
"Caroline's already left."

Peter had met Shazia's roommate, a tall and imperious girl from
South Africa. He'd heard Caroline was a whiz in nanotechnology.
"Where's she going?"

"She's assigned to Tower West, too."

Good. Maybe they could room together. That would make the
transition smoother for both girls.

Shazia slid her keycard into the box mounted beside the door.
Turning the knob, she pushed it open to reveal a small square space
filled with the usual scarred oak furniture, doubles of everything—beds, dressers, desks. It didn't take long for her to fold garments and pack them away. She placed some framed pictures

between her sweaters before zippering the suitcase closed. She filled a second suitcase with towels and some personal items.

It felt sad, this brisk uprooting.

She straightened and glanced around. "I guess that's it."

Tower West wasn't far.

The tall dormitory was ablaze with light. Buses idled at the curb, as people scurried across the bright courtyard. Peter pulled the pickup onto the grass at the end of a row of parked cars. Campus security wouldn't be issuing parking tickets tonight.

Lines of students snaked through the lobby, jockeying for position in front of the three card tables that had been set up by the elevators. A uniformed guard stood there, arms crossed.

Peter and Shazia joined the crowd.

When it was their turn, the woman at the small table looked up through the narrow glasses perched on the tip of her nose. "ID?"

"Yes, of course." Shazia set down her suitcase and dipped her hand into her briefcase.

The woman took the laminated card and squinted at it, then reached for her keyboard. She tapped a few keys and frowned. She looked at the card again, then retried the numbers. "Are you a current student?"

"Yes. I just arrived this semester."

"Maybe they haven't inputted your number into the system yet. Let's try your name."

Shazia spelled it out.

The woman typed. Then she shook her head. "That doesn't work, either. You sure you're current?"

"They might have her in the general student population," Peter said. "Maybe we should check Tower East."

"Tower East's already full. We're taking their overflow."

Something knocked the backs of Peter's legs. He turned around to see a tall boy standing close behind, burdened with backpack, sleeping bag, and a row of bags. "Sorry," the kid said.

Peter nodded and turned back. He held out the card he wore clipped to his pocket. "I'm her advisor," he told the woman. "I can vouch for her. Could you assign her a room now and we'll straighten out the details later?"

"I'm sorry, Dr. Brooks. You're not the first person to ask me that tonight. If I bend the rules for you, I'll have to bend them for everyone." She handed Shazia back her card.

"But she's entitled to temporary housing."

"Only if she's a currently registered international student."

Peter was losing his patience. "She *is* a currently registered student."

"Not according to my records. Maybe there's some problem with her tuition payments."

Peter glanced at Shazia.

She looked helpless. "I don't know."

"Whatever the problem is," Peter told the woman, "I'll get it sorted out tomorrow. Let's just find her a room now."

"I'm sorry, Dr. Brooks." She looked pointedly behind Peter. "Next."

"Her dorm's closed. She has nowhere to go." His cell phone was ringing. He could feel it vibrate against his hip. He pulled the phone from his pocket.

"Fine." The woman sighed. "Tell you what. Why don't you wait against that wall and I'll find someone to help you."

Sure she would. He glanced down at his phone and flipped it open. "Excuse me," he said, then spoke into the phone. "Kate, honey, can I call you back?"

"Dad? Where *are* you?" She sounded teary.

"I'm at work. Why? What's the matter?"

"Mom said she'd be gone an hour, but it's been way over two hours. She's not answering her phone." Her voice went up, sailing clearly from the tiny mouthpiece. "I just saw on the news that someone got shot at Kroger."

"Dr. Brooks?" the clerk said impatiently.

"Is that where she is?" Peter asked Kate, alarmed.

"I don't know. She told me she was just going to the store. She didn't tell me which *one*."

"Dr. Brooks, I have to ask you to step out of line."

"It sounds like your daughter needs you." Shazia put her hand on his sleeve. "You go, Peter. I'll figure something out."

He hesitated, feeling torn. He looked around at the crowds

shoving to get into the lobby. How could he abandon Shazia in the middle of this chaos, with no certainty that she'd find a place to stay? But how could he ignore his daughter's plea, especially now, after a year of virtual silence on her end? He couldn't even remember the last time she'd turned to him for help.

"Dad?"

Shazia placed her palms on his chest and gently pushed. "Go."

# TEN

J ACOB WAILED THE ENTIRE TRIP HOME. ANN SAT IN THE backseat beside him, rubbing his cheek with her thumb and holding the pacifier in his mouth. "Hang on, little guy. We're almost home."

Her leg was throbbing. She'd have to ice it the minute she got a chance.

"What's he doing here?" Libby asked.

There was a pickup parked in her driveway. Though it was too dark to make out the color, Ann recognized the shape immediately. Peter. He didn't usually stop by unannounced. "I have no idea."

Libby began hauling out sacks of groceries and lining them up in the driveway. Ann limped around the back of the minivan and lifted out a heavy bag. "I've got it. You go home and feed Jacob."

Libby put her hand on the door handle and jerked her chin toward the pickup. "Call me, okay?"

"Sure."

As the SUV backed down the driveway, Ann punched in the code for the garage door. The outside lights flashed on and the garage door rumbled up. Kate and Maddie stood there on the threshold.

"Mom!" Kate had her hands on her hips. "Where have you *been*?"

"Getting a tattoo."

Maddie skipped over. "Really?"

"No, not really." Ann handed Maddie the toilet paper. Why was Kate so annoyed? Certainly not because dinner was going to be late. Maybe she was just pissed she'd been stuck at home with Maddie. Or maybe it had something to do with Peter's unexpected arrival. "You know where I've been. Grab the milk, Kate."

Maddie wrapped her arms around the huge bundle. "Daddy's here." She beamed at Ann.

"I see that." Ann glanced back to find Peter standing in the kitchen doorway. He wasn't alone. Someone stood closely beside him, a tall, slim woman wearing a neatly belted coat and high-heeled boots. Her dark hair gleamed in the light from the kitchen behind her. A girlfriend? The possibility stung. Ann thought of her own hair hanging in straggles to her shoulders, her lipstick worn off hours ago, her baggy jeans and the hole in the toe of her sneaker, the ugly pulsing lump on her shin. *Oh, God.* She didn't feel like dealing with this right now. Peter should have given her some kind of warning, allowed her the chance to prepare mentally if not physically. She lifted her chin and tried to look calm.

"Need help?" He grabbed two bags by their corners.

"I'm okay. What are you doing here?" They faced each other. No necktie. Today must have been lab day. He wore a yellow shirt, one Ann had never seen before, in a vibrant shade she might not have selected. She wondered who was picking out his clothes these days. Peter had always been so hopeless about the details, willing to fudge sleeve length and collar type just to get the job done. Ann had enjoyed lingering in the men's department, running her hand across the smooth cottons, holding silky ties up to match. She glanced toward the woman standing behind them and wondered if she took the same delight in taking care of Peter.

"The girls called me," he said. "They couldn't reach you."

They'd stopped that sort of manipulating ages ago. "My phone was buried at the bottom of my cart."

"Kate saw something on the news. She tried you for over an hour. I tried, too."

"I told them to keep the TV off. She couldn't wait till I got home?"

"She was scared, Ann."

Was he questioning her decision to leave the girls alone while she ran to the store? "Giant was a zoo, Peter. People were behaving like monsters. The girls were better off home alone. Just because Kate was freaking out—"

"I wasn't freaking out." Kate stomped over. "I was mad. You said you wouldn't be gone long, but you were gone forever. You didn't even tell me what store you went to."

Ann was puzzled. What did that matter?

"At least *Dad* answered his phone." Kate pronounced this with as much venom as she could possibly pack into those few words. "Jeez, Mom. How much milk did you get?"

*As much as I could.* "Put it in the big freezer." Kate whirled away, but not before Ann glimpsed her puffy, reddened face. So she really had been upset.

The young woman still stood in the kitchen doorway. She moved awkwardly aside to let Ann pass.

Ann paused. "Hello."

She was a lot younger than Ann had first thought. Midtwenties, say. Thirty, tops. And she was very, very pretty.

The girl smiled shyly. "Hello, Mrs. . . . I mean . . ." She had a lovely accent. Her gaze fluttered over to Peter, clearly wondering what name Ann went by now.

"I'm Ann," Ann said.

Peter stood on the step behind them. "This is Shazia Massri, one of my PhD students."

*A student?* Peter had never said a word, never given her a clue he'd started seeing someone. And here he'd brought this . . . child . . . over and introduced her to the girls. Peter never thought. He was so determined to avoid conflict that he nevertheless managed to rake it up anyway.

"May I help?" Shazia said.

"Thank you, but I can manage." Ann walked into the kitchen.

Peter glanced down as she limped along. "I'll get the rest."

Ann opened the refrigerator and began fitting things inside. "Do you want spaghetti or ravioli for dinner, Maddie?"

"Tacos." Maddie emptied a bag and lined up the contents on the counter.

"We had tacos last night."

"But I *hate* ravioli!"

"Spaghetti it is." Ann fitted blocks of cheese into the bottom drawer and pressed in a bag of cheese sticks. She wriggled the drawer shut.

Kate came in. "The milk's done."

Ann nodded toward the bag on the counter. "Take care of that, will you?"

Kate heaved a sigh but pulled the bag toward her.

Peter came in with two bags cradled in his arms and two more dangling from his fingertips. "That's the end of it." He set down the bags and pulled out a box of cookies. He turned to the pantry.

"Not there, Daddy." Maddie pointed. "Up there. And these go up there, too."

Peter took the box she handed him and slotted it up high.

Ann watched him covertly. It felt strange having him carrying in the groceries and putting things away. She'd gotten used to doing it on her own. She had to admit she didn't like the tweak of pleasure she was feeling from having him here in her kitchen doing something so mundane and so normal, something he'd done a million times before but not once in the past twelve months.

Shazia stood by the door, not exactly in the room, not exactly out. Maybe she was waiting for Ann to offer her something to drink or to engage her in meaningless chitchat, but Ann just couldn't muster up the energy. It had been a rotten day. She longed for it to be over. She wanted to have a hot meal and a long bath, tuck her girls into bed, and curl up among her own covers with a good book.

She put in the last container of cottage cheese and closed the refrigerator door. "Thanks. I can take it from here."

Peter nodded and pulled his keys from his pocket.

Kate crossed her arms. "What are you going to do about Shazia, Dad?"

Ann stopped in the middle of folding a grocery sack and looked at Peter. What was Kate talking about? Was there more brewing in this Peter-Shazia relationship than Ann suspected?

Peter stood there, keys dangling from his finger, looking confused.

"I heard you on your cell phone," Kate said. "She doesn't have anywhere to go, does she?"

Ann was surprised. "I thought the university was providing emergency housing for international students. You were on that committee, Peter. Did the plans change?"

"There's been some kind of bureaucratic screw-up. Shazia's not on the list."

"He's been calling hotels," Kate told her. "There aren't any rooms."

"There are dozens of hotels in Columbus," Ann said. "There has to be something."

He shrugged. "No one's answering the phones." His voice was light, but his eyes were serious. "No big deal. If we have to, we can camp out at my place."

That rankled. The divorce wasn't even final yet.

"Ha." Kate leaned against the counter. "You should see Dad's apartment, Mom. It's teeny."

"It's not that bad," Peter said.

"It's pretty bad," Kate said. "Dad, you don't even have a stove."

"Enough," Peter said firmly.

Ann had no idea what Peter's place was like. She'd never wanted to know the details about how Peter was moving on without her.

"We'd better get going," he said.

Ann nodded. "All right."

Peter kissed Kate's cheek and ruffled the top of Maddie's hair.

She protested, swatting at him and giggling. Then she threw her arms around him. "I love you, Daddy."

"I love you, too, princess. I'll call you guys later. Bye, Ann."

"Bye."

"Nice meeting you," Shazia said, and then they were gone, the kitchen door shutting with a click.

"Mom," Kate said.

"Try not to worry, honey. Your dad'll be fine." Ann took out a jar of spaghetti sauce and stuck a pot on a burner. She couldn't bear to look into Kate's accusing eyes.

"What is *this*?" Maddie had pulled a tin from the bag and was staring at it.

"Protein powder. You make shakes with it."

"Like milkshakes?"

"Something like that." Ann heard the soft grumble of an engine starting up. Peter would cobble together some sort of solution. But what if he couldn't? Would he end up sleeping in his truck? She thought of the crazy crowds at the grocery store, the man and woman who'd stolen her bottles of water. What if there were actual riots? It was inconceivable. She unscrewed the jar of sauce and dumped its contents into the pot. She looked down into the red liquid.

She felt Kate watching her. She looked up and met her daughter's gaze. "I'll be right back."

As she stalked down the driveway, she could see Peter and Shazia talking in the cab of the truck. Shazia saw Ann first. She straightened in her seat and said something to Peter.

He rolled down the window. "Something the matter?"

Ann said nothing. She could feel the huge house looming behind her. All those rooms, so many of them empty. She had to.

"Ann?"

"You should stay here," she said. He looked surprised. How awful. Had things between them so deteriorated that he'd be taken aback by a simple act of civility? "Both of you."

"Ann."

"There's plenty of room." Four bedrooms and a pullout sofa in the basement. He paid the mortgage. He'd been generous, letting her take the house and its contents, leaving with just his clothes and some audio equipment.

What was she doing, persuading her soon-to-be ex-husband and the girl who was probably his young lover to move in?

"I know it's weird," she said. "But these are unusual circumstances."

He looked at Shazia, then back to Ann. "Maybe just until I can straighten things out."

The relief on his face was plain. He'd been worried. It was now full dark, and cold. There probably wasn't even any food in his apartment. How could she have hesitated? She put her hand on the metal rim of the window. "It's settled then."

Ann turned to go back into the house. Behind her, the engine shut off and the car doors opened. First one and then the other.

Unusual circumstances indeed.

# ELEVEN

$P$ETER WEDGED HIS JACKET INTO THE HALL CLOSET BE-
side the girls' coats, their cheerful colors standing out against
the tan of his jacket and the sober maroon of Ann's coat, the same
one she'd had for years. Boots stood on the floor below—Maddie's
mauve leopard print, Ann's stubby brown ones, and a sleek black
pair with designs stitched into the leather with white thread. Kate's,
probably. She'd always loved cowboy boots. He remembered her
first pair, a bright cherry color, that she loved so much she insisted
on wearing them everywhere, to the store, on playdates, even to
bed. After she'd fallen asleep, either he or Ann would tiptoe in and
gently ease the boots off her feet. But then, sure enough, the next
morning she'd appear in the kitchen doorway, yawning, still in her
nightgown and wearing those boots. How old had she been, two?
Maybe three. She'd cried so when she finally outgrew them and Ann
couldn't find a pair in a larger size.

In the kitchen, Ann was tearing open a box of pasta and dumping its contents into a pot of bubbling water. She looked up as he
approached, and she swept back a strand of hair from her face with
the back of her hand. "It's just sauce from a jar tonight."

Peter thought of her homemade marinara, rich with chopped
onion and garlic and bell peppers. He wondered if this hasty meal

was a result of her working full-time or if this was just the way she and the girls ate now. Somehow, he'd thought all three would be frozen in time, doing the same things the same way they always had, just without him. "Smells good."

"Get out the Parmesan, Maddie," Ann said. "Kate, please set the table." She glanced over her shoulder at Peter. "I think there's a bottle of wine in the basement if you want to hunt it up."

"Sure."

He found it easily enough, lying in the wine rack above the mini-refrigerator, just where he'd left it. Rubbing away the dust from the smooth glass shoulders of the bottle, he came back into the kitchen. Maddie was pouring cheese into a small bowl while Kate spread place mats across the kitchen table. Shazia stood by the sink, a water glass in her hand.

He winked at her and she smiled.

Ann stirred the pasta. "Do you have a lot of family in Cairo, Shazia?"

"All my family's there," Shazia replied. "My brother, my sister, my parents. My father comes from a large family. He's one of ten children."

"Ten!" Maddie said. "That's practically a soccer team."

Shazia smiled. "I have a lot of cousins."

"I can imagine," Ann said. "What does your father do?"

"He's a medical doctor."

"And you're getting your PhD. He must be very proud of you."

"Shazia went to Oxford." Peter opened a drawer and began hunting for a corkscrew among the rattle of spoons and spatulas. "And she got her DVM in Cairo."

"Impressive." Ann brought out a loaf of bread and began to slice it. "So, you're making the switch from veterinary medicine to research?"

Peter knew what Ann was thinking. He'd made the same career jump. He remembered telling Ann he was entering research. He'd leaned across the table and clasped her hands in his. Later, she'd confided she thought he was about to propose. When that time did come, it was over a table, too, and there was candlelight and wine. He looked down at the bottle in his hands and got busy.

"I read one of Peter's articles online," Shazia said. "It was very persuasive. He said the best way to make a real difference in animal health was through research."

"I like your phone," Kate said. "It's such a cool color."

"Look how tiny the keypad is," Shazia said, pulling it from her pocket.

"Wow."

"How are you finding Columbus?" Ann asked. "It must be quite a change from Oxford and Cairo."

Shazia laughed. "In many ways, yes. But it's actually been an easier adjustment than I expected. People have been very welcoming. There are lots of international students here."

Peter held up the wine bottle and Shazia shook her head. She set down her water glass. "If you don't mind, I think I'll go lie down. I have a terrible headache."

"Of course." Ann wiped her hands on a dishtowel. "Let me show you your room and get you some towels. Peter, would you dish the girls up?"

She said it so casually. *Dish the girls up.* One of the shorthand expressions they used to use all the time. Surprising how nostalgic he felt hearing it again. Staying here was going to be more difficult than he'd realized. He watched Ann climb the stairs, her voice floating lightly down as she talked to Shazia, showing her around, welcoming her into what would be her home, too, for a little while.

AFTER DINNER, PETER STOOD IN THE DOORWAY OF MADDIE'S room. Dishes clattered from the kitchen below as Ann cleaned up. Shazia was in the guest room down the hall. He heard the soft murmur of her voice and guessed she was on the phone.

He put his hands on his hips. "You're *sure* you brushed your teeth, Maddie?"

She giggled from where she lay in bed. "Yes, Daddy."

"Because I'm not coming in if you haven't."

"I have. I swear."

"With toothpaste?"

"With toothpaste."

"All right then." He reached down to turn on the nightlight, then straightened and switched off the overhead light. The room was bathed in a soft glow. He made his way to her bed and sat down beside her.

Maddie lay back against her pillow and looked up at him seriously. His eyes adjusted to the darkness, and now he could see her features, the rounded curves of her cheeks, the sleepy slants of her eyes so like Ann's. He'd noticed that she'd lost another tooth, a bottom one along the side. What was the Tooth Fairy bringing these days? The going rate used to be five bucks. Once they couldn't rummage up enough bills between them to slide under seven-year-old Kate's pillow. In triumph, he had produced a Lowe's gift card. So much laughter. They should have saved some of it for the years to come.

Maddie said, "My teacher told us that birds are making people sick."

"Uh-huh."

She frowned. "You're around birds all the time."

"Well, that's true. But I wear a special suit. Did you know that?"

"Like Superman?"

"No. It has a mask and goggles to keep infection from getting through and gloves to protect my hands. Sometimes I put on white overalls so I don't spread the infection around."

"And you wear that *all* the time?"

"Oh, yes. Whenever I go in the field. I keep all that stuff in my truck."

"Do we need suits? Kate, Mommy, and me?"

"No. I don't think so." He brushed the hair back from her forehead. "Now I lay me down to sleep."

"I pray the Lord my soul to keep. May God's love be with me through the night and wake me with the morning light." She yawned and smiled up at him.

He kissed her cheek, so soft and warm. He'd missed this. "Good night, Maddie girl."

He was at her doorway when she spoke up again.

"Daddy?"

"Hmm?"

"Are you and Mom still having a divorce?"

Poor Maddie. This turn of events must be so confusing for her. "Yes, sweetheart," he said gently. "We are."

Kate was a mound of blankets in the deep gloom of her bedroom, leaning up against her headboard, waiting for him. "Hey," she said as he sat heavily on her bed.

He leaned forward and kissed the top of her head. "Hey. You ever clean this place?"

"Only when Mom threatens to take away my phone."

She'd been dabbing on perfume again, its sweetness mingling with the fruity aroma of her shampoo and the mint of her toothpaste. He remembered the days when they had to plead with Kate to take a bath. When she was six, they had to stand over her to get her to brush her teeth.

"How long are you staying?" she asked.

"Maybe a few days. We'll see."

She bit her lower lip. "This is really serious, isn't it?"

"Yes."

"People are dying, right?"

"Yes."

"Do you know anyone who's died?"

He thought about that, then shook his head. "No one I know of, honey. Certainly no one here."

"Are we going to die?"

He picked up her stuffed owl, limp with age, its beak hanging on by a few stitches. Where had this come from? He hadn't seen it in years. She leaned forward, and he settled it behind her head. How his daughter could sleep without a pillow was beyond him, but she never complained of a sore neck. "I know things seem to have happened awfully fast. But scientists and governments have been working on this problem for a long time. We knew this was coming. We just didn't know when. There are all sorts of plans and procedures in place to protect us."

"Like closing school?"

"Exactly. Which is a very smart thing to do. If we can keep people from catching it from one another, we can give scientists time to work on a vaccine."

She made a face. "That means a shot."

If only it were that simple.

"Just think," he said, rising. "No school tomorrow. You can IM to your heart's content."

"No one IMs anymore, Dad."

"No?"

"They text."

"Ah." These were the things he missed so painfully: the lost tooth, the backpack exchanged for a floppy bag, no more chocolate syrup stirred into milk. These next few days would be an unexpected gift, a chance to reconnect with his daughters. "Well, then you can text to your heart's content."

"Right. Tell Mom that." She yawned and turned over. "Good night, Dad."

That was another thing: Dad instead of Daddy. Maybe that was the thing he missed the most.


ANN WAS UP WHEN PETER CAME INTO THE KITCHEN EARLY THE next morning. She stood by the coffeemaker, her hand on the pot handle, waiting for the water to stop dripping. She wore her old blue terry robe with the sagging pockets, and her hair was mussed. She wasn't one for predawn conversation, so he was surprised when she spoke. "Coffee?"

"Please." He'd missed her coffee. Every pot he brewed was either bitter sludge or tasteless brown water.

"Sleep okay?"

"Fine."

"Really." She handed him a mug, the one Kate had painted at a long-ago birthday party, the orange happy face faded now from so many washings. "Beth says that sofa's a medieval torture device."

Ann's sister had known what she was talking about. There was a certain pernicious spring that dug into his ribs whenever he turned over. "It's like the Four Seasons compared to the one in my apartment. Speaking of which, I'm going to head in and grab some clothes."

She nodded toward the television set playing quietly in the family room. "They're reporting a few cases in Mexico now."

*Already?* He lifted his mug so she couldn't see his expression. Mexico was close. There were all sorts of migrations between Mexico and the United States, human and otherwise. So the latest modeling studies had been correct: restricting air travel had had little effect on containing the spread of the virus.

She poured coffee into a second mug and pushed the pot back onto the burner. "Nothing in Egypt, though. Did Shazia reach her parents?"

"Not that I know of." He drank some coffee. No cream, of course, but he could make do with some milk.

"They must be so worried. Well, maybe they'll talk today." She sipped her coffee. "Hamburgers sound okay for dinner?"

"Sure." He'd forgotten this, the way-too-early decision-making about what to have for dinner. He didn't care what they ate. He never had, but Ann had always needed to regiment her day into segments. Errand time, laundry time, mealtime. It was how she'd coped as a stay-at-home mother. He wondered if things were different now that she'd gone back to work.

He reached into the refrigerator for the milk. "How are you for cash?"

"The ATMs were cleaned out by the time we got to the bank."

"They should be up and running now. I'll get water, too."

"It was horrible last night."

"Sounds like it." At least she'd come away with only a bruised shin. It could have been worse.

"That shooting at Kroger?" She shook her head. "They said on the news that it was over a parking space."

He couldn't believe it, either. "Well, things should have calmed down." He was here now. If anyone would be going to the store, it would be him. "Ann?"

She looked over.

"You know we can't let the girls play with their friends."

"For the whole three months, do you think?"

"We'll have to take it a day at a time."

"It's going to be so hard on them. Especially Kate."

"It's better than the alternative."

She looked at him over the rim of her cup and nodded.

TRAFFIC WAS FAIRLY LIGHT UNTIL HE NEARED THE AIRPORT. Then the highway jittered with cars, brake lights flashing irritably, no doubt filled with students trying desperately to get home. An airplane thundered across the sky, its lights twinkling red and white in the darkness. Peter broke free of the backup and headed for the side streets. Here, the neighborhoods were still half-asleep, just a few cars working their way down the road. People yawned at bus stops and slumped against walls, waiting for rides.

Up ahead, Tower West rose against the lavender sky, dark except for the bright band of light that glowed through the glass of the first-floor lobby windows. Cars packed the lot and overflowed onto the grassy spaces between the buildings. A uniformed man was just coming out of the building. The guard from last night. Peter recognized the weary set of his shoulders. He slowed and rolled down his window.

"We're full up," the man said in response to Peter's question. "We had to turn away a lot of kids. They just kept coming." He shook his head, his gaze distant. "You plan for the worst. And then when the worst happens, you find out just how useless your planning was."

Ten blocks away, a brick apartment building held down the corner, squat and square. The lobby doors stood open. The building manager was a stickler for keeping them locked. Peter stepped inside and listened. A television muttered in the apartment to his left. Bikes leaned against the wall. Normal. He shrugged and closed the door behind him. Taking the stairs to the second floor, he unlocked the far door on the right. Here, too, everything appeared the same. The narrow bed in the corner, its covers pulled taut. The battered table that served as both nightstand and kitchen table, holding a gooseneck lamp, coffeepot, and alarm clock. The folding chair in the opposite corner beside the small bookcase. The framed photographs of the girls, Maddie's duck painting taped to the wall. He'd left the drapes half-open. Pale sun streamed across the worn carpet. He filled his suitcase and slung some things into a duffel bag. He unplugged the television and DVD player, and drew the curtains shut. He stood and stared around at the small space, his home for more than a year.

Out in the hallway, a man and a woman trooped up the stairs toward him. He recognized them as his next-door neighbors, both college students. Peter had learned to work late on weekend nights to avoid the inevitable parties and to close his ears to their early-morning lovemaking. They pressed themselves against the wall to let Peter and his bags squeeze past.

"Take care," the woman said.

First time she'd ever spoken to him. It sounded so final. Peter nodded. "You too."

She continued up the stairs, the man's arm around her shoulders.

The streets had perked up during his brief absence. The coffee shop on the corner was doing a brisk business. People thronged the patio and overflowed onto the sidewalk, chatting as they waited for their morning brew. People swooped past on bikes. Others walked hand in hand down the sidewalks. Downtown was beginning to have a carnival air about it, everyone hanging out, enjoying the unexpected day off from school and work.

Peter shook his head and loaded his bags into the back of the pickup.

He drove by playgrounds that an hour before had been empty. Kids ran everywhere, calling out to one another. Their parents stood in idle clusters, rocking strollers and no doubt negotiating how to manage this day and all the suddenly school-free days to follow. Movie theaters would be swamped. So would the mall, fast-food restaurants, the library, and rec center, anyplace that welcomed kids. A mistake.

This wasn't the time for celebration. These people shouldn't be standing out here, laughing, gossiping. He considered stopping, rolling down his window, and telling them to go home. But of course he didn't. They wouldn't listen. They'd think he was a madman.

"LISTEN TO THIS." SHAZIA SAT ON THE FLOOR IN THE CORNER of the den, laptop balanced on her knees, her hair loose about her shoulders. She was playing with her barrette, snapping and un-snapping it. "RNL is working on a vaccine."

"Who isn't?" Peter looked back to his computer screen and typed a few commands. He had to download his lectures for the week and then post the exam. It was all master's-level work. At that point, students could be expected to follow the honor system.

"But it looks like they may have something. They've already moved on to Phase Two of clinical trials."

Peter swiveled in his chair to look at her. "Really?"

She nodded. "A Dr. Liederman's leading it."

"Albert Liederman?"

"You know him?"

"My old doctoral advisor. I haven't talked to him in months." Which had been a worry. Over the course of the past year, Lieder-man had stopped attending conferences and returning phone calls. Peter had thought the old fellow was slowing down, but now it seemed he had simply diverted his energies elsewhere. "I've been after him for years to write a memoir about the '78 influenza out-break. We came that close to a full-blown pandemic." He held up his thumb and forefinger pinched together.

"In 1978?"

She had probably never even heard about it. Few people had.

"You should hear him talk about it. That guy could send shivers down your spine."

But talk was all Liederman would do. How many times had he grumbled, "I can't write a book, Brooks. That's your job."

Peter leaned back in his chair. "He gave me his notes a while ago. Told me to take a crack at putting together a book. Maybe you could help me organize the material."

"I'd like that."

He saw a movement out of the corner of his eye, and he looked over to see Ann standing in the doorway of the den. "Want to light the grill?"

Shazia set down her laptop. "I'll help."

"Stay put." Peter waved his hand. "Tonight I'm cooking."

Shazia looked at him. "That'll be nice."

He knew what she was thinking. What kind of dish could she expect from a guy who ate from vending machines and take-out restaurants?

Peter walked beside Ann down the hall. "I might have found Shazia a place. The school's going to open up Baldwin Hall. I persuaded them to take her even if she's not on the official list."

"It's too bad she won't be with her roommate."

"There'll be other international students there. She'll know someone."

Maddie sprawled on her belly in front of the television set. He had no idea what shows were her favorites these days. He'd never seen this particular one before, something involving preteen girls arguing with a man in a hotel uniform. He stopped beside the couch where Kate sat, laptop propped before her. His old computer, outdated but powerful enough for her to play around on. "Who are you talking to?"

She answered without looking up. "Michele. Claire. John. Andrea. Scooter."

He looked over at Ann. "John? Scooter?" These weren't names he'd heard before. What kind of name was Scooter? He couldn't even tell what gender it belonged to.

"John is Michele's boyfriend." Ann handed him a platter of hamburger patties. "And Scooter's a boy in one of Kate's classes."

Peter looked down at Kate. Pink blossomed across her cheekbones as she stared at her computer screen. He glanced back at Ann. She was frowning slightly. Then she shook her head. *Don't say anything,* she was telegraphing, and he nodded.

So soon. He slid open the screen door and stepped out onto the patio. Too soon. Kate had just turned thirteen. He looked back through the glass at his daughter cross-legged on the sofa, coltish, long brown hair falling forward. She tapped gracefully at the keyboard, her hands all smooth motion, sitting back and laughing. The sight of it made his heart twist.

He turned the dial and was glad to see the answering flame. He hadn't thought to check the propane level. He shoveled the burgers onto the grill and set down the empty platter.

It was a crisp evening, cold enough to cloud his breath into soft puffs. Streetlights burned up and down the dark sidewalks. He'd missed the sunset.

A dark SUV glided past. The driver lifted his hand in greeting. It was that doctor who lived beside the Guarnieris, what was his name? Singh. That was it. He'd moved into the neighborhood a few months before Peter moved out. They used to nod politely at each other as they crisscrossed their lawns with mowers. The vehicle slowed in front of the driveway and Peter saw a figure step in front of the headlights, followed by a smaller, shaggier shape.

Walter Finn and his dog. The animal was genial enough, but you couldn't say the same about the man. Finn was forever circulating petitions against one thing or another: too many weeds in a neighbor's yard, bikes left scattered across sidewalks, snow going unshoveled, all the petty grievances that sprang up in a suburban community, which most people ignored but onto which Finn fastened greedy claws.

Peter stabbed at the burgers and flipped them over.

The dog tugged at his leash, wanting to come over and investigate the meat he was cooking. Finn lifted his head and spotted Peter standing conspicuously against the bright light shining from the kitchen behind him. Peter braced himself for another round of what's-this-neighborhood-coming-to, but Finn jerked the leash instead and tugged the dog away.

"Heel, Barney," he ordered, and the dog shambled over to check out who'd been visiting the tree on the far corner.

Peter had been afforded a reprieve. Finn must have figured out he wasn't the go-to guy of the house any longer. Turning back to the grill, he saw Smith standing at his own grill just across the yard.

"Dude," Smith said. "Good to see you."

"Been a while."

"Crazy times, huh? Libby sent me out for water today, but all I could find was that fizzy designer stuff."

"I got lucky at a gas station on Franz. A delivery truck was just unloading when I pulled up. We've got extra you can have."

"I'll take you up on that. Libby's been a wreck about it."

They talked back and forth across their patios. Would the NFL adjust to a few missed games? How much farther would the Dow Jones skid before recovering? Was there any end in sight to the price of gas? Libby came out, the baby in her arms, and handed Smith a platter.

"Hey," Peter said.

"Hello," she said coolly.

Well, at least she wasn't pretending he was invisible. This was progress. Peter pushed his luck. "Jacob's gotten big." Last time he'd seen the baby, he'd been cradled easily in one arm. Now the kid straddled Libby's hip, reaching forward with one plump hand for the piece of bun Smith held out.

Smith said, "Gonna grow up to be a linebacker, just like his old man."

The coals glowed softly. The smell of cooked meat rose. Peter pressed the spatula beneath the hamburgers and lifted them onto a plate. Picking up the platter, he dialed off the heat.

"Hey," Smith said. "I got an idea. Why don't you guys come over?"

An old tradition, combining their cookouts onto one patio or dining room.

"Smith," Libby said.

"Jeez, Libby. Come on. If Ann's cool with it—"

"Actually," Peter said, "Libby's right. We should probably be keeping our distance."

Silence.

"Christ." Smith's voice came to him out of the darkness. "Right. I guess I saw something about that on the news. You really think it'll do any good?"

"It's all we can do."

The clatter of a grill lid lowered into place. "Well, good to see you, Peter."

"You too."

Peter looked around at all the houses, large, dark squares rising out of the ground, windows glowing bright, islands separated by lawns and closed doors. The empty patios, the tables with the chairs stacked and the umbrellas furled. No one else was out enjoying the spate of clear weather.

He looked back at his own house. Through the glass he saw into the kitchen—Ann reaching down a stack of plates from the cabinet, Maddie collecting her drawing materials, Kate pouring a glass of milk. It all appeared normal, but it wasn't. Everything had changed.

"Listen, if our government's too chicken to force people to isolate themselves, then Americans should take it upon themselves to stay away from each other."

"You know how many businesses are going to fold if we do that? Hotels, restaurants, any kind of retail establishment. The stock market will crash."

"Maybe. In the short run, business, particularly the service industry, will take a hit. But it's better to field it in the beginning than to have their entire customer base disappear forever."

"Right. Can you imagine the long-term effects of people locking themselves up for extended periods of time? The 1918 pandemic lasted eighteen months. We'll be a nation of blubbering idiots if we lock ourselves away for that long."

"Better than relying on soap and face masks."

"Oh, come on. Face masks are a proven health precaution."

"Not necessarily. Their effectiveness hasn't been established."

"If you're so afraid of getting sick, why are you even here today? How do you know that I'm not contagious?"

"Well, you're right about one thing. It's probably too late for any of us to do a damn thing. So, on that note, if any of us is still here, next up we have the secretary from the Department of Health and Human Services. Our phone lines are open. Here's your chance to ask those questions nobody seems to have answers for."

Colby and Company,<br>
WTTM

# TWELVE

---

ANN STEPPED OUT INTO THE BRIGHT NOON SUN. ZIPPING her coat, she scanned the grass.

A sharp rap on the glass made her look over. Libby stood waving behind the window next door. She held up a finger—*hold on*. Sure enough, a few moments later, Libby came out through the front door, pulling on her puffy blue coat. She stopped in the middle of the lawn and stood there, facing Ann across the grass. "I've been wanting to call, but Smith's had the phone all day. How are you?"

"Fine. How are you? How's Jacob?"

"Just peachy. He adores having Mommy home twenty-four-seven. Mommy, however, wants to bang her head against the wall, repeatedly, until she's unconscious." She put a hand on her hip. "But that's not what I asked you. Come on, Ann. How are you, really?"

"I'm okay. Really."

"Uh-huh." She hiked an eyebrow. "I see Peter's still here." She shook her head. "What were you thinking, letting him come back and bringing that girl with him? Don't you think you've got enough going on without having to deal with him and his I-don't-love-you-anymore crap?"

Actually, that wasn't what Peter had said, Ann wanted to

protest. What he had said was, *I love you, but I'm not in love with you anymore.* Ann would have settled for that; she *had* settled for it.

"It's not that simple. He can't find a place for Shazia. He's tried everywhere." The university hadn't been able to find the staff to open additional dormitories. Soon, the housing administrator kept promising Peter. Soon.

"Why doesn't she just move in with him?"

"His place is too small."

"Serves him right."

"Listen, if one of my daughters was stranded in a foreign country, I'd want someone to take her in."

The look on Libby's face softened instantly. "Well, of course you would. Sorry. I'm being a bitch, I guess. It's been only a few days and already I'm stir-crazy."

"Tell me about it. Maddie and Kate have been sniping at each other all morning." Ann spotted the newspaper on top of the lilac bush. "This is a new one," she said, stretching up to tug it free.

"The delivery guy doesn't get out of the car, you know. He just wings it out the window. Pretty soon, he'll just dump the whole lot on the corner and let us paw through."

WHEN ANN CAME BACK INTO THE KITCHEN, SHE FOUND THE table empty. The girls had fled, leaving behind their books and worksheets. Where were they?

Peter walked down the hall toward her. "Have you seen the phone?"

"Maddie had it last." A shout came from outside. Setting the newspaper on the counter, Ann walked over to the sliding glass door and looked out.

"God. It could be anywhere, then." Peter got to his hands and knees to look under the coffee table.

There the girls were, jumping on the trampoline. "What are they doing?"

"Taking a break. Kate said you said they could."

Ann was annoyed. Peter should have seen right through that one. "They just had a break. They've got to finish their homework."

"What's a few minutes? It's good for them to burn off a little excess energy."

"They don't have excess energy. They have assignments due at three." She slid open the door. "Kate! Maddie!"

Maddie sat in the middle of the trampoline while Kate made huge jumps all around her. They were both laughing. Kate turned. She wobbled on the elastic surface of the trampoline, grinning at Ann standing there in the doorway. "Five more minutes?"

Ann couldn't recall the last time she'd seen the two girls getting along like this. She couldn't possibly order them back inside. How terrible would it be if she ended up emailing their homework in a little late? At least they were doing it.

"All right. Zip up your coats, both of you." She shut the door and glanced at the television. Sound muted, it was showing the same video clip it had been showing all day: masked people lined up outside a clinic. How many of them would test positive?

She moved to the refrigerator. "Have you heard anything new?"

"They're working on sequencing."

Ann imagined it, lab-coated scientists bent over lab equipment, not even taking a break to eat or sleep. *Good*. They could eat and sleep later. The cases in Mexico had been confirmed, people who'd slipped into the country before the air travel restrictions had been imposed. She thought of the virus silently creeping its way across the vast border that stretched between this country and Mexico. Ohio was a long way from the border, though. Maybe the flu would be halted in its tracks before it got anywhere near Columbus. She shivered. "I thought we'd have chicken tonight. We can still eat that, can't we?"

"Definitely." He began digging among the sofa cushions.

That was a relief. She'd hate to throw it out. "Have you talked to your brother yet?"

"I emailed him, but I haven't heard anything."

Mike was good about staying in touch. Even after Peter moved out, Mike emailed the girls regularly and, like as not, included a note to Ann. "Do you think they have him doing hazardous duty?"

"You know Mike. He can never say what he's doing."

Ann still had a hard time picturing such a jovial guy as a code-cracking spy. She wondered how Bonni and little Mikey were doing. Although Mikey wasn't so little anymore. Last time he visited, the teenager had towered over Ann.

"I called your mom a few weeks ago to wish her happy birthday," Ann said. "The girls got on the phone with her, too."

Ruth Brooks had had no idea who they were. "Kate?" she'd said. "Maddie *who*?"

"That's nice," Peter said.

Ann didn't know what nice was anymore. Was it at all kind to call and force her mother-in-law to face all that she was forgetting? Or was it kinder to abandon her to what little memory she retained? Ann removed a can of crushed tomatoes from the pantry and found the garlic.

The phone rang, startling them both.

"Aha." Peter stood up. "Here we go. Want me to answer it?"

How awful. There he stood, phone in hand, asking permission. She hated this awkwardness. It was a miserable reminder of how things had failed between them. She merely nodded.

"Hey," Peter said into the phone. He chuckled.

Obviously someone he knew. She peeled the garlic and squeezed it through the press.

"I know, I know." Peter stood by the glass door, watching the girls play. "I've been meaning to call, too."

His voice had a friendly, almost conspiratorial tone. This was no business call. It had to be one of Ann's friends. She stood there, can opener in hand, waiting for him to speak again so she could guess whom he was talking to.

"I was as surprised as anyone when WHO went to Phase Five." A small laugh. "No, they didn't consult me first."

Someone he liked, that was evident. Someone he hadn't talked to in a while. She caught herself. Was she really eavesdropping? How horrible. She set the chicken breasts back into the refrigerator to marinate and went into the laundry room, where she could no longer hear Peter's voice.

The jeans were piling up again. Sometimes the girls didn't even bother to wear them; they just consigned them to the dirty pile. Well, Kate could learn how to use the washing machine. Ann could start her on the basics, like towels. And Maddie was certainly old enough to sort socks and put things on hangers. It would be good for both of them to accept a little responsibility.

Peter poked his head around the door and held out the phone. "It's Beth."

So that explained his happy voice. Ann took the phone. "Hey."

"Peter sounds terrific." The pleasure in her sister's voice was unmistakable. Beth had always liked Peter. She'd once told Ann she thought of him as the brother they'd never had. "He says you're letting him and his student stay until he can find her temporary housing."

Ann closed the door and leaned on it. "She's more than just his student."

"Oh." A pause. "Wow."

A world of sympathy floated within that single word. Ann pressed the receiver to her ear. "You should see her, Beth. She's so young and pretty and . . . nice."

"Well, that sucks. Don't tell me she's rich, too."

Ann laughed despite herself. "I have to admit they've been pretty circumspect. I don't think the girls have put it together yet."

"I should hope not. Maybe this is just one of those things he has to get out of his system."

Beth was just like their mother, hoping against hope that Peter would see the light and change his mind. It came from their fondness for Peter, not out of any real understanding of the situation.

"Beth, he still wants the divorce." After all this time, why was it still so hard to say that word? "The papers came a few days ago. I don't know whether I should mail them or hold off until things calm down. I tried my lawyer's office and left a message, but no one's called me back."

"What does Mom say?"

"I haven't told her yet. I was going to when we came for Thanksgiving." Was Thanksgiving even worth celebrating now? As soon as she had the thought, she dismissed it. Maddie loved holidays, all causes for celebration, even Groundhog Day. She was always urging

Ann to decorate and make special things to eat. Even though there'd be no turkey or pumpkin pie, even though they'd be stuck here and not with her parents, they'd be together, she and the girls. That was worth being thankful for.

"Well, I won't say anything if you don't want me to," Beth said.

"Thanks. So, how come you're not at the hotel?"

"Carlos let me take the day off."

Her boss never let her take a day off from the front desk. It was as though he thought Beth was the only one who could check guests in. Ann reached for the basket of clean clothes and began folding. "How come?"

"That big convention we had scheduled canceled. Most of housekeeping didn't show for work yesterday. Neither did room service. Which turned out to be okay, since we didn't get our food service delivery. Everything's a mess."

Ann ran a hand across the soft flannel of Maddie's pajamas. "You need to be careful. Don't hang around crowds—"

"I know, I know. Carlos makes everyone wear these stupid masks and gloves all the time. No wonder we don't have any guests."

Ann heard a soft sucking noise and frowned. Was Beth smoking again?

"I'm having trouble getting Dad's prescriptions filled," Beth said. "The insurance company will pay for only one month's worth, so we asked the doctor to intervene. It still didn't do any good. We ended up paying full price and hoping the insurance company reimburses us later. Talk about a pain in the ass."

"What about you? Are the grocery stores open? Do you have enough food?"

Beth snorted. "Since when do I ever have any food?"

True. Her younger sister seemed to subsist on diet soda and hastily grabbed meals from the employee cafeteria. Her refrigerator probably contained an ancient box of baking soda and a bag of withered carrots. "You'd better stock up."

"Relax. Mom could feed an entire army. But that's not why I called."

Ann set down Kate's turtleneck. "What is it? Is Dad okay?"

"He's coughing some, but he's not running a fever. It could be just a cold, but I'm taking him to see his oncologist. I wanted to let you know."

"I appreciate that. Call me later, okay?"

"Sure. Love you, big sister."

Ann smiled. Beth could never pass up an opportunity to tease her about being the older, and therefore more decrepit, sister. Only fourteen months separated them, but this was payback for all those early years when Ann boasted that she was the authority because she was older. Beth had been utterly gleeful when she realized that at some future point being older wouldn't necessarily be so desirable, and she'd been hammering at that discovery ever since. "Love you, too."

Ann set down the receiver and walked into the kitchen. A burst of laughter came from the backyard. There was Maddie's giggle and Kate's chortle, but what was that higher-pitched noise? Ann glanced out the window. Kate was doing a flip. Ann had told her a million times not to do that unless a grown-up was present, but there she was curling herself into a ball in midair. Maddie sat along the perimeter, clapping and yelling. Kate landed, arms outstretched, toppling backward into another girl.

There were *three* children jumping up and down, bumping into one another. Was she seeing things? No, there were definitely three bodies leaping around. Her stomach dropped. Who was that third child?

She yanked open the door and stepped out onto the patio. "Kate! Maddie! Come here right this instant!"

Kate stopped and looked, but Maddie, oblivious, continued jumping up and down in great big pushes. As Ann watched, she reached out her hands toward the third child.

"Madeline Ruth Brooks!" Ann marched across the grass and clapped her hands. "That's *one*!"

Maddie stopped jumping so suddenly she fell back against the net.

"That's *two*!"

"Okay, okay. I'm coming."

Kate was already scrambling through the opening in the mesh. Both girls came running across the yard toward her, leaving the third person to walk unsteadily across the surface of the trampoline to watch Kate and Maddie's progress, hooking her fingers through the net and pressing her face against it. "Hi, Mrs. Brooks."

Ann's heart was thumping. "You need to go home, Jodi. You can't play on the trampoline anymore."

"Why not?"

"Haven't your parents explained to you?"

Jodi climbed down from the trampoline.

"Mom," Kate whispered, "her parents aren't home. They're in Las Vegas. Her grandma and grandpa are watching her."

She'd forgotten that.

Jodi trudged over to where Ann stood.

"I'm sorry, Jodi," Ann said. She really was. "But you'll have to go home."

The child shrugged and turned away.

"We'll talk to you later," Kate said.

Jodi lifted a shoulder and let it fall.

Kate whirled around. "Why did you have to yell like that? It was so humiliating."

Ann pulled the girls inside and shoved the door closed. She snapped the lock. "What were you two thinking? I've told you, no playdates." The girls didn't even like Jodi. Why would they play with her now, of all times?

"But she came over," Kate protested. "What were we supposed to do, tell her to go away?"

"You're always telling us to be nice to people." Maddie's eyes shone with tears.

"I know." Ann pulled her girls close. "But things are different now. We just can't be near other people." Then she thought of Maddie stretching out her hands toward Jodi and her blood chilled. "She wasn't coughing, was she? Go wash your hands."

"God, Mom." Kate pulled away. "Why do you *always* have to be like this?"

"Two Americans have been hospitalized with what appears to be bird flu, hospital officials at Ramsey Medical Center announced just minutes ago. One is a baggage handler at Minneapolis–St. Paul International Airport and the other a mayoral aide who had recently arrived here from Washington, DC. No official travel advisory has been announced, but Minnesota officials are urging people to stay in their homes."

*ABC Special Report*

# THIRTEEN

*I*T WAS HERE.

Who would have predicted Minnesota? Peter would have thought Los Angeles, New York, Texas, somewhere along America's vulnerable coastlines. But instead of lapping at the shores, the virus had reached over the borders and struck right into the heartland of America.

Since the special report last night, Peter had been on the CDC, WHO, PubMed, and PandemicFlu websites, obsessively clicking to refresh. He hadn't slept since the announcement, staying up instead to check email, make phone calls, and watch news bulletins on TV. There'd been a marathon of information exchanges, but nothing new had been reported.

The two cases had been confirmed more than twenty-four hours ago, and both patients were holding their own. No additional cases had been reported, which was surprising and could be saying something about the nature of this particular virus. It might be weakening.

"Peter?"

He'd like to run those samples he'd collected from that second die-off. Who knew? Maybe the link was hidden there. The strain might have mutated to become less virulent. It was a remote possibility, true, but still a possibility. He needed only to get into his lab for a few hours a couple of days in a row. What was the danger?

"Peter."

The way he figured it, he had a fifty-fifty chance of getting into the building. If Hank was on duty, forget it. But the man had to sleep sometime. So if it was Arnold, he was golden. Arnold didn't even look at the name tags. He was more interested in his *Sports Illustrated* and quizzing passersby about the football teams' bowl chances.

He realized Shazia had skewed in her chair to face him. "Sorry. What was that?"

She turned her laptop so he could read the screen.

HE SMELLED DINNER COOKING BEFORE HE WAS HALFWAY down the hall.

The girls were in the family room, Maddie with a sketch pad propped across her bent knees, Kate hunched over her laptop, iPod wires trailing from her ears.

Maddie spotted him immediately. She scooted to a kneeling position so she could look at him over the back of the sofa. "Daddy, can Hannah come over?"

"Why don't you go over there?" Kate said. "In fact, *stay* over there."

Maddie made a face at her sister, then turned her attention back to him. "Come on, Daddy, please. I bet Cindy and Sarah are together."

"No, Maddie," he said. "I'm sorry. We've talked about that."

She turned around and slumped in her seat.

He rested his hand on the top of Maddie's head. "Where's your mom?"

"In the garage."

He found Ann rummaging around in the tall metal tool chest. Beside her stood the freezer stuffed with the groceries she'd bought the other night and the shelving unit stacked with cans and boxes.

He watched her as she picked up first one thing, then another. "Looking for something?"

"A screwdriver."

He reached up to the Peg-Board mounted on the wall, un-hooked the tool, and handed it to her. "What are you doing?"

"Taking down the trampoline."

He felt a small twinge. He'd been the one to give it to the girls. "I should do that."

She nodded and set down the screwdriver. "Anything new?" She'd been quiet since hearing the news last night, keeping her thoughts to herself. Ann was like that. She held tightly on to the things that worried her most.

"Tennessee just reported a pintail die-off."

"What about Minnesota? Any more cases?"

"None that I've heard of."

"That's good." She began collecting the girls' soccer balls and tennis rackets and fitting them into the big bin beneath his old tool bench.

She was hoping for a miracle. Well, weren't they all? "Tennessee thinks it's high-pathogenic." He fished out a tennis ball from behind the gardening supplies and tossed it into the bin.

"So it's slowed down in humans but picked up in birds?"

She was quick. He'd always liked that about her. The mower looked rusty. Its blade probably needed sharpening, too. "Different strains. It'd be interesting to figure out what's happening in birds. It might be able to help us identify how the human variant's changing. Ohio and Tennessee are both on the Mississippi flyway. It could be that all these die-offs are related."

"What die-offs?"

That's right. She didn't know. "There were two up north recently, a day apart."

Just more than a week ago. It didn't seem possible. He opened the stepladder and lifted first Kate's bike, then Maddie's, to the hooks screwed into the rafters.

"As bad as that botulism one?" She was remembering that first die-off, years before.

"Worse, if you can believe it." He climbed down and dusted off his hands. "I analyzed the first batch but got kicked out of the lab before I could get to the second one. Those samples could tell us a lot. The best thing would be to compare them with Tennessee's re-sults."

She put her hands on her hips and sighed. "You're thinking of going in, aren't you?"

He heard the longing in her voice. This had been a break for her, coming out here for a change instead of roaming around inside the house. The girls weren't the only ones getting restless. "Want to take a walk?"

IT FELT GOOD TO BE STRIDING ALONG IN THE COLD. PETER scanned the bright, cloudless sky. Not a duck or goose in sight. But the weather was changing. He could feel the air gathering itself up. "They predicting snow?"

"Tomorrow."

"The girls will be happy."

He glanced at Ann walking beside him. He could tell her mind was a million miles away. "Dinner looks good."

"It won't be the same without turkey."

"Chicken's close enough."

"I guess. But there won't be any leftovers."

A real loss. He loved Ann's open-face turkey sandwiches the day after Thanksgiving almost as much as he loved the huge meal itself. "I should try the stores again. Maybe something will be open." Though he didn't hold out much hope. Now that H5N1 was here, all bets were off.

"I don't get it. Beth says her Safeway's open."

"Luck of the draw."

"Some luck."

Here was where the Hummer dealer lived, Stan Fox. Peter had to admit he hadn't missed being wakened early on Saturday morn-ings by the roar of his lawnmower. The man was in his yard now, looping green strands of Christmas lights over his shrubs. The aroma of cooked meat wafted past. Someone was barbecuing.

"Shazia's cousin emailed her last night," he said.

"Does she know why Shazia's parents haven't called?"

"Sounds like they're on the move."

She took that in, then said, "I'm worried about Shazia. She's not eating."

"Of course she is."

"Not really. She skips breakfast and she just nibbles at her dinner. Maybe she's vegetarian or something, and is too polite to say anything."

He knew Shazia wasn't a vegetarian. They'd split a million tuna subs. "I'll talk to her."

They paused to let a car pull into a driveway, one he'd never seen before. "The Guarnieris get a new car?"

"Not that I know of."

Brake lights flared, then the trunk popped ajar. The engine silenced and doors swung open. Al and Sue got out, looking rumpled and tired. Al had put on some weight, Peter saw, and Sue had done something different with her hair. It stood up in reddish tufts all about her head.

"Hey, Al." It felt awkward not striding forward to shake the fellow's hand. "Hi, Sue."

"Brooks," Al said. "Good to see you."

The four of them stood there looking at one another, keenly aware of the wide grassy strip stretched between them.

"How was Las Vegas?" Ann said.

Al reached into the trunk and pulled out a set of suitcases. "Sue won a couple hundred bucks. We took in a show. Then WHO made that announcement and everything went to hell. The airport was a zoo. People everywhere and not a single open parking space."

"You drove the whole way back?" Peter said.

"Straight through." Sue reached up to fluff her hair with her fingertips. "We were afraid to stop."

"Got stuck in Oklahoma. Ran out of gas and couldn't find a station open. Highway patrol had to rescue us." Al slammed the trunk lid.

Sue shook her head. "Wait until the rental car company finds out we still have their car. I don't know how we're going to get it back to them."

Al looked down at his wife and put an arm around her, drawing her close. He kissed the top of her head. "Don't you worry, Susie Q. They'll get their money."

"I suppose."

The front door opened and Jodi came running out. "Mommy! Daddy! Mommy!"

She flung herself at Sue, who gathered her close, laughing. "My goodness. What are you doing still in your pajamas? And why aren't you wearing any shoes?"

Al wagged a playful finger at his daughter. "Well, now that we're back, young lady, you're going to have to toe the line. No more sleeping until noon. No more ice cream for breakfast."

Jodi giggled and tugged at her father's arm. "What did you get me?"

"Careful, careful," Al said. "Come on. We got something for Nana and Poppa, too."

Peter frowned, watching the three of them. He couldn't help it. He thought of all those miles Al and Sue had traveled, all the ways they could have come in contact with the virus.

"Jodi's one of my students now," Ann told him as Jodi and her parents trooped up the front walk to where the grandparents stood waiting.

"Really?"

"She's not a very popular kid. I've encouraged Maddie to be kind to her, but Jodi's tough. I can't really blame Maddie for wanting to keep her distance."

"How is teaching going? Is it as bad as you thought it might be?"

She glanced at him with an expression of surprise. He looked back at her. Of course he'd remember she was anxious about the whole business. He'd worried about it, too, for her sake.

"It's been all right," she answered. "Teaching isn't the same as doing."

They came to that big white house with all the columns. "Does that boy still live here, the one who used to stand on the sidewalk and yell for Maddie?"

"Now he's sticking poems in the mailbox."

"Sounds like I'd better have a talk with him."

"Well, here's your chance."

The garage door was gliding up. A car backed out, the father driving, the wife sitting beside him. Peter and Ann stopped short of the concrete apron. Suitcases were strapped to the top of the vehicle. The little Marlon Brando was in back. He pressed his face to the glass and stared at them.

"I wonder where they're going," Ann said.

"Disneyland."

"Really?" Ann looked at him quizzically. "How do you know?"

He shrugged. "Why not? The lines have got to be really short right now."

She made a face at him. "Ha, ha."

He felt pleased that he'd dragged a smile from her. They passed Singh's house. The doctor was on the front porch, picking up his newspaper and shaking off the condensation.

"How's it going?" Peter said.

"Oh, hello, Brooks. Good to see you." Singh nodded at Ann. "Actually, it's been quite busy, as you can imagine. I've been called in to staff the ER." He pulled off the plastic bag from around the paper. "Well, if you'll excuse me." He turned and went into his house.

"He's not an ER doc, is he?" Ann asked.

"I think that's right. I guess the hospitals are being overrun with people worried that every sniffle's the flu."

Walter Finn marched toward them, Barney trotting alongside. The man looked as though he were ready for mortal combat, with that heavy black thing across his lower face. He even had thick, rubber-rimmed goggles balanced on his nose. He glanced up, then yanked the leash and swerved across the street, dragging the dog with him and keeping his face averted as though eye contact might be dangerous. Barney grinned at them as he was tugged across the asphalt to the opposite curb.

Peter stared after him. "He looks like Dr. Demento."

Another brief smile from her. "They're saying respiratory masks won't do any good."

"There's some controversy about that. The standard N95 filters out anything bigger than .3 microns, but an influenza virus can be as small as .08. This one, though, seems to be holding at .5."

She looked over at him, then shrugged.

"You talk to your folks today?" Peter asked.

"Beth says the hotel's completely empty. She's really worried they're going to start laying people off."

"She'll be all right. Your sister's socked away every nickel she's made."

"It's just that she's worked so hard to get where she is."

"How's your dad's chemo going?" He'd hated learning about it months after the fact. The old guy had always been good to him.

"He's got five more weeks of treatment. Then we'll know if it's done any good."

"He's a fighter. He'll beat this thing."

Ann scuffed her shoes through the crumpled leaves. She had her hands jammed in her coat pockets. Her cheeks were pink, her hair bright in the sunlight. They used to love taking walks. Most of their courtship had been conducted on Georgetown's buckled sidewalks and the dirt paths that wound alongside the Potomac.

The sun was going down, hitting windowpanes and the chrome of a parked car. Two teenagers were shooting hoops in their driveway. One boy set up the ball and threw. "Loser," the other boy taunted as the ball missed the basket.

"Peter?"

"Hmm?"

"Has Maddie ever talked about William to you?"

Where had that come from? He glanced at her, but she was watching the basketball players. "No."

"You never told her what happened?"

"Not specifically." There had been no reason at all to delve into that. Where was Ann going with this? "Why?"

Ann stopped. He stopped, too.

"She said something to Hannah. I had no idea she'd been thinking about it. I don't know if I should say something to her or not."

"I wouldn't. Let her bring it up. Otherwise she'll think there's something to it."

She shot him a look. "There *is* something to it."

But there didn't have to be. "That's not what I meant, Ann. I'm sure she's all right. It's normal for kids her age to have questions."

"You always dismiss my concerns."

Did he? "I'm not trying to dismiss your concerns. It's just that you always have so many of them when it comes to the girls. It's hard to give them the same importance that you do. It weighs you down, Ann. You know it does. I don't want to be dragged down, too."

"Dragged down," she repeated. Her gaze returned to the boys. "It fell on Thanksgiving this year."

What was she talking about? He looked at her.

She looked back. "You forgot, didn't you?" She looked sad.

He paged rapidly through the days and came up empty.

"William," she said. "He would have been ten today."

It was a physical blow. Ten years? How was that possible?

She had turned her head to watch the boys again. "Do you think he'd have played basketball?"

No. He hated this. He couldn't bear it. "Ann," he began, but she went on as though he hadn't spoken.

"Maybe he wouldn't have liked sports. Maybe he'd be more into dismantling the toaster or firing off rockets. Your mom said you used to drive her crazy doing that stuff. I think about that, about how he would have been just like you. I imagine looking at him and seeing you, the both of you wrapped up in one small person, and my heart would just *stop*, it would be so full." She shook her head. "Maybe not. I don't know. I'll never know."

He didn't want to be standing here in this soup of raw emotion. He wanted to keep walking, feel the autumn air brisk on his face, scan the sky for a faraway hawk. His breath was coming in short puffs.

She was nodding. "So it's up to me."

"What does that mean?"

"I'll be the one to remember. I'll be the one to keep him alive."

"You can't do that, Ann. Don't put that on me. You grieve in your way. Let me grieve in mine."

"Have you ever really grieved, Peter? Or have you just pushed everything away?"

He clenched his fists. "Look. I have my apartment. I can—"

Ann looked at him and laughed, a bitter staccato burst. "Right." She walked away, leaving him standing there on the sidewalk.

For Immediate Release

## *AIRPORTS TO CLOSE,*
## *HOLDING SAYS*

---

WASHINGTON, DC—Secretary of Transportation Frank E. Holding has announced the Federal Aviation Administration will close airspace around thirteen metropolitan areas, effective immediately. These cities include New York City, Washington, DC, Boston, Atlanta, Miami, Chicago, Minneapolis–St. Paul, Detroit, Denver, Las Vegas, San Francisco, Seattle, and Los Angeles.

Commercial and general aviation flights will not be permitted to fly within fifty miles of these cities. These restrictions are not expected to be lifted any time in the near future. Airline passengers who had planned to travel in and out of these cities are urged to seek alternate arrangements.

The secretary also announced that additional airports might be closed, as necessitated by the spread of avian influenza.

*Public Affairs*
*U.S. Department of Transportation*

# FOURTEEN

---

$T$HEY ATE IN THE DINING ROOM.

     Ann removed the thick felt covers from the table to reveal the gleaming red wood beneath, then shook the folds from her grandmother's soft linen tablecloth, the cloth so old the white had turned to cream. Peter came in as she was removing the china from the hutch.

He set down the wine bottle in his hand and looked around. "Everything looks great, Ann."

He was asking her to pretend everything was all right. She carried the stack of delicate plates over to the table. He was right. They needed to get past the day, to focus on making this Thanksgiving seem as normal as possible. She stood back and studied the table, the gleaming silver and the rich linen, the elegant plates with their thin gold bands. She'd forgotten nothing. Everything was the way it used to be. "I think we're ready," she said. "Do you want to call everyone in?"

When they were all seated, there was an awkward pause while she and Peter looked down the table at one another and silently conferred over whether to follow their old tradition of giving thanks. It might flay open old wounds barely healed, so she shook her head and he nodded.

Picking up the serving fork from the platter of chicken, he turned to Shazia. "May I have your plate?"

Maddie reached for the bowl of stuffing. "Kate's got a boyfriend."

Ann looked at Kate, who blushed furiously. What wonderful, charming news. It had to be Scooter, that boy she'd been texting incessantly.

Peter had been in the middle of pouring wine into Ann's glass, and now he stopped and looked from Maddie to Kate to Ann.

"She was telling Michele about it." Maddie dumped a spoonful of stuffing on her plate. "He asked her out and she said yes."

Kate pointed a fork at her. "You should mind your own business."

"Out, like in a date?" Peter frowned. "I don't think that's at all appropriate."

He looked so alarmed that Ann couldn't help smiling. "Don't worry. It's just a figure of speech. When a boy asks a girl out, it doesn't mean they'll actually go out on dates. All they do is text each other and talk on the phone." And maybe meet up at their lockers and hold hands in the hall. But of course there wouldn't be any of that. Kate's first crush would be played out entirely long-distance.

Kate was literally writhing. "Can we *please* change the subject?"

"Maddie, may I pass you the green beans?" Shazia said, and Kate heaved a sigh of relief.

Maddie started to shake her head, then caught the look Ann gave her. "All right," she said reluctantly. "Thank you."

Ann smiled at Shazia. "I hear you heard from your cousin."

Shazia nodded. "She says my parents are going south to stay with my brother." She shook her head as Peter offered the bowl of mashed potatoes. "It's more rural where he lives. They think it will be much safer there."

It had been over a week and Shazia had yet to reach her parents. Maybe conditions overseas were worse than Ann realized. Maybe things were going to get just as bad here, too, now that the airports were closing one by one.

"Is your cousin going with them?" Ann asked.

"No. She's remaining in Cairo. She's a pharmacist. She couldn't leave her job."

Couldn't, or wouldn't? Perhaps in the end it was the same, one person doing the hard, difficult thing. "She sounds very brave."

"Do you have Thanksgiving in Egypt, Shazia?" Maddie carefully lifted her milk glass with both hands.

"Well, sure," Kate said. "Only the Pilgrims are called pharaohs and Plymouth Rock is shaped like a pyramid."

Maddie looked uncertainly at her.

Sometimes Kate was mean just for the sake of being mean. "Enough, Kate." Ann passed the glass bowl of cranberries to Shazia and reminded her older daughter, "When you were Maddie's age, you thought money really did grow on trees."

Kate opened her mouth to retort, then shrugged. "Whatever."

"We don't have Thanksgiving like you do, Maddie." Shazia took a tiny spoonful of the jellied fruit before handing the bowl to Peter. "But my country does have important feasts. There's the Festival of Sacrifice and the Ramadan feast."

Maddie nodded. "I've heard of Ramadan."

"Yes. Those who are Muslim fast for a month and then they have a four-day festival."

"*Four* days?" Maddie repeated.

Shazia smiled, shook her head as Ann held out the rolls. "And there's Christmas, too, only we celebrate it in January."

"Christmas!" Maddie turned to Ann. "Will Santa still come this year?"

Ann hadn't even thought about it. She hadn't started her shopping. She'd been planning to take advantage of the Thanksgiving sales. Now what would she do?

"You bet," Kate said. "And the Tooth Fairy and the Easter Bunny are going to help him, because the elves got H5N1."

That term didn't belong in Kate's mouth. Ann reached over and gripped Kate's hand. Surprisingly, the girl didn't pull away. Ann said to Maddie, "We'll have to see, honey."

She had a month. She'd figure something out.

Maddie turned to Peter with a bright smile. "Guess what? I lost a tooth last week. It fell out while I was drinking chocolate milk."

"I can see," he said. "Must've been pretty chewy milk."

Maddie giggled.

"How about you, Kate?" Peter ladled gravy over his potatoes. "You got any dental issues I need to take care of?"

Kate rolled her eyes. "Like I'd ever tell you." She sank her fork into her potatoes and took a bite.

Maddie set down her glass. "Remember that time you chased Kate around the house with the pliers?"

Peter nodded. "That silly girl." He made a face of comical disbelief. "Can you believe she wouldn't let me tie a string around her loose tooth?"

"That's because," Kate said, "I let you do it that one time, and when you slammed the door, the doorknob fell off."

"So she *bit* me." Peter pulled a face at Maddie. "I still have tooth marks to show for it."

The house had always been so noisy when Peter came home from work. All the laughing and running up and down the stairs. It had been so quiet this past year.

Shazia was looking from Kate to Peter, a half-smile on her face.

"How about when she smashed your finger with the hammer?" Maddie said.

"Oh, yeah." Kate's eyes were bright. "When we were building that tree house with Granddad."

The four of them had had so much fun. Ann and her mother-in-law had watched from the kitchen window, holding on to each other, helpless with laughter, as first one board was nailed sideways and then the other.

"Tree *hut*, you mean," Ann said.

"Only because you made us put it on the lowest branch." Peter shook his head. "Dad and I twisted like pretzels trying to get those boards in place."

He'd referred to his father so easily. Her heart lifted. "Well, it's a good thing I did."

Kate nodded. "Because it broke when Grandma crawled in."

"Poor Mom." Peter smiled. "At least she didn't fall far."

Peter and Ann smiled across the table at each other. She felt happiness sail between them, limned with sorrow, too. They'd never make happy memories again. But how nice to find this joyful memory among all the sad ones. A gift.

"Oh, wow." Maddie pushed back her chair and pointed to the window.

A faint spray of tiny colors shone between the slats of the blinds. It was too bright inside the room to get the full effect. Ann stood and turned off the dining room light, and now the bright colors outside sharpened into points.

They crowded in front of the windows. Peter pulled the cords and the blinds rolled up, revealing the Foxes' holiday display in full rollicking motion on their lawn across the street.

"Look." Maddie's voice was full of wonder. "They've got a Santa on their roof."

There he sat, red-cheeked and waving a green mittened hand, as his reindeer pawed the shingles.

"They still have Frosty," Kate said. "And that snow globe thing."

The enormous inflatables towered on the lawn below. A set of white wicker reindeer pranced beside the sidewalk, and elves lined the front path, bending and straightening as they pretended to build toys. Candle flames flickered in each window, and every bush was draped with lights that twinkled like emeralds and rubies, sapphires and diamonds.

"When are we going to put up our lights, Daddy?" Maddie asked.

A simple question, but it brought with it so much. The girls unwinding the cords as Peter checked the bulbs, their thoughtful discussions about trees versus bushes, whether they should go all-white or stick with the traditional multicolored.

"We didn't have any last year," Kate said.

"You do this, too, Peter?" Shazia sounded amazed.

Peter laughed. "Nothing like it, believe me. I usually toss up a few strings of lights, but that's pretty much it."

Even so, the house had always looked so cheerful in the dark. Ann would be out with the girls and they'd pull onto their street and there would be the sparkling colors, flashing happily on and off, welcoming them home.

"Peter has more of a Fauvist approach to holiday lighting," Ann said, and Peter laughed.

"More like a bunch of elves barfed on the bushes," Kate said.

"Hey," Peter protested.

Maddie doubled over. "But it's so true, Daddy."

Kate leaned into Ann, and Ann put her arm around her. In a few short years she'd be taller than Ann. Ann kissed her daughter's temple, the skin so warm and Kate-fragrant, the pulse so steady beneath her lips. She drew Maddie's small hand in hers and clasped her fingers tightly. She was glad for this Thanksgiving and all its strangeness. Maddie was right. Things didn't have to be perfect to be celebrated. Sometimes it was enough just to *be*.

The three of them stood there, close together, with Peter and Shazia on the other side, and watched the joyful spectacle blink on and off across the street.

THE LAUNDRY DETERGENT BOTTLE WAS COVERED WITH SHINY black bugs. They swarmed over her fingers. Stifling a scream, Ann flung them off and hurriedly backed away. The beetles dropped to the floor and streamed out the laundry room door.

Now she had a sword in her hand. It was long and curving, with an ornate handle. She swung it. The insects, a black flowing river speeding across the kitchen floor, spread to the steps that led upstairs.

Peter was working on his laptop. She called to him as she ran past. He didn't lift his head. But then he was there, standing in the front hall. He was wearing his coat and carrying a suitcase. "I have to talk to Liederman," he told her, slamming the door behind him.

Now she was stomping the beetles, the flats of her feet crushing their bodies. When she lifted her feet, they skittered away unscathed. They were crawling across her toes. They flowed to her ankles, swam to her knees. She was wading in them. She grabbed the banister and pulled herself up the stairs. It was a lake of small grasping bodies. They swarmed over her shoulders, her throat. They filled her mouth and pressed against her eyes.

Her eyelids flew open to blackness. She was in her bed. She

pushed herself up and looked at the clock on the nightstand. Three-thirty. Earlier than usual.

Maddie had left her overhead light on again. Would she ever outgrow her fear of the dark? Her sheets were twisted around her legs, and she had an arm across her face. Ann stepped in to switch off the light and tug the blankets up to her daughter's chin. Maddie remained motionless, as though lost in some dreamy valley from which she could never be roused. How many nights had Ann stood by her crib, watching?

Down the hall, Kate's door stood open. Ann paused and heard her daughter shift in her sleep. Reassured, she moved on.

Silence came from the guest room. The door was firmly closed: no light shone around the frame. Shazia must have finally fallen asleep. Ann had heard her crying earlier. She'd gotten out of bed, but when she reached the hallway, the muffled sound had stopped. Shazia had to be sick with worry. Here she was, marooned with this family and so far from her own. She'd heard from her cousin only the one time. Her parents had remained unreachable. She must lie in this strange house and hold herself very still in the darkness.

Moonlight followed her down the stairs, disappeared as she passed the dining room, reappeared as she stepped into the kitchen. She set the kettle on the stove and went into the family room. Settling back against the sofa cushions, she wrapped the afghan around her shoulders and fumbled for the television remote. She turned the volume down low. A man stood canting into the wind, his face grave. More bad news.

The next station was playing the same scene. The home-and-garden channel was, too, and all the movie channels. Where was the station that played reruns of old black-and-white shows? She liked those. She'd watched them during middle-of-the-night feedings, rocking her babies to sleep. No, it was playing the same scene as the others, all vivid color and jerky motion as the newscaster spoke into the microphone, stepping sideways to allow the camera to pan across the metal structure jutting from the surface of the ocean. The picture changed to a man speaking into a nest of microphones. Even the children's stations were showing the same images.

The creak of a step. She looked over to see Peter.

"I thought I heard someone," he said.

He was wearing his tattered university sweatshirt and sweat-pants. Was that what he was sleeping in these days? "Did I wake you?"

"I couldn't sleep." He sat down in the armchair, sighing.

She was glad to see him, glad for company in these echoing, dark hours. That dream had been so unsettling. "I'm making tea."

"Sounds good." He nodded toward the television set playing quietly, its face a bright square in the darkness. "Any news?"

"A crew's gotten sick on an oil platform in the Gulf of Mexico. The oil company and the CDC's arguing about getting medical assistance out to them."

"There'll be gas shortages."

Of course. She hadn't thought through the implications. But now her mind was working, going down all the awful possibilities. Gas shortages meant trucks couldn't make food deliveries. Trains couldn't reach warehouses. Factories would shut down. "For how long, do you think?"

"Well, prices will skyrocket in the short term, but then they'll settle back down. There are all sorts of plans in place to handle this sort of situation. The President can always draw on our emergency fuel supply." He yawned. "How much gas do you have?"

"A full tank. I filled up on the way home from school." Eight days ago. It seemed like eight years.

The minivan got only nineteen miles to the gallon. A full tank took her three hundred miles. Three hundred miles was nothing; it was partway to nowhere. "Maybe they'll get a new crew out there soon."

Peter didn't say anything. He was no longer listening, intent on the words creeping across the bottom of the television screen. She squinted to make out the tiny type. Both Minnesota patients were dead. Chicago was reporting additional cases. So was New Orleans. Detroit had one suspected.

"Minnesota," he said. "Illinois, Louisiana, Michigan. They're all on the Mississippi flyway."

So was Ohio. While they'd been sleeping, the virus had been busy, spiraling ever closer to where they lived. She thought of her dream again and shuddered. "You think that means anything?"

"It's interesting."

The kettle whistled from the stove. She got up before it started shrieking. "Decaf?"

"Thanks." He followed her into the kitchen.

The kettle was shaking on the burner. She poured steaming water into two mugs, dunked in the tea bags. "When are you going in?"

He took the mug she offered him. "A couple of hours. When I get those samples ready, I can start working with the people in Tennessee. We'll isolate various bits of RNA and try to see whether it's grown more virulent. With both of us working, we'll cover twice as much ground."

"But it's avian. Why take the risk of exposing yourself for that?"

"Everyone's working on human cases. No one's paying any attention to the avian form. But the human outbreaks seem to be following the avian, at least here in America. My thinking is, they've got to be related somehow. So anything I learn about the avian form might shed light on the human."

Still, she didn't like the idea of him venturing downtown. Who knew how bad things had grown? Who knew how desperate people had become? Peter was so trusting. He'd pull over in an instant if he thought someone needed his help. He wouldn't give the least bit of thought to his own safety. There had to be another solution. She remembered the guy on the federal side who'd worked with Peter in the past. "What about Dan? Wouldn't this be his job?"

"Yes, but he can't get anywhere near his lab. All nonessential state workers are strictly off-duty now. If they caught him, he'd be fired."

She tried one last gambit. "The university's closed. You could get fired, too."

"I'll be careful."

The same way he'd always pushed her away. *It'll be all right. Don't worry. I'll be careful.* As if saying those things actually reassured her, as if they reduced her fears to mist. They never did. They only made her feel more alone. "Is Shazia going with you?" she heard herself ask.

"No. It's a one-person job. I've asked her to stay and sort through Liederman's notes for me. You know that book I've always wanted to write?"

"I remember." She set down the spoon and looked at him. His face was dappled with red light. The kitchen was filled with it. She turned her head to see the source. They both leaned over the kitchen sink.

An ambulance, red and white lights flashing, was pulling into a driveway down the street. They weren't running the sirens. Maybe they didn't use sirens in the middle of the night.

"You think it's Al?" Peter said.

"Probably. He had that bypass last year. But he looked okay this afternoon." He'd stood there and clasped Sue to him. Ann had watched with a kind of longing, remembering how she and Peter had once been so easy together.

"He might have been having symptoms we don't know about."

The driver's door opened. A man appeared and walked around to the back of the vehicle. He swung open the door and pulled out a stretcher. Another man was there now. He hoisted a big bag onto the stretcher, and together the two men wheeled the stretcher along the path. They paused by the front door. It yawned open, and they entered.

"Shouldn't they be moving faster?"

She felt Peter shrug.

One of the EMTs backed through the doorway. He lifted the stretcher down the front steps. A second man appeared.

Ann strained to see beyond him but spotted no one standing in the doorway. Sue must be inside, getting ready to go. Her parents had already gone back home. They had a cat they were worried about, Ann knew. She'd seen their car earlier, accelerating down the street. She should run across the street and offer to take Jodi. She actually put down her mug before she caught herself. Of course she couldn't. She could only stand here and watch helplessly.

At the bottom of the steps, the two men released the wheels and guided the stretcher down the path. They were moving so slowly. They both had their faces covered with masks and dark goggles, making them look strangely insectile. "Do you see that?" She hoped Jodi was still asleep. She didn't want to think of a child witnessing this.

"I guess it's standard practice now."

She saw his worried frown. She supposed that what he said made sense.

They came down the path, the stretcher between them. She couldn't make things out. One of the men was blocking her view. He walked backward onto the driveway and swept the stretcher into position to face the back of the ambulance. Now Ann could see the stretcher bed. Its surface was completely white, the sheet draped all the way around. It appeared empty. Had this simply been a false alarm? "Why are they leaving?"

"Ann," Peter said, "it's not Al."

She looked again and saw that there was a small lump beneath the sheet. She gripped the rim of the sink. *Oh my God. Jodi.* Her heart thudded. It wasn't possible. She was just a little girl. "But she was fine. She looked fine." She'd come running across the lawn just that afternoon. She'd thrown herself, laughing, into her mother's arms.

"Hmm."

"Could it happen that fast?"

He nodded.

Ann started to tremble. "Couldn't it be something else?"

"It could."

"But you know it's not."

*Jodi.* And she'd found her so annoying. She'd scolded her just the day before. She'd told her to go home. She blinked away tears.

The stretcher collapsed and the men worked it into the back of the ambulance. An EMT climbed into the driver's seat. Taillights flared.

Her throat felt tight with fear. The steel of the sink bit into her palms.

"Peter," she whispered. "She was here. She was on the trampoline with the girls."

# FIFTEEN

$P$ETER BANGED ON THE DOOR. "HELLO?" HE CUPPED HIS hands to the glass and yelled. "Anyone there?"

Fifteen minutes and still no sign of the security guard. Peter could see the circular desk just on the other side of the glass, the top of the computer monitor, but no one sat there. Hank or Arnold must be doing rounds. *Come on.* How long did it take to walk four floors? Could be he was in the bathroom. In which case, Peter might be here a while longer.

He stamped his feet to keep warm and pounded the door again.

Movement on the other side of the glass. *Aha.* Someone was walking toward him. Peter squinted. Not Hank's broad stride, slighter than Arnold. As the man approached, he pulled a mask up over his lower face. He twisted the dead bolt and held the door open. "Thought I heard something."

"Lewis?" What was he doing here? His lab animals. Right, someone had to feed them. "Where's Hank?"

Lewis shrugged. "Who knows? When I got in this morning, no one was here. Good thing I have a key."

"Anyone else around?" They began walking down the corridor.

"A few, in and out. It's busier over at the medical school."

They came to a stop by the elevator.

"You hear the latest?" Lewis said. "Christ, it's right here in Columbus."

Jodi's body had been so small it had barely lifted the sheet draped around her. When he left the house that morning, Ann was staring out the kitchen window, her face pale, cup held motionless to her lips. He knew she hadn't slept.

"See ya." Lewis turned and headed for the door to the basement.

Peter unlocked his lab door and stepped into the pungency of solvents, a sweetish aroma that was familiar and comforting. He gloved up, slid his arms through the sleeves of his lab coat, and opened the freezer.

The sampling tubes sat there, the swabs stiff inside the clear plastic. He started to shut the freezer door, then paused. He counted to be sure. One of the Sparrow Lake samples was missing. He'd ask Shazia about it later. Maybe she'd neglected to extract the right number.

Setting the tubes on the counter to warm up, he carried the centrifuge to the hood and plugged it in. Selecting the boxed test kits from the shelf, he brought those over, along with the bag of Eppendorf microtubes.

It was strange, working in this utter silence. Peter was used to some background noise. The ringing of a phone, a door squeaking open then shut, someone coming up and asking a question. Shazia had wanted to join him, but he'd persuaded her to stay put. "Stay online. Let me know if anything changes." No sense in both of them taking the risk.

He stopped the centrifuge and carefully removed each swab, pipetted the remaining material into fresh tubes. Measuring out the chemicals from the test kits, he dripped each mixture into the raw material to melt away lipids, bacteria, proteins. He held up a tube. Now it was pure RNA, harmless as water. The little savages were gone. Standing and stretching, he walked over to his laptop and sat down at the counter to email the lab in Tennessee. Maybe he'd check in with Shazia and ask her about that missing sample.

Ann answered. "Peter?"

He heard the girls calling to her in the background. There was some urgency in their voices. He thought of what Ann had said.

Kate and Maddie had been around Jodi. The incubation period was about right. "Are the girls okay?"

"No, no. They're fine. Did you just get in?"

"A little while ago. I wanted to get this batch in."

"How much longer are you going to be?"

"I'll be home by dinnertime." He hoped. Once he got the PCR running, it would be another four hours before he knew whether or not it was avian influenza.

"Hold on, Kate," he heard Ann say. "I'm talking to your father."

"I've looked everywhere." Kate's voice. "I can't find them."

"Look in the blanket chest." A pause, then Ann came back on the line. "Sorry about that. Kate can't find her snow pants."

It wasn't that cold outside. "Why does she need her snow pants?"

"Peter. Don't you know? It's snowing."

He walked to the window and looked out. Tiny white flakes spiraled downward against the tan and brown buildings. There were a dozen or so people walking along the sidewalks below, no one side by side. Snow already covered the grass below. The streets looked slushy with it. The sky stretched above, a solid gray wall desolate of birds. Odd. Ducks headed inland when the weather turned miserable. Unless they were dead. All of them? That would be millions. That wasn't possible.

"Peter?"

"Sorry. Yeah, I see it's really coming down out there. Let me get back to this before it gets too deep."

MADDIE LOOKED UP AS PETER STEPPED THROUGH THE SLIDING glass door and onto the patio thick with snow. She was jabbing a stick into a snowman. It hung there, lopsided. "Daddy!"

"Hey, Maddie girl." Through the slanting curtains of snow, he glimpsed other families playing in their yards. He heard the scrapes of shovels, hoots of laughter.

Kate knelt by a ball of snow. "Help."

"Please don't tell me that's the daddy snowman." He waded

across the yard through the snow to her. It was so cold and crisp out here. They hadn't had a snow like this in years. Most storms disdained them, sweeping farther north or south, leaving Columbus with dreary skies and cold temperatures. "Come on. This guy's nowhere near tall and broad-shouldered enough. Nothing like your real dad."

Kate rolled her eyes, but she put her hands alongside his.

"Lean into it," Peter said, and they pushed the ball of snow in long, uneven tracks through their yard back to where Maddie was working.

Maddie had her knitted hat perched on top of her snowman and one of his old scarves wound around its neck. "What can we use for noses?"

"Carrots," he said.

"Mommy said no."

Right. He'd forgotten. "Well, I'm sure we can find something."

The sliding glass door opened. Ann stepped over the threshold, rotund in a big quilted coat, hat, scarf, mittens.

He grinned at her. She always pulled on every warm thing she had when it snowed, as though she'd freeze into a human Popsicle otherwise. "They teach you to dress like that in DC?"

She ponderously made her way over to where he stood. "The three times we had snow." She hiked an eyebrow at Peter's bare head and his feet clad in loafers. "I found these," she said, shaking a Baggie. "They could be noses."

Maddie took it. "Buckeyes. Thanks, Mommy."

Ann pulled bright yellow daisies from her pocket. They sprang into her hand, unchastened by having been cramped into tight quarters. "I got these out of my craft box. Maybe they could be buttons or something."

Kate snorted. "Hippie snow bears. Perfect." But she took the silk flowers and plunged them down the front of one fat snowman.

"There's Shazia." Maddie straightened and waved. "Shazia! Come play."

Shazia wore an old down coat of Peter's and a pair of his snow pants, cuffs folded. Her cheeks were flushed. "I've never seen so much snow."

"My parents say it's coming down hard in DC, too," Ann said. "They say it's beautiful."

Her voice sounded wistful.

Shazia said, "I've finished sorting your notes, Peter."

"That was fast."

"She worked straight through lunch," Ann said. "Shazia, I left a plate out for you."

"Thank you."

"Help us make a snow fort, Shazia," Maddie said.

Shazia looked around. "I've never made a snow fort."

"What about snow angels?"

Shazia shook her head, her dark hair sliding this way and that over her shoulders.

Kate looked at her, hands on her hips. "Have you ever gone sledding?"

It was clear from the expression on Shazia's face that she had never done that, either.

"Well," Peter said, "we'll just have to take you to the park so Kate can teach you all her special tricks, like plowing into trees and skidding down the hill on her rear end."

"Funny, Dad," Kate said.

"I don't know," Ann said. "There might be a lot of people there."

She had a point. Jodi had contracted H5N1 from someone. It might have been Sue or Al returning from their cross-country trip, or it might have been someone from the neighborhood. In either case, they now knew that H5N1 was here. "We'll be safe as long as we stay three feet away from other people," Peter said.

Ann chewed her lower lip.

Kate groaned. "Mom. Come *on*. It's like we're prisoners or something."

Ann looked at Kate and her expression softened. "Just promise me you'll stick with your dad and that you won't go running around."

"We promise, Mommy," Maddie said.

Ann kept her gaze on Kate. "Even if Michele's there."

"My God." Kate threw her hands up in the air. "If I see Michele, I'll run screaming all the way home."

"What about Scooter?" Maddie said. "I bet you won't run screaming home *then*."

She ducked, giggling, as Kate threw a snowball at her.

Libby came out onto her patio, Jacob in her arms. She twirled around, lifting her baby to the falling flakes. "It's his first snow," she called over, laughing. "He loves it."

Peter remembered Kate's first snow. They'd been living in Greensboro and he'd bundled her up and brought her outside and set her little booted feet onto the ground. She'd taken one look around and howled, lifting her arms to be picked up again. Peter had been bent over with laughter, but Ann had rushed outside barefoot to scoop up the baby. "There, there, darling," she'd crooned. "It's just snow. Look." She'd held out her palm to show the flakes harmlessly alighting and melting.

Maddie had been a different story altogether. They'd been visiting his parents in Michigan and a few inches had fallen overnight. She'd demanded to be let out, standing unsteadily by the window, holding on to the sill, flexing up and down on her toes. When Peter had finally taken her out, her little hand firmly in his, she'd lifted her foot and stamped it, chortling at the resulting squish. She spent the entire afternoon stomping around in the snow, tipping over and righting herself. She'd cried when Peter had at last carried her back inside to dry off.

"How about a snow tiger?" Maddie asked. "There's enough snow for that."

"There's enough for an entire snow zoo." Ann plucked Maddie's hat from the snowman and shook it. "Put this back on, honey."

Maddie brushed her hand away. "I don't need it. I'm fine."

A sudden wailing filled the air.

Shazia stopped and looked around.

"It's the tornado sirens," Kate said.

But tornado season was over.

"They'll stop in a minute." Ann fitted the hat back onto Maddie's head. "I'll get your snowman another one."

The whooping noise ceased and the loudspeaker started. Peter lifted his head. It wasn't the usual broadcast. Ann had heard it, too. She'd stopped and raised her head to listen.

*"Please tune in to your local news program for an update."*

He slogged through the drifts of snow, sliding open the back door and coming inside, snow falling from his shoes to the floor. Ann reached the remote first, pressing the buttons and stopping at the sight of the governor speaking into the camera, his face grave. They stood together, listening.

The girls arrived, breathless, Shazia beside them.

Peter stared at the screen.

*". . . following reports of multiple outbreaks in Columbus, Cleveland, Cincinnati, Toledo, and Dayton . . ."*

All those cities?

He felt a tug on his coat sleeve and glanced down to see Maddie looking up at him, her blue eyes wide and her cheeks rosy. "What's he saying, Daddy?"

He put his hand on her shoulder. "Hold on, honey."

*". . . closing our state borders to all incoming and outgoing traffic, excepting deliveries of essential food, medicine, and fuel."*

Quarantine.

The cities that locked themselves up during the 1918 flu pandemic had suffered fewer casualties. Philadelphia had been the slowest to react. The city had been decimated.

LIFTING HIS HEAD FROM THE PILLOW, PETER YAWNED AND looked around. The room was full dark, the snow packed tight against the small windows set high along the basement ceiling. He had the vague sense that a lot of time had passed. Groggily, he got to his feet, found his slippers, and made his way upstairs.

Brilliant sunlight assailed him as he stepped onto the first floor. He blinked.

All the softness of last night's slanting flakes was gone. Harsh brightness poured in through the windows, the result of sun glinting off mounds of snow, the sky beyond white with the promise of more. The sun was high. It had been up for hours. The snow had blanketed the house and coerced his sleeping mind to stay huddled beneath the covers for as long as possible. He'd make some coffee and head straight in to the lab.

The house was quiet. Everyone else was sleeping in, too. Then he heard the strangeness, the absolute stillness that saturated the room and pressed against him, and realized this was no ordinary silence. No refrigerator humming, no furnace clicking off and on, no television playing. Now he felt the chill. How long had the power been off?

Ann came down the stairs, a befuddled expression on her face. Her gaze found his. She was hearing it, too.

"We've lost power," he told her. "I've got to go in."

She pulled her robe more tightly around her. "Are the roads clear?"

He went to the sliding glass door and looked out.

Everything was white. It covered the patio and the bushes. It swelled up to the bottom of the trampoline. He couldn't see where the sidewalk ended and the road began.

Ann came up behind him. "Oh, no."

He wouldn't be going anywhere anytime soon. The lab was over ten miles away. Even if he walked the entire distance, forging through the snow that would reach his knees, he'd never make it in time.

He looked out at the stillness and felt despair. His lab wasn't on a generator. With every minute that passed, the temperature inside the freezer was rising. The viruses he'd prepared were thawing. Some of them might already be dead. Before too long, they'd all be dead. Whatever answers they'd held would be lost forever.

# SIXTEEN

---

ANN ELBOWED HER WAY INTO THE KITCHEN, HER ARMS full. The snow had started again, no longer a charming dance of flakes but a relentless slanting white the same hard color as the sky. She dumped packages on the counter. "Peter, would you light the grill?"

Peter was emptying the refrigerator shelves into bags by his feet. "It's not even noon."

"I know. But we need to cook the meat before it spoils." If they got a sudden warm spell before the power returned, they'd lose all of it. This way, they could eke out a few more days. Cooked meat lasted longer than uncooked. Didn't it?

He looked thoughtful. "All right. Why don't you bring it out to me in batches?"

Thank goodness he was here. It was reassuring for all of them to have another adult around, helping to work things out.

"Kate says the lights don't work, either." Maddie held her spoon poised over her yogurt cup. She was bundled in sweaters and mittens, a bright pink scarf tied around her throat, its ends trailing down her back.

"Don't worry." Peter shrugged into his coat. "Your mom's got lots of candles."

No, she didn't. Ann had a couple of boxes of tapers for the dining room candlesticks, that bizarre collection Peter's mother foisted on her before she went into the assisted-living place, and a bunch of tea lights left over from Halloween. With any luck, the power would be back on before she had to resort to using any of them.

"You still good for firewood?" Peter opened a drawer and removed the box of matches.

"I think so." She hadn't touched the half-cord he'd bought before he moved out. It lay as he'd left it, covered by a tarp at the back of the yard.

"Good. I'll get a fire going in a little while." He winked at Maddie, slid open the sliding glass door, and stepped outside into whiteness.

Kate shuffled into the room and slumped into her seat at the kitchen table. She was the picture of mourning in her black turtleneck and skullcap pulled down low. "Is it *ever* going to stop snowing?"

"Daddy says we have to shovel," Maddie said. "And *you* have to do the front walk all by yourself."

Kate glared at her. "Don't talk to me." She reached for the container of yogurt in front of her and scowled. "I hate yogurt."

"I know." Ann unwound butcher's paper from a rib roast. "But eat it anyway." That yogurt was already a week past its expiration date. Perfectly okay, but a few more days might render it inedible.

"I should've charged my iPod last night. It's totally dead." Kate peeled back the foil cover. "And my cell phone's dead, too."

Kate had drifted all morning, opening her laptop and staring at the blank screen, picking up her hair dryer and dropping it back onto the bathroom counter with a groan, as if by sheer *want* she could make them spring to life.

"You can use the phone in the den." Ann set the roast aside and reached for another package.

What a relief it had been to lift the receiver and hear the steady thrum of the dial tone. Though the den was an inconvenient spot for their only line to the outside world. She'd have to plug it into the family room outlet later.

"I can?" Kate regarded her with suspicion. "How come?"

"We got lucky. We never upgraded to digital, so the landline still works."

"What does that mean?" Kate demanded.

Ann ripped open the paper and found pork chops. "To tell you the truth, I don't have a clue. Your dad might be able to explain it."

"So, would Michele's phone work, too?"

"You'll have to try her and see." She mentally crossed her fingers.

"Don't forget to call your *boyfriend*," Maddie said slyly.

Kate dipped her spoon into her yogurt. "I told you. Don't talk to me."

"So, wait." Maddie looked up at Ann. "What about the TV? Is there one that works?"

"No, honey. I'm afraid that's a different thing." Ann snipped through the thin plastic and dumped the chops into a bowl.

"Oh." Maddie's voice sagged with disappointment.

Ann looked across the counter at Maddie staring down into her cup, clearly trying not to cry. "You know how you're always trying to get me to play Monopoly?" An eternally endless game when played at an eight-year-old's level.

Maddie shrugged elaborately.

"Well, consider me fair game." Ann smiled. "So to speak."

Maddie straightened in her seat. "O-kay!"

"We'll all play." They could divide into teams. The girls would love that, even Kate, especially if Shazia joined in. "Let me take care of the food first, okay?" Ann turned and almost bumped into Shazia.

"Excuse me." Shazia balanced a stack of packaged chicken breasts and ground beef in her arms. "This is the last of it." She set them carefully on the counter.

Just a few days ago, their meat supply had seemed so ample. Whenever Ann opened the freezer, she had been reassured to see the packed shelves. But now that everything was spread out before her, it seemed woefully meager. Well, she could make soup from the bones. She could use the fat to cook with. And at some point, the stores would reopen. The city would step in. Ann's wasn't the only family watching its food supply dwindle.

"Do you want me to empty the rest of the freezer?" Shazia said.

The fewer times they opened the door, the colder its contents would keep. Still, it would be a challenge to figure out when things were no longer safe to eat. Meat would give off a rancid odor. Ice cream would form a furry skin, but how did frozen peas signal rot? She'd make a new rule—no one opened the freezer but her. "Better leave it as it is. But you could help put away the food Peter took out."

"Okay." Shazia picked up two bags and elbowed her way through the back door.

"Listen, guys. We're all going to sleep down here tonight. I'll set up the air mattresses. Your dad will light a fire in the fireplace."

"Why can't we sleep in our own rooms?" Kate said.

"It'll be too cold up there. It'll be nice down here, I promise. But no more reading in bed, Kate. I'm sorry, honey." Ann turned on the faucet and washed her hands.

"Why can't I use a flashlight?" Kate asked.

"We need to conserve our batteries."

Maddie licked her spoon. "What does that mean?"

"That means nothing works," Kate said. "Not even your CD player. Not even your DS."

Maddie turned to look at Ann. "Is that true?"

"Hey," Ann said cheerfully, drying her hands on a dishtowel. "It'll be all right. We've lost power before. Remember?" *Not like this. Never like this.* "The lights will come back on any minute now. Until then, it'll be a big party. I mean, how many times do you get to sleep in the family room?"

"Big whoop." Kate pushed herself up from the table and brought her yogurt container over. Ann put a staying hand on Kate's arm. Kate rolled her eyes, then held out the cup.

Ann looked inside. It had been scraped clean. "Good girl." She put her hand to Kate's forehead, then the backs of her fingers against her daughter's pale cheek. "How are you feeling?"

"Freezing."

Thank God that was all. There was no evidence of fever, no complaint of a headache. She pulled the scarf up to Kate's chin and put her arms around her daughter's shoulders. "Daddy'll get a fire going soon." Kate's hair smelled of Kate and cold.

Kate pulled away and dropped the yogurt container into the trash. "Can I call Michele?"

"You bet. If a call comes through, pick it up."

Maddie brought over her spoon and dropped it into the bowl of soapy water. "Can we play Monopoly now?"

"Not just yet, sweetheart. Why don't you find a book to read?" The chicken breasts were frozen solid. She'd have to defrost them before she could peel off the plastic wrap. She plugged the sink and turned on the faucet.

"But I've *been* reading. I'm *sick* of reading."

Growing up, Ann could read for hours and hours. Her idea of heaven was to stay up late as the house ticked into nighttime silence and read by the cozy light from her lamp until her mother called down the hall, *Time to go to sleep, Annie.*

"Well, how about cards?" Ann set the packages of chicken into the cold water and balanced a heavy pot on top to keep them submerged.

"There's no one to play with."

*True.* She trotted out the one sure thing. "Why don't you draw?"

"I guess." Sighing, Maddie dragged herself away. "Can I bring my markers downstairs?"

"Of course." Ann slid open the door to an elemental rush of cold that sucked away her breath. Peter stood in a drift of snow that came up beyond his knees, scraping the grill rack with a wire brush. "Here you go." She reached the platter of food out to him. "I've got more coming."

He nodded absently. She guessed he was thinking about his samples again. Had he really been onto something? Would it have made any difference, in the end? They'd never know.

Back in the kitchen, she crossed to the refrigerator, picked up the bags still sitting on the floor, and nudged the door closed. Now it was just a big, empty, expensive box.

The garage was a frigid slap. She pulled up the hood of her sweatshirt and felt her way around the strange shapes that loomed out of the gloom. Bikes, sleds, lawnmower. Shazia crouched in the corner and fitted things into the big bin Ann had emptied earlier, light from the small window falling onto her.

"Do you want me to open the garage door so you can see?"

"It's all right." Shazia reached out and took the bags from her.

The girl's teeth were chattering. The sweater she wore wasn't heavy enough to keep her warm. "Shazia, you're freezing. Go inside. I'll do that."

"No, it's okay. I'm almost done."

Ann hadn't seen the girl in anything but blouses and thin sweaters. She should have figured it out sooner. Maybe Shazia didn't have any winter-weight clothes. She was probably too polite to say anything. "Do you have anything warmer to wear?"

Shazia glanced down at herself. "I didn't realize how cold it got here."

"We'll go through my closet." Nothing would be a perfect match, Shazia was so tall and slim, but they'd figure something out.

"All right. Thank you." Shazia folded up the plastic bag and reached for the next.

In the kitchen, Ann found Maddie kneeling by the bin of markers, poking through them. "Hey, Mom—Kate's been calling you. Libby's on the phone." She uncapped a marker and scrawled something across a piece of paper. "These are all dried up."

"Check the school-supply box."

Kate stood in the den, an impatient look on her face. She thrust the receiver at Ann. "I was talking to Michele."

So Michele was just on the other end of the phone line. Thank goodness. Something was going right. "I'll let you know when I'm off. Go round up the pillows from everyone's bed, please, and put them in the family room." Ann put the receiver to her ear. "Hey. How are you guys doing?"

"Can you believe this?" Libby sounded on the verge of tears. "My mom was all set to come, then this . . . stupid . . . quarantine."

"I'm so sorry, Libby."

"I mean, how are they going to stop people?"

Ann leaned back against the desk. Peter's laptop sat there, its lid yawning hopefully open. She pressed it shut. "They'll shoot them."

"Oh, come on! This is America, not some Third World country."

"They will, Libby. You can't risk it."

Libby let out a shaky breath. "How are your folks doing?"

"My dad had a rough night. His cough is back. But at least they have electricity."

"Nice to know it's civilized somewhere."

"I don't know how civilized it is there. Beth's apartment was broken into while she was at work. The cops didn't even come out to write a report. They just took her complaint over the phone."

"Oh, God. I hadn't thought of that. What if someone broke in here? We don't have a gun. We don't have *anything*."

"Libby. It's all right. No one's going to break in." Still, Ann glanced to the window. Of course, no one was out there. She was being foolish.

"I'm so tired of this, Ann. I just want a hot cup of tea and to read the newspaper without freaking out over what it's saying."

"I know. Well, at least we still have the phone."

"I'd lose my mind otherwise." There was a muted shout in the background. Libby sighed. "I'd better go. Smith needs something. Probably forgot how to change a diaper again."

Ann smiled. Libby already sounded better. "I'll call you later."

THE BASEMENT WAS SHROUDED IN DARKNESS. ANN REACHED automatically for the light switch and caught herself. She stepped into the utility room and waited for her eyes to pick out even the faintest images. No use. It was utterly black in here. She shuffled forward a few steps until her feet bumped into something. She bent and extended her hands and touched the smooth contours of a storage bin. Prying off the lid, she patted around, feeling smooth metal and stiff canvas. Pushing the tent aside, she reached deeper, hooking her fingers onto something ribbed and rubbery. She drew out her find and dropped it to the floor. There should be another underneath, and sure enough, there it was. She brushed off dust and a sticky wad of cobweb, hoping the spider that constructed it had moved on. Say, to another solar system.

After dragging both air mattresses up the stairs, she spread them across the family room floor and manually pumped them up. Each one could hold two people. There were five of them. Someone would have to sleep on the couch. She and Kate would take one mattress, Peter and Maddie the other. Shazia could sleep on the couch. It was long enough, and she was slim.

Back down in the basement, she unearthed the collection of sleeping bags: the two brightly colored ones emblazoned with cartoon characters, which the girls took to sleepovers, the more durable pair from when Peter and she had gone camping in West Virginia years ago, and the old black one from Peter's college days, which she really should return to him. Well, it would come in handy now.

Coming back up to the family room, she unzipped each bag and shook it out over the mattresses, and spread one across the couch for Shazia. Now, upstairs to retrieve comforters and pillows from the beds. When she came back into the kitchen, she found Maddie sitting at the kitchen table.

"Hi, Mommy."

"Hi, honey."

She layered the comforters across the sleeping bags, folding down the tops and tucking in the ends, and plumped up the pillows and set them out. At last she stood back, hands on her hips, and studied her handiwork. It looked cozy. Those big windows would be a problem, though. She could already feel the cold seeping in from where she stood. She'd have to fashion some sort of weatherproofing system with plastic wrap and duct tape.

"That looks nice," Maddie said.

Ann turned to smile at her.

Maddie was holding a paintbrush. Not one of those thin plastic ones that came in all those crayon colors but a full-sized brush with a real wood handle. It looked, in fact, exactly like the very expensive sable one Peter had given her for their first anniversary. The one she knew they couldn't afford but which she couldn't give up. The one she'd used to paint her first watercolor, the deep vibrant purples of violets against the rich green grass.

Ann sucked in her breath. "Where did you get that?"

Maddie swirled bristles across a sheet of paper. "This box."

"Where's this box?"

"Downstairs."

"On the top shelf?"

"Uh-huh."

Ann came over. She plucked the brush from Maddie's hand and plunged it in the cup of water.

"Don't, Mommy. What about my picture?"

Twisted tubes of paint lay scattered across the table, alongside a plastic palette still smeared with the last colors Ann had ever used. She couldn't bear to look at their hopeful brightness. "Did you open the other box, too?"

"No."

Ann reached for the tube of aquamarine and screwed the cap tight. The umber lay uncapped, too, and the ebony. "You should have asked me first." She had taped those box flaps shut. Maddie would have had to work to open them, and that should have signaled to her that that box wasn't to be touched. "This isn't for you." Her voice trembled with anger.

"Then who is it for?" Kate said from behind her.

"Me." Everything seemed intact. She would retape the box and hide it in her bedroom closet.

Maddie pushed herself back from the table. "But you don't use this stuff. Why can't I?"

All those things had given her so much joy, but they'd belonged to a different Ann. The person she was now couldn't bear to look at them.

"Shut up," Kate said. "She's just telling you."

"Mommy, she said 'shut up' to me."

But Ann wasn't listening.

"DON'T GO, MOMMY," MADDIE SAID.

"I won't, sweetheart." Ann held the red-and-white candy-striped candle steady on a plate. It gave off a halo of light, enough for them to see by.

Maddie pulled the nightgown over her head. "Are you still there?" Her voice was muffled by flannel.

"I'm right here."

Maddie poked her head through the neck and pushed her arms through the sleeves of her nightgown.

"See?" Ann said. "Here I am."

The candlelight cast Maddie's face in shadow, played over the smooth curves of her cheeks, made her eyes huge and watchful. Ann set down the candle and helped her daughter into her flannel bathrobe. "You look beautiful," she said, tying the sash securely. "Just like a princess." She held out her arm. "Are you ready, Your Majesty?"

Maddie giggled, a sound that lifted Ann's heart.

She clutched Ann's elbow as they went down the stairs. When they rounded the landing, Ann saw flames leaping in the hearth. It looked so warm and inviting. "See?" she said to Maddie. "Just like camping. Only without the bears."

"Can I sleep with you tonight?" Maddie asked.

Ann glanced at Peter. It'd be a tight fit for him to share the mattress with Kate. He nodded. Maddie had been so subdued all evening.

They arranged themselves on the air mattresses, the girls in the middle, Ann and Peter on either side. Shazia curled up on the couch. The candle flickered on the table in the corner. Ann would have to wait for Maddie to be ready before she could blow it out.

"I'm f-freezing," Kate said. "How long before the power comes back on?"

Peter said, "I'm sure they're working on it right now."

"So, tomorrow?"

"I hope so." Ann reached over and tugged the blanket to Kate's chin. "The homesteaders were just fine without electricity."

"We're not homesteaders," Kate said, flipping over on her back and out of Ann's reach.

"Who are they?" Maddie said.

"The people who settled the American West," Ann said.

"Oh. People from long ago."

"That's right."

The fire crackled. Kate glared at the ceiling. Maddie was pressed up against Ann. Ann slid an arm around her and leaned in to kiss her daughter's cheek, so soft and full. She'd get Maddie her own paint set. Maddie turned nine in March, only three months away. It could be her birthday present. By then, everything would surely be back to normal.

"So, Maddie," Peter said. "Tell me something."

Maddie lifted her head.

"Would you rather ride a magic carpet or shake hands with a leprechaun?"

Ann smiled and waited for her daughter's reply.

"Could a magic carpet take me anywhere?" Maddie asked.

"Sure," Peter said.

"Like to Disney World or Toys 'R' Us?"

"You bet."

"I guess I'd shake hands with a leprechaun. Then I could ask him where the end of the rainbow is."

That was pure Maddie, taking an opportunity and cracking it wide open. Ann squeezed her close.

Maddie said, "Kate?"

Kate's voice was muffled by her pillow. "What?"

"Would you rather have to read the dictionary or go to school in your underwear?"

"They both suck. This is a stupid game."

"Come on, Kate," Maddie said. "Play."

"It's all right." Ann leaned over Maddie and rubbed Kate's back. "She doesn't have to."

Kate shrugged off Ann's hand and rolled away.

"Well, I want to," Maddie said. "Daddy?"

"Yes-s?" Peter growled out the word.

Maddie giggled. "Would you rather eat a cup of sugar or have an extra toe?"

"Hmm. A toughie. I'm going to have to go with the toe. How about you, Maddie? Would you rather be ten inches tall or . . . ten feet tall?"

"Um. Ten feet."

"Ten feet's ridiculous," Kate said. "Your head would bump the ceiling."

"I thought you weren't playing," Maddie said. "Shazia? Would you rather have to walk around the world backwards or swim through every ocean?"

"Oh. Well, I like swimming. Can I say that?"

"There aren't any rules. You can say whatever."

"Okay."

"You take a turn. You ask someone. Ask Mommy something."

"I can't think of anything."

Orange embers glowed. A soft chunk from the fireplace as a log collapsed, a shower of bright sparks. Ann rose up on an elbow and blew out the candle. The warm smell of burned wick spiraled into the air.

"I've got one," Kate said. "Would you rather live forever or save someone else's life?"

"Who are you asking?" Maddie said.

"Mom."

Ann sank back against her pillow. Where was Kate going with this? "That's a hard one. I'd have to think about it." But she couldn't think about it. She wouldn't.

"Wouldn't that depend on whose life it was?" Shazia said.

"Maybe not," Peter said.

Ann felt him looking at her across the bodies of their children. What did he want from her? Did he think she would believe him now, after all these years?

"Anybody," Kate said. "It doesn't matter. Hitler."

"Santa Claus," Maddie said. "Would you save Santa Claus?"

"How about a homeless drunk?" Kate said. "Mom?"

Maddie yawned. "I bet the power will come back on tomorrow."

"Dream on," Kate said, but her voice had no heat to it. She'd grown sleepy.

Ann lay there, staring unseeing at the ceiling. After a while, Shazia sighed and Ann knew she'd fallen asleep, too. The fire died down, shrouding the room in darkness.

He wouldn't want to be called William. He'd go by Will. He'd crouch beside Peter, watching his father's every move as he built the fire. By the next day, he'd have mastered fire building. *I got it*, he'd say. He'd lug in the log and heave it onto the fireplace, wipe his palms on his pants. *Better stand back, Mom. I've got to close the grate.*

"Ann," Peter said.

She knew what he was thinking. It was all she ever thought about. Rolling over, she stared into darkness. She'd had her chance to save someone's life. And they both knew how that had turned out.

"The pileup on I-71 is estimated to have resulted in thirteen deaths so far. Rescuers are still working to reach travelers who have been trapped in their cars since Friday. The highway remains closed. Police are cautioning people to find alternate routes.

"Over six hundred thousand households remain without power. Crews have been called in from neighboring jurisdictions to assist in restoring power. A power company spokesman cautioned that difficulties in obtaining parts from overseas could result in an additional delay. Citizens are asked to call 911 to report any downed wires.

"We are in a Level Three Snow Emergency. All cars must be removed from primary and secondary routes. Vehicles will be towed at the owners' expense.

"The quarantine remains in effect. Public gatherings for any reason are discouraged. People experiencing flu symptoms, or those who suspect they may have been exposed, are advised to stay home."

*WTVN News Radio*

# SEVENTEEN

P ETER SNAPPED OFF THE RADIO, CLIMBED OUT OF THE truck, and slammed the door. The sound echoed around the garage.

Three days without electricity, seventy-two hours without so much as a brief flicker to suggest anyone was working on it. The only vehicle going up and down the street had been Singh's powerful SUV, and even that had gotten stuck the first time out. Peter had helped push the vehicle onto the main road. Wherever the plows were, they hadn't ventured out here to the suburbs. Singh told him that he hadn't seen an open grocery store in over a week. "I don't think they're getting deliveries. This snow only made things worse."

"What about the hospital? Are you getting supplies?"

"Yes, but it's sporadic. Better keep that to yourself, though. We don't want a riot on our hands." Singh shook his head and climbed into the driver's seat. "I'll let you know if I see anything open. I'll put a note in your mailbox."

But so far, their mailbox had remained empty.

Going in through the back door, Peter bent down and untied his boots. It felt as cold in here as it was out in the garage. He could see his breath.

Ann stood in the family room, her hand on the phone. She was staring out the window. Upstairs, he could hear raised voices—Kate and Maddie, bickering again. A door slammed. He winced, but Ann was motionless, her gaze distant. "You okay?"

"Dad's treatment is being postponed."

"I'm sorry."

"What can you do? Everything's on hold." She turned and looked at him, her face taut with worry. A length of hair had escaped her clip and curved along her cheek. There was nothing he could say to reassure her, nothing that she wouldn't see through to the false hope it held. "Any news?"

"They've raised the number of fatalities to thirteen. They still haven't gotten everyone out."

"Those poor people."

"They're telling people to stay home if they're sick."

"But what if you develop pneumonia? You'd have to see a doctor."

She watched him, waited for him to confirm this. Wanted him to. It was an unbearable notion, thinking that medical assistance wouldn't be available if you needed it. The announcer hadn't mentioned any exceptions, but of course people would still flock to their doctors' offices. A radio announcement wouldn't keep them from lining up outside the hospitals. It was human nature. If one of his girls got sick, he'd be the first to pound on the emergency room door.

"Of course," he said, knowing better. Those resources were rapidly being depleted. Soon doctors would be unable to get medical supplies, most of which were imported from China. That country had been virtually shut down. Antibiotics, too, were in finite supply. "I'm going to drive around the neighborhood. Maybe I can learn something."

She frowned. "It's not safe. The roads aren't even plowed."

"The sun's been working on them. Singh's been able to get in and out."

"What about the gas?"

"I won't go far."

"All right. Just . . . be careful."

He backed his pickup out of the driveway and bumped into the grooves Singh's SUV had carved. They carried him down to the main road. There, a pair of parallel ruts ran down the middle, snow packed high on either side.

A cement-colored sky hung above, showing no sign of sun or cloud, nothing to indicate whether or not more snow was on its way. Everything was draped in snow dirtied by the passage of time. Nothing moved but smoke trickling from chimneys. No hawks wheeled overhead. No little fat chickadees hopped from branch to branch. The virus had gotten to them. There was no other explanation. He gripped the steering wheel and stared hard at the road before him.

The tracks swerved around a fallen tree, swung back, vanished beneath blowing snow. He slowed to a crawl and they reemerged.

Glancing down side streets, he saw people out working the snowbanks with shovels. They paused to watch him drive by. He lifted his hand in greeting, got some nods and waves in return. Kids sledded down a far embankment. The day before, he'd persuaded the girls to go sledding. Shazia had ended up staying home, so it had been just him and his girls. It had been fun at first, Kate and Maddie laughing and rosy-cheeked, traipsing alongside him through the deep snow. But when they arrived at the park and saw the masked children and the parents standing guard at the top of the hill, his daughters' moods turned somber. They'd refused to go anywhere since.

He was getting warm, thawing out for the first time in days. Pulling off his hat and gloves, he rolled down the window. It might have been a good idea to bring the girls along and let them warm up, too, but he knew Ann would never have permitted it.

A gold sedan appeared in the distance heading toward him. Peter slowed, wondering how they were both going to manage to stay on the road. One of them would have to leave the safety of the ruts. Peter, probably, since he was in the bigger vehicle. But then the car turned onto an adjacent street. It was gone by the time Peter reached the intersection.

He heard a droning noise. He lifted his foot from the accelerator and listened. The sound grew louder and took shape, attenuated into the wasplike whine of a power tool. A few blocks away, he found its source—two men standing beside a red minivan, knee-deep in the snow. One held a power saw, working it through a fat tree limb. The other man grabbed hold of the drooping branch and tugged. Snow sifted down. The second fellow caught sight of Peter's truck and elbowed his buddy, who turned and stared. The power saw muttered into silence.

Peter leaned his arm out the window. "Hey."

"Hey."

Both men wore caps and quilted jackets, heavy boots, and gloves. Peter flashed back to the father and son up at Sparrow Lake all those weeks ago. These two bore a similar guarded watchfulness, but for a different reason. They were illegally chopping down street trees. "Cold day," Peter said.

In other words, *I'm not here to bust you.*

The men exchanged a glance.

"Least it stopped snowing," the shorter one said. "You look familiar. You got a kid who plays soccer?"

Peter nodded. "My eight-year-old."

"Yeah, okay. I guess I've seen you at games."

"Know whether any stores are open?"

"I heard there was one out in Galway," the shorter fellow said.

Galway was thirty minutes away. Was it worth the gas to check and see? They weren't that low on food yet.

"Don't even bother going out to Lancaster," the guy continued. "Farmers there are chasing people away with guns."

Peter frowned. "Hear anything about when the power might come back on?"

"Matter of fact, a guy from the power company just went by. Said they've got parts of downtown up and running."

His apartment was downtown. If the power was on there, he could load everyone up, toss in some sleeping bags and some food. It'd be cramped quarters, but at least it'd be warm. They'd have running water and the use of a bathroom. And the Internet. "You know which areas?"

"Nah." The taller man picked up the branch, dragged it over to the minivan, and pushed it through the yawning trunk door. "Dude was in a hurry to get going."

"What about the university? Did he say anything about the power being on there?" They could camp out in his office. He could move his desk into the hall to make room. There was a kitchen, with a refrigerator, microwave, and coffeemaker. That'd be the better bet.

A shrug. "You could ask him yourself. He's working that substation down on Summit."

"South of Brant?"

"That's the one."

As Peter put the truck in gear, the shorter fellow took a step toward him. "Mind me passing on a piece of advice?" He nodded at Peter's truck. "Better keep an eye on your vehicle. People have been going around puncturing gas tanks on big trucks like yours and siphoning off the gas."

A few miles down the darkening road, Peter spied the fenced enclosure, the tall metal structures inside pointing skyward. A white van sat tilted off the road by the gate. Peter could see a man on the other side, shoveling. He rolled his truck to a stop and got out. The fellow looked over his shoulder, then turned and stopped, shovel clenched between both hands. "Don't come any closer, sir."

"Got it." Peter stopped a good ten feet away.

The man wore a hard hat and an orange safety vest over a bulky gray jumpsuit. "You need something?"

"I hear you got the power on downtown."

"That's right. Where the hospital is."

There was a bit of good news. Peter's office was just a few blocks away. No doubt it was on the same power grid. "I'm surprised you haven't gotten the whole city back up yet."

"This one's been a real bitch. The storm took down a transmission tower and tripped failures all along the line." He leaned the shovel against the fence. "Fire broke out. We lost a couple guys."

"I'm sorry to hear that."

"Spooked my line crew. Half of them didn't show this morning. Couple called in sick, but you ask me, it wasn't H5N1 that got them. They got family and they're afraid to leave them. My foreman's worried about his cat. Who'll feed it if he gets stuck on the job?" The man laughed sourly. "Times like these, you can't pay people enough.

We tried to call in crews from other locations, but the storm hit them pretty hard, too."

The radio announcer had been wrong then. No help was coming.

There was a crackle of static. The man fumbled for the radio clipped to his shoulder. "Go." He bent his head, listening. "You sure about that?"

This substation fed his house. Maybe he could wait out the evening and see if the power came back on there. Otherwise, first thing in the morning, he'd load everyone up and head out. It was getting too late now. Ann would balk at driving after dark.

The man hooked the radio back into place. "Mind moving your truck?"

"Sure." Peter stepped back from the fence. "You're done here, then?"

The man crunched over and retrieved his shovel. "Haven't even started. The tower went down again."

"So, the power's back off downtown?"

"Looks like it." He stood by the gate, shovel in hand, and waited. He wasn't going to move until Peter was far enough away. Peter backed up and the man worked the lock on the gate. "I'm not looking forward to trying to get back into the city."

"I hear I-71's closed."

The man looked up. "You been down there?"

"No. Is it bad?"

The man shook his head. "Worst thing I ever seen, all those burned-out cars jammed end to end." He slammed the gate shut. "There was nowhere for anyone to go. They just sat there and let the fire take them."

THE SLEDDERS WERE GONE. ALL THAT REMAINED OF THE TWO men stealing firewood was a scattering of fir tips staining the snow where they'd been working. Headlights blinked in the distance, then vanished. The sky above was turning black. Peter headed west, drawing the night with him.

By the time he pulled onto his street, it was full dark. His headlights threw up slanted cuts of snow and shadowed the gray slush hardened now into ridges. Windows flickered with candlelight. The brick house with the columns stood somber and unlighted. Was it better wherever that family had fled to? The small house beside it stood dark as well. Peter eyed it as he drove around the corner.

Light burst from a window onto the snow-packed bushes below, illuminating the wooden windowsill, a section of brick wall, and the spiky holly bushes beneath. Then just as suddenly, the light winked out.

Peter braked. There was no mistaking what he'd seen. He hesitated, then bumped the truck up onto the sidewalk. Anybody trying to get under his fuel tank would have to tunnel through the snow first.

He worked his way through the unshoveled snow and pounded on the door.

A dog barked from inside.

"Finn? It's Peter Brooks. Your neighbor from down the street."

"I know who it is," said a voice behind him.

Peter wheeled around. A figure stood by the back gate. There wasn't enough starlight to discern the man's features, but he'd recognized the brusque voice. Walter Finn.

"What do you want?" the man asked.

"I saw your light. You have a generator, don't you?"

"None of your business."

"All I want is some information."

A curt laugh. "Here's some information for you, free of charge. Hell's freezing over."

"What about the vaccine they're working on? You hear anything about that?"

"Come on, Brooks. You don't really think there's a vaccine, do you? They're just shining us on, big G's way of keeping the little people from complaining and asking too many questions."

*Big G* must mean the government. "I know the guy leading up the effort. I've worked with him. It's not a lie. There really is a vaccine in the works."

"I wouldn't have taken you for such a fool."

"I can prove it."

A pause. "How?"

"Let me online. I can show you."

A beat, then Finn said, "Get your mask first."

He meant a respiratory mask, and he was right. Peter should be wearing one. "Hold on. I've got one in my truck."

A minute later, the front door creaked open as Peter worked his way back up the walk toward the house. A flashlight suddenly switched on. In the long beam of light, Peter saw heavy boots and work pants, four brown paws. He glimpsed the heavy black respirator strapped to Finn's face. The light moved up and flared in Peter's eyes.

He blinked and threw up his forearm. The light dropped away. The dog tried to push past, but Finn shoved him back with his knee. The door banged open. The dog panted happily up at him.

"This way." Finn led him downstairs, shutting the door after them and switching on the light. In the sudden brightness, Peter saw concrete-block walls, small windows covered with black plastic, and a naked lightbulb screwed into the middle of the low ceiling. He rounded the steps and saw Finn's work space. The man had everything.

On the large wooden table tucked into the corner sat a desktop computer, a short-wave radio, and a small television set. A portable heater glowed beneath, and a table fan whirred on top of the small bookcase. A sleeping bag had been unfolded across a narrow cot. Finn was living down here. It was definitely warmer. Barney trotted over to the folding chair and sat on the floor, looking expectant.

"Go on." Finn's voice was muffled behind the mask. "Show me about the vaccine."

Peter tugged his gloves off and pushed them into his jacket pocket. He flexed his fingers. It felt good tapping the keyboard, seeing the screens pop up one by one. "Do you mind if I look around a little?"

"Two minutes."

Barney nudged his cold nose into the palm of his hand. Absently, Peter rubbed the dog's head, tugged an ear. He scrolled down the WHO website. The hourly bulletins had slowed, coming now every day or so. The last update had been over twelve hours ago. He scanned the headlines. They were still in Phase Five. Good to know they hadn't reached Six, the final, irreversible phase. Vaccine trials were ongoing, but preliminary results showed that two innoculations might prove necessary. Peter wasn't sure how to interpret that. He wished he could talk to Liederman directly.

He moved on to the CNN website and halted at a photograph of uniformed soldiers rolling bodies into a huge pit. Men, women, children, they were all jumbled together. A jolting sight, one that instantly reminded him of all those poor dead birds heaped along the shore. Mourners stood on the bank, their faces covered with shawls. He glanced at the caption. Cairo. Shazia's hometown. *My whole family lives there,* she'd said.

Finn nudged him and made a circular motion with his hand. *Wind it up.*

Peter let out a breath, moved to the university website, and followed a few links. Liederman's bearded face grinned out at him. "See? The man works for a private company." Peter accessed his email system and found the last message Liederman had written to him. "Check the date. It's not a long message. He was too busy for that, but in it he refers to how far he's gotten on testing the vaccine."

Finn leaned nearer to read. Then he straightened and jerked a thumb upward. Visiting hours were over.

Reluctantly, Peter stood. He had no idea whether he'd been persuasive. He'd have to finagle another visit somehow.

Barney pushed alongside as he walked up the stairs. A slight tug at his pocket made Peter look down to see that the dog had one of his gloves in his mouth.

"Hey." Peter took a few steps after him and stopped suddenly. He was in Finn's kitchen. Cabinet doors stood open. The counters were heaped with cans, boxes, bags of food.

Peter stared. The man even had those military rations, the smooth white packs clearly labeled in black. Meat loaf. Chicken cacciatore. "Hey, how'd you get those?" He turned.

Finn stood there, a long black rifle pointed straight at Peter's face.

# EIGHTEEN

---

*L*IKE THIS, MOMMY?" MADDIE LOWERED HER CHIN TO the floor, her bottom sticking up to the ceiling.

Her daughter looked like an inverted V. "Perfect," Ann said, suppressing a smile. "Ready, Kate?"

"Ready. But I'm only doing ten."

"I'm doing twelve," Maddie said.

"Suck-up," Kate said.

"One, two, three, go." The girls levered themselves up and down, collapsed to the floor. They both needed their hair trimmed. Maddie might oblige, but would Kate? "Time for sit-ups." Peter had been gone over an hour. He'd be back any minute now. She'd hated to see him leave the safety of their home, but it would be good to know what was going on. "Remember how I showed you?"

"This is so *boring*." Kate flopped onto her back and stared at the ceiling.

"Come on, sweetheart. Do some sit-ups with me. You'll feel better if you get moving a little."

"Right."

"Maybe we could clear the driveway and you could work on that backhand of yours."

Kate turned her head and looked at Ann with narrowed eyes. "I told you. I hate tennis. I am never playing tennis again."

The season was over anyway. "How about playing a board game? How about Clue?"

"Maddie cheats."

"I do not," Maddie said.

"Ugh." Kate pounded the carpet with her fists. "I am so *bored.*"

"You said that already," Maddie said. "And I do. Not. Cheat."

"Why don't I see if Shazia will play with us?" Ann asked.

"I guess." Kate rolled back to stare at the ceiling. "She can help make sure Maddie doesn't cheat."

"Mommy!"

Ann fled.

The guest room door was closed. All was quiet beyond. Ann hesitated. She rapped on the wood.

"Yes?"

The chilly room was bright with sunshine. Shazia lay on the bed. She pushed herself up drowsily from her pillow.

"I'm sorry." Ann halted halfway into the room. "I didn't realize you were napping."

"That's all right." Shazia yawned and swung her feet to the floor. "Do you need my help with something?"

"The girls and I are wondering if you'd play a board game with us."

"Oh. Okay." She slid her feet into the flannel bedroom slippers unearthed from the donation pile, a pair that had been Peter's. Lifting her hands, she swept back her gleaming dark hair and tugged the rubber band from around her wrist to form a ponytail.

The girl was truly exotic-looking, with her smooth skin and almond sloped eyes, her heavy hair and the languid way she slid her gaze to a person and let it rest there. Did she have any idea of the effect she had on people? Ann thought not. She seemed almost careless of her good looks, the way only the truly beautiful can be.

Ann looked around the room, at the suitcase beneath the desk, the other one against the wall. That was all Shazia had brought with her. Two suitcases. A framed photograph sat on the desk. A chubby boy with black curls grinned out at her.

Ann smiled. "Who's this cute little guy?"

"My nephew. He just turned two." Shazia leaned over and picked up another framed picture from the nightstand beside her. She held it out for Ann to see. "These are my parents."

Ann came over and saw a man and a woman in elegant clothes leaning toward each other, their clasped hands folded on the linen-covered table before them. "They're a good-looking couple."

"Thank you." Shazia rubbed a thumb across the carved wood of the frame. "This was taken on my father's sixtieth birthday. My sister sent it to me."

Twelve days. Ann had never gone that long without talking to her mother and father. Maybe Shazia had a different relationship with her family. Perhaps it was normal for them to go for extended periods of time without speaking, but things weren't normal now. This protracted silence could mean only one thing. "Have you talked to your roommate?"

"Yes. The dorm lost power, too. She has to walk all the way down to the lobby if she wants to use the telephone. She's on the fourteenth floor, so I don't expect to hear from her again for a while." She shrugged. "She sounded okay, though. Her floor does a different theme every night. Last night was Hawaii. Tonight's Dungeons and Dragons."

Put a bunch of twentysomethings together and that's what you'd get, Ann thought, luaus and swordplay. Put a bunch of fortysomethings together and you'd get recipes and strategies for organizing your clutter.

"She says the only lights are in the hallways. She has to leave her door open if she wants to see inside her room."

How grim that sounded. "Did she say whether anyone has gotten sick?"

"The first two floors are reserved for H5N1 patients."

*You'd stay in your room, then. You wouldn't dare go past those doors on your way to the phone. You'd keep your door closed and accept the dark.*

Shazia leaned over and set the frame back down on the nightstand. As she did so, Ann caught a glimpse of a navy leather photo album lying open there. It looked like one of hers. What was it doing here? It belonged in the family room.

Shazia saw her looking and blushed. "I'm sorry. I hope you don't mind. I didn't have anything to read."

"Not at all." Ann tilted her head, curious as to which album had captured the girl's interest. She saw photographs of pine trees, a weathered building, scruffy-bearded men grinning at the camera.

Shazia picked up the album and held it in her lap. "It's the lodge at Sparrow Lake, isn't it?"

"One of Peter's favorite spots." And there he crouched, grinning, his forearm resting on his bent knee. Three other men stood ringed around him, wearing camouflage and ball caps.

"He took me there my first week to introduce me around. He was worried the old men wouldn't work with me if he sent me up there to test alone."

"Peter told me they could be a rough group."

Shazia turned a page. "Once they realized they couldn't shock me, it was fine."

Peter came home from those trips reeking of fresh blood and cigarette smoke. Ann made him change in the garage before she let him in the house. Once she asked to accompany him, when the sky had sparkled blue and the trees shimmered gold and ruby, but he'd shaken his head. *You'd hate it,* he'd told her.

But he'd taken Shazia.

Ann studied the photographs. They'd been taken a few years ago. Peter's hair was longer, his face less careworn. Ann had been the one to develop the film and slot the pictures into the album sleeves. No doubt she'd glanced at the images but had never stopped to question Peter about these friends of his. "I don't know those people."

Shazia tapped a short, clean-shaven man. "Victor works in Peter's lab. So does Sam." She moved her finger to a slight fellow standing apart from the rest. "Harold works with Dr. Lewis. I can't imagine how Peter persuaded him to go. Harold hates doing fieldwork. He's always asking to stay back and monitor the experiments. But Peter says you have to get out and meet the animals you're trying to save."

Ann had always teased him that it was a good thing he didn't study lions and tigers.

"I'd never been in the woods before," Shazia said. "Watching the sun set over the lake . . . It was amazing."

Peter loved sunsets. During their courtship, he'd often show up at her door with a bottle of wine and some cheese and bread, and suggest they go find a view. "Sounds like you had fun. I guess the hunters weren't too hard on you."

Shazia ran a hand down the page and smiled. "They were wonderful."

Ann stared at her. How had she missed the signs? The flush on Shazia's cheeks, the longing in her voice, the way she was looking at Peter's photograph. This was no schoolgirl crush. The girl was in love. She felt hot and cold at the same time. Beth had been wrong: this wasn't just something Peter had to get out of his system. He and Shazia shared something deeper. Why was she so surprised? The casual way Shazia and Peter were around each other had fooled her. Well, now she knew. Now she could prepare herself.

Ann straightened. "You can have those pictures if you want."

Shazia sat back, her eyes wide. "Oh, no. I couldn't possibly take them."

"I'm sure Peter won't mind."

Shazia was looking at her. Understanding moved across her face. She looked uncertain. "All right, Ann. Thank you."

Something thudded against the wall below. Ann felt the vibration beneath her feet and automatically looked down. There was another shuddering sound of impact, and this time she placed it. "Someone's banging on the garage door."

Oh my God. The girls were alone downstairs.

Ann whirled around and raced to the stairs, taking the steps down two at a time. "Kate, Maddie! Where are you?"

"Here."

She reached the landing and looked down. Maddie stood by the front door, zipping up her coat, Kate beside her, jamming her feet into boots.

"Where do you think you're going?" Ann said, running down the rest of the stairs.

"Outside," Kate said, eyes bright. "This is war."

Ann pushed past her daughters to look out the window beside the door. Brightly garbed figures flitted around the yard across the street. She heard shouts and far-off laughter.

Shazia said, "It's children, throwing snowballs."

"You can't go," Ann told her daughters, watching through the glass as the children crisscrossed one another, ducking and throwing. Where were their parents? What were they thinking? Just because the children were outside—did they think that made them safe? Hadn't any of them heard? Jodi had *died*. She'd run around the neighborhood just like these children and raced directly into the flu's path. She was only eight years old.

Maddie yanked a hat down over her ears. "Daddy says if we stay three feet away from people, we'll be okay."

Ann turned and looked down at Maddie. "This is different. You are *not* going out there."

Kate tied a scarf around her neck and reached for her gloves. "Right. Like we're going to get cooties from snowballs."

"You don't know that. I'm sorry, girls, but you have to stay inside."

Maddie stared up at her. "Everyone else is outside!"

"I know, but that doesn't make it right."

Maddie's eyes shone with tears. She stamped her foot. "I hate you." She unwound her scarf and tossed it to the floor. Shazia quickly bent to retrieve it.

Kate looked out the window. She shrugged. "It doesn't matter anyway. They're gone."

Ann hated the hopelessness in her daughter's voice. "How about . . . ?" she began, but Kate just looked at her, her eyes bottle green and just as hard.

"What about that game your mom was telling me about?" Shazia said. "The one you wanted me to play?"

Maddie crossed her arms and stared at the floor. In a grudging voice she said, "Clue."

"Oh, yes. I've heard about it. But I've never played."

"It's easy."

"Anything's easy when you cheat." Kate tugged off her gloves, finger by pissed-off finger.

Maddie whirled around, ready for combat, but Shazia extended her hand. "Will you show me?"

Maddie hesitated, then, shooting Kate one more hostile look, allowed herself to be led away.

Ann said gently, "I'm so sorry, Kate. I wish—"

But Kate lifted her head. "That's a car."

The passage of a car was a rarity these days. Now Ann heard it, too. She came up close to the glass but saw nothing. There'd been teenaged boys among those snowballers. Maybe they'd decided to stop and hotwire someone's car. A frightening thought. Would they try her garage next? "Stay here," she told Kate. How could she possibly stop them? Of all times for Peter to be gone. "I'm going to take a quick look."

She stepped out. The rumble of a car engine came more clearly. The street spread out before her, white and gray and black. The houses all stared back with blank windows. But someone was there, someone just out of sight. She turned her head and peered in the direction of Libby's house. Now the cold seeped through her clothes, pressed icy fingers against her skin. Shivering, she wrapped her arms around herself and tucked her hands into her sleeves. She walked out to the edge of the porch, and now she saw the black SUV backing down the driveway.

"It's Libby." Kate had come out, too, and stood beside Ann, leaning into her for warmth. "Where's she going?"

"I don't know." Ann put her arm around her daughter. "I talked to her last night. She didn't say anything." If she was headed out to try the stores, she would have phoned Ann first to see if she needed anything. And she'd have sent Smith.

They watched the ordinary progression of vehicle heading to road. Then someone appeared around the corner of the house, a man laboring through the snow. Smith.

"Libby!" he yelled.

"What's the matter?" Ann called.

Smith ignored her.

Ann glanced over at Libby to see what she was making of this. Libby stared through the windshield at her husband, her face set with determination.

"He's not wearing any shoes," Kate said.

It was true. As Smith lifted each knee, Ann could see a naked foot. His coat flapped open, and he was bareheaded. Were those pajamas he was wearing?

Libby revved the engine. The SUV fishtailed at the bottom of the driveway, plowed into a snowbank, and hung there.

Smith had reached the car. He stood there in knee-deep drifts and pounded on the driver's window with his fists. "Libby! Don't be stupid. Come inside!"

Kate slid a cold hand into Ann's.

Libby flung open the door into her husband. He lost his footing and skidded sideways, his legs sliding beneath the car chassis. Ann held her breath. He lay directly beneath the car. The engine was still running.

Kate squeezed her hand. "Mom. Do something."

She should call the police. But the phone was all the way in the family room. Did she dare leave them alone? "Libby!"

Libby made no sign that she'd heard Ann. She kicked at Smith.

Ann gasped. "Libby! What is the matter? Libby, stop!"

A door across the street opened. Mrs. Nguyen poked her head out for a moment and surveyed the scene. She glanced over at Ann, shook her head, and closed the door.

Smith rolled to his feet, hand to his forehead, and backed away from his wife. "Jesus, Libby."

"Just get away from me." Libby climbed back into the driver's seat.

Smith caught the door. "Calm down, will you? You're overreacting."

Tires churned. Exhaust swarmed blackly into the air.

"Mom, call the police," Kate pleaded.

"I don't know if they'd come."

Smith wedged himself behind the SUV's door and reached back to fumble with the lock.

Libby smacked at his face, his shoulder and arm. "Get away, I said!"

Smith pulled himself along the side of the SUV to the back door and grabbed hold of the door handle there. It swung open. Now he was crawling inside.

Libby almost fell out of the vehicle. She grabbed the opened door and banged it against her husband's legs.

"Libby!" Ann took an involuntary step toward them. "Smith!"

Smith backed out, clutching a car seat. A baby's cries sailed out, thin and high-pitched. The blanket slid, revealing Jacob, his mouth in an open howl, his cheeks red and eyes squeezed shut.

"He's hurting him, Mom."

"It's okay, Kate. Jacob's fine. He's just upset."

Libby grasped the handle of the car seat. "Don't you *dare.*"

"You're acting crazy." Smith swung away from her, still holding on to the baby.

Libby pounded his chest with her fists. She flailed at his shoulders. He elbowed her aside and tramped back to the house, lugging the car seat with him. Libby stood staring after him, her chest heaving; she looked wildly all around. Her gaze halted at Ann and Kate standing there on the porch.

Ann yearned to go over and put her arms around her friend. "Libby, are you all right?"

"Go away." Libby slid into the driver's seat. After a moment, the engine silenced. She leaned forward and rested her forehead on her crossed arms.

"Mom?" Kate's voice trembled.

Ann drew her daughter to her. "It's all right, honey." Maybe this sort of thing happened all the time between the two of them. What did anyone know of someone else's marriage? She wouldn't have expected Libby and Smith to brawl like this, but then she wouldn't have expected Peter to walk out on her.

Libby had abandoned the SUV. She was trudging up the driveway toward her house. After a moment, she disappeared from view. Ann heard the garage door rattle down, and then all was quiet.

"I thought Libby and Smith loved each other."

"They do. Of course they do." Kate sounded so disconsolate. Ann squeezed her daughter close. "But you know, honey, marriage is complicated."

An inadequate comment, and Ann felt the weight of it.

Kate threw off Ann's arm. "So why do people even bother to get married in the first place?"

She wheeled around and swung open the front door. The soft click of the latch as the door closed quietly behind her was as loud to Ann's ears as if her daughter had slammed it.

ANN WAITED UNTIL IT WAS ALMOST TOO DARK TO SEE BEFORE lighting the candles. Shazia fed the fire and they all ate dinner at the kitchen table, accompanied by tiny orange points of flame. Libby hadn't answered the phone. All was silent from the house next door.

"Why is Daddy taking so long?" Maddie tapped her fork against her plate.

Ann reached out a hand to quiet her. "He'll be back soon." Even she heard the lack of conviction in her voice. Peter had been gone all afternoon. What should have taken minutes was consuming hours. Maybe he'd stopped to help someone. Maybe he'd had engine trouble. Or gotten stuck in a snowdrift. The possibilities were endless. There was no use worrying through them. Still, she found herself listening hard for the sound of Peter's truck. "So, what else did Hannah say?"

"She hurt her ankle playing kickball."

"Ouch. What was she doing playing kickball?"

"Well, it wasn't really kickball. It was more like snowball. Get it? *Snow*ball."

Ann smiled, happy to see that afternoon's recrimination gone from her child's face.

"Hilarious," Kate said flatly. "If the power comes back on, can I dye my hair, Mom?"

*If*, she'd said, Ann noted sadly. Not *when*.

"What color?" Maddie was fascinated.

"The power *is* coming back on," Ann said, "and why would you dye your hair?"

"Michele's having Claire and Hilary over tonight to do make-overs. She asked me, too, but I knew you wouldn't let me." Kate stabbed a piece of food with her fork.

That couldn't be true. Kate had to have misunderstood. "Are you sure about that?"

"Uh-huh." Kate pushed the food around on her plate. "Everyone *else's* parents said it would be okay."

Meaning Ann was the only mean one. "I'm sorry, Kate, but it's too risky. We all need to sit tight for just a while longer."

"That's what you always say. I don't want to sit tight. Sitting tight is *boring*."

"Oh, Kate. A little boredom never hurt anyone." Ann was bored, too. Bored of washing clothes by hand, of cooking in a fireplace that had never been intended to be anything but ornamental, of worrying about having enough food and how her parents were doing.

"So, I can't go?" Kate dropped her fork and crossed her arms.

"Of course not."

"Mom, come *on*. Michele says since no one's sick, it's okay."

"That's my point, Kate." How many times would she have to explain this? Perhaps Kate couldn't be expected to grasp the concept, but she had to learn to accept the fact. She couldn't be around other people. Period. "Michele can't know that no one's sick. People can be sick and not know it."

"Yeah, yeah." Kate rolled her eyes.

Ann bit back a sharp response, exasperated. She and Shazia exchanged a glance, then Shazia leaned forward. "Your mother's right, you know. People are the most contagious the day before they show symptoms."

Kate refused to look at her. "You're a grown-up, too," she muttered. "You don't understand."

"Daddy's home!" Maddie cried.

Ann cocked her head, listening. Now she heard it, too, the garage door groaning along its tracks. "You're right," she said, pushing back her chair with relief.

Maddie flew at Peter as he came in through the back door.

"Hey," he said, stumbling a little. "Was I gone that long?"

"You were gone *forever*."

"It seemed like forever to me, too." Peter swung Maddie down, kissing her as he did so. "Hey, Katydid." He leaned over and ruffled her head and she smacked at him, stepping back to smooth it down again.

*Katydid?* He hadn't called her that in years. Ann watched him. Something was wrong. There was something he was holding back, something that he wasn't going to volunteer. "So, did everything go okay?"

"I ran into a guy working on the substation down in Hilliard." Peter bent to untie his boots. Pulling them free, he thumped them against the tiles and stood them up to drip-dry.

"That's great." Hilliard was only a few miles south. "Is the power coming back on?"

"It could be a while longer. They're having trouble getting work-ers. But they did manage to get downtown up and running for a few hours."

Ann smiled at Kate. "You hear that? The power company's work-ing on it. The electricity should be coming back on any minute now."

Kate put her hands on her hips. "That's *downtown*. What about *us*?"

"They'll get to us," Peter said. "But they have to follow a certain order. Everything's linked together. First they have to fix the substa-tions, then they'll get to the individual power lines." He hung his jacket on the hook and dropped his keys onto the counter. "I'm starving."

Ann sat down across from him so she could watch his expres-sion. Maddie climbed onto her lap, and Ann wrapped her arms around her daughter's small, warm body, pressed her cheek to her daughter's hair, a little stiff with residue from last night's shampoo. Maddie had refused to stay still for one more cupful of icy rinse water.

"I saw lights on at Finn's house," Peter said. "So I stopped to pay him a little visit."

"No way. He just invited you in?" Walter Finn was the last per-son Ann would have expected to stop and chat. Just the other day, he'd practically set the sidewalk on fire in his haste to get away from them. *Wait.* Just how close had Peter come to the man? "You wore a mask, didn't you?"

"And gloves," Peter mumbled through a mouthful of pasta.

Shazia looked around the table. "Who's Finn?"

"Our neighbor down the street," Kate said.

"He's mean," Maddie said. "He never gives out candy for Halloween. He *yells* at you if you walk on his grass, even if you didn't mean to."

Peter wiped his mouth with his napkin. "Turns out the guy's some kind of survivalist. You should have seen his place. He's got water, batteries, every kind of food you could possibly imagine."

"Like candy?" Maddie's eyes were round. "Like grape jelly?"

Ann smiled into Maddie's hair.

"Probably," Peter said.

Maddie sighed. "Lucky."

"Peter." Shazia tilted her head. "What did you mean when you said you saw the lights on at this man's house?"

That's true. Peter had said that. Ann looked at him.

Peter paused, his fork halfway to his mouth. "Finn has a generator."

Ann sucked in her breath.

Kate looked at Peter, then at her mother. "So?"

"That means this man has electricity," Shazia said.

"Hold on," Kate said. "He's got TV?"

"TV?" Maddie squealed. "No fair."

"How come we don't have one of those things?"

"They're expensive, for one thing. And they're all sold out, for another."

Shazia said, "Did you go online?"

The Internet. Of course.

"That was the only reason he let me in, so I could prove to him there really is a vaccine in the works." He chewed, swallowed. "This is great, Ann—I could eat a bear. The President's asked Congress to authorize emergency spending toward additional vaccination research. And he's set up a national database to track outbreaks and identify where to channel federal resources."

"Like food drops?" Ann asked.

He held her gaze for a moment. "Possibly."

So he was worried about their food supply, too.

"What about manufacturing the vaccine?" Shazia said. "And with the gas shortages, how are they going to distribute it?"

"He's negotiating with other countries on both those fronts. There was some talk that he'd open the national fuel reserve, but that wasn't confirmed." He lifted his fork to his mouth, then paused. "He's bringing the troops home. He says we need them more here."

"The war's over?" Ann asked. "Mike will be coming home?"

"Uncle Mike?" Maddie clapped her hands. "Yay!"

Peter smiled at her, then turned to Ann. "No one's talking about war. It's all about the pandemic."

There it was. Her heart skipped a beat. He'd actually used the word. *Pandemic.* Things had gotten that terrible.

"So, listen," Peter said to his daughters. "You know that snowstorm we got? They're calling it the storm of the century. It went all the way up the East Coast. Buffalo got over six feet."

Maddie said, "That's a lot, right?"

"That's a whole lot." Ann tightened her arms around her daughter. Maddie leaned back to push her head against Ann's shoulder. She smelled of wood smoke and crayon. "That's almost as tall as Daddy."

Peter turned to Shazia. "You'll never believe what I read on the WHO website. There's an Aboriginal tribe in Australia that's showing immunity."

Shazia blinked. "But that's fantastic! Do you suppose it has something to do with their avian migration patterns?"

Australia had a huge migratory bird population, Ann remembered. Peter had always talked about doing a sabbatical there, and taking her and the girls. Another time, another place, and they could have been there right now, safe in a little bubble where people didn't get sick.

"Aborigines?" Maddie twisted in Ann's arms and looked up at her. "The same ones who do dot painting?"

Ann smiled down at her. "Maybe."

"So, wait." Kate looked from Ann to Peter. "You mean there are people who can't get sick?"

"Apparently," Peter said.

"But . . . how?"

"No one knows. WHO's sent a team of biologists to try and figure it out."

"Dr. Antony's in Stockholm." Shazia pushed back her chair. "He might be on the team. It would be good to talk to him. Would Mr. Finn let us get online?"

He shook his head. "We'd have better luck phoning."

Shazia glanced at her watch, then stood. "The long-distance charges—"

Ann waved a hand. "Don't worry about that." At this point, she'd be thrilled to get a phone bill with a whopping charge on it, anything to signal someone was out there, someone was keeping track.

Maddie slid from her lap. "Are you done eating, Daddy? Can you read to me now?"

"Sure," Peter said.

"You're eight," Kate said. "You're old enough to read to yourself."

"You're thirteen," Maddie retorted. "Old enough to butt out."

So it was official now. They were in a pandemic. Ann thought of those haunting photographs in the books on the 1918 pandemic, the ones that depicted rows of anonymous white cots spreading out as far as the camera's eye could see, all of them filled with the sick and the dying. Somewhere, maybe even in this city, were rooms filled with sick people. But they wouldn't be enough to contain all the sick from this pandemic. They would have to use warehouses. Air hangars. All the cornfields of Ohio couldn't hold them all.

She watched her children leave the room, the man she'd married pick his plate up from the table and turn to talk to the young woman who'd been orphaned by circumstance. As long as they remained within these walls and as long as they kept others away, there was no way they would end up nameless in a photograph for future generations to page past and wonder.

———

ANN WAS SMOOTHING THE BLANKETS ACROSS THE SLEEPING bags when Peter came into the room. The girls were at the kitchen table with Shazia, playing some sort of game that involved slapping cards and a great deal of argument. "Peter," she said in a low voice, "we need to keep an eye on Kate. I have a feeling she's going to try and sneak out."

"We're crammed in here like sardines." He reached up to press a loose bit of tape holding the plastic against the window. "We'll know if she goes anywhere. Besides, the minute she tries something, Maddie will rat her out."

"I suppose that's true. But still. Help me keep an eye on her."

"Sure." He stabbed the poker into the flames, sending sparks spiraling. "Listen, we have to keep the cars locked in the garage. People are going around stealing gas."

She rocked back on her heels and stared up at him. "In this neighborhood?"

"In *every* neighborhood. Folks are out of work. They're getting desperate."

Her sister had been fired that morning. Beth had gone in to find the doors locked and all the lights off. A piece of paper had been taped to the door. "Has Shazia heard back from Sweden yet?"

"She left a message. Antony'll call when he gets the chance."

"Wouldn't it be easier for her to email him?"

"Of course." He set the poker back in the stand and drew the grate closed. "But Finn, prince that he is, doesn't want anyone to know he's got power. He's terrified the whole neighborhood will be at his door if they find out."

Ann thought of Libby struggling to keep the baby warm, and elderly Mr. Mitchell, who lived across the street and was particularly frail, and felt a spurt of anger. "He can't expect to keep something like that a secret for long."

"I know." Peter brushed the ashes from his hands. "Tell you the truth, I feel sorry for him, holed up like that. He has no one to talk to but his dog."

They were all feeling the strain. "Libby and Smith got into a terrible fight this afternoon."

"Is that why their SUV is backed into the street?"

"It was awful, Peter. I thought Libby was actually going to run him over." She and Peter had never fought like that. They'd retreated into cold silences instead, stamped with their own kind of ugliness. "Kate saw everything."

"It'll be better when the power comes back on."

Bringing with it heat, light, television, the Internet, cell phones—all their old friends. "I called over there, but no one picked up the phone."

"Maybe they're making up."

"Ha, ha." Another thing she didn't know about. She and Peter had never used sex to make up. Nothing could have brought them back together, so they hadn't even tried.

Peter stood watching the threesome at the kitchen table. "I'm going to try the stores again. Even with the power out, they might have rigged up a manual system."

"We need milk and bread. Vegetables would be a godsend." She couldn't even bear to think about fresh fruit. Her mouth practically watered at the possibility of an orange. A banana. "Stores may be posting information. We should ask Finn to check."

"I told you. We can't."

"We can at least ask him to take a look."

He glanced at her and softly said, "Finn pulled a gun on me."

"What!"

"I was on my way out when I looked into his kitchen. Guess he didn't want me seeing his supplies."

She would never have guessed the man would be capable of violence. But wasn't that a lesson she'd learned that very afternoon, watching Smith and Libby? "That's no reason to pull a gun on someone."

"I wasn't going to point that out to him."

"I'm glad you didn't." So, this was what he'd been holding back. "What a horrible, selfish man. What harm would it do him to let you check in every now and then?"

He shrugged, his gaze on the flames. "Well, what goes around comes around."

"Your dad used to say that all the time." His father had had a saw like that for every situation. Trying to hold a conversation with him had been like thumbing through a book of old folk sayings.

Peter refused to meet her gaze. "I better bring in some more firewood."

Apparently, talking about his father was still off-limits.

He strode over to the back door and reached for his coat. Ann turned to the window, to the black night pressed against the glass. She couldn't see past the pane, but somewhere out there was Walter Finn. He probably wasn't the only one with a gun. He probably wasn't the only one going a little crazy. There was a lesson there for all of them. It wasn't just the virus they needed to worry about.

# NINETEEN

---

$P$ETER TURNED THE KNOB AND PUSHED THE BUTTON. A flame sputtered to life. He set the kettle on top of the grate.

It was cold out here, cold enough to show his breath before him in little flags of white that held themselves suspended in the air before dissolving. It was almost as cold inside. His ears and nose tingled. It was difficult to draw a deep breath. He hunched his shoulders and slid his hands into his armpits and stomped his feet. He wore two thick pairs of wool socks and heavy work boots, and yet his feet still ached. Ann had been checking the girls every day for signs of frostbite.

The whine of a car engine made him look up the street into the blue dawn light. Dr. Singh's SUV was stuck again. Gears ground, then the vehicle pulled itself up and out and crunched past. The man lifted a hand and was gone.

The street lay rutted and piled with brown snow crumbly as sugar. Some neighbors had cleared paths. Others still had snow heaped in front of their doors. The sun had helped a little, melting the drifts into soft mounds, which the moon then hardened into crisp crusts.

The birch in the back corner looked strong. It had tripled in size over the past few years, and now it looked as though it owned its patch of yard. A nest clung to a forked branch, a wispy brown cup. He wondered if the birds that had built it would return, if they'd safely completed their trip south.

Smoke puffed from a chimney across the way.

He turned his attention back to the grill. No steam yet emerged from the spout.

A nearby snuffling sound made him glance over to see a dog nosing his way down the sidewalk toward him. Finn's dog. The animal stopped and pawed at the snow. Peter crouched. "Hey, boy," he said. "Hey, Barney."

The dog lifted his head. His eyes were dull. His fur lay matted against his body. Where was Finn? What was he doing letting his dog wander around like this? Peter had never seen the dog without the man and vice versa. Had Finn run out of food and released his dog to fend for himself? No. Only ten days before, the man had had a kitchen full of food. Finn could have decided to move in with someone and been unable to bring the dog with him. Hard to imagine the guy would've left his dog to take his own chances, but maybe he'd felt he had no choice. Maybe the man had gotten sick. Peter thought of him alone in his basement with all his electronic toys, his gun at the ready. How could any of it help him now?

The dog lowered his head, watching.

"C'mere, boy."

He was hungry. And thin, his ribs clearly delineated beneath his filthy coat. Peter patted his jacket pocket and fumbled out the bit of granola bar. It was Maddie's. She hadn't wanted it and had given it to Peter to hold a day or two back. He peeled back the wrapper and extended his hand. It would be good to get the dog close enough for even the most cursory examination. Roaming around out here, the animal was subject to all sorts of hazards—infection, hypothermia, dehydration. Peter held the food steady. "Come on, boy."

The dog slitted his eyes, backed up a step, and growled.

Wary, no more the friendly pet. What could have happened to make him this way?

The kettle on the grill began to hiss.

The dog would come investigate after Peter left, he decided. He dropped the granola bar onto a flattened section of snow and stood. Switching off the flame, he lifted the kettle and heard the *whoosh* of heated water slide against metal.

Ann had the glass carafe ready on the kitchen counter, the paper filter in the holder, the coffee spooned out. He poured until the filter was full of bubbly grounds, then lifted the lid from the teapot Ann had prepared for Shazia and filled that, too. Now the bowls lined up, the instant oatmeal carefully measured.

Ann closed her eyes. "This is what heaven must smell like."

She wore a woolen hat and thick woolen mittens. Her hair waved around her face, out of its usual smooth style. When had she given up wearing lipstick and mascara? Probably weeks ago and he was only just now noticing. He'd always preferred her this way—the soft intelligence in her eyes, the gentle coloring of her mouth. "I thought you said it would smell like new books."

"It does."

They were speaking quietly so as not to waken Shazia and the girls, sleeping in the next room. "And magnolias."

"Peter. There are rooms in heaven that have different smells." She put her hands on her hips. "Duh."

A perfect Kate imitation. He grinned, lifted the kettle, and poured in more water. "That was the last of the propane."

"No more coffee?" She looked stricken.

"We can use the fireplace."

She shook her head. He knew she was thinking about how low their firewood supply was. They'd been conserving it for night, when the cold became unbearable. She gave him a rueful look. "It's all right. The power should be back on soon."

Every day they said the same thing. It had been thirteen days. Peter was beginning to fear the worst—that the power might never return. That everyone at the power company was sick or gone. That they might have to wait until spring to feel warm again.

Ann poured a cup and lifted it to her face, breathing in the aroma. "I'm going to wash clothes today."

"Thank God. I'm down to those boxers my mom gave me."

"The ones with the reindeer?"

"The very same."

She looked at him over the rim of her cup. "But Peter. She'd be so thrilled to see you wearing them."

She was teasing him. This was the Ann he remembered from before. The Ann who'd been lost to him for so many years. How surprising that these strained circumstances would reveal her to him again. He'd missed her. "Well, at least they're not as bad as the necktie she sent me for Easter."

She sucked in a breath. "Tell me."

"It has little bunnies all over it. Cute until you look close and realize what those bunnies are doing."

"Oh, Lord—don't tell me you wore it to work!"

"I was in a hurry. I just pulled it on."

"Oh, Peter."

"Shazia finally said something, but by then my students were calling me Peter Cottontail."

She laughed.

He shook his head. "I think one of the nurses must be helping her pick out stuff. Mom didn't used to be . . ." He was going to say *nuts*, but he stopped himself. That was exactly what she was now.

"Oh, I don't know. Your mom's always gotten into the spirit of the holidays. As soon as it's time to take down the New Year's stuff, she puts up the Valentine's Day stuff."

"True."

"You should call her, you know."

Her voice was light. He'd never have the relationship with his mother that Ann had with her parents, especially not now. It wasn't as if he or his mother got anything out of their brief phone conversations. "Peter?" she'd say in a fuzzy voice. "What a nice name. I've always liked that name." And then they'd both wait for him to make an appropriate response.

He lifted the carafe over his cup. "How's your dad doing?"

"Still fighting that cold. Beth's really worried about him."

Beth had moved in with Ann's parents. She'd packed up her small apartment and loaded everything into her car. With no paycheck coming in, it made sense. But he felt sad that his sister-in-law had had to give up that small bit of independence. "She'll get him in soon."

"Maybe."

"The Guarnieris have their chimney going."

A shadow crossed her face. "I wonder how they're doing."

"Al was out shoveling yesterday. I waved, but he didn't look over."

The man had stood there staring at the snow. At last he flung his shovel aside and went indoors. Peter went over later and finished the job. Underneath the snow he'd discovered petrified newspapers and a bright green mitten. He pried it loose and placed it on the doormat. When he looked later, the mitten was gone.

"I wish there was something we could do." She held her cup between her palms. "Has Kate or Maddie said anything to you about Jodi?"

"Not a word."

"They must suspect something, but I don't dare bring it up." She took a sip. "I heard Shazia on the phone last night. Was it her family?"

"No. Dr. Antony's secretary returned her call. She confirmed that he's in Australia with that aboriginal tribe. So it must be a legitimate lead."

"Australia. It's summer there right now, isn't it? Just think of it. No peeling ice off your toothbrush, no scraping frost off the windows."

He'd always promised to take her to Australia. He'd forgotten that, too. He felt a pang of guilt. "I'm going to get you some new pots and pans."

She looked at him, surprised. "Where did that come from?"

"Look at that kettle. It's filthy. There's no way you can get all that soot off, so stop scrubbing. When this is all over, I'm getting you a new set. Anything you like."

"Even that super-expensive copper-clad stuff?"

"You bet." He smiled at her.

She smiled back, a faraway look in her eyes.

He watched her. "Ann," he said gently.

She turned her gaze to him.

"It won't be this bad much longer." He didn't say anything about the second wave of deaths that was surely coming after this one ended, or the third. She already knew.

She studied him for a long moment. Then, at last, she nodded, accepting the only thing he had to offer her: hope.

# TWENTY

ANN CAUGHT SIGHT OF HERSELF IN THE MIRROR AS SHE pulled the towel from the bathroom rack, and stopped to stare. When had she become so pale, her cheeks sharp and her eyes sunken? She'd lost weight. They all had. Peter's pants were so droopy he'd taken to wearing belts, and the girls . . . She shook her head to clear it. No. She couldn't bear to think about the girls.

In the laundry room, she turned on the faucet and squirted dish soap into the sink. She swirled her hand around but the water was too cold. The bubbles formed reluctantly and broke apart as soon as she dropped in the socks and underwear.

They were getting precariously low on food. They'd run out of so many things. All the fresh food was long gone; they were now steadily working their way through their dwindling supply of frozen and canned foods. She worried about the girls' calcium intake. The milk and yogurt had been consumed first, and they were down to a single block of Swiss, the girls' least favorite kind of cheese. Time to dig into her stash of vitamins to try and stave off any deficiencies until she or Peter could get to the store. They couldn't stay trapped inside forever. At some point, they'd have to risk venturing out, quarantine or no quarantine.

In the meantime, they still had flour and sugar, and seasonings.

She was going to experiment with making biscuits in the fireplace today, keeping a close eye on the pan to make sure they didn't scorch or become hard as rock. Everything took so much effort. All their energy seemed to be directed toward maintaining the basics: food and heat and shelter. She marveled at the ancestors who found time to sew clothes, fashion furniture, tend livestock.

Peter came through the back door, whistling, stomping the snow noisily off his shoes. His hair stuck up on one side, and he'd missed a spot shaving along his jaw. His eyes were bright blue, and he had two spots of color on his cheeks. He brought with him the smell of icy air and frozen vegetation. He'd been on one of his mysterious excursions again. He hadn't asked her to join him and she hadn't offered, sensing his need to be alone. She felt the same need. Sometimes she went upstairs to her bedroom closet and huddled in a blanket on the floor and put her forehead against her bent knees. She'd sit there in the dark, quiet cold, breathing in deep gasps of air, until the fear inside her subsided to a murmur and it was safe again to be around the girls.

"The mail hasn't come," she told him. "No paper, either."

They were down to the telephone and the truck radio, and the latter was increasingly playing more music than news.

"We've got a bigger problem," he said. "The garbage is getting out of control."

"I know." Ann squeezed moisture from a pair of socks. Everyone in the neighborhood had been lugging trash to the curb and leaving it there. The entire street overflowed with cans and bags stiff with frost.

"When this cold snap lifts, things will start rotting. There'll be bugs." He leaned against the jamb and crossed his arms. "Not to mention rodents."

She gave him a sharp glance. "We don't have rats in the suburbs."

"I'm not kidding, Ann. If it's not rats, it'll be other wild animals."

"That's just fantastic. Our own private wildlife refuge. Maybe we can sell tickets." She wrung out a pair of Maddie's underwear and draped it over the side of the laundry basket. "Will you tell Kate to bring down her things?"

"Sure." He walked into the next room.

Maddie's nightgown went in, and one of her turtlenecks. The water was turning brown. It was all the smoke from the fire. It coated their skin, slid down their throats, and sank deep into their hair. She thought of standing in a steaming shower, upending shampoo into her palm and soaping, letting warm water sluice down her skin.

Kate whirled in and dumped clothes onto the floor. "Here."

Ann eyed the pile. "You've worn everything three times?"

"Oh, believe me. They're disgusting."

"That's the spirit." Ann picked up Kate's green shirt from the pile and pressed it deep into the water. The iciness of the water shot straight through the thin rubbery skin of the gloves she wore and penetrated deep into her bones. Her hands throbbed.

Kate stood there watching. "I don't get it. How come we still have water?"

"They're different systems. But we have to be prepared to lose the water. That's why I keep the bathtubs and sinks full." Every day, she'd work through their laundry. As long as they had running water, she'd wash their clothes. "That's why you can't bathe in my bathtub. That's drinking water."

She shuddered. "I would so *never* drink that water."

"Oh, yes, you so would." Ann brought up the shirt and squeezed. She switched on the water and rinsed the garment. "Did you reach Michele?"

"She didn't pick up. No one did."

That was a bad sign. That was the one thing people did, if they could: they answered the phone. And Kate knew that. "Try not to worry. They were probably on the line with other people. She'll call you back."

"She had that party, remember? Maybe you were right." She wouldn't meet Ann's gaze. "Maybe someone came who was sick."

It had been painful for her to admit it. Ann wanted to put a reassuring arm around her daughter, but Kate would see that as confirmation of her worst fears. "That was over a week ago," she said instead, keeping her voice light. "Michele wouldn't be getting sick now."

"I guess." Kate didn't sound convinced.

"You've been talking to your other friends, right? And everyone's okay."

The phone rang and Kate's face lit up. "Maybe that's her," she said, and went toward it.

Ann fervently hoped so. She pulled the plug and watched the dirty water swirl away. Into a fresh soapy sinkful, she plunged jeans.

"Mom," Kate called, "it's for you."

She heard the disappointment heavy in Kate's voice. Sighing, she tugged off her gloves and hung them over the faucet. Her fingers ached. She curled them and pulled down the cuffs of her layered sweaters. Shazia sat folded into the armchair, staring out the window at who-knew-what, Maddie curled beside her, turning the pages of a book. She'd read it a dozen times. Now she was just looking at the pictures.

"Mommy, can I color these?"

Ann put a hand on Maddie's head. "Let me think about it, okay?" She hated the thought of Maddie marking up her books.

"You're so spoiled," Kate said to her sister. "Mom would never let me draw in my books."

"Leave me alone," Maddie said. "I wasn't talking to you."

"Leave me alone," Kate said, mocking. "I wasn't talking to you."

Maddie looked up at Ann, scowling. "Mommy," she began, and Ann patted her head.

"Ssh," she said, and took the phone from Kate. Maybe it was Libby. She was still refusing to answer Ann's calls, but Ann had caught glimpses of her through her kitchen windows. Libby never waved back, never ventured out onto the patio to talk.

"Hello?" Ann said.

Beth said, "Mom's sick."

Ann sank onto the couch beside Kate, suddenly boneless. "With what?" she asked her sister. But she already knew.

Shazia glanced over.

"Stop it," Beth said. "You know with what. GW and Sibley are full up, so I'm driving her to Charlottesville."

Charlottesville was over a hundred and fifty miles away from where her parents lived. All those hospital systems in the DC area, and yet they had to go all the way into the heart of Virginia? Ann started to ask why, then stopped. The implications were too worrisome. And Beth had enough on her hands now.

"I have to hurry, Ann, but I wanted to let you know."

"How's Dad?" she said, but Beth had already hung up.

Kate had her chin to her chest, flipping her cell phone open and closed. Ann reached over and put an arm around her and squeezed her daughter close. Surprisingly, Kate allowed this. Ann breathed deep. It was Kate's smell, with the underlying fruity fragrance of the perfume she still rubbed behind her ears every morning.

Years ago when they'd been living in North Carolina, a storm had swept through one evening, coating tree branches, telephone wires, cars, sidewalks, and streets with ice. In the morning, she and Peter had strapped Kate onto a sled and pulled her around the block. Nothing moved, not smoke from a chimney, a car, a curtain, at their passing. The entire world, it seemed, had fallen into an enchanted sleep, suspended in crystal. They marveled at the laciness of tree branches, the way the sidewalk glittered as though made of crushed diamonds. They rounded a corner and discovered a huge fallen oak with its enormous root system exposed, pale and vulnerable. The layer of topsoil had been too thin to hold the shallow roots. All that week, more trees succumbed to the weight of the ice pulling them downward. There had been fender benders, a house fire from a snapped electrical wire, but the only real casualties of that storm had proven to be the elms and oaks of Greensboro.

It had seemed like such a calamity then. Peter had grumbled about traffic being diverted around closed streets, but it had really just been an annoyance. Normalcy had soon reasserted itself. They had all known it. Everything would be fine soon. It was just a matter of time.

Ann pressed her lips to her daughter's temple and felt the pulse beneath the skin. Dear Kate, opening her bottle of perfume each morning and looking in the mirror.

Someday her girls would tell their children that they lived through the Pandemic. With any luck, this would be just a memory for them, too.

THERE WAS NO JOY IN FOLDING THESE THINGS. THE NAP WAS rough, the cloth unyielding, and here and there, a faint smokiness lingered. Ann flattened a sleeve, brought it over and made a rectangle. She set it in Peter's basket. The jeans were the worst. The denim was so stiff that she weighed it down with books to force the fold and make a tidy square. This pair went into Kate's basket.

A gentle rattling told her the water had begun to boil. She glanced at the fireplace and saw steam rising from the pot at last. It'd taken almost an hour. It had been so much faster on the grill. The next time, they'd have to start the process earlier.

"Peter," she said, picking up the plastic bowl, "it's ready. Shazia, would you put dinner on the fire now?"

Shazia rose and walked into the kitchen, where the pot stood waiting. Spaghetti and meatballs. Their last can.

Peter lifted the big pot from the flames and carried it up the stairs, water slopping up the sides and over. She worried that he'd burn himself, but he met her gaze, reading her mind, and smiled.

"Girls," Ann said, "we're coming in."

Kate and Maddie stood in the bathroom in their bathrobes, looking equally mutinous. Peter stepped to the bathtub and emptied the pot to mix with the cold water already there. He gave Ann a nod and shut the door behind him.

"Why can't I have some privacy?" Kate snapped.

Ann hated to deprive her of this, too. Kate had looked horrified when Ann had torn off four squares of toilet paper that morning and pressed it into her palm. Ann had stood outside the bathroom door and after the toilet flushed, opened the door and came in to measure out the dollop of liquid soap.

"We can't waste the hot water." Ann dipped in two washcloths. The water was warm and gentle on her skin.

"We have tons of water."

"But not tons of firewood. Come on, my little ones. You know how you love bathtime." Ann rubbed the cloths in the bar of soap and squeezed to make suds. She sang, "Rubber ducky, you're so fine . . ."

Kate groaned. "Please, Mom. Stop. We're not babies anymore." But she untied her bathrobe and let it fall to the floor.

"Don't look." Maddie tugged the belt of her robe.

"As if." Kate tugged off her socks.

"You too, Mom." Maddie was beginning to shiver.

"I won't," Ann said, though it was impossible not to catch glimpses of her daughters' pale, slender forms. She was shocked to see how skinny they both had become.

It had been years since she'd seen either of her daughters naked. At least two since Maddie announced she was taking her showers by herself from now on, eight years for Kate. Ann couldn't recall the last time Kate had stripped with abandon and stepped into the tub, her baby self focused on the bubbles and not the parent crouched watchfully beside her. Now Kate stood there shivering and hunched, her back to her sister and Ann, her arms crossed over her top and bottom. Kate was thirteen and a half, and she hadn't menstruated yet. Her pediatrician had told them it could start any time now. Of course that was then.

Ann handed a washcloth to Kate and ran the other cloth down Maddie's back. Her shoulder blades protruded, her spine rounded bumps of bone. Now Maddie's tummy, so flat, her hip bones little scoops.

"Mom," Maddie said, "are you looking?"

"No."

Now Maddie's arm, thin in Ann's grasp, the knobby shoulder, the pointed elbow, the little vulnerable wrist. "Turn around," she told Maddie. "No one's looking."

She scrubbed one leg, then the other. Maddie's skin was all gooseflesh, the downy hair golden.

"I'm done," Kate said, her teeth chattering. She climbed into the tub.

Ann handed Maddie the washcloth. "Do your toes," she said, then stood and dipped the bowl. She brought up a wave of water and poured it down one side of Kate, then the other.

"My turn," Maddie said. "Hurry. It's getting dark."

Kate stepped out and wrapped herself into a towel.

"Tomorrow, you two can wash in front of the fire," Ann told

them. "We'll make sure Daddy and Shazia stay in the den. And maybe we can do your hair in the powder room sink."

"Yippee." Kate stepped into her room and slammed the door.

"I'm done," Maddie said. "You can go now."

"Your clothes are on your bed," Ann said.

This was what she wouldn't give up. Neatly folded clothes, warm baths for her children, their nightgowns waiting on their beds.

On her way downstairs, she glanced through the window to the shifting colors of the sky. Streaks of orange and lavender along the dark horizon, weighed down by navy. When had she last stopped to watch the sun set? She'd always been so busy at this time of night. There had been after-school activities to shepherd the girls to and from, dinner to prepare while she caught up on the day's worth of phone calls and emails, lunches to assemble for the next day, homework to supervise. Now there was nothing to buoy her, nothing to keep her from sinking into thought, and memory. Picking up a blanket from where it lay over the back of a kitchen chair, she slung it around her shoulders and went outside.

Her skin felt taut with the cold, and she drew the wool tighter around her. But the chill felt good, welcome. A sharp reminder that she'd let down her guard. Again.

The quiet slide of the door behind her released a burst of noise—the girls squabbling and Shazia's low, interceding voice—then the door closed again to silence. Footsteps crunched toward her.

"Mind some company?" Peter said, coming close but not touching.

A narrow strip of salmon pulsed along the horizon, broken by the dark shapes of her neighbors' houses. A delicate web of clouds floated above. Now only the barest shell pink remained above the spiky treetops, and higher still, a deep band of violet.

"Beth hasn't called." It was a three-hour trip, and it had already been seven hours. Beth knew Ann would be watching the time. Beth knew Ann would want to hear the moment they'd arrived.

"Maybe she's not there yet."

"What can they do for Mom?"

"Put her on a respirator. Give her antiviral medication."

If they had any. And maybe not even then. Her mom wasn't in a category to merit special consideration. She wasn't a first responder. She wasn't a politician. She wasn't a scientist working on a cure. She was just a retired schoolteacher. A nobody. Just like everyone else Ann loved.

# TWENTY-ONE

*P*ETER STEPPED OUT ONTO THE PATIO.

Three days had passed since Beth had called. Ann had been phoning every hospital between DC and Charlottesville, with mixed results. Sometimes the phone rang endlessly; sometimes it was answered but no assurance given that Ann's mother had checked in. Yesterday afternoon, she'd picked up the receiver to make another round of calls and had turned to Peter with an expression of mute horror. He'd grabbed the phone from her and pressed it to his ear, hearing for himself the dead silence on the other end. The dial tone had vanished, taking with it their sole remaining lifeline to the outside world.

"Oh, Peter," Ann had said, her voice hushed. "What will Kate do now?"

Crusted snow squeaked beneath his boots. He took a few steps and leaned to look at the far window at the back of the house.

Ann was doing laundry again. That was all she did these days, it seemed. She was keeping herself busy. It was a mindless task, yet she'd be so fiercely intent on it, measuring out the soap, dropping the clothes to bob in the sink, that she wouldn't be looking out the window. Still, he checked the laundry room window, then the sliding glass door in case one of the girls was walking past, and finally the row of family room windows. The glass panes stared blankly back through a freckled film of frost and soot. No one stood behind them.

A small grating noise made him glance toward the street: Kate, opening the mailbox for what had to be the tenth time that day. Of course, the box was empty. They'd have heard the irregular rumbling of a mail truck making its rounds. The sound would have galvanized them all. He saw her shoulders slump. Then she turned and trudged back to the house.

When he was sure she was back inside, he stooped and reached beneath the stiff khaki of the grill cover. Dragging the bowl forward, he discovered it filled solid with ice. The water had frozen before the dog could get to it. But the second bowl had been licked clean. Peter crouched and scraped the insides of the cans he'd smuggled into the bowl, tapped the fork on the rim, and straightened. He checked the windows again. No one.

A gust of wind whipped past, carrying the odor of smoke. Someone had their chimney going. He sniffed. Not wood smoke. This had a bitter tinge to it. He turned around and lifted his gaze. There, above a peaked roof, he saw a plume of black smoke bullying its way into the sky.

The cans clattered to the patio pavers. He ran around to the garage, grasped the handle, and heaved the door, shuddering, upward. He plunged inside. The hose was around here somewhere.

Ann appeared in the doorway, the cuffs of her sweater pushed up, soap bubbles clinging to her knuckles. "What is it?"

"The Guarnieris' house is on fire."

She went pale. "I'll try the phone again."

He spied the garden hose lying in great loops on a back shelf. He yanked it free and raced across the street. Neighbors were collecting.

Singh appeared. "Use mine."

They ran between the two houses. The reek of smoke grew dense. Singh threw himself to his knees to twist the hose onto the spigot and turn the handle. Peter stood back, gripping the nozzle, and stared aghast at the smoke billowing behind the windows. A pane snapped, then cracked. The flame was out, licking at the sill. Orange raced along the eave.

Water sprayed from the nozzle, a pitiful stream useful for watering a lawn, useless to quell a conflagration. Still he aimed the hose at the roof. The water splattered against the siding and dripped down. He pressed a thumb to the nozzle to intensify the flow. Not good enough. They couldn't wait. He thrust the hose to Singh and stepped forward to force his way inside.

"Peter." It was Ann. "No!"

The front door was locked. The metal handle was hot. Peter lifted the heavy, dirt-filled flowerpot squatting beside the mat and heaved it at the window beside the door. He raised his foot and smacked his heel against the crazed glass. Crooking an elbow over his face, he reached through, fumbling for the lock. He found it, twisted it, withdrew his hand, and swept the door open. Smoke billowed around him. Blinded, coughing, he pushed forward. The heat shoved him back.

Someone had his arm and was pulling, screaming at him. He stumbled down the steps and fell to his knees.

Ann was beside him, wiping at his cheeks and forehead with her shirttail. She hissed, "What were you thinking?"

He rubbed his eyes and looked around. Singh stood aiming the hose at the house. Other neighbors had their hoses going, standing far apart on opposite lawns, eyeing each other nervously as they soaked the roofs on either side. He looked back to the small brick house. Flames leaped in every window. The entire roof was ablaze. Helpless, he watched the fire engulf the front door. A timber on the porch collapsed in a shower of sparks.

A gasp went up.

He'd been standing there only moments before. He felt for Ann's hand and squeezed it hard.

A kind of hopeless frenzy filled the afternoon. Everyone ran around, yelling, aiming hoses, dumping buckets of water, smacking at errant sparks with brooms. But the flames were ravenous. They whooshed across the bricks and leaped to the bushes lining the front path, driving everyone back. The fire roared and hissed and sputtered, and finally subsided. All that remained was the eerie outline of a home, the doors and walls and windows still standing but the roof and floors gone, the interior burned down to ash and tall spectral things poking skyward that had once been pipes and beams. Al and Sue had never appeared. Maybe by some miracle they'd escaped unharmed. They could have gotten in their rental car late one night while everyone was sleeping and headed somewhere else, somewhere with fewer painful memories. But even as Peter had the thought, he dismissed it. He'd seen the hulking thing in what used to be the garage; he knew it was a four-door sedan with Nevada license plates.

Dusk arrived. One by one, neighbors picked up their hoses and buckets and dispiritedly traipsed back to their dark houses. Peter came around the house and saw his daughters standing between Ann and Shazia on the sidewalk. His heart leaped at the reassuring sight of them.

Maddie began jumping and waving. "Daddy!"

His precious child, made so joyful by such an ordinary thing, her father appearing out of the gloom. He smiled tiredly at her. "Have you been standing there this whole time? You must be freezing."

"I've been *looking* and *looking* for you."

"I told her not to worry," Ann said. "I told her there was no way you'd get too close."

He heard the accusation in her voice. He *had* tried to get too close. He'd done it without thinking. "I'm fine, princess. See?" He held out his arms in a wide gesture of bonhomie.

Kate stood slightly behind her mother, her hands stuffed into the pockets of her ski jacket, watching him intently. When she realized he was looking at her, she lowered her head and turned away.

"It's late." Ann put her arms around the children. "Are you coming?"

"I'll be in soon."

She nodded, and they all crossed the street and went inside.

Peter rolled up the garden hose. He coughed and spat onto the ground.

A small light bobbed in the distance.

"Singh?" Peter called. "Is that you?"

The line of light turned and flared. "Be careful. There are hot spots everywhere."

Peter worked his way around the building, stepping carefully around the smoldering tide of debris and the slippery patches of re-frozen snow, and came up to where the man stood in a ghostly door-way.

"There," Singh said.

Peter peered into the murk. He followed the bright beam of light as it dove past cobwebbed sheets of ash, timbers corrugated and puckered from the heat, greasy puddles speckled gray, to hover on the rounded corner of a white porcelain sink. So this had been the kitchen. The wind shifted, bringing with it the stink of melted plastic, sulfur, copper, and something richly sweet. His eyes wa-tered. "Is that . . . ?"

"I'm afraid so." Singh held the light steady.

Peter cleared his throat and leaned forward. There, nestled by the foot of the sink, he saw the instantly recognizable curve of a human skull burned to mahogany with gaping holes where the eyes had once been, the mocking grin of teeth.

"That's Al." Singh shifted the beam, and Peter glimpsed a sec-ond skull and a length of hunched spine wrapped in brown ropes of sinew. "The smaller one's Sue."

Peter looked away, sickened. It felt wrong, looking. He thought of Jodi rocketing into her mother's arms Thanksgiving Day, Sue laughing with pure delight, Al slinging an arm around his wife's narrow waist and following his dancing daughter up the path to their front door, all three of them so glad to be safe and together and home. He swallowed, hard.

Singh shook his head. "First their little girl. Now this."

Peter realized his face was wet, that tears were sliding effort-lessly down his cheeks. He made no attempt to stop them or wipe them away.

Singh patted him awkwardly on the back. They stood close to-gether as the smoke twisted into the night sky and embers flared red and hissed into the kiss of slush.

At last, Peter said, "You think it was smoke inhalation?"

The man's fingers dug into the material of Peter's sleeve. "We can only pray so, but we'll never know. They'll never get to a morgue."

Peter cleared his throat. "Things are that bad?"

"We're almost out of medicines. The morgue is overflowing. Our director died two days ago."

"We can't just leave them here."

"When things cool down, I'll collect what I can and keep them for any relatives who may wish to bury them." Singh shook his head. "At least they were together."

Peter was frozen by the time he returned home. The sweat of exertion dried icy across his back and down his sides. He felt impossibly tired. Coiling the garden hose in his hand, he heaved the length of rubber inside the garage. A yelp and then a dark shape streaked past. Finn's dog? The animal was gone, swallowed into the shadows that claimed the sidewalk. He'd probably been looking for a place to sleep. A shame Peter had frightened him away. No chance he could coerce the dog back. Barney was long gone by now.

He dragged down the garage door with a mighty clatter, kicked off his boots, stripped off his outer layers and spread them out in a far corner of the garage to air. Shivering, he opened the door into darkness.

"Peter, is that you?" Ann called.

"Be right there."

Groping in the shadows, he washed up in the laundry room, his teeth chattering harder now. His head ached. He located a pair of pants Ann had washed and hung to dry. A bathrobe hung there, and he pulled it on. When he stepped into the kitchen, he saw a glow from the hearth. Used to be he was the only one in the family who could lay a fire.

The four of them sat there in the golden glow, cross-legged on sleeping bags, their faces turned toward him and deeply shadowed. He took his place beside Ann, and she handed him a plate.

He lifted it and sniffed. No use. He couldn't smell anything but smoke. Looked like crackers with something piled on top. He brought one to his mouth. He chewed and swallowed with effort, his throat dry. He wasn't hungry. "What is this?"

"Tuna," Ann said, watching him. She handed him a smooth small box.

He squinted at it.

"It's a juice box," Maddie said happily. "Mom's been saving it. Because it's Christmas Eve, Daddy."

That's right. He'd forgotten.

"Here we go again," Kate said.

"Shut up," Maddie said.

"I wonder when Santa's going to get here," Kate chanted in a singsong. "I sure hope Rudolf doesn't have the flu. That'd slow things down for sure."

"Kate," Ann warned softly.

"Well, I've been thinking about it," Kate persisted. "And I've decided I'd like an iPhone. What about you, Maddie? What do you want Santa to bring you?"

Maddie looked up at Ann. "Does this mean no Santa?" she said tearfully.

"Shh." Ann patted Maddie's knee. "You know how sometimes we have to postpone birthday parties?"

"Uh-huh."

"Well, it's the same thing with Christmas this year."

"Does Jesus know we're putting off his birthday?" Kate said.

"Enough," Peter snarled, and she sat back, surprised.

He peeled the cellophane from his straw and tried to poke it into the tiny hole. His fingers were clumsy with cold, and the dancing shadows from the fire weren't making it easy for him.

Shazia reached out. "May I help?" She poked the straw into the tiny hole.

He drank. The cold, sweet liquid slid down. Under the sweetness, though, he tasted ashes.

Ann said, "How do you think it started?"

"It was probably their camping stove. Singh thought they'd been using it for heat."

Everyone was quiet.

"Are they . . . dead?" Maddie's voice wobbled.

"Honey," Ann began, but Maddie insisted, "All of them, Daddy? Even Jodi?"

The firelight played over their young faces. Kate had her head lowered as she jabbed the rubber of her shoe with the tines of her fork. Maddie's gaze was full on him, her eyes shiny with tears. He made his voice gentle. "You know, you've got to be very careful using a stove indoors. We wouldn't do it."

"That's right," Ann said.

Kate twisted the fork into her shoe.

The truth had come out about Jodi, though not in the way he'd have predicted. Maybe this was for the best. Maybe it was better for the girls to believe the fire had taken Jodi. He didn't know. He couldn't tell. The girls had given him no signals at all as to how deep their awareness ran. Ann had been right. Kate and Maddie were both unnervingly quiet on the subject.

Maddie rubbed her nose. Then she sagged into Ann and her shoulders shook. Ann put her arms around her and kissed the top of her head. "Shh," she crooned. "It's all right, honey. It's going to be all right."

Kate hurled the fork clattering across the floor and pushed herself up.

It was his fault. He shouldn't have snapped at her. He started to follow her, but Ann said, "Give her a few minutes."

A door slammed.

Maddie wept. "I hate Kate."

"Hush," Ann said, smoothing her hair from her damp cheek. "You don't mean that."

"I do mean it. I hate her. I wish she'd never been born."

Ann tensed for a moment, then pulled Maddie closer.

A whole family was gone. Peter reached over and took one of Maddie's hands.

The fire had drawn out the neighbors. Some of them. It had been a small group, smaller than he'd have expected. "Did you see Libby or Smith?"

Ann shook her head without looking at him. She had her cheek pressed to Maddie's and was softly humming, rocking Maddie in her arms. He glanced at Shazia. She shook her head, her face in shadow.

That was surprising. Smith was the kind of guy Peter would have expected to be the first to come running to help.

# TWENTY-TWO

WHERE WERE THEY? Ann stood on the patio and watched Libby's house. A wet smokiness blew across from the still-smoldering house behind her. Soot peppered the snow about her. She shivered.

Maybe Libby was driving up to her parents' adobe house surrounded by beige sand and purple mountains. She was lifting Jacob from his car seat and handing him to her mother, happy to be home. "Merry Christmas," Libby was saying, and Smith was putting his arm around her. They were all trooping inside.

Ann thought about pulling into her own parents' driveway. The front door would bang open and her parents would stand there grinning, the lights on the Christmas tree glowing gaily in the room behind them. Maddie would leap about, and Kate would come close for hugs. Her dad would insist on carrying in the suitcases. Ann would scold him and shoo him away.

She stopped herself.

Her parents weren't home. They were still in Charlottesville. Assuming they'd made the trip successfully. Of course they had. Beth was smart. She was clever and determined. She'd let nothing stand in her way.

Not knowing was the hard part. There were so many things she didn't know. She was marooned in silence. It pounded against her eardrums. It mocked her as she watched out the windows for signs of life. Who knew what was happening in the hospitals, the medical labs, other towns and cities? She didn't even know what had happened next door.

Her mother, her sister, her best friend, they were all gone. There was no one left.

She stepped back into her kitchen and locked the door.

"Where is it?" Kate yelled from somewhere upstairs.

"Say *please*!" Maddie sang from the family room.

The girls were at it again. Ann could feel a headache punch its way between her eyes. She turned and saw Peter bringing down the first-aid bin. Fear stabbed her. "Who's sick?"

"I'm just seeing what we have." He pulled things out and stood them on the counter. "Do we have any more cough syrup?"

He was taking inventory? He'd never been one to track the mundane. That sort of thing had always been Ann's domain. Now that there were no stores or gas stations, maybe he'd begun to realize their limits. She didn't know if this reassured or worried her. "There's some in the girls' medicine cabinet. Why?"

Stomping footsteps upstairs.

Maddie called out, "Did you check the toilet, Kate?"

"Mom! Maddie flushed Owl down the toilet!"

Aghast, Ann marched into the family room, where Maddie sprawled across a chair, her book in her lap.

"Did you?" she demanded.

"She took all my crayons, Mom, and broke them into pieces."

Ann tipped back her head and stared at the ceiling. "Did you flush Owl down the toilet?"

Maddie licked her lips, then leaned forward to whisper, "No, Mom. I didn't. But don't tell her."

"Ann?" Peter called from the kitchen. "I can't find a thermometer."

"Honey," she said to Maddie, "it's terrible she broke your crayons, but you just can't take Owl away."

Maddie stuck out her lower lip, thinking, then lifted a shoulder and let it drop. "Whatever." She pushed herself up.

Ann walked back into the kitchen. "I keep the thermometers in that tin," she told Peter.

He dug out the small container and pried off the lid. "Here it is."

"There should be two."

He shook his head. "Nope. Just the one."

Ann pulled the bin toward her and shifted things around. A thermometer was small enough that it was probably lying at the bottom unnoticed. "What's this about, Peter?"

"We need to consider pooling our resources."

Ann stared at him. "With who?"

"After what happened with the Guarnieris—"

"You're not talking about getting together with our neighbors!"

"It's the only way we're going to make it through this." He pulled out a bottle of ibuprofen and shook it.

She pictured those children the other day, running around, mingling germs from all their various households. All it took was one sick person, one sneeze, one cough. Panic squeezed her chest. Peter couldn't be serious. A thousand protests bubbled to her lips, but all she could manage was one shocked "No."

He set the bottle down. "What if one of us gets injured? You only have a couple rolls of gauze. Singh probably has an entire storage unit of the stuff."

"He's around sick people all day. There is absolutely no way I'm letting my girls near him."

"By building one fire to heat three families, we could triple our firewood. What about antibacterial ointment?"

Peter was still reeling from Sue and Al's deaths. "Maybe earlier we could have considered something like that. But not now, not when the flu's everywhere."

"Three bottles of rubbing alcohol. Good." He began returning things to the bin. "By driving one car to the store, we can halve our fuel expenditures."

He wasn't listening. She rapped her knuckles on the counter and he looked up, startled.

"Peter," she said. "I said no."

"You're not thinking of the bigger picture. It's not just the flu we have to worry about."

My God, he could be so patronizing. "This isn't some lab experiment, Peter. This is real life. These are my daughters, and I say we
are not getting anywhere near our neighbors. It was bad enough
yesterday, all of us running around outside like that. I stayed up half
the night worrying that one of us might have gotten exposed."

He looked at her for a long moment. Then he took on that stubborn expression she knew only too well. She'd come at him too directly. She sucked in her breath and released it. "Listen. You said it
yourself, Peter, remember? You said the girls couldn't play with
their friends. There's no difference between that and this."

"Ann." His voice was cold. "We're not talking about playing with
friends. We're talking about the difference between surviving and
not."

"Don't you think I know that?" she snapped.

Shazia came down the stairs. "Is Kate okay?" she asked. "I
heard . . ." She halted, hand on the banister, her gaze moving from
Peter to Ann and back again.

"Kate's fine." Peter turned and set the bin on the pantry shelf.
"Do you need the girls for anything, Ann? I've got a project I'd like
their help with."

"Good. Take them." She reached for the broom. The floor was
dirty again. She could feel grit rolling against the soles of her shoes.
And there was a smear of something on the floor by the sink.

Shazia made up the bucket of bleach solution. She carried it
across the kitchen, leaning to one side to offset the weight, and went
into the bathroom. That was the routine. Bathrooms first, door
handles, kitchen, twice daily, morning and night. A spoonful of
bleach poured into the sinkful of water, dishes set in to soak till
noon. Everyone got one set of dishes each day. If they lost water,
they'd switch to paper and plastic.

Ann stepped into the garage and held the dustpan over the
nearest bin and gave it a quick shake. The stink made her eyes
water. She'd have thought the cold would have kept down the
stench. She turned to leave. Then she paused.

A small white bag lay across the top of their food, not tucked to
the side where she kept it. It had been torn in two and its contents

were gone. Blueberry muffins. She'd been saving them for the girls. No toys, no gift cards in their Christmas stockings, no new pajamas—just one small package of blueberry muffins, and now, not even that.

Could Kate or Maddie have pilfered it? No, they wouldn't have left the evidence lying around for her to discover.

"What is it?" Shazia stood on the step, clutching her sweater around her.

"I think we have a thief."

Shazia picked her way over to where Ann stood. She frowned down at the bin and then crouched, moved things aside. She picked up a Baggie containing doughnut crumbs, its corner shredded. "It looks like an animal got into this."

"A raccoon?"

"Maybe rats."

*Rats? My God* . . . in her home? Those horrible, dirty creatures rummaging around, their noses twitching and their long hairless tails flicking. Her lip curled. Disgusting things. They got into everything. They were indiscriminate. They had ticks and lice, and who knew what else? Then a new, more terrible, thought struck her. She turned to Shazia. "Don't they eat human flesh?"

Shazia was scanning the garage. "If they can."

Ann put her hand to her throat. They could find their way into the house and nip them as they slept. "We'll keep the garage door closed."

"I doubt it will do any good. They can chew their way through it or crawl underneath."

Ann stared at the door. It was at least two inches thick. How was that possible? "They can chew through the *door*?"

Shazia studied the bin, moved back to stare at the floor. "Concrete, too."

"Are you *kidding* me?"

"We need to locate their nest."

Ann looked around. What did a rat's nest look like?

Shazia lifted up a box. "Ideally, they'd dig a burrow somewhere outside, but the cold might have driven them indoors."

So, wait. They could still be in here? She curled her toes in her shoes, shuddering. The way Shazia was shifting things around, a rat could leap out at any moment. She picked up a shovel. "What are we looking for?"

"If it's just one, he'd have a pad, a few flat items stacked high enough to raise him up from the floor. If it's more, they'd have shredded stuff into a cup shape."

The very thought of rats organizing themselves in this scheming fashion nauseated her. She poked the garden pots in the corner with the tip of the shovel. Shazia was flipping through the stack of paper bags they'd been using as kindling.

"See anything?" Ann gingerly lifted aside garden gloves, a trowel, and a bag of topsoil.

"Not yet."

The door opened. Kate stood there, Owl tucked into her crooked arm. "Mom? Dad wants to know if he can have some envelopes."

"Close the door." Ann poked the shovel blade into a dark corner. "Get out of here."

"I'll tell him you said 'Go ahead.'" The door shut.

There were so many hiding spaces. Storage shelves lined one wall. There was Peter's workbench and tool chest. The bin of sports equipment. "Find anything?"

"No. Perhaps they've made their nest elsewhere. I think the freezer out here is okay."

"You think?"

"They can't get through metal. But if we remove their food source, they'll just search out another." Shazia rubbed a forefinger along the crack where the door met the step. "They don't need much space. Maybe only half an inch."

So not even the food in the kitchen was safe from the filthy little beasts. Disease carriers. They'd have to block the door somehow, but how certain could they be that they'd keep them out entirely? She narrowed her eyes. "How do we kill them?"

"We could try some sort of poison."

"Like what?"

"I really don't know. Arsenic, I suppose."

"We don't have anything like that."

"I don't know how successful we'd be anyway. Rats are wary. They'll take a small taste of something new and wait to see if it makes them sick." Shazia straightened. "It'd be good to have a cat."

"Maddie's allergic."

"I see."

Shazia turned and left. Was she actually looking for poison? Was that the sort of thing she'd have brought with her? Ann quickly followed. The girls sat at the kitchen table, pushing folded sheets of paper into envelopes and licking the flaps.

"Don't go into the garage," Ann told them. She heard the sharpness in her voice.

So did Kate. She raised her head, staring at Ann, her brows drawn together.

"Want to see what we did?" Maddie said.

"In a minute."

Instead of heading for the stairs, Shazia veered into the dining room. "Peter?"

Of course, Ann thought.

He looked up from the notebook opened before him. "What's the matter?"

"We've got rats," Shazia said.

Ann said, "They've gotten into the food."

He set down his pen and pushed back his chair. "I was afraid of this."

They followed him through the house.

"Did you see any droppings?" he said.

"No," Shazia answered.

They crowded around the food bin.

Peter ran fingertips across the concrete and rubbed them together. "Any sign of nesting?"

"No," Shazia said. "We could sprinkle baby powder around the bin and watch for tracks."

Ann shook her head. "We can't leave the food out here for them to get into again."

"It's no good now anyway," Shazia said.

The pickles, olives, the salad dressing, the last slices of bread . . . "None of it?"

"No tail whips or paw prints, no grease marks." Peter frowned. "I don't think rats got into this stuff."

Thank God.

"You think it was another sort of animal?"

He nodded. "Still, it's just a matter of time before rats follow."

"There haven't been any documented cases of rats spreading H5 to humans," Shazia said.

"But we know rats can be infected with it," Peter said. "And we've been out of touch for weeks now."

Ann stared at him. "Wait a minute. Are you telling me these rats could be carrying the flu?"

"I don't think we have rats."

"But if we did?" she said impatiently. "Could we be exposed?"

Peter turned his gaze to her. "Yes."

# TWENTY-THREE

PETER LIFTED THE KEYS FROM THE HOOK AND CALLED into the kitchen, "Girls, are you done with those?"

"Almost."

"Bring them out, will you?" It must have been Finn's dog, Barney, who'd gotten into their food supply. The animal must have been after more than just shelter the night before. The poor creature was probably starving. In a way, Barney had done them a favor, reminding them of the risks they took leaving their food out like this. A dog today, rats tomorrow.

Ann and Shazia backed up to let him go to his truck. Peter reached into the toolbox in his truck bed and pulled out a pair of latex gloves.

"We'll have to do the whole neighborhood, won't we?" Ann looked grim. "If rats get into one house, they'll make it to ours, too."

"Yes, that's true," Shazia said.

He pulled the tarp from the shelf and shook it across the bed of his truck. Ann and Shazia helped him tuck down the corners.

Maddie came running. "Here, Daddy."

"Good job, honey." He took the envelopes.

"What are those?" Ann said.

"The girls and I wrote a letter to the neighbors." He tucked the envelopes into his coat pocket.

Ann had been walking around to the passenger side, and now she stopped and looked at him.

"Listen," he said, wanting to forestall any more arguments. "We can do this without coming into contact with anyone. We'll work up some sort of system where we leave things on each other's front porch."

She narrowed her eyes. "You have a far greater trust in our neighbors than I do."

In some ways, that had always been the problem. It was one of the reasons they'd left North Carolina. "I'd better get going," he said. "There's no need for you to come along. I can manage this." He got into the truck and slammed the door.

Ann stood back, looking uncertain. Shazia stood beside her. The engine rumbled to life, a welcome, clearing sound. He backed the truck out of the garage.

Averting his eyes from the black thing that had been the Guarnieris' home, he started at the house on the opposite corner. Small grocery sacks littered the ground around the driveway like huge misshapen snowballs. He grasped a handle and lifted. It resisted. The plastic had melted to the icy slick of the pavement. He tugged harder and the bag ripped, dribbling sodden tissues and fireplace ash. He'd have to scrape it up by hand. Before he drove on, he opened the mailbox, fitted in one of the envelopes, and pulled up the red metal flag. Sooner or later Stan Fox would notice and come investigate.

Metal cans lined the pavement outside the Nguyens' house. Peter had to work to loosen the lids hammered on too tightly. The cans were too unwieldy to lift over the side of the truck, so Peter pulled out the bags they contained and rolled them onto the tarp. Mrs. Nguyen came out onto the porch and watched. Peter pointed to the mailbox, and she nodded.

A can lay half-buried in the slush in the next driveway. Large bags listed at the one beyond. He let his focus grow distant. He didn't need to know the Mitchells drank tea and ate pudding from cups, bought this brand of detergent. He wouldn't match the apple cores to the Hutchesons or the coffee grounds to Singh.

The street curved, and Peter pulled up in front of the yellow ranch at the bottom of the cul-de-sac. He hadn't been down here in a while. He recalled seeing two small children riding their tricycles in the driveway. Didn't they have a cat, too? Yes, an obese, yellow creature that had streaked out in front of his truck one spring morning when he'd been on his way to work, the woman of the house running after. "Sorry!" she'd called as Peter screeched to a stop. She'd scooped the cat into her arms and stood back, waving.

Now Peter looked down at the front yard. Soda cans and crushed juice boxes, Styrofoam trays, flattened waxy boxes, and cans with their lids at sharp angles. Empty wine bottles and baby-food jars. Everything had just been tossed onto the snow and left there to be blown away. He looked at the house. The curtains were still, no smoke from the chimney. He turned off the engine and climbed out of the cab, reaching for his gloves. This would take a while.

Finally, the truck bed was too full to accept another bag. He reached in and tamped things down with the flat of a shovel to keep stuff from flying out the minute he picked up any sort of speed. He peeled off his gloves and squirted hand sanitizer onto his palms. Rubbing them together, he swiped his temples with a forearm.

As he drew past the house, he spotted Ann standing on the front porch, watching. He slowed and rolled down his window. "I won't be long," he called to her. He wondered if she'd reply, was relieved when she called back.

"Be careful."

"I will." He pulled away from the curb, eagerly accelerated through the stop sign at the bottom of the street. It had been weeks since he'd ventured beyond their neighborhood. Had anything changed during his absence?

The roads were unexpectedly clear, the snow gone from the pavement but still standing on the grassy medians and hills. At an intersection, the stoplights dangled overhead, useless. Cars waited to take their turns. Peter drew alongside a minivan the same make and color as Ann's. He glanced over to see the passenger, a young woman with a hand to her face. She refused to look over at him.

Static hissed from his usual radio stations. Two days before, they'd all sparked out like old Christmas lights. It had been an unwelcome surprise. The AM stations were dead, even the ones the government used to disseminate public information. He'd thought they were foolproof. It must have been some glitch that brought them down, maybe a sequence of glitches. He flicked off the radio and settled back into his seat.

There was the library, the gas station, and the Chinese restaurant, all dark and silent. Normal for Christmas Day, but now they had a more abandoned look, with their long, blank windows completely unadorned by any attempt at holiday festiveness. A fire engine sat skewed in the empty parking lot. No one was around it. There were no lights flashing. Had they run out of gas in the middle of a run?

The dump wasn't far, five miles perhaps. The map showed it standing off a long curving county road Peter had never been down before. He looked to his gas gauge. The arrow pointed to the halfway mark, more than enough to make it to the dump and back. There was enough to tack on a quick trip to the university. Depending on how long this job took, he might head down there afterward. The power had to be on by now. He wondered about Lewis. Had he been able to tend to his lab animals?

He drove under the freeway and past a sprawling housing development. Everything looked closed and quiet. He slowed as he reached the turnoff and took the left. The road surface changed from asphalt to gravel. Trees crowded in on both sides, and the snow grew thick in the shadows. He bumped over the ruts. A signpost pointed right. The road flattened and he broke through the tree line. Two metal posts stood on opposite sides of the road with a heavy chain lying on the snow between them. The guard box sat empty.

Someone had been through here recently, though. Tire tracks cut through the slush. He could see where they turned around on the berm ahead. He angled into the clearing and rocked to a stop. A mountain of trash rose before him, vast and multicolored, sprawling across the flat Ohio terrain.

White slabs of Styrofoam. Black tires, bundled red and blue rags, steel pipes, yellow plastic buckets. Thousands of twisted bags, their contents undecipherable. The snow had settled, filling in the gaps and softening the edges.

Something was wrong, but he couldn't put his finger on it.

He edged his truck right up to the very perimeter. The air was still and frosty. The stink seeped in through his closed windows. His eyes watered, and he tried to breathe through his mouth. He sat there and looked at the heap that filled his windshield.

It wasn't the presence of something that bothered him, he realized, but the absence. Where were the cawing gulls circling above?

Climbing out of the truck, he slammed the door shut.

He tugged on a fresh set of gloves, unfastened the back gate, and reached in for the first bag. The ride had jostled things around, and the first bag he picked up split open. He did what he could to scoop up the mess before heaving it onto the slope of refuse. Things broke apart and rolled toward him. He stepped back out of their reach and began tossing bag after bag, building up a kind of rhythm. Reach, flex, heave.

When most of the truck bed had been emptied, he retrieved the broom he'd brought along for this purpose and climbed up to sweep out the bed. The tarp that he'd spread to protect the truck bed lay wrinkled and slick. He removed his gloves and left them and the broom in the bed, lifted up the back gate, and latched it into place.

He climbed into the cab and turned on the engine. His entire truck would need to be hosed out and disinfected. The sweat he'd built up earlier made him clammy, and he blasted the heat into the cab. The clock on the dashboard read just after three. He put his truck into gear and backed out through the gate. Time for round two.

He took a different route home, slowing as he approached the grocery store. Someone was there, walking toward the lone car parked in the lot. Peter swung the wheel hastily and bumped into the shopping center. He rolled down the window. "Hey."

The man turned and looked over. Middle-aged, bulky in a quilted navy coat, he wore a red apron tied around his neck and waist. He had his hand on his car door handle, and he looked impatient. "Yeah?"

"Are you open?"

"We were. You just missed it." The man swung himself into the driver's seat. "We'll open again the next time we get a delivery."

"Any idea when that'll be?"

"All I can tell you is keep checking back. Like I do." He slammed the door and started the engine.

Peter looked to the store. Plywood had been nailed over the picture glass. Shards of glass twinkled on the pavement. The sound of the car engine faded into the distance. Peter slowly pulled forward, loathe to leave.

The little potted fir trees, the empty concrete benches arranged in the little courtyard at the end of the parking lot. There was the mailbox on the corner and a squat metal box beside it.

Braking to a stop, he turned off the engine and patted his pockets. They were empty, of course. Would he have to break the glass? No, wait. The ashtray. He usually kept spare change in there. He fingered out some coins and stepped out of the truck.

The newspaper was thin, the size of the free community papers that used to appear in their driveway every week. He climbed back into the truck and checked the date. Six days old. Still, Ann would be pleased. She'd been hungering for news. They all had.

The front page was completely devoted to H5N1. The vaccine Liederman had been working on had failed and was being pulled. Patients had died. Terrible news. Peter guessed Liederman's group had been working too fast. The reporter was writing fast, too. He hadn't even mentioned any other ongoing vaccine programs.

The CDC estimated thirty million Americans were going to die. Ten percent of the U.S. population. A staggering number, but one that came in far below what Peter would have guessed. H5N1 had a fatality rate closer to fifty percent. That translated to one hundred and fifty million American deaths. Either CDC was buffering the numbers or the virus had mutated to a milder form. Peter hoped for the latter, suspected the former.

On the next page was a photograph of a tall building, one side sheared completely off. Steel beams bristled like chopped arteries. He read the caption. Japan had had an earthquake. Thousands of people had died because international relief couldn't be mustered. All those desperate people waiting for help that never arrived. He read the story below. Militant Pakistanis had marched on Islamabad and overthrown the government. These were headlines that would have carried the front page but which were now relegated to the inside section.

Here was a black-bordered list of things they were supposed to have at home. Below it was an article on caring for the sick. He paused at the next headline. *Mass Fatalities Overwhelm System.* Morgues and undertakers all across the country had resorted to hiring freelancers to collect the dead. Health departments were lagging in issuing death certificates. Thousands of deaths might end up going unreported. The President's national database was struggling, and gaps were appearing in the more rural areas. At the bottom of one page was a photograph of a familiar curved structure, the ice hockey rink where the girls had learned to skate. Columbus was storing its overflow of dead bodies there.

He glanced around the empty parking lot. His was the only car there.

Maybe it wasn't that people were staying home. Maybe they were all dead.

He climbed out of the truck and crammed the newspaper past the metal lid of the nearest trash bin.

# TWENTY-FOUR

*T*HEY'D GONE THROUGH SO MUCH FOOD.

Ann counted the cans and boxes once again, as if by doing so she could magically multiply their number. Of course she'd thought she'd be feeding three, not five.

"Tell us another story, Shazia."

"Like what?"

"Tell us about your family."

All the food she'd tossed out over the years without the least bit of remorse. The leftovers too scant for a meal. The lengths of spaghetti used to carry flame from birthday candle to birthday candle. Altogether, a dinner's worth. The lettuce gone limp in the bottom of the refrigerator drawer. Maybe she could set everything on a table on her front lawn and barter with her neighbors. One jar of pine nuts for one jar of grape jelly or, hell, an apple. She craved the sensation of biting into sweet crispness, the flood of juice filling her mouth. A glass of cold milk. Broccoli. Green, the color of life.

"Well, let's see. My father's a pediatrician, and my mother's a beautician."

"What's that?"

"A beautician? She does people's hair and makeup. Mostly women. Egyptian men don't tend to wear much makeup."

Christmas. One day since the fire, four without phone service, twenty-eight since the power had gone out. A series of losses that she tracked, marking off each day and fixing it in her mind. Today was Wednesday. Tomorrow would be Thursday. All the cues that normally kept the calendar for her had vanished, and she had to keep it for herself.

"Did she show you how to do your makeup?"

"A few tricks, like curling your eyelashes before you put on mascara. And if you line your lower eyelids, you will make your eyes look smaller."

Shazia was counting off the days, too. Ann had come upon her studying her planner, moving her finger along the small squares, her lips soundlessly forming the numbers. Now she sat with the girls cross-legged on the floor in the family room. They'd pushed aside the sleeping bags and pillows and arranged themselves in a semicircle. In a little while, one of them might come into the kitchen and get a cup of water. Or they might go to the front door and look out through the glass. They brushed their teeth in the tiny powder room, got dressed in there, stood in front of the mirror and ran a washcloth around their face and neck. No one ventured upstairs anymore. No one went down to the basement. Their whole world had shrunk to these few rooms.

"Why didn't you become a . . . beautician?"

"Well, when I was a little girl, we had a dog. Her name was Fila. I loved her very much. She would eat her food right out of the palm of my hand, and when she wanted something she would lift her paw and cock her head. She was very cute. At night, she slept on a pillow beside my head."

Ann leaned her forehead against the sliding glass door. Nothing moved outside. Everything was painted in dreary shades of black, brown, and white. She was so tired of looking at the same houses, the same trees, the same empty sidewalks. She should have gone with Peter.

"What happened to her?"

"She got sick. The doctor said there was nothing he could do about it. She got very thin and then one day she died. I was quite sad for a long time. So my mother suggested that maybe when I grew up I could become a doctor who would help keep little girls' dogs from getting sick."

"So, that's what you do?"

"Not exactly. I wanted to study with your father. So I changed my field of research. Your father tells people he talked me into leaving Cairo and coming here, but that's not how it happened. I talked him into taking me on."

Ann had stood on the porch as Peter drove up and down the street. No one had come out to help. They'd been watching, though. She'd seen the curtains twitch and shadows move behind the glass. That's when she realized that there was no risk of Peter's plan to coordinate supplies and resources working. She wouldn't have to say a word. The silence from the neighbors would say it for her.

"Because he's so smart?"

"Your father's more than that."

She could have run across the lawn and caught him before he pulled away, opened the truck door and climbed in beside him. Shazia could have stayed with the girls. She could have leaned back in her seat and felt something move other than the sky. But in the end the opportunity to go with him had come and passed. She couldn't risk both of them being exposed. There were the girls to consider. Always.

MADDIE RAPPED HER PAINTBRUSH AGAINST THE RIM OF THE drinking glass. *Tap. Tap. Tap.* Papers were spread before her, revealing splotches of emerald grass and blue sky.

Ann put a hand on her daughter's arm. "Maddie, please. Stop that racket."

But Maddie just hit the glass harder.

Ann sat up with a start and realized she'd been dreaming. The room was dark, the fire in the hearth reduced to glowing orange embers. The rapping noise was still there. It was coming from the front hall. She looked around. Everyone was fast asleep—Kate, Maddie, Peter, Shazia.

She unzipped her sleeping bag and crawled out, stepping unevenly onto the quilted fabric. Who would be knocking at this time of night? She felt a sudden surge of hope. Mom, Dad, Beth.

She ran to the front door. The floor was cold against her stockinged feet. Moonlight gleamed through the window on the landing. A dark shape moved behind the glass inset beside the door. Someone was standing there. Ann automatically reached for the porch light switch, but of course nothing came on. She pushed her face to the pebbled glass and peered out. "Who's there?"

"Ann?"

A woman's voice, familiar, but not her mother's. "Yes?"

"Ann? Oh, thank God."

Libby!

"Where have you been? We've been so worried." Ann lifted her hand to the sliding bolt. So Libby and Smith hadn't driven off to Arizona. They'd been trapped here all along, just like them.

"Let me in."

"Of course! You must be freezing."

Ann slid the dead bolt almost all the way, then heard it—the thick, wet coughing on the other side of the door. She froze. "Are you all right?"

"Can you let me in? It's so cold."

"Are you . . . sick?" In the narrow space of quiet, Ann heard another noise. Someone was crying. Jacob.

"Please, Ann."

A shuffling sound, and Ann turned to see Peter emerging out of the gloom behind her, yawning.

"Who's out there?" he asked.

"It's Libby. She's got Jacob."

"Well, let them in." Peter strode over and reached past her, toward the door.

Ann put her hand on his forearm. "Hold on."

Libby coughed that awful croupy cough.

Ann felt something dark grow inside of her. She reached up and shot the dead bolt home. The sound filled the hall.

The doorknob rattled.

Peter frowned, confused. "Why'd you do that?"

"She's sick." My God. Libby.

"But . . . we can't just leave them out there."

Libby's voice was hoarse between coughing fits. "Jacob's okay. I promise. He's already had it."

"If he's already had it, he's immune," Peter said.

In Libby's place, Ann would say the same thing. Her heart was thumping. She needed to think. Could she possibly take the baby? He was so small. She could confine him to one room, but not downstairs. All the rooms there fed into one another. She'd have to take him upstairs. But it would be too cold up there for the baby. Maybe she could stay downstairs, while Peter and the girls moved up. What if she got sick? How could she keep the girls safe then? Her mind whirled with possibilities. One by one, she discarded them.

"Mom?"

Kate and Maddie stood in the hallway, Shazia behind them.

"Who's at the door?" Maddie said, rubbing her eyes.

"Shazia," Ann said, "take the girls into the other room."

Shazia hesitated, looked at Peter.

"Please, Shazia," he said.

She put an arm around the girls and led them away.

The knob rolled back and forth more urgently. "Ann? Please!"

"If he really did have it, he's fine," Peter said. "Let him in, Ann."

"What if she's lying?"

"What if she's not?"

She chewed her lips; she tasted blood. "I just can't take that chance, Peter. I just can't."

"We have to."

Now Libby was thumping against the wood.

"Ann," Peter said.

The dark thing inside swelled and filled Ann completely. Her head buzzed. "I won't risk our children's lives for someone else."

"It's not just someone else. She's your best friend."

"She'd never risk Jacob for the girls." Was that true? She couldn't think.

"You don't know that."

Wait. She did know it. She did. What mother would risk her children's lives for anything? No, Libby would do just as she was doing; she was certain of it, no matter how it hurt her to do so. "We are not opening this door."

"This is wrong."

"Peter." He had to hear her. His eyes were dark chips. "Listen. It kills half the people who get it. You know that. One out of every two. That means we're sacrificing one of them." Her eyes ached, her throat. She saw Jodi, just eight years old, jumping on the trampoline, her hair flying up and down, her laughter sailing into the sky. She was suddenly so furious she couldn't breathe. She needed him beside her, not against her. How could he not understand? "Kate or Maddie. Which one of your daughters do you want to die?"

"For Christ's sake, keep your voice down."

She pressed herself back against the wood, horrified by her own words. The wood vibrated. Easy enough to fight when the monster kept its distance, easy enough to draw the line. But when the monster was literally outside the door, that's when your actions mattered. The hard choice wasn't opening the door. The hard choice was keeping it closed. Peter couldn't see that. He never would.

"Just go back to sleep." She'd never felt more alone. "Let me handle this. As usual."

"What the hell does that mean?"

"You always take the easy way out. Our marriage, your mother. You're weak. Just like your father."

He flinched.

"I'll go away," Libby pleaded, scrabbling at the door. "Just please help Jacob. Ann, please. Please help my baby."

The flu had taken so many. It wouldn't take Kate or Maddie. Ann leaned against the door with all her weight. She wouldn't let Kate or Maddie be hurt any more than they already had by this unspeakable thing.

Peter said softly, "And you think this makes you a good mother?"

Her gaze floated to his face, rigid with anger, his lips thin, his eyes narrowed. She hated what he saw.

"It's all I know," she whispered.

The thumping stopped.

"Just take my baby." Libby's voice receded. "I'm in the yard. I'm in the yard."

Ann's legs couldn't hold her. She slid down the length of the door and bowed her head, clenching her eyes shut and pressing her hands over her ears. The monster raged all around. She was the monster.

Silence.

She lifted her head. The hall was empty. Peter had left. She rose shakily and looked out through the window at the empty landscape. All she saw was the snowy slope of yard and the line of dark houses beyond. Libby was gone. Her gaze dropped to the porch. What was that?

Libby had left the baby. He lay in a laundry basket mounded with blankets, with just the tip of his nose peeping out. Ann pressed her palm to the window. Her breath frosted the glass. In the fitful moonlight, she thought she saw a tiny foot push against the curve of blanket.

*Libby, come back.*

Everything outside was still. Even the trees were holding their breath. Libby was nowhere in sight. What if Ann was wrong? What if Libby had told the truth? All Ann had to do was twist the dead bolt. He lay right there outside her door. She wouldn't even have to step outside. Maybe he wasn't sick.

*Libby, please. I can't do this. Come back and take this burden away from me.*

Ann put her face into her hands.

# TWENTY-FIVE

PETER LOPED AROUND TO THE FRONT OF THE HOUSE looking for Libby. No sign of her standing by the front door, but there was something on the porch. He stepped closer. She'd left Jacob.

He crouched, slid his hands beneath the blanket. The baby had been there only a few minutes. Not long enough for hypothermia, but he was so still. Peter brought him to his shoulder and patted the small back. A tiny hiccup. He let out the breath he didn't realize he'd been holding. He'd come back for the baby's things later.

He stepped into the kitchen and found Ann standing there.

She stared at him, hollow-eyed. Her gaze dropped to the baby in his arms. She looked back at him. "Girls," she said in a choked voice. "Go upstairs, please."

"You and Daddy were *yelling*." Maddie was tearful. "Why were you *yelling* like that?"

"We'll talk about this later," Ann said. "I want you both upstairs. *Now*."

"Fine," Kate said. "Don't tell us anything. Treat us like babies. You always do!" She whirled around and stomped up the stairs.

Maddie followed, her hand trailing on the banister as she

looked back at him and Ann. "You're coming, too, aren't you, Mommy?"

"I'll be right there." Ann kept her gaze on Peter.

"I don't get you," Peter said. The baby squirmed, and he shifted him to his other arm. "Your priorities—"

"Our daughters are my priority." She said it flatly. "They should be yours, too."

"They don't have to be the only thing."

"Yes. They do. And they always will be. Even if you never understand that."

He watched her march up the stairs. She was a stranger to him. He couldn't believe they'd ever shared a life together, made plans, raised children.

Shazia said, "Are you all right, Peter?"

He glanced at her standing there in the gloom, a blanket draped around her shoulders. She looked fragile, buffeted by the anger between him and Ann. "I'm fine. Why don't you go back to sleep?"

"You're sure?"

"Sure. No sense in both of us staying up."

"Let me know if you need me." She turned and went into the family room.

After a moment, he heard the rustle of covers as she settled herself onto the sofa.

Peter patted the baby's back and paced.

Murmuring drifted down the stairs. Ann was talking to the girls. Maddie's voice. Now silence.

A log broke apart in the hearth. A shower of bright gold sparks. It was the last of their wood.

The baby relaxed. Peter carried him into the family room. He started to lower himself into the chair and the baby stiffened. Up Peter went.

The baby twisted his head, trying to look at Peter.

"You know I'm not your dad, don't you, buddy?"

There was no mucus, no sound of labored breathing. He put his fingers to a soft, cool cheek. The baby balled his little fists against Peter's shoulder and reared back. He opened his mouth to wail. Peter pressed the baby to his shoulder and drummed his back. Up and down, up and down. They walked the house in a dreary circuit. Dining room, kitchen, front hall. Dining room, kitchen, front hall. Around and around and around.

The baby slumped. Peter sat down. Jacob's eyes flew open. Peter groaned and stood back up. He'd forgotten these times.

They walked to the dining room window and looked out. Moonlight bathed the stripe of the street and the shapes of the trees. The baby raised his head. Searching for his mother?

"She'll be back," Peter murmured against the soft ear. He swayed the baby from side to side. "She'll be back," he promised.

A THIN GRAY LIGHT SEEPED THROUGH THE WINDOWS. DAWN. Shazia was sitting up in the family room, blankets tented around her. He'd kept her up.

"Sorry," he said. "It's been a while since I took care of a baby."

"It's all right. I'll help."

"Would you hold him? There's some stuff for him on the porch. I need to disinfect it."

"Sure." She held out her hands.

*Just like that.* Why couldn't Ann see that?

Crouching on the front porch, he scoured the jars and spoons and toys with a towel dipped in bleach solution. So much stuff to take care of one little baby. He dropped the clothes into the bucket of soapy water and pushed them down. He'd let them soak for a while. Nothing could be done about the disposable diapers and the baby wipes. He hoped a night in the open air had killed any viable viruses. The house next door was dark. Was Libby standing by a window? Could she tell the basket was gone?

He lifted his hand. If she was watching, she'd see. She'd know Jacob was safe.

Going inside, he found Shazia standing by the fire, jiggling the baby up and down.

"He probably needs changing." Peter took the baby and lowered him onto a swirl of blanket. Jacob arched his back and waved his arms, whipped his head from side to side. "Hold on there, little man. I'll make this super-quick. Shazia, want to get me a diaper from one of those bags?"

"Sure." She rummaged around, pulling things out. At last she lifted a package of diapers. "So, how old is he?"

Peter didn't know. He tried to recall when Jacob had been born. He remembered coming to visit his daughters and seeing the blue helium balloons bobbing out front next door. There'd been tulips around the mailbox. Had to have been April or May. "Six months. I think." He unsnapped the sleeper, reached in for the plump little legs and pulled them free. Off came the sodden diaper. No need to bother with a wipe or ointment. Peter spread out the diaper, grasped the baby's ankles, and lifted, hoisting the little bottom into place. He pressed the sticky flaps into place, tugged up his sleeper, and snapped the front. Sliding one hand beneath Jacob's head and the other beneath his bottom, Peter put Jacob to his shoulder. He sat back to find Shazia staring at him with amazement.

He smiled at her. "I've done this before."

A step creaked. He glanced over and saw Ann standing there at the foot of the stairs.

Her arms were crossed, and she was watching them impassively. "How is he?"

"No coughing. No fever."

"But he could still have it." Her gaze lingered on the baby.

"We won't know until tomorrow night." Forty-eight hours was the standard incubation period for this virus. Unless, of course, it had mutated. The baby gnawed his fist. "Libby left jars of baby food, some diapers and things."

Ann's frown deepened. "We'll have to sterilize everything."

"I've already done that. The clothes and bibs are soaking. I'll rinse them later." He gave the baby to Shazia.

"Come, baby," Shazia crooned. "We can read a book while we wait for the girls to get up."

"No," Ann said.

Shazia looked at her.

"My daughters don't go anywhere near Jacob. Not until we know he's not contagious."

Shazia glanced at Peter.

"Look at me, Shazia," Ann said. "I'm the one who's talking. This is my home."

Peter rose. He didn't trust himself not to say something that would only make things worse. He avoided Ann's demanding gaze. "We need firewood."

She moved aside to let him reach his jacket on the hook. Shutting the back door between them, he scanned the interior of the garage and spotted the sled balanced on the rafters. That would do.

Ann had called him weak, but she'd gotten it wrong. He didn't run away from things. He accepted them. There was a difference.

As he strode past Smith and Libby's house, he glanced over. The front door was shut. No one stood at a window. So far as he could tell, Libby hadn't crept back to check on her son. And he hadn't seen Smith at all.

# TWENTY-SIX

WHAT HAD THEY TOUCHED? ANN STARED AROUND THE kitchen. She'd left them alone down here for hours. Right now, viruses could be swarming over the faucet, countertops, cabinets. Pick up a sponge, it was on your hands. Rub your eye, blow your nose, now the virus entered your bloodstream and raced to your lungs.

She'd have to assume everything. She pulled on a pair of latex gloves from the medicine bin. The bigger risk came from directly inhaling the virus. A sneeze could spray droplets as far as three feet. Should she put on a mask? No, not yet. Not unless she heard one of them sneeze or cough. A horrible thought. She couldn't think that.

She pulled out the bottle of bleach. Only a few inches remained. She poured some into the bucket and added water. She scrubbed everything, even the refrigerator and oven handles. One of them might have rested a hand there. The baby might have coughed. She could spend an entire day going around, scouring those places the girls might come in contact with—toilet handles, doorknobs, banisters.

She glanced into the family room and saw Jacob sleeping in Shazia's arms. The baby curved into the girl's body, the round top of his head showing above the blanket, his small hand splayed against the front of her sweater. What if he had the flu? He might seem perfectly healthy now, but with every breath he could be expelling billions of lethal viruses. Shazia hummed as she rocked him in the chair. She wouldn't be so calm if he got sick. All the misery of a sick infant, the sudden spikes in temperature, the eyes squeezed shut, the clenched fists and stiff back, impossible to console. You couldn't put him down and back away. You had to hold him close and wait for the medicine to take effect. You had to watch.

Ann crushed granola bars into bowls, dropped in a handful of dried cranberries. She tapped out the remaining flakes of powdered milk and stirred in some water. It had been ages since they'd had fresh milk or cheese. She once read that to dogs humans smelled like sour milk. What did they all smell like now?

She carried the bowls upstairs and set the tray down on the nightstand. There was only one narrow lump in the bed. She sank down on the mattress. "Maddie."

Her daughter groaned and buried her head beneath the pillow.

Ann pulled the pillow from Maddie's grasp. "Sweetheart, wake up."

Maddie rolled over and blinked. Then she smiled up at Ann. "Morning, Mommy."

"Hi, honey. I brought you breakfast."

Maddie struggled to a seated position and took the bowl Ann held out. "Where'd Kate go?"

"She must be in the bathroom."

Maddie looked into her bowl. "What *is* this?"

"Cereal."

"It looks weird." But Maddie fished out a granola bit with her fingers. "We're not allowed to eat up here."

"Jacob might be sick," Ann said. "Remember? So until we know for sure, I want you girls to stay in here."

"So, we can't play with him?"

The first spark of hope she'd heard in Maddie's voice for days and here she was, quashing it. "No."

The light went out in Maddie's eyes. "For how long?"

"Until tomorrow morning." Ann reached over and tucked a strand of hair behind Maddie's ear. "I thought maybe we could make sock puppets today."

"What about Daddy?"

*Daddy can't come near you. He's a walking time bomb. Daddy's put you at risk, not to mention the rest of us.* She'd stood against the door and Peter had opened it. He knew the risks and he'd still brought the baby in. If the baby was sick, they'd all get it. There would be no escaping the virus then. "He went out for wood."

"It's really cold up here, Mommy."

"I know, honey." Ann pulled the blanket up around her daughter's shoulders. She'd never imagined a situation in which she'd be denying her daughters warmth. But there was no question about what was right. She never would have guessed that she'd turn her back on her best friend. Life was hard. Life demanded impossible choices. You never knew who you truly were until you had to make them. "The baby's littler. He needs to stay downstairs."

"I guess."

Kate shouldn't be taking so long. It had to be absolutely freezing in the bathroom. Kate should have scurried back to bed as soon as she was able. Maybe she was sick. Ann stood and almost ran to the bathroom door. She knocked. "Kate?"

There was no reply. She knocked again. "Kate?" She turned the knob and pushed the door wide open. Sunlight streamed into the tiled room, revealing the white sink and tub, the toilet beyond. Kate was nowhere to be seen.

Ann hurried back into the bedroom. Maddie had set her bowl down and was looking worried.

"Kate?" Ann called, going out into the hall. She checked the girls' bedrooms, their bathroom, even went down to the guest room. She ran down the hallway. "Shazia?"

"Yes?" Shazia came to the foot of the stairs, Jacob in her arms, and looked up at Ann. "What is it?"

"Is Kate down there?"

Shazia shook her head.

"I can't find her."

Shazia looked puzzled, then her expression cleared and something like guilt swept over her features. "Ah."

"What?"

"I heard the door close a few minutes ago. I thought it was Peter, returning. But when I went to check, no one was there."

"Kate's *gone*?"

Shazia bit her lip and bounced the baby in her arms. "Maybe."

# TWENTY-SEVEN

A N OLD MAN HUDDLED IN THE SHADOWS OF HIS FRONT porch. White-haired, a brown coat parted around a big gut, tan hunting cap with furred flaps. Peter lifted his hand in greeting.

The man leaned forward in his chair. "They making any food drops?"

His voice sounded thick with phlegm. Was he sick?

"I don't think so," Peter replied.

He couldn't remember the last time he'd heard the drone of a plane overhead. One of those small daily annoyances that he'd always taken for granted. He'd be happy enough to hear one now, though.

"The plows never did come."

"They never did." Peter looked at the man. "Are you alone?"

The man shook his head. "Everyone's asleep."

Still Peter hesitated. "You need me to bring you something?"

"Nah." The man sat back. "I'm good."

Straggly eskers of snow marked the passage of the sun as it slanted over the roofs. Peter trudged on, the sled scraping along the pavement behind him. It was a solitary feeling, pulling an empty sled.

He spotted a stick poking up from the grass beneath a gingko tree. It was small, more like a twig. Something to spear a marsh-mallow with, not something to warm yourself by. Still, he picked it up and placed it in the sled. Here was another one, lying across the path. It was pale green inside and tipped by buds. A young branch. Someone or something had torn it from the tree. He placed it in his sled. It'd have to dry before he could light it.

He followed the path into the woods.

The air felt good and clean. It forced the stuff up from his lungs. He coughed. They'd all been walking around in a haze of wood smoke. He smelled it on his daughters' hair, his clothes, the blankets they used at night. Ann tried to keep up with it, but he didn't mind it so much. It was a comforting smell, one that reminded him of the good part of his childhood. Every fall, his dad would take him and Mike up to the cabin to go hunting. At night, they'd build a bonfire and look out over the water. Their dad would start to talk. His voice would be scratchy after a day of not speaking.

They'd hear about the hills of Kentucky, blue with dawn, eight of them crammed into two rooms. Building the railroad through North Dakota, losing a thumb when the hammer skidded. Sailing to Europe on a transport ship at the end of the war and rescuing French maidens. Wrestling a bear in the Black Hills, made an honorary Navajo in Minnesota.

Peter and Mike recognized fiction blended with fact. The stories didn't matter. The sound of their father's voice did. How often had he told them a man is measured not by what he says but by what he does? He'd never once told Peter that he loved him. He'd just loaded up his old pickup and taken his boys out hunting.

Peter wandered deeper into the woods.

Sugar maple and black walnut, red oak and hickory. Cold and shadowy, a burst of sunlight across a clearing. The smell of wet earth and moldering leaves. He came to the creek bubbling over the rocks, the muddy bank dotted with coiled brown lumps of fern, stiff marsh grass, slick slabs of creamy gray limestone. A willow bush arched gracefully amid a cobweb of brown.

He snapped off a branch. It would look pretty in a vase on the kitchen table. Later, when the catkins had shriveled and dropped off, they'd use it for kindling.

From the narrow bridge, he could see down into the clear water and the pebbles that lined the bottom. There, just beyond the first curve, he spied a sizable branch half in, half out of the stream. He grasped the wood and tugged it free from its nest of vines. He raised a boot and stomped, breaking the stick into usable pieces. Enough to heat the room for fifteen minutes.

Here was another prize, a fat, knobby limb. It had the look of age, a white smear of mold along its side. It released a puff of decay. Enough to heat a can of soup. He swiped his face on his jacket sleeve.

A random series of turns and he found himself in a different neighborhood. The houses were large and set well back from the street. Peter glimpsed a covered swimming pool in the backyard of one, a pond in another. The Scioto ran behind these houses, a dark ribbon of water unspooling in the distance. Oaks and redbuds and locusts spread a canopy of branches across the avenue. These were mature trees, and they'd dropped dead limbs to the ground. A bonanza. He gathered all he could, quickly stacking them in the sled, taking care to pack them as close together as possible. He straightened.

Across the street, an iron fence ran along the road. The house behind it stood three stories tall and had stone archways, twin chimneys, a paved courtyard, tennis courts on one side. The heavy metal gate sagged crookedly across the driveway, bent in the middle as though something had rammed it from its moorings. It was a disturbing sight. Farther on, someone had painted a bold black circle onto the stone gatepost with a slash mark through it. It didn't appear to be a typical kind of graffiti. This symbol seemed to have some sort of purpose. He glanced around but saw no other evidence of vandalism other than the busted gate.

"They went away," someone said.

Peter spun on his heel and saw a little girl watching him from across the street. She looked about Maddie's age, with a similar disheveled appearance. He smiled at her.

She came closer, picking her way around the lumps of icy snow and beaten grass, coming up to the fence that bordered her yard. "The big truck took them." She curled her fingers around the metal bars. Her blond hair hung in straggles to her shoulders. She wore a white wool coat with a broad black fur collar. "If the truck comes, you have to let them in."

She must be talking about some sort of moving truck. Maybe the driver had overshot the entrance and accidentally rammed the gate. But that didn't explain the painted circle.

"I see," he said.

She studied him. "You're not allowed to come in. Mommy said."

He nodded. "Your mommy's right."

"Amelia!"

A woman came running down the wide lawn toward him. She came up to the girl and grabbed her arm and yanked her back. She crouched, ran her hands down the girl's coat. "Did you touch her?" she said to Peter. She gave Amelia a little shake. "Honey, did he come close to you?"

Peter said, "No, of course not."

She rose and glared at him. "Shame on you. You should know better."

The way she stood there, so pure and self-righteous, so sure in her conviction. And then the traitorous thought slithered in, forming itself before he could stop it—*just like Ann.*

What kind of person didn't rescue a baby?

# TWENTY-EIGHT

ANN RAN DOWN THE STREET, HER BOOTS SLIDING IN THE half-melted slick snow, her unzipped coat flapping, searching frantically for a glimpse of a slim girl in a bright red coat. "Kate!"

Past the burned-out house, no one there, just the terrain bumpy with black and broken things, past the Foxes' house with its Christmas display frozen in mid-frolic and looking ludicrous, looking so terribly sad, past Finn's house—Kate wouldn't have ventured anywhere near him—all the way down to the end of the street. Mr. Nguyen was out doing something to the side of his house. He merely shook his head at Ann's shouted question—no, he hadn't seen Kate—and went back to work.

Had one of Kate's friends come and picked her up, persuaded her parents that Kate had permission? Surely Ann would have heard the car. Surely, even inside the house, she would have heard the growl of a car engine. The sound would have seemed to split the air. Still, she ran out into the avenue and scanned both directions for a departing car. But there was nothing.

She turned all around, despairing. Then she thought, *the park.*

Ann ran the whole way, dodging the piles of snow along the curb, the trash, an abandoned bike. She made the final turn and the park spread out before her: the snowy field, the abandoned tennis courts, the playground, and yes! Kate, hunched on the swing, her head against the chain, pushing herself idly back and forth with the toe of one boot.

Ann halted by the stone pillars, not daring to believe Kate was truly there, alive and whole and *alone*. She put her hands on her knees and panted, trying to collect her breath. Her headstrong daughter. Thank God she had found her in time.

Kate didn't look up when Ann marched right up and stared down at her bent head.

"What were you thinking?"

Silence.

"I thought we'd talked about this. I thought you understood. My God, I was so worried." She wanted to shake her child, hard enough to rattle the words right out of her. She wanted to fling her arms around her and never let her go. "Kate. Talk to me."

Kate slowly swung back and forth.

"Are you okay?"

She looked okay. Had anyone else been here with her? Ann scanned the area, noted the heap of twisted cigarette butts beside the sandbox, saw with relief how dirty and soggy they were. They'd been there a while. The round metal trash can lay on its side by the water fountain, spilling black soot onto the slush. Someone had lit its contents on fire, but no smell of soot lingered. So that had been a while ago, too.

What was her daughter doing all the way out here in this deserted park?

Ann sat down on the swing beside her. She thought about what to say.

"Been a long time since I sat on one of these things. I can't say I miss it."

Kate had her hands folded in her lap. She wasn't wearing gloves, and her knuckles were white with the cold. Ann wanted to take her hands in hers.

"Remember how you wouldn't swing unless I sat on the swing beside you? My rear end would go numb and I'd walk funny all the way home."

Kate pushed her toe against the ground.

A car rolled slowly past on the street. Ann kept her gaze trained on it until it turned the corner and disappeared. Maddie had promised she'd stay in the bedroom. Shazia had nodded agreement: she wouldn't venture upstairs. She wouldn't let Jacob anywhere near Maddie. But Ann had seen the flicker of doubt in Shazia's eyes.

"The only thing worse was when you made me play in the sandbox. It wasn't enough for me to sit on the side like all the other moms. No, I actually had to get into the sandbox so you could make me into a castle or something." The sand would creep into her shoes, her socks, somehow even into her hair.

Leaves rotted inside that wooden box now. Every spring, the park people dumped fresh sand on top of the old. How many times had Ann dug down through the layers of sand with Kate's toy shovel and unearthed a cicada shell or a girl's little plastic barrette? It was like an archaeological dig.

The chains creaked as Kate swung back and forth.

A gust of cold, wet wind. Ann pulled the lapels of her coat closer about her neck. "Looks like they've finally fixed the slide. Thank goodness. That old one was so cracked, I was always afraid you were going to get hurt. I tried to talk you into going on the monkey bars or the whirligig, but you never did."

"I hated that slide."

Ann closed her eyes with relief. So Kate was going to talk. "I know. You just went down it to make me crazy."

Voices made them turn their heads. There by the tennis courts stood three figures, two women and a boy. They stopped, catching sight of Ann and Kate at the same moment. Ann held her breath, ready to grab Kate's hand. A long moment, then the older woman nodded, and the three of them turned and walked in the other direction. A minute later, they stepped off the path and vanished into the woods beyond.

They needed to get home. "Kate," Ann began, and Kate said, "I thought Libby was your friend."

Was that what this was about? "I know."

Their friendship was over. Ann didn't know what stood in its place. Even as she thought this, she knew better. Libby had been sick enough to risk everything. She'd been sick enough to wrap up her child and abandon him on a porch to freeze. Sick enough to leave him behind. That hadn't been the product of fever. That had been Libby seeing the future and trying to change the outcome. She took a deep breath. People *did* recover. Half of them survived.

"She asked me to do something I couldn't do, Kate. I wanted to, but I just couldn't." How could she make Kate understand that things weren't always black and white, that there were endless variations of gray? But Kate was thirteen, that jagged sliver of time between childhood and young adulthood. Thirteen-year-olds saw the world very clearly. People were good or mean or stupid. Things were right or they were wrong. There was no *maybe* about it.

"Dad did, and she wasn't even his friend. She didn't even like him."

Ann heard the confusion in Kate's voice. A bubble of anger rose to the surface. Peter had just gone ahead and brought the baby in. "I know."

Kate rolled her toe in the slush. "I would be there for *my* friends." Her breath fluttered out in a small white cloud.

"I know you would."

"Michele never did call."

It had been weeks since Kate last talked to her friend. "They must have left town."

"You always say that."

Maybe Ann did. But it was so much harder to think of the alternative. It was so much better to offer Kate hope than despair.

"She would've let me know," Kate said. "She would've put a note in the mailbox or something."

So that's why Kate had been constantly checking the mail. Ann had thought it had been searching for contact from the outside world, but instead it had been from one very small piece of it. Michele.

Kate said, "She hated that slide, too."

Ann smiled, remembering the two girls at the top of the curving yellow slide, arguing over who had to go first. "But she still went down anyway."

"She was my best friend."

"We don't know, Kate. Michele could be perfectly fine."

"No one is." Kate leaned her head against the chain of the swing. "I've been waiting, but no one came."

"Your friends have been meeting here?"

Kate gave her a sidelong glance. "Some of them."

Ann tightened her grip on the chains. She'd come so close. Kate could have caught up with them. "Let's drive over to Michele's house. We can honk the horn and see if someone comes to the door."

"And what if no one does?"

"Then we'll check Scooter's house, and Claire's . . ."

Kate was shaking her head. "Stop it, Mom." Her voice was weary. "You can't fix everything."

No, Ann couldn't fix everything. Some things were completely out of her grasp. Some things were just broken forever.

"Listen." Ann turned her swing so she was facing Kate. Their knees gently bumped. "You can't do this again." She tilted Kate's chin up, forcing her daughter to look at her. "Got it?"

After a moment Kate said, "All right."

She'd never survive losing another child. Never.

# TWENTY-NINE

PETER UNSCREWED THE JAR OF BABY FOOD. JACOB SAT in Shazia's lap, watching Peter's every move. Ann knelt at the hearth, holding the pot over the flames, crouched as far away from him and Shazia as she reasonably could.

Peter dipped in the spoon and captured a smear of creamed carrot.

Shazia bounced the baby on her lap. "Open up," she commanded. "Yummy, yummy."

Obediently, Jacob took the spoonful and swallowed. Carrot dribbled down his chin.

"Did you see anyone, Peter?" Shazia said, wiping his face.

"A little girl."

"And?" Ann rocked back on her heels. Her cheeks were flushed from the heat of the fire.

"And her mother came and got her. I barely got within ten feet of her." Ann's vigilance was relentless. It strained against him.

Jacob reached out a chubby hand toward the spoon filled with food.

Shazia caught his wrist. "No, no, baby."

Maddie's voice floated down the stairs. "Can I *please* come down?"

"I told you, Maddie. Not until tomorrow." Ann carried the pot to the counter. She spooned out the bits of chicken and dropped them in the girls' bowls. She'd added an extra can of water, too. The result would be more the idea of soup than the reality.

"But there's nothing to do up here. Kate's still sleeping. And I'm so *bored.*"

"It's almost dinnertime. We can play cards afterward."

"Why can Daddy be with Jacob and we can't?"

Ann set the pot down. "Because."

Jacob swatted the spoon held too long before him and chortled at the answering spray. Shazia grasped the baby's hand. "No, no."

Ann put on her coat and tugged down her hat. Lifting the bag of trash from where it leaned against the cabinet, she unlocked the sliding glass door and stepped outside. Wintry air sliced inside, then vanished as she closed the door again.

"Jacob seems fine," Shazia said to Peter. "Maybe his mother was telling the truth."

"Maybe." Ann had refused to consider that possibility. She knew what it was like to bury a child. How could she be so willing to let another mother bury hers?

"She and Ann are good friends?" Shazia said.

Since the day they moved in and Libby had come over to welcome them with a plate of scorched brownies. "Ann is Jacob's godmother."

He'd stood in the back of the church, having been invited by Smith, and watched Ann as she took the baby from Libby at the altar. The sadness in her expression had been impossible to bear. He'd turned and slipped away.

"That explains the way she looks at him."

The compassion in Shazia's voice was clear. He looked at her. "Don't tell me you agree with what she did."

Shazia shrugged and swiped a cloth across the baby's chin again. "Ann's a mother. I don't know what that's like."

Was this a glimmer of female bonding? Peter would have never expected it. Shazia had always been so logical, driven more by the objective rather than by the subjective. Give her facts, not feelings.

He'd never imagined that she and Ann might share a common perspective.

The sliding glass door opened again. "Peter, would you come here?"

Ann stood in the doorway. She sounded upset. Wearily, he stood and handed the spoon to Shazia. Lifting his jacket from the hook, he slipped it on and pulled his gloves from the pockets. He stepped outside and closed the door. "What?"

She pointed to the ground.

He followed the rigid line of her finger to the two bowls lying on the pavers just beneath the apron of the grill cover.

"You're kidding me, right?" she said.

"I only gave him the things we didn't eat." She reminded him so much of his father. His dad had had the same look of disappointment when he caught Peter undoing the traps he'd set.

"What didn't we eat, Peter? Name one thing. Today I gave the girls crackers with mustard for lunch." Her voice caught. "And they ate them."

He looked at her, her lips chapped, her hair combed back into a messy ponytail. He thought of her picking out the bits of chicken and placing them in the girls' soup bowls. She'd play games with the girls to make sure they finished every drop. She'd do what she could to make sure no one noticed her own bowl was half-empty.

He put out his hand. "Ann, I didn't mean what I said. You are a good mother."

She jerked back. "It's always been like this for us."

"No, it hasn't. Don't you remember?"

"I wasn't enough. Our children weren't enough. Our life together wasn't enough."

"It wasn't that. I got so tired of being unhappy. You deserve to be happy, too."

She jammed her hands in her pockets. "Just . . . stop."

He knew what she was thinking about, what she always was thinking about. "You know I don't blame you."

He'd told her this a million times. But it didn't matter. She blamed herself. Nothing he said would ever change that. Her guilt took her to a faraway place, out of his reach. Her guilt had made strangers of them.

She shook her head, her lips pressed tightly together. "You can't be here anymore. You left, and you should have stayed away. Together, we just don't work. We make everything worse."

"Ann," he tried, but she wasn't listening.

"We don't know how long this quarantine will last." Her face was white. "But you need to think about where you can go."

After William died, she couldn't bear to go near the nursery. They kept the door shut for months. One day he'd come home early from work and found Kate napping in her room. He'd followed the quiet rustling noises down the hall to the nursery, where the door stood wide open. Ann was inside, kneeling by the bureau, folding tiny white undershirts and little blue sleepers into boxes. He had stood there in the doorway watching her, worried at the furious way she was emptying the drawers. She'd caught sight of him standing there and rocked back on her heels to look up at him. "I can't live here anymore, Peter. We need to move."

He'd phoned Liederman the next morning, got the job offer in Columbus the next month. At the time, he thought she was running away from the memory. Now he realized she'd been running away from him.

"You want me to explain to the girls?" he said.

"Yes."

# THIRTY

---

THE RAIN STARTED IN THE MIDDLE OF THE NIGHT.
Ann had always loved the steady pattering against the panes. Her moody Irish heritage, her mother used to say. Everything washed clean and new, all the dirty ridges of snow rinsed down the storm drains. The streets would gleam like silver ribbons. The trees would be brighter. The grass might show some green instead of dreary ochre. Bushes would be coaxed to bud pink and yellow and white. The crocuses might poke through. The cold would ease. The girls could bathe in a real tub instead of shivering before the sink. Everyone could take off a layer and move more normally. A break before the rest of the winter roared back.

The house creaked.

One flight of steps separated her from Peter. It might as well have been a mountain range. She had no idea what time it was. After midnight, probably. The room bore the solid darkness of predawn hours. She punched her pillow into shape. The material was icy against her cheek.

*You know I don't blame you.*

His leaving would be so hard on the girls. There would be tears, questions, accusations. It would feel as raw as the first time he'd left.

A second creak, longer this time. Someone was up and walking around downstairs, treading over and over the same spot in the kitchen. She heard a weak cry. The baby. She sat up. Was Jacob sick?

Someone stood in the dark kitchen. The figure turned. Shazia. "Something's wrong with the baby," she whispered.

"Does he feel hot?" Ann said softly.

The baby whimpered.

"No."

"Has he been sneezing or—"

"No. I think it's just baby stuff. Oh, Ann, I don't know."

The baby rubbed his face against the girl's shoulder. Ann saw that and knew. The relief made her knees weak. Jacob was fine.

"He's hungry." The incubation period was over. And all they had was a hungry, sleepy baby.

"But he had dinner."

Libby had been trying to wean him from his midnight bottle. Ann didn't know how far along she'd gotten in the process. But this was definitely hungry behavior.

"Try his pacifier." Ann reached for the can of formula on the counter and pressed the can opener into the metal. How many ounces would he need? She tried to remember how many Libby had been giving Jacob at his feedings, somewhere between six and eight ounces. Six, she decided. They'd need to conserve every ounce. Who knew when they'd get more? She held the bottle up, trying to see in the gloom, and twisted the nipple onto it.

Shazia sat rocking the baby in the living room, trying to push a pacifier into his mouth. Every time Jacob opened his mouth to tongue it out again, Shazia shoved it back in. "He reminds me of my nephew," she said softly. "Such a temper."

The longing in her voice was plain. "Would you like to feed him?"

"I think he wants you." Shazia stood and ladled the soft, squirming baby into Ann's arms.

"Hey, buddy." Ann clasped him tight and settled herself on the chair.

Jacob opened his mouth wide. The pacifier dropped. She pushed the bottle's nipple in. His lips clamped on and his eyes opened. He stared at her. As if unwilling, he gave a tentative suck. His eyes drifted shut and his body relaxed. She rocked, listening to the sound of the rain, loving the simple joy of feeding a baby. She brought him closer to her, bent and kissed his warm, downy forehead, breathed in that delicious baby smell. Innocence. She rubbed her cheek against the top of his head, slipped a forefinger into his hand, and felt his fingers tighten around hers.

Shazia sat down on the couch opposite. "Does the rain mean winter is over?"

"No, unfortunately. We sometimes have these warmer spells. They don't last long. It could snow again tomorrow."

Shazia shuddered. "Don't even say it. I never want to see snow again. I don't care if I never go sledding."

Over Jacob's head, they shared a smile.

Shazia lifted her feet and tucked them beneath her. "In Egypt, our biggest problems are sandstorms. You can't possibly be outside in one of those."

"I've never been there. I've studied the art, though. I'd love to see it in person."

"You should go in February. That's the best time of year."

February was only weeks away. Ann imagined it, wandering along warm, sun-baked streets with a gorgeous azure sky above, her girls running and laughing as they discovered one miraculous sight after another.

"I can't bear it."

Ann lifted her head and saw Shazia staring out the window.

"I just can't, Ann."

Ann felt a rush of sympathy for this stoic young girl who'd uttered not one single word of complaint. "Oh, Shazia. I know. It won't be for much longer." The same words she used with the girls, the same soothing tone. "You're just having the middle-of-the-night blues." Ann knew what that was like. She'd paced this house a million times, despairing, waiting for the sun.

"I don't know what to do. Peter's gotten so strange, too. Have you noticed? After that house burned down . . . he doesn't talk."

Peter had been the same way after William's death. If he did talk, it was about the inconsequential things. Maybe they could get another year out of the car. Maybe Kate would like to see that play, the one with the dancing mushrooms. "We're all feeling the strain. We just need to hang on. You know that as well as anyone."

"That's what makes it so much harder, Ann. I know this is just the first wave. How can we possibly survive two more waves of this?"

"We can't think like that. We can only go one day at a time." Ann was rocking harder. Jacob gave a small mew of protest. "Sorry, baby," she murmured. "Sorry."

"My grandfather died last year. He suffered for weeks, refusing water and food. He didn't recognize us. He cried out to ghosts only he could see. He shriveled and became a stranger. It was a relief when he finally . . . just . . . stopped." Shazia was crying now. Ann could hear it in her voice.

Ann needed Peter to wake up. She glanced at him, but he was lost in a sea of blankets. Could she reach him with her foot? The baby reached up and batted her chin. She caught his fingers in hers and held them to her lips.

"I saw my best friend die, too." Shazia swiped at her cheeks with her fingers. "A motorcycle ran onto the sidewalk and hit her. One moment she was alive and talking to me about a boy we both liked and the next moment she was gone. She was eleven."

Ann and Libby used to talk about everything—relationships, motherhood, whether true happiness was real. They'd taken their friendship for granted. They hadn't stepped out of the way of tragedy, either.

"Tell me, Ann. Which do you think is the better way to die?"

Ann put the baby to her shoulder and rubbed his back. He wriggled his head into the crook of her neck just the way William used to, his breath coming in soft little feathers. She pressed him close. A sudden death was the worst way, she knew. "Oh, Shazia," she said, helpless.

Rain streaked the glass and puddled on the sill. A silvery light seeped into the room. Dawn was coming. Ann could see the outline of Shazia's profile, the curve of her cheek, the slope of her shoulders.

"Peter said he is leaving in the morning." The girl's voice was low. "I'd like to go with him."

It sounded like she was asking Ann's permission. Of course, it wasn't hers to give. She couldn't bless Shazia's relationship with Peter. She didn't even want to. "Where will you stay?"

"The dorm. I'm sure something's opened up there by now."

"You can't possibly do that. It wouldn't be at all safe. You know that." Ann resettled the baby and fitted the bottle back into his mouth. He looked up at her with wide, trusting eyes. It had been so long. She kissed the top of his head. "This is your home now, Shazia." It was the truth. "Besides, your parents think you're here."

"My parents expect me to take care of myself."

What a strange thing to say. Ann looked at her. "What is it, Shazia? What happened?"

Shazia shrugged and gazed out the window at the lashing ropes of rain. Her hands remained folded in her lap.

"Shazia?"

But the girl refused to meet her gaze.

Ann found herself staring at the girl's cupped fingers. Shazia had picked at her food for weeks. All that crying behind closed doors. All that endless napping, her studying the calendar when she thought no one was watching. The pieces rushed together into one telling whole. Ann caught her breath.

Shazia was pregnant.

Then . . . who was the father?

Ann shifted her gaze to Peter.

# THIRTY-ONE

---

MADDIE LEANED AGAINST THE LAUNDRY ROOM DOOR and thumped the back of her heel against the wood. "But I don't *want* you to go."

Peter rolled up a pair of jeans and shoved them into his duffel bag. "I won't be far, honey. I'll just be a few minutes away."

Twenty minutes or ten miles. Somewhere along the way he'd stop and get some supplies. He might chance upon an open grocery store, or perhaps a convenience store. Even a gas station would do. There were several between here and his place. He didn't need much. He could manage a long time on peanut butter and candy bars. If those didn't pan out, well, surely he'd figure something out. He zipped the bag shut and glanced over at Maddie. She had her mouth turned down and was blinking rapidly to keep the tears back. He came over, knelt, and took her small hands in his. "As soon as I get settled, you can come for a visit."

"Why can't I come now?"

Kate spoke from the doorway. "Because he doesn't want you to."

Peter looked up. Kate's face was pinched white with anger. "Kate," he began, but she whirled around and stormed off. A moment later he heard her say something, heard Ann's muted reply.

"Is that true, Daddy?"

He gripped Maddie's hands tightly. It had been hard enough leaving them the first time. He looked into her eyes. "Of course I want you and Kate to stay with me, but you've seen my place."

She pushed out her lower lip. "It only has one bed."

"Right. I have to get things set up. Hey, I have an idea. Why don't you draw me another picture to put up on my walls? How about a sunset?"

She kicked the door some more, then slipped her hands from his grasp and trudged off.

Peter pushed in a shirt and zipped the duffel closed, then dumped the bag on the floor outside the laundry room.

Ann glanced up from where she sat on the couch, Jacob on her lap. Kate sat hunched and scowling on one side of her, Maddie on the other, her box of markers opened in front of her.

"I think that's everything." Peter picked up Jacob's blanket, his teething ring and picture book with the gnawed corners.

"You're not planning to take the baby?" Ann said.

He straightened and looked over at her. It was a strange thing to see Jacob in her arms. All babies looked alike, soft and sweet and generally bald, but there was something about the way she was holding him that made Peter think of William. Maybe it was the blue cap fitted onto the round little head. Maybe it was the way she held his little hands in hers. "Well, sure."

Maddie lifted her head from her drawing. "That's not fair, Daddy."

Kate said, "What about when Libby comes back for him?"

Ann glanced at Kate. "Right. Jacob should stay here."

He looked at her with surprise. All those memories that Jacob had to be churning up for her, too—was she truly ready to wade through them and take care of the baby for who knew how long?

Maddie scowled. "If you're taking Jacob, you have to take me, too."

"Now *that's* a good idea," Kate said.

"Shut up," Maddie said. "Please, Daddy."

He rested his hand on Maddie's head and kept his gaze trained on Ann. "You sure?"

Jacob rocked back and forth in Ann's lap, and she lifted him up to stand on her knees. He chortled with glee and clapped his chubby hands together. She pressed her cheek to the top of his head and looked at him. "I'm sure."

Something had changed for her. He wondered when.

Maddie was looking from Ann to him. "Does that mean you're still going?"

"That's right, honey." He set down the things in his hands and glanced at the fireplace. "But I think I'll scrounge up some firewood first. You guys are pretty low."

Ann shook her head. "You shouldn't be on the road when it's dark."

"That's hours away. I have time."

"Kate, take Jacob, please." Ann kissed the baby and placed him in Kate's lap, then stood. "Can we talk for a minute, Peter?" She led the way into the den and closed the door. "Shazia wants to go with you."

He was surprised. "Really?" She hadn't said anything to him. In fact, he wasn't even certain where she was right now. He'd been looking for a chance to talk to her before he left, but she'd made herself scarce all morning. Last he remembered, she'd been closeted in the upstairs bathroom.

"I don't think she should."

"Agreed." He wasn't at all comfortable leaving Ann alone to care for the children. It was safer for all of them if Shazia stayed. "I'll talk to her."

"She's made up her mind."

Was Shazia worried she'd outstayed her welcome? "She's a smart girl. She'll listen to reason."

Ann had her hands on her hips and was staring at the floor. "Peter." She breathed in some air and let it out. She brought her gaze up and looked at him. "I know about the baby."

"Okay." He said it slowly. "The baby's healthy. Just like Libby said."

She shook her head. "Not Jacob. Shazia's baby."

"Shazia has a baby?" He stared at her. Shazia had gone straight from college to graduate school. When had she found time to start a family? And why hadn't she once mentioned it? And where was this child? Ann had to be mistaken.

"She's going to," Ann said grimly.

"She's pregnant?" He stared at her, dumbfounded. "She told you that?"

"She didn't have to."

He scrubbed the back of his neck. Jesus. Now what? "How far along is she?"

"Early. I'd say first trimester. She's barely showing."

All the risks Shazia had taken. He'd never have allowed her to work with the die-off samples if he'd known. "Why didn't she tell me?"

"I don't know the answer to that, Peter." She crossed her arms. "But I bet that's why she wants to go with you."

He nodded. "I'll talk to her," he said again. Shazia was pregnant. That changed everything.

THE RAIN WENT ON, AN IRRITABLE DRIZZLE THAT SWITCHED from sleet to water to sleet again. Peter was thoroughly soaked by the time he arrived home. He spread the wet branches on the floor of the garage, stripped off his coat and hat, and hung them over the handlebars of the wheelbarrow.

Ann stood at the sink, washing dishes. She wore layers of clothes, all somber colors that covered every inch of her but her head and fingers. Still, she looked cold. She glanced over at him. "Any luck?"

"Everything's too wet to burn. I left the wood in the garage to dry. I checked next door. No one answered."

She turned off the water and picked up a dishtowel. "Did you look in the windows?"

"I walked all around. The fire's out in their family room, but there's candlelight coming from upstairs."

"Okay." She exhaled. "That's good."

"It's getting dark. I'd better go soon."

She nodded.

Maddie and Kate sat before the fire with Jacob, Shazia cross-legged beside them. They were playing some sort of game that involved running a toy truck through the folds of the blankets. Jacob chortled and smacked his hands down, leaning forward and almost toppling over.

"Whoa," Kate said, grabbing his shirt. "Look, Jacob. Look at the truck."

Peter had a sudden flash of little Kate leaning over William's crib, reaching out to make the mobile dance. "Look, baby," she'd said. "Look at all the pretty flutter-byes."

Maddie glanced up at Peter. She'd been crying, her eyes swollen and pink. "Why do you have to go, Daddy?"

"That's what Dad does," Kate said. "He leaves."

That pierced him to the core. Was that what she really thought? And was she wrong? "Kate," he said, but she refused to meet his eyes.

"Jakey," she said instead, "don't you want your truck?"

"Stop, Kate," Maddie said. "I had that first."

"Don't be such a baby."

Ann had come in behind him. This protracted leave-taking was agonizing for all of them. Better to just go. He glanced at the fireplace. The fat log he'd wrestled onto the grate just that morning was now a smoldering lump, just a few flames licking its surface. He could already feel the chill gathering in the room. "That fire's going to go out pretty soon."

"It's getting late, Peter," Ann said, worry in her voice.

Shazia started to rise. "Peter?"

"I know we need to talk," he said to her. "Let me work on the fire first, okay?"

Shazia sank back down. "All right." Her tone was puzzled. She knew something was up.

He still hadn't decided how to broach the subject with her. How did you talk about something like that? *So, I hear you're going to have a baby.*

The flashlight was in the server drawer with the candles. He pushed the button, checked the light.

The basement was dark; the feeble daylight barely penetrated through the small windows set high. He shone the beam of light around the storage room. He couldn't use anything precious. Not the disassembled crib upright in pieces against the wall or his father's battered Army trunk. Nothing painted. It might release toxic fumes. So Maddie's dresser was out, unless he manually sanded the white paint off first. That would take a while, though, and there wasn't much daylight left. He held the flashlight beam steady on his parents' old oak dining room set. That might work, though he'd have to saw it up into usable pieces. The beam of light played over something that threw back pointy shadows at him. The stack of Ann's frames. So many that she'd never used. Some of them were gilded. None of those would do. He came closer and something squelched beneath his shoe. He backed up and directed the flashlight beam to the floor. What now?

He was standing in a puddle. He cast the beam upward. No rusty filigree traced the ceiling tiles. The water wasn't coming from there. Back to the floor, where a faint line spidered the outline of where the water had stood for a while then retreated, leaving dampness behind. The puddle shimmered.

He went upstairs. "Ann?"

She turned around from the kitchen sink.

"We have a problem."

She frowned at the flashlight in his hand and reached for the faucet.

"When was the last time you were in the basement?"

She snapped off her rubber gloves. "Two days ago, I guess. I was looking for games for the girls."

He held the flashlight beam on the stairs so she wouldn't stumble. She followed him into the utility room.

She stopped and stared at the puddle, then started to laugh. "What's next, a plague of locusts?"

A smile twisted his mouth. "I was thinking the same thing."

She pushed her hair back from her face with the flats of her hands. "How did this happen?"

"It's the rain. With the sump pump off, all that water has nowhere to go. We've got to move everything out and mop the floor."

Together, they worked the dresser through the doorway of the utility room and into the main room beyond. The flashlight lay on top, rolling this way and that and throwing up crazy angles of light. The trunk, heavy with the smell of mildew. The tall mirror, the old lamps, the rolled-up rugs. Now the cartons, the cardboard soft and crumbling.

"All our books," she said sadly.

Not all of them. But her old books, the ones she'd been saving for the girls, and the old board books that he knew she'd been saving for future grandchildren.

"At least the Christmas ornaments are okay." He pulled the plastic bin away from the wall.

"What's that?"

He was carrying out an armload of curtains. "Hmm?"

"That humming noise." Ann straightened. "What is it?"

"Mom?"

"Hold on," Ann called.

Now he heard it. He turned around, searching for the source.

Ann said, "I think it's coming from over here."

She walked to the corner by the sump pump. Peter went over and looked down.

"It's working," she said. "Maybe it's on battery power."

Sure enough, he could see the water moving at the base of the pipe. "Could be. Maybe something came loose and we accidentally pushed it back into place."

"But we haven't been over here yet."

There was a sudden burst of light. Blinking, he turned to see Kate in the doorway, hand on the light switch.

"Look." Sudden darkness, sudden brightness. Kate stood there, hope naked and shining on her face. "Does this mean it's over?"

# THIRTY-TWO

A NN PRESSED THE CHANNEL BUTTON, SKIPPING PAST faces, test patterns, and bright colors.

"Hold on." Maddie sat cross-legged with the baby in her lap. "I like that show."

"In a minute. Kate, find my cell phone and plug it in."

Here was CNN. Ann stood back. The regular anchorman was gone, replaced by someone Ann didn't recognize, an older man who kept clearing his throat and looking offscreen. What was he saying, something about riots? She watched jerky footage of a military vehicle rolling past the Watergate Hotel. She recognized the place instantly. She'd driven past it a million times on her way to the Kennedy Center. She'd gotten her wedding cake from the bakery on the first floor. Now below the familiar curving line of windows was the strange sight of running people and burning cars. The camera halted and showed a man cracking a bat through a store window, glass splintering everywhere.

It was impossible to gauge what was going on from what she was seeing. Words scrolled across the bottom of the screen. A fire raged uncontrolled in Hong Kong. New York City was storing its dead on barges. A governor had committed suicide. A preacher had convinced his congregation, all two hundred of them, to swallow cyanide. This was all happening now? Kate had come close and was reading the same things she was. Ann reached for the channel button. "Did you plug in my phone?"

"Uh-huh," Kate said. "It says, 'searching for service.'"

The system could come back on at any moment. "Keep an eye on it for me, will you?"

"Okay." Then Kate said with sudden urgency, "I'll be right back. I've got to see who's online."

Ann stopped at a cartoon. "Here you go."

"I've already seen that one," Maddie said, but she scooted over with Jacob in her lap. "Look, Jakey. TV."

In the den, Peter and Shazia tapped away at their laptops. Ann was glad to see the relaxed concentration on the girl's face. Whatever demons plagued her now seemed quieted.

"Based on the numbers, though, wouldn't you say we're cresting?" Shazia leaned back in her chair.

First trimester, all right, though it was hard to be certain given all the layers the girl was wearing. That meant she'd conceived sometime in early fall. She'd just arrived at Peter's lab. It must have been instant attraction. Right after that, Peter had asked for a divorce. The shock on his face when Ann told him about the baby had seemed genuine. Ann felt guilty being the one to tell him.

"If the numbers are right," Peter said.

Ann turned on the desktop computer and reached for the button on the monitor. It buzzed to life. Four hundred eighty-seven messages sat in her mailbox, most of them junk. She rapidly weeded out the discounted mortgage rates, insurance quotes, bookstore coupons, offers to cure male impotence and hair loss—special deals on air purifiers and UV lights that promised to kill the flu virus on contact—and scanned the few personal notes remaining. Nothing from Beth. She was probably somewhere without power. That was the only reason her sister wouldn't have written. *Not the only reason,* whispered a little voice. But Ann couldn't think about that.

Peter said, "UCLA's got something on a vaccine."

"I see it," Shazia said.

They were all hunched over their individual keyboards. Ann

typed a message. She didn't bother to check spelling or punctuation. *Beth—we're fine. Please write ASAP. Love you.* She punched the Send button.

Crossing to the dining room, she turned the thermostat dial. A click, then a whoosh, as the heat came on. The sound was so wonderful, it brought tears to her eyes. She flicked on lights as she went, pushing back the gloom of the rainy day that pressed against the windows. Each pop of light felt like a small victory. She scooped up the sleeping bags and sheets from in front of the TV. Maddie scooted over to let her pull an end free. Kate sat at the kitchen table, her laptop opened before her.

"Who's online?" Ann asked.

"Everyone but Michele and Hilary. No one's talked to them."

Hilary. Ann recalled a bright blonde who giggled at everything and worked once with Kate on a social studies project. Every teenager who was able was plugged into a computer right now, and still no word from Michele. Ann came up behind Kate and put her hand on her daughter's shoulder. She looked down at the screen, at all the white rectangles there, popping up one on top of another. "What's everyone saying?"

"Claire's at her uncle's house. John's got a bunch of strangers living in his basement. Scooter's mom got sick, but she's better now."

*Really? Sick how?* "Ask him what her symptoms were."

"Mom, that's weird. I don't want to do that."

Ann went into the laundry room and shoved sleeping bags into the washer, slammed the door shut, poured in detergent, and set the dial. Water sprayed across the washer window. It was all so lovely. Things were getting clean. The lights were on. Heat was beginning to seep through the vents. No more filthy fireplace and murky splatters of candle wax. No more feeling their way around corners at dusk.

In the kitchen, she pulled out the coffeemaker from beneath the counter. *Hello, old friend.* She tapped the remaining grinds from the bag into the filter, poured in water, and pressed the button. An answering hiss. The kettle went on the stove.

She pulled down the dishes and loaded the dishwasher. Everything was going to go through the sani-cycle. She pushed the button. A low churning sounded. Who'd have thought such a simple noise could be so thrilling? "As soon as the water heats up, I want both of you in the shower."

"Scooter's mother was throwing up a lot," Kate said. "They think it was something she ate. Thanks for making me ask, Mom."

Her voice sounded so much lighter. It was good for her to be on-line again, good for her to be chatting with her friends. Maybe one of them would know what was going on with Michele.

Ann glanced at Maddie sitting transfixed before the television set. She looked content. In a little while, Ann would roust her and suggest that she email Hannah.

The delicious aroma of coffee warmed the room. Ann couldn't wait for the coffeemaker to finish brewing. She pulled out the pot, poured an inch into her mug, and sipped. Weak—she'd been sparing with the grounds—but definitely coffee. She took another sip. The house was beginning to fill with heat. She could feel her muscles relax. She'd had no idea she'd been holding herself so stiffly.

Her gaze fell to the floor. In the brightness of the overhead light, she could now clearly see the scuffed brown footprints and the streaks of soot along the walls. Everything needed a good scrubbing.

The washer beeped, signaling the end of the cycle. She pulled long, sopping nylon sleeping bags out of the washer and forced them into the dryer. Now a load of towels. She mopped the floor. As soon as she was done, she was going to scrub her hair and blow it dry. The house hummed with busy noise. She hadn't realized how muted her world had grown.

On her way through the kitchen, she picked up her cell phone from the counter. The tiny lighthouse swept its beacon from side to side. Still no connection. The towers must be out.

The coffeemaker wheezed behind her. She filled two mugs, made a cup of tea, and carried them into the den. "Anything more on the vaccine?"

"Thanks," Peter said as she set his mug down on the desk. "I've emailed people at Hopkins and Harvard, but I haven't heard back yet."

Shazia was typing, her gaze on the laptop screen. Had Peter

convinced her to stay? Ann would have to find an oblique way to encourage her to start taking multivitamins. There was a bottle in the cabinet. Not prenatal vitamins, of course, but they were better than nothing.

She put down the mug of tea. "Here you go, Shazia. It's decaf."

Shazia moved the mouse and the MapQuest image slid away. "Thank you."

Peter lifted his mug and sipped. "I sent Mike a message, but Mom's nursing home is offline. And I can't get through to the bank."

The last time Ann had talked to her sister-in-law had been three weeks before. Bonni had said Mike was okay, just out of range. Whatever that meant.

It wasn't too alarming about the nursing home. They probably had more important things on their hands right now than checking their email. But the bank was another story. "Do you think they're shut down?"

"I don't know. I keep trying to access our accounts, but the system's frozen. I have to keep rebooting."

"Maybe too many people are trying to get in."

"That's got to be it."

Shazia still hadn't reached for her mug.

"Everything okay?" Ann said.

"I don't know." Shazia sounded confused. "There's a note here from my cousin. She says my parents didn't make it to my brother's."

Peter lowered his mug.

"And my nephew is sick."

"Oh, Shazia," Ann said.

"But that was a week ago. I don't know anything more." She reached for her cup. "There's a message from Harold."

The name sounded familiar, one of Peter's students Shazia had mentioned the other day. Ann glanced at Peter, who was looking interested.

"Floyd?" he said.

Shazia nodded. "He's been on a farm. He's learning how to milk a cow." She smiled. "Can you picture it?"

A farm. That would have been a good place to stay. Fields of food, milk, no one around for miles.

Ann went to pull out armfuls of heated sleeping bags from the dryer. She dumped them on the family room floor. "You two spread these out to finish drying, okay? I'm going to put the towels in now."

Slowly, both girls moved toward the pile.

Ann was making her bed when she heard the baby fussing downstairs. She went out to the landing and called down, "Is Jacob okay?"

"Yeah," Kate called back.

"Have you checked his diaper?"

"Ew."

"Don't forget your showers."

The house was so toasty. She was going barefoot, digging her toes into the plush of the carpet. She folded clothing, fragrant and still warm from the dryer. She took Shazia's things and laid them on her bed. At some point Shazia would be unable to wear her regular size. They could sew inserts into some of her looser pants. Shazia could wear Peter's shirts.

Ann placed the last of Kate's jeans in the dresser and pushed the drawer closed. Everything in the house had been scoured clean. She'd heard the girls troop up the stairs for their showers and heard them go back down again. Now it was her turn.

She came out into the hall and heard the baby crying fitfully. "Girls, what's going on down there?"

"We don't know," Maddie called back.

He was probably hungry.

Maddie sat on the floor of the family room, trying to hold Jacob on her lap. She had his toys spread out in front of him, but he kept batting her hands away and sobbing.

Kate was at the kitchen table, tapping at her laptop.

"Give him his pacifier, Maddie, and I'll heat up a bottle. Guess what, Jacob? You get warm milk today." She opened cabinets. Where had Peter put the baby's stuff? Not in the cabinet. There was nothing in the pantry. The counters were bare. She frowned. "Kate, where's the formula?"

"I don't know."

Here were two solitary jars of baby food but no tall cans of formula.

She lifted the baby from Maddie. Walking with him to the den, she halted in the doorway. "Peter, where's the formula?"

He stood staring down at a paper in his hand. "In the pantry."

"Oh," Shazia said. "I used the last of a can this morning."

The baby was arching in Ann's arms, wailing. Peter was focused on what he was reading. He needed to stop paying attention to whatever he was doing and start worrying about what was going on right here, right now. "Peter," she said sharply.

He glanced up. His face was blank.

"Jacob's hungry."

He blinked, then frowned.

So there wasn't any more formula. The look on Peter's face told her he'd just realized it, too.

# THIRTY-THREE

W HAT ABOUT POWDERED MILK?" PETER SAID.
Ann shook her head. "There are only two jars of baby food. After that, it's sugar water."

Jacob rubbed his face against her shoulder. Ann patted his back and murmured in his ear.

Peter folded the paper in his hand and tucked it into his pocket. He'd find a way to tell Ann about its contents later, when they could grab a few quiet minutes alone. He went to the den window. The rain was slashing down. "Do you think they have any more?"

Ann came up to stand behind him.

The porch light next door burned through the mist. There was a faint glow from an upstairs window.

"The lights are on," Peter said.

"They came on with the power," Ann said.

They looked at each other. *Of course.* "The stores are probably open," Peter said, deciding.

"Do you really think so?"

"I'll go check."

Ann nodded and stepped back, biting her lower lip, holding the baby and bouncing him. "We need baby food, too."

"Got it." He shrugged on his coat. "I'll be as quick as I can."

A LONG LINE OF PEOPLE STOOD AGAINST THE WALL. BEHIND them, light shone around the planks of plywood nailed here and there across the windows. The store was open.

Peter found an empty spot along the back, then got out of the truck and hurried through the cold drizzle.

Two men stood at the store entrance, arms crossed. Men and women, some children, huddled in their coats and hooded jackets, like moths drawn by the light. Many of them wore masks. No one looked at him. It felt strange to see a crowd, especially one that was so quiet. Peter pulled up his mask and joined them.

"Do they still have anything in there?" he said to the woman in front of him.

She turned. She was round and dark-skinned, with a red bandanna stretched across her nose and mouth. The only thing that was doing was keeping her face warm. Above the fold of cloth, Peter saw her eyebrows pinch together in a frown.

"I don't know," she said. "I'm out here, aren't I?"

He tried to see around the lengths of wood fitted across the glass. Was there enough of everything in there for all these people out here? He looked back to the line. There had to be at least sixty people in front of him. "How come we're not moving?"

"They're letting people in five at a time. I been waiting an hour already." She crossed her arms as if to say, *Don't even think about butting in front of me.*

Time passed. People drifted into place behind him. Peter stamped his feet to keep warm. The rain drilled the awning overhead, splashed onto the pavement. It stopped, then started again.

Down the line, there was a raised voice, then some shouting and pushing. The people in front of him hurriedly edged back. Someone stumbled to the curb and the line reassembled.

"What was that about?" Peter said.

The woman in front of him didn't answer.

He leaned back against the wall. Another eighteen minutes crawled by. At this rate, it'd be dawn before it was Peter's turn. They might be out of everything by then. The store door opened. The line straightened, then arced as people at the end moved out to see what was going on.

Out came a woman, pushing a shopping cart in front of her. A man walked beside her, hand on her elbow. Plastic bags sat heaped in her cart. Peter strained to see what they held. There were some long, narrow boxes of what could be pasta. A fat jug of water. Maybe a loaf of bread balanced on top, baked somewhere where there were still ovens that worked. The line shuffled forward.

Peter leaned out of line and called to the man holding the door. "Excuse me." It came out muffled, so Peter pulled down his mask. "Sir."

The man stopped and looked down the line. He had the name of the store and the word *Manager* embroidered in red over his pocket. He also had a nasty black eye.

"Can you tell me if you have any baby food?" Peter said.

"Wait your turn."

"But you do have formula?"

"Get back in line, sir."

The other man had returned from walking the woman to her car. He shook out the umbrella in his hand, then walked over to the manager. The two of them went back into the store, leaving the first two outside guarding the door. Peter shoved his hands into his pockets. This place couldn't be the only option. He thought about Jacob squirming in Ann's arms, crying with hunger. How long could he wait for food? Now that the power was on, maybe other stores had opened up, too. He pulled his car keys from his pocket and stepped out of line.

PETER PEERED THROUGH THE SLANTING RAIN, WATCHING FOR a lighted storefront. He slowed at one, saw that it was a liquor store, and drove on. Here was a gas station awash in activity. Cars were lined up for the fuel pumps, going all the way to the road. That little store wouldn't carry anything but cigarettes and snack foods, anyway.

The drugstore where they got their prescriptions sat in darkness.

There were lights on at the next intersection. Peter turned into the lot jammed with parked cars. He came to the end of an aisle and saw the crowd mobbing the door. He rolled down his window. Rain splattered in with the noise of their shouting. Glass shattered and a siren shrieked.

He took the highway. He turned the wipers on high and fiddled with the buttons on the radio dial. Maybe the radio had come back on with the power. Nothing. Nothing. Nothing. Then a blip of sound surprised him and he skipped back. The music came through, a song from his teenage years. He hadn't liked it all that much then, but now it sounded fantastic. He hummed along.

Here was the exit for the small plaza where he got his hair trimmed. A fast-food restaurant, a dry cleaner, and yes, some sort of mom-and-pop place. He'd noticed it as he'd walked past on his way to the barber's. There were always hand-lettered signs taped to the windows offering deals on shampoo or cheese curls. There weren't any cars out front.

A bell chimed as he stepped into the store. A man stood behind the cash register. A white mask covered his lower jaw. "Good evening."

Peter smiled back, stamped the water from his shoes, and brushed it from his sleeves. "Glad to see you're open."

"You looking for anything in particular?"

"Baby food."

"Aisle three."

There was music playing. It sounded like the same station Peter had been listening to in the car. Peter pulled a cart from the line by the door and headed down the aisles. Here was the baby section, and there was plenty of formula. The cans stood in rows, powdered and liquid. He scanned the shelves and recognized a yellow label. He reached for several cans and piled them into his cart. Jars of strained peas, applesauce, pears, squash, green beans, a couple boxes of baby cereal.

He turned into the next aisle. Diapers. What size? The packages were labeled. Stage 1, Stage 2. He couldn't decipher what those meant. Crawlers, Walkers. Okay, these made better sense, but where was the one for a baby who could only sit up and roll over?

He pulled one from the shelf, turned it around in his hands. Ah, it went according to weight. How to estimate Jacob's weight? He tried to think of how much babies weighed at birth. Seven pounds? Ann would shake her head at his ignorance. Boys were probably bigger. So, say eight pounds. He'd told Shazia that Jacob was six months old. Babies probably doubled their weight by that point. Did Jacob have the feel of a sixteen-pounder? He held his arm crooked around an imaginary baby. No. More than that. Jacob had to weigh closer to a turkey. Say twenty pounds.

He reached out and selected two of the blue packs.

He turned into the food aisle. Everything looked good. He put whatever he could think of into the cart. Beef jerky. Crackers. Tuna. A bag of chocolate bars. Maddie loved potato chips. Ann didn't like them in the house, but that was then. He set a big bag on top of everything else. Kate was fond of grape jelly. He put in a jar of that, too. Ah. Coffee.

The pet aisle was up next. Adult, midsized breed. He lugged a big bag of kibble onto the bottom of the cart, went up to the register, and began placing things on the counter.

"Find everything?" the clerk said. He held a scanner to each item, set each can into a plastic bag.

"And then some."

"Big storm we had."

"I'll say. Good to have the power back on." A nice, normal conversation, nothing doom-and-gloom about it. Inside this warm, bright place, Peter could pretend it was an evening like any other and he was just stopping by to pick up a few things on his way home. He pulled his wallet from his back pocket. "How much do I owe you?"

The clerk punched a button. "That'll be three hundred and eighty-two dollars and fifty-nine cents."

Surely he'd heard that wrong. Peter glanced down at the digital display and saw the line of glowing numerals. "Three hundred and eighty-two dollars?" he repeated dumbly. "How did it get to be so much?"

The clerk put a hand on one of the bags. "Let's see. Tuna's nine bucks."

"Nine bucks?"

The guy shrugged. "Prices have gone up a little. I don't know when I'll get my next delivery."

"Right." Still, nine bucks for a can of tuna. He couldn't even imagine what the coffee was going for. "All right, forget the tuna. How about I just take the baby food and the diapers?" He'd take them home to Ann and Jacob, then come back out and try their regular store for more groceries. A big chain like that wouldn't do something like this. "How much is that?"

The man sighed heavily. Reaching into one of the bags, he pulled out a canister of formula and scanned it. "Thirty-five dollars."

"Thirty-five dollars?" Peter took the canister from the guy's hand and turned it around to see the small label affixed to one side. "But this says twenty-one."

The man took the formula back. "Like I told you, prices have gone up a little."

Peter could accept some fudging with the numbers in these circumstances, but this was outright gouging. "Gone up a lot, more like."

The man's expression darkened. Without a word, he pulled out a can of tuna, lifted the scanner to it, and pushed a button on the register. The numbers on the register flickered.

"All right." No use arguing with the guy. "I'll take it." He slid a credit card from his wallet and held it out.

The man shook his head, pulled out another can and scanned it. "Cash only." He turned and set the can behind him.

"I don't have that kind of cash on me." The bank website had been frozen all afternoon. The ATMs weren't up and running, either. "I'll write you a check."

"No checks. No credit cards. Cash." The man scanned a box of macaroni and cheese.

Peter watched with a sinking feeling. The girls loved that stuff. He looked into his wallet and fingered the bills. "Look. I've only got sixty dollars on me. Would you give me two cans of formula for that?"

"I told you. Formula's fifty bucks."

"You said thirty-five."

A shrug. "Now it's fifty."

The man was making some kind of point. Peter had offended him. He'd crossed some invisible line. "Fine." Peter worked at keeping the anger from his voice. "I'll take one can of formula and whatever jars of baby food you'll give me for sixty."

"I changed my mind. Nothing's for sale."

Peter stared at the man, but he refused to look up.

Two jars of baby food, Ann had said. After that, they'd have to feed the baby sugar water.

"We're talking about a baby," Peter said, biting off each word. "We've run out of food. He's going to starve. Don't you get it?"

The man shook out a now-empty bag, pressed it back into its original folds, and placed it beneath the counter.

Peter stared blankly at him. "You're crazy."

The man halted. He put his hands flat on the counter and leaned over. Fiftysomething, dark wavy hair, cheeks plumped up over the white of his mask. Evidently, he hadn't been missing any meals.

"Sorry," Peter said. "I didn't mean that. Look, what if I throw in my watch?" His father's old Omega. But watches could be replaced. The baby needed food now.

"Do I look like a pawnshop? Get outta my store."

"Come on. One can of formula."

"Get out." He pulled out a package of diapers and turned to add it to the growing pile behind him. Things started to tumble, and he reached out a hand to catch them.

Peter stood there. His pulse raced. He stared at the two bags on the counter. Another moment and they'd be empty, too. He reached out and grasped the neck of one of them.

The clerk whirled around at the rustling sound. "Hey!"

Peter pushed through the door and into the rain. He fumbled

for his keys and pulled them from his pants pocket. He pressed the remote.

The door banged open behind him. "Stop!"

Peter fell into the front seat, slammed the door, and shoved the gear into reverse. He accelerated backward. Raindrops mottled the windshield. He couldn't see.

"You son of a bitch!"

Peter roared out of the lot, squealed onto the highway and toward a pair of headlights. A car horn blared. Peter swerved. He pressed the gas pedal to the floor. His heart pounded. He couldn't swallow. He switched on the wipers. The highway carried him up and away. He lifted his foot, slowed to sixty.

He took the first exit, pulled off the road, and sat there in the dark. Rain pattered overhead. He leaned forward and rested his forehead on his steering wheel. What had he done?

With shaking fingers, he reached for the bag he'd thrown onto the seat beside him. He held it open and looked inside. In the dim alien-green glow from his dashboard, he saw what he'd gotten. Beef jerky and chocolate bars.

# THIRTY-FOUR

M ADDIE CLAPPED HER HANDS TO HER EARS. "MAKE him *stop*, Mommy."

Jacob smacked the spoon. Food sprayed across his face, and he howled.

"She's trying," Kate snapped. "Don't be such a brat."

"Mommy—"

"Hush!" Ann wiped the baby's face with a cloth. Jacob couldn't help it. When babies wanted a bottle, that was what they wanted. She picked up the bottle and lifted him from where he leaned in Kate's lap. "Let's try this again." She cradled him and rubbed the nipple of the bottle against the baby's lower lip. Jacob hiccuped and opened his mouth. A tentative suck, then a look of horror crossed his face. He reared back, pushing at her with tiny fists.

"No, no. Give it a try." She coaxed the bottle's nipple back into the baby's mouth and tickled his tongue with it. Again he spat it out. "Come on, sweetheart. Hold on. Just a little longer."

Peter had been gone for well over an hour. Surely he wouldn't be much longer.

She held the baby firmly in the crook of her arm and pushed in the nipple. Jacob stiffened and twisted his head. He automatically swallowed. Another suck, another swallow. He squirmed, then brought up his hand and put it on hers as she held the bottle.

"Good boy," Maddie said.

Everything depended on whether or not Peter had found anything open and how long the lines were. She'd feel much better knowing exactly what the situation was. She wished she could just call him. She wished she could just hear his voice. How easy it used to be—pick up a cell phone and press buttons.

Jacob's arm fell to his side. His mouth stopped working. She held up the bottle and checked the level of fluid remaining. He'd managed to finish half. Worn out from struggling against the bottle, he'd fallen asleep before he was anywhere near full. "Turn the TV down, honey," she said to Maddie. "The baby's sleeping."

Ann lowered him onto the pile of blankets. She crouched there, placed a cupped hand to the baby's head. How long would sugar water satisfy a baby?

"Kate." Ann went over to stand behind Kate, who was sitting at the kitchen table. "Show me how to IM."

Kate gave her a sidelong frown. She'd taken her shower and her skin was rosy, her wet hair combed back from her face. "Why?"

"Let me talk to someone's parents." The power had come on, but the phones were still out.

"Mom."

"Just for a minute." Ann pulled out a chair.

A heavy sigh. "Hold on." Kate tapped the mouse pad and a rectangle popped up. She typed *POS* then hit return. "Like who?"

Ann knew what that meant. Parent Over Shoulder. "Ask Claire if her mother or father can talk."

Kate typed quickly. Ann read the response. *BRB.* Be Right Back. The cursor blinked. *My uncle's here,* came the message.

Kate said, "Is that okay?"

"Sure." Ann had never met the man. Who cared? "Ask him if he knows whether any grocery stores are open."

Kate typed. A moment passed. The answer box appeared. They both leaned forward to read the response.

*Don't know. Phone service spotty. 70 and 75 closed. Curfew 9 PM throughout city.*

How did he know these things? "Ask him—"

"Can't you use your computer?"

"Yes, but you're the only one who knows how to IM."

"Shazia knows how. She can show you."

True. Shazia had gone up to take her shower after Peter left. Surely she'd be done by now. Ann tilted her head, listening for the rush of water in the pipes, and didn't hear anything. She pushed her chair back. "Anyone know where she is?"

Maddie said, "Gone."

Ann looked over. Maddie knelt by the television set, pressing buttons. "What?"

"She's gone."

"Don't wake Jacob. Come over here."

The baby murmured, and Maddie looked down. She stood and came over to where Ann and Kate sat. "She went out."

Out? Out to stand on the porch? Out to check the mailbox? No—it was pouring out there. But maybe she'd just wanted a few minutes alone. "When did she do that?"

"When you were busy with Jacob. She just said goodbye and went."

Kate pulled the laptop toward her. "She said it to me, too, Mom."

People didn't say goodbye just to go stand on the porch. Ann stepped out quickly onto the cold, damp concrete of the front porch. Shazia wasn't there. Ann looked all around and saw empty streets glistening beneath the streetlights.

Upstairs, Shazia's bed was made. A navy suitcase stood against the wall. Shazia had had two. Where was the other one? Ann checked the closet and under the bed. A picture frame lay facedown in a puddle of broken glass on the nightstand. Ann turned it over and discovered a small heap of shredded paper beneath. The photograph of Shazia's parents, Shazia's mother gazing up at Ann from her small bit of paper, accusing.

The small counter in the guest bath was clear, bare of the toothpaste and toothbrush Ann had glimpsed there earlier. She'd noticed the foreign brand, had wondered what sort of flavor the little yellow leaf on the tube indicated. And here, against the back of the counter, lay a thermometer. One of hers, the one that had gone missing from the first-aid bin. Why had Shazia been checking her temperature?

She headed for the den. Shazia's laptop no longer lay there on the desk. Her long coat was missing from the hall closet.

"Girls," she called, coming back into the family room. "What exactly did Shazia say?"

"We told you," Kate said. Her fingers flew over the keyboard. "She said goodbye. Oh, and thanks."

Goodbye and thanks. What else could that mean? "She didn't say where she was going?"

"No."

But she'd been looking at MapQuest.

"I'll be right back," Ann said, and Kate nodded absently. Maddie returned to sit close to the television.

The rain was pelting down now in fat, angry drops. Ann pulled her coat firmly about her and went to the edge of the porch to peer down the street. "Shazia?"

House lights gleamed through the foggy sheets of rain, a friendly sight after so many weeks of darkness. She went down the steps and onto the dark front path. Raindrops spattered the hood of her coat and tapped her shoulders. A gust of wind splattered cold water against her pant legs. Streetlights shone steadily. Here and there glowed a bright square of window or a lit patch of driveway. She tried to see beyond the shimmering lights and through the rain for a dark moving shape, but it was impossible to see anything clearly.

"Shazia!"

Ann walked to the curb. Water streamed toward the gutter. The trees shivered in a gust of wind. How long ago had she last seen Shazia? Maybe twenty minutes. Thirty, tops. Long enough that she'd be well out of sight by now, especially if she was moving purposefully.

Ann should take the car and go look for her. She had a full tank from when she'd stopped on the way home from school, the last time she'd gone anywhere. She could at least make sure the girl had a plan and that she knew what she was doing, that she wasn't going to thumb a ride with a stranger or attempt to walk all the way out into the countryside.

She'd have to wake the baby, though, and take the children with her. Kate could hold Jacob in the back. Ann had never driven with a baby not strapped into a car seat. Could she really rouse him and drag him out into the wet cold, after he'd finally fallen into a fitful sleep?

She could leave him be and let Kate watch him. Kate was old enough to babysit, certainly, but she'd never taken care of a baby before. If Jacob happened to wake, Maddie could help distract him. The house was warm and the lights were on. They'd keep the doors locked, of course. They'd be perfectly fine. After all, Ann would be gone only a little while, just long enough to drive around the neighborhood.

She reached the front porch and her resolve trembled and disappeared. Of course she couldn't do that. She couldn't possibly leave her daughters alone. Not under these circumstances.

Ann turned around and stared into the shadows. She pictured Shazia hunched over, ducking the rain that came in curtains now, holding her suitcase in one cold, numb hand. She'd have stopped to put her laptop inside it, probably wrapped it up in her sweaters for added protection. Her laptop. Of course. There it was, the solution. Ann could email her and make sure she was okay. Just as she had this thought, the world fell dark. The streetlights vanished. Where the houses once stood, throwing out bright beacons of light and warmth, there was now complete darkness.

Everything was gone. Ann stared around her in disbelief. All that was left was the steady downpour of rain and the twin headlights of a car pulsing toward her.

# THIRTY-FIVE

$T$HE RAIN CAME HARDER NOW, POUNDING THE WIND-
shield. The wipers swept across the glass and thunked back.
Peter accelerated down the exit ramp and slowed to a stop at the red
light.

He was a thief.

The store owner might have seen Peter's license plates and jotted down the numbers. The police would find out where he lived
and come pounding on the door. Ann's door. How would he explain
this to Ann and the girls? No. Ann would understand. In fact, she'd
be furious at the shopkeeper. The girls need never know.

He gripped the steering wheel. He was overreacting, his guilty
conscience imagining the worst. The police wouldn't bother re-
sponding to such a minor incident. They had bigger issues to handle. Most likely, the shopkeeper wouldn't even file a report, not if he
wanted to avoid explaining his own behavior. Peter squeezed his
eyes shut and shook his head. He had to get hold of himself. After
all, what was he talking about, maybe ten bucks' worth of stuff?
Later, when this was all over, he'd pay for the things he stole. He'd
pay double.

Just as quickly as the rain had built up, it fizzled. Fog filmed the
windshield. Peter turned on the defogger to release a blast of cold

air. The radio was playing another song from the seventies, something about being hopelessly in love. He felt like he was drowning in syrup. He needed some old R&B or even some of that urgent hip-hop Kate loved. Peter jabbed the button on the dashboard and silenced it. The cab filled with the rhythmic swishing of his wipers.

The traffic light flared green, and he accelerated. He'd try the grocery store again. After all this, he couldn't go home empty-handed. Better to stay out a little longer and come home with something for the baby. The clock on the dashboard read 8:23. He'd been out here for over three hours. He checked the gas gauge and was dismayed to realize he was down to a quarter of a tank. After the grocery store, he'd stop at that gas station he'd seen open earlier. The lines might be shorter by now. He wished he could phone Ann and give her a heads-up. He wondered how the baby was doing.

The store was just a mile or so away.

The windshield slowly cleared. In the tunnel of light his headlights threw out, he saw a figure materialize out of the gloom in front of him.

What the hell?

Peter pounded the brakes. Tires screeched. The truck swung one way, then the other. His headlights crossed the curb, swept across a pair of legs. He gripped the steering wheel. A long, slow arc, and then the truck shuddered to a stop. He stared through the glass but saw nothing in front of him. He'd felt no sickening thud of impact. Where had the man gone? Had he somehow fallen beneath Peter's truck? Peter glanced through his side window and saw someone standing there in the rain, a man wearing dark clothes, his pale hands shoved into pockets.

The fellow came up to Peter's window. He wore a hood pulled low over his forehead, hiding his eyes. Why was he sauntering like this? Didn't he realize how close he'd come to being run over? Peter rolled down his window. Water dripped in.

"Jesus. I almost hit you."

The stranger lifted his chin, revealing a soft mouth and nose, an uncertain beard. Not a man. More of a kid, really. Eighteen, tops. "Get out of the truck."

"What?"

"Move it."

Peter looked at him, disbelieving. What was this, a carjacking?

"Come on, come on."

The kid bounced a little on his toes. Was he high on something? Two other people appeared on the road behind him, shadowy figures, malignant in the way they stood there.

Peter shook his head and reached to roll up his window. He didn't have time for this.

"Let's go, old man." The kid's voice had changed.

Peter's passenger door opened. Before Peter could do anything, there was a boy leaning in across the seat. A soft snicking sound to his left, and Peter turned back to look through the window. Moonlight gleamed down on cold metal. The first boy was holding a switchblade.

So, this was to be a night of everyone for himself.

Peter leaned close. As if to oblige him, the boy leaned closer, too.

"Fuck you," Peter said.

The boy blinked. Then he coughed, a deep phlegmy sound that bent him almost double.

Droplets sprayed across Peter's face. He reared back.

The boy straightened, wiped the sleeve of his coat across his face. And smiled.

# THIRTY-SIX

A NN STOOD ON THE PORCH AS THE HEADLIGHTS GREW larger. *Peter?* But even as she hoped so, she knew it wasn't. The headlights were too oblong, for one thing. They were set too far apart. Sure enough, the car swung by without slowing. Someone else returning home, someone else's glad reunion.

She turned to go back inside. In the disappearing light from the headlights, she caught sight of the folded piece of paper taped to the door. A note. She peeled it free and held it up, squinting to make out the words. But it had grown too dark to read. Then she caught herself. The girls! They'd been alone in the sudden darkness. Maddie would be scared.

She swung open the door and stepped into the blackness. "Maddie? Kate?"

"Here," Kate called back.

Her voice sounded calm. There was a dim glow from the room beyond.

It came from a candle on the mantel. Another one burned on the buffet. Here were the girls, sitting on the floor with the baby.

"Look, Mom," Maddie said. "Jacob woke up and he's trying to crawl."

The baby was on his hands and knees, rocking back and forth.

"Who's a big boy?" Maddie crooned. "Who's the big Jakey Wakey boy?"

Ann shook her head. She couldn't believe what she was seeing. "Did you find Shazia?" Kate said.

"No." Ann sagged against the wall. Her first thought was relief, then something different. Sorrow. Her two little girls, who'd had to grow past the luxury of being afraid of simple things.

ANN FED ANOTHER DAMP BRANCH INTO THE FLAMES. IT WAS A thin and petulant fire, spitting hisses and pops.

The girls nibbled crackers as they played a game. Jacob sat cradled in Kate's lap as she selected a card. Ann had fed him the rest of the baby food. She'd set aside some crackers to mash with water for later. She hoped it wouldn't get to that.

"Why isn't Daddy home?" Maddie said.

"He'll be back soon," Ann said.

"So what?" Kate slapped down a card. "He's only going to leave again."

There was no answer for that.

Ann wandered into the dining room. The rain was unceasing. Surely by now Peter had found a grocery store open. But still the niggling thought intruded—what if he hadn't? What would they do then? She glanced back toward the children. Jacob was gripping a playing card and waving it around as Maddie giggled.

The house was growing chilly again. She would have thought the heat from the furnace would have lingered longer, but the warmth was running out as quickly as it had rushed in.

The girls got ready for bed. The house seemed so empty without Peter or Shazia. Ann tucked her daughters into clean, dry sleeping bags. Jacob sighed and settled on his mat of blankets. She'd dressed him in triple layers and pulled socks over his tiny fists to keep them warm.

Rising, she peered at her wristwatch in the candle's glow. It was already ten-fifty, much later than she'd realized. She blew out the small flame and the room fell dark.

*Peter, where are you? Are you all right?*

It was possible that he'd run out of gas. He wouldn't have any way of letting her know. He could have had an accident. The thought speared a blade of fear between her eyes.

She went to the phone and picked up the receiver. Silence.

The rain slowed and at last ceased. She took the blanket from the couch and wrapped it around her shoulders. She paced, going from window to window. What was taking him so long?

The baby whimpered, and she went to check on him. He was sodden. Careful not to jostle the girls, she removed his diaper. He didn't wake. Pulling the last diaper from the plastic wrapping, she slid it beneath him. She stretched the tabs across his hips and folded the covers back around him. Peter might have thought to pick up diapers. Back when the children were babies, buying diapers was one of the things they did every time they went to the store. The practice might have come back to him. If not, they could make do for a while, fashion something out of a washcloth and safety pins.

She couldn't possibly sleep. She needed to keep busy. The vacuum still sat in the middle of her bedroom. There were towels to put away, blinds to shut. She went upstairs, not even bothering to bring the flashlight or a candle. She'd gotten used to wandering around in the dark. It was amazing what she could distinguish now by moonlight. She stood by the bedroom window. A quarter moon peeped from between drifting clouds. She glanced at the street. Someone was walking down the sidewalk. She stared hard at the scene below. The moonlight faded, grew stronger. It was a man. He had his head down, but he looked like Peter. He had the same general build and way of walking. But it couldn't be Peter. Where was his truck? The figure disappeared around the corner of the house toward the garage.

She raced downstairs to the dining room and looked out the window there to see if whoever it was was coming around the house on the sidewalk. Then from the side of the house, she heard the telltale rumbling of the garage door going up.

The sound froze her in place for an instant. She made her way into the kitchen and came up close to the door. "Peter?"

"Yes."

*Thank God.* He was home. Her fingers closed around the door-knob's smooth surface. It refused to turn.

"Stop." His tone was low and urgent. "Don't come out here."

"What?" She stood there, bewildered. It was Peter and yet it wasn't. His voice was wrong. Deeper.

"Stand back from the door."

"But why? Peter, what's going on?"

"Stand back, Ann."

"Tell me what's going on," she insisted, not moving.

"I've been exposed."

# THIRTY-SEVEN

SILENCE, ANGUISH ALONG THE LENGTH OF IT. AT LAST she whispered, "Peter."

His heart ached. For her, he realized with some surprise. The familiar feeling had slid in, unguarded. "Can you get me a blanket, some dry clothes?"

"Of course. I'll be right back."

He'd never been colder in his life. All those predawn hours spent crouching in frozen fields, all that time standing on the shore as icy winds blew across the lake. He'd thought he'd been cold then, but now he knew what true coldness was. His teeth clicked so violently together his jaw throbbed. He'd lost all sensation in his feet. His hands pulsed. He leaned against the wall and felt as though he might fall down.

"Peter?" Ann was back.

"Yes." He roused himself. "Set everything down, then back away. All the way into the kitchen."

Silence.

"Ann?"

"All right."

He counted to ten, then unlocked the door and swung it open. Moonlight shone through the laundry room beyond and illuminated the bundles of soft things lying just inside the door. Superstition, not science, kept him from turning his head and looking into the kitchen's interior, where he knew his wife stood. He couldn't see her, but he sensed her worry and fear radiating palpably toward him through the dark. *It's all right,* he wanted to tell her, but she'd have seen right through him. They knew each other that well. He scooped up the bundle and shut the door.

He stripped off his cold, wet things and dropped them to the concrete floor. He held up various garments, trying to sort through things. He tugged everything on, underclothes, sweatpants, a T-shirt, a knitted pullover, and put a hand on the wall to steady himself as he pulled on socks. "Are the doors locked?"

"Yes."

"Are you sure?"

"Yes."

"I couldn't get any formula. I'm sorry. I tried."

"That's all right. Peter, how did it happen?"

"Go to bed, honey. We'll talk in the morning."

"But where will you sleep?" Her voice trembled.

He longed to hold her. Another surprise, a welcome one. He drew the blanket around his shoulders. "I'll figure something out. Good night, Ann."

A long moment before she whispered back, "Good night, Peter."

IT WAS DARK AND HE WAS COLD AND SOMETHING WAS JAMMED into the small of his back. He turned over. Why couldn't he extend his legs? He stretched and his knees bumped something unyielding. This wasn't his pillow against his cheek but something hard and scratchy. He opened his eyes.

He stared up at a gray ceiling with a small plastic dome light embedded in its center. He turned his head. Now he saw a swoop of molded black plastic, a steering wheel protruding from the opposite end. He was in Ann's minivan.

Right.

He lay on the passenger side. He'd pushed the seat back as far as it would go and reclined it to its limit. Not the most restful of circumstances, but it had been dry and out of the elements, and it had worked for—he brought his watch up to his face and peered at the dial—ten hours. He couldn't believe he'd been asleep for so long. It was already midafternoon.

He groaned and pushed himself up. His back ached from where the armrest had dug into him. His legs were stiff. One arm had gone numb. He opened the door and made his way out of the car, came to full height, and stretched.

All was quiet. He wondered where everyone was. He came around to the back of the van. Bending down, he grasped the garage door handle and heaved it open. That ache in his legs. Was it anything more than overexertion? That clearing of his throat. Could it be the preamble to a cough?

"Hi, Daddy."

He squinted, poked out his head from the garage's dim interior into sunshine. It was Maddie, and she was running toward him across the yard. Ann was right behind her, grabbing her arm and pulling her back. "Remember what I told you." Then Ann looked at him and smiled, a hopeful look. "Hi."

Kate came up behind them, the baby on her hip, and stood there, biting her lip.

They all looked so wonderful. Watery sunlight shone on their hair. Their cheeks were pink from the cold. They stood together, ranging in height, different versions of the same model, impossibly beautiful to him. He smiled. "Hey, you guys. What've you been up to?"

Maddie said, "We put Jacob on the trampoline."

"Sounds like fun." Peter leaned against the doorjamb. "How's he doing?"

"Holding his own," Ann said. "Turns out he likes cracker mush."

Kate lifted Jacob higher on her hip. "Are you okay, Dad?"

"I feel fine, honey."

Ann said, "Girls, take the baby in and change him, okay?"

Without a word of argument or disagreement, they traipsed away. Peter watched them go in amazement. He looked back at Ann. "I'm going to take off. It'll be a hike, but—"

She was shaking her head. "You can't go now."

"Now's exactly when I should go."

"What happens if you get sick, Peter?"

"Exactly."

"No."

They looked at each other across the span of driveway and grass. She'd locked the door on Libby. He couldn't understand why she was opening it wide for him.

"Please," she said.

A gust of wind blew her hair across her face. She was wearing one of the girls' headbands, a pink elastic thing. She looked so young and earnest, just like she had when they'd first started dating. He couldn't help it. He grinned. She blushed, then smiled back. The long years of strain between them wavered. Something else began to grow in their stead, something that didn't yet have a name.

"All right," he said.

She let out a breath. "How are you? How do you really feel?"

"Thirsty. And I have to use the bathroom."

"I'll keep everyone outside. I'll wipe everything down afterward."

"Make sure the girls are washing their hands."

"What happened, Peter?" She looked beyond him into the garage. "Where's the truck?"

"They took it."

She looked back to him. "Who?"

"A bunch of kids ambushed me. One of them coughed on me."

She stared at him.

"I'm okay," he said. "A little shook up, that's all. It's just a truck."

"He coughed?" Her voice was a whisper.

He could barely hear her across the distance that separated them. It seemed like they were standing miles apart. "He wasn't that close." A small lie. The boy had been plenty close enough. He imagined he could still feel those moist droplets on his face. He pushed the thought away and looked around. "Where's Shazia?"

Ann's face changed. "She's gone."

"What?"

"She left a note. I read it before I realized it was intended for you."

"That's all right. What did she say?"

"She wanted to thank us for letting her stay, but that she needed to be with her friends now. I really don't understand that. I've been so worried about her. I didn't go after her. I wanted to, but I couldn't leave the girls alone."

She was looking at him, asking him to forgive her. Well, there was nothing to forgive. "She knows where we live. She'll come back if she wants to."

Ann drew her brows together. "I think she might have gone to be with her friend on the farm, the one who emailed her."

"Harold? That makes sense. They're in love."

She stared at him. "What?"

"They hit it off the minute they met." He shrugged. "No one else can stand the guy. Hard to picture the two of them together, but what do I know?"

She was giving him the weirdest look.

"What?" he said.

"Nothing." The wind lifted her hair from her shoulders. "Did she tell you where that farm is? Is it in Ohio, or—"

"I don't know." He didn't want to talk about Shazia anymore. "She's a grown woman. She knew what she was doing when she walked out. She knows the risks as well as I do. She'll be fine."

"I hope so. I really do." She looked away, then back at him. "I'll move the kids upstairs so you can come in, then I'll get you water and something to eat."

It was strange, though. He wasn't the least bit hungry.

PETER KICKED OVER A BUCKET AND SAT DOWN. PEELING BACK the wrapper on the granola bar, he took a bite. Water dripped leisurely from the eaves and trickled down the street. Fat white clouds mounded in the northern sky.

One cough.

Peter had scrambled out of the truck, stood well back as the boys shoved past him and climbed in. He'd lifted his face and let the rain sluice across his skin. He'd scrubbed his mouth and nose and cheeks with his coat sleeve, bent and spat onto the ground. Whatever the boy had coughed on him couldn't have made it into Peter's respiratory system. But they'd know for sure later.

He couldn't wait for later to arrive.

An angry shout from down the street brought him to his feet. More shouting, then a high-pitched yelp, the sound of an animal in distress. He strode out onto the driveway. A man stood in the middle of the street, hands on his hips.

"What happened?"

The man turned and glared. Stan Fox, the Hummer dealer with the perfect lawn and the neatly tied trash bags. "Goddamned dog stole my stuff. I came out onto my porch to get something and found him digging around."

Barney? The man had probably thrown something at the dog, maybe gotten close enough to kick him. "Where'd he go?"

Stan jerked a thumb in the direction of Finn's house. Barney had headed home. "Goddamned dog. Goddamned dog owners."

The small house stood at the bottom of the street, awash in clumps of melted snow. The drapes were drawn tight. No smoke puffed from the chimney. No sign of Barney anywhere, but he was probably curled up somewhere nearby, licking his wounds. Dogs were solitary creatures when they were injured. But where? One quick glance at the handkerchief porch and the scrawny azaleas fronting the house told Peter the dog wasn't anywhere out here.

Maybe around back.

The side gate stood ajar. Peter pushed it open and stepped into a small walled garden. There was an amoeba-shaped swimming pool, covered for the season, a big barbecue grill, also covered, a tidy stack of outdoor chairs. Picture windows along the back of the house overlooked the pool. Nice. Who'd have known this was here?

A bug buzzed. He absently swatted at it, eyeing the potting shed in one corner, the burning bushes that had dropped their magenta leaves and were now a web of straggly branches. He could see right through them to the brick wall behind. No dog hunkered down there. Pacing the perimeter of the yard, he came full circle and stopped beside the lounge chair standing in the shadows beneath a window. He crouched. "Barney?"

Soft panting.

Peter brushed aside another insect, then gently lifted the chair and set it down a few feet away. The dog lay pressed up against the side of the house. He didn't raise his head but rolled his eyes to watch Peter.

"It's all right, fella." Peter extended his hand and let Barney take a tentative sniff.

A weak thump of tail.

Without moving closer, Peter examined what he could see of the dog. Barney's eyes looked clear. That was a good sign. His coat was matted and stiff with mud. His ribs protruded, and his abdomen was arched. Poor fellow had starved down to muscle and bone. No rash or infestation along the rib cage or on this flank, but there on his hindquarters was a streak of something dark and crusty. Old blood.

"What happened here, boy?" Peter moved around to get a better look.

Barney watched him warily.

A two-inch gash had split the skin. The flaps on either side were swollen and angry. The injury wasn't recent, maybe a day or so old. The redness indicated that infection had already begun to set in.

"Looks like I found you just in time." He rocked back on his heels and regarded the dog. "What did you do, wedge yourself into a tight spot? Duke it out with a raccoon?"

Barney had his head down now. Weariness had made him submissive. He'd be receptive to the granola bar Peter was still holding on to.

"All right, boy. You'd better let me take care of that."

He stood and saw through the glass into the room on the other side. The padded hump of a green sofa, a matching chair angled beside it, the corner of a fringed Oriental rug. Nice bachelor furnishings. Something black and tiny crawled along the glass—a fly. In the middle of winter? But then he remembered. Finn had heat. Inside, it wouldn't feel like winter.

The insect swept up, then lighted onto the floor, just out of his range of vision. His gaze followed it and sharpened.

A red and black plaid bedroom slipper lay on the rug just beyond the curve of the chair, a cuff of blue material curving over the rubber heel. Peter moved down the glass and saw the rest. The cuff became pajamas. The slipper matched the bathrobe. Beneath them sprawled something brown and viscous, covered with writhing white worms. Knobby yellow bits protruded from the ends of the sleeves. A larger rounded part lay at the farther end. He recognized them, pale bones and a skull. Walter Finn. The brown mass must be what remained of his flesh, and it swarmed with maggots and buzzing flies.

Peter took a step back.

The man had collapsed alone in his fortress of a house. Despite all his precautions, the virus had still found a way in.

For the first time, Peter felt truly afraid. They were on their own. Nothing was going to save them. They had to save themselves.

# THIRTY-EIGHT

ANN OPENED THE CABINET IN THE LAUNDRY ROOM AND looked at the pile of canvas bags, freebies that Peter had brought home from conventions. How many should she take? She held one up by its straps. It looked awfully small. She brought down the whole pile.

"Don't worry about Shazia," Peter had said.

Ann still couldn't believe it. She'd been entirely mistaken. He and Shazia were just colleagues. The relief was enormous. She didn't know why she felt so happy.

She lifted the key from where it hung on the brass hook beside the back door and went into the family room. Maddie was on the floor, kneeling on her sketchbook to hold it open. She pinched her nose with her other hand.

Ann stopped. "Where's Kate?"

Maddie jerked her chin toward the closed powder room door. "Washing her hair for like the millionth time."

Poor Kate. The water was freezing, but she'd persisted in the process, dunking her head into icy sinkful after icy sinkful, emitting little shrieks as she did so. She refused Ann's help, emerged red-faced and shuddering, her hair piled into a towel. Silence came from there now, so maybe she'd reached the towel part. Or not.

Ann strode over and rapped sharply on the door.

"What?" came Kate's irritated response.

"Nothing," Ann said. She looked down at Maddie. "Why are you doing that?"

Maddie glanced at Jacob, who lay on his tummy beside her. He'd risen up on his forearms to watch her work. "What if he goes?"

Ann bent down to pull the covers back up over the baby's bare legs. She'd smeared him with Vaseline and was letting him go bare-bottomed in the hope he could heal from the hideous case of diaper rash that had bloomed across his bottom and thighs overnight. Washcloths were a terrible substitute for diapers.

"Try and keep him covered up." She stood, tugging on a pair of latex gloves. "I put Daddy's lunch on the back step. He might knock to let us know he's finished, but don't answer the door."

Maddie unpinched her nose. "Okay."

"I'll be back in a few minutes."

She thought Maddie might question where she was going, but her daughter merely nodded and returned her attention to her drawing.

The grass was boggy and yielded to the pressure of her steps. Afternoon sunshine swam about her. She came up onto the other porch and lifted the doorknocker. The sound fell away unanswered. She peered through the narrow window and saw the long, empty hallway stretching away before her.

She slid the key into the lock and turned it. An answering click. She stared at the doorknob. The virus could survive only a few hours out in the open. It had to be dead by now. She was wearing gloves. The minute she got back, she'd toss them. So why was she standing out here like this, her heart drumming away? It wasn't the virus she was terrified of. It was what it had left behind.

The doorknob moved easily in her grasp. Stepping across the threshold, she felt the gaze of unseen witnesses follow her inside. She swung the door closed behind her.

She stood in the shadowy foyer.

Then the smell hit her. Thick and cloying, and inexpressibly foul. She recognized it. It was the same reek as when that songbird had died in their garage the previous spring. By the time Ann had discovered it, maggots were crawling across the feathers. The odor had literally sent her reeling.

Now she knew for certain. She swallowed hard. *Where?*

The rooms on either side of her were empty, the den with its shelves full of books, the dining room with its gleaming table and ornate server in the corner. Ann had helped Libby hang those watercolors on the walls. She'd helped load that heavy mirror into the back of her car and later had celebrated its discovery over a shared bottle of wine.

A soft ticking came to her. It was the clock, its pendulum swinging. She'd never heard it before. Libby's house had always been noisy with talk, laughter, ringing telephones, televisions going in several rooms, toys that sang or beeped or chimed.

She walked quickly to the kitchen and let out her breath when she saw that no one was there.

A bottle of cough syrup lay on the floor in a splatter of bright orange. Dishes were heaped in the sink and on the counter. Crumpled tissues trailed across every surface. The refrigerator door was ajar, releasing the smell of must.

In the cabinets, Ann found cans of formula, jars of baby food, two boxes of baby cookies. She sagged with relief at the sight.

The pantry revealed cans of soup and vegetables, boxes of macaroni, peanut butter, cereal, rice. Tears stung her eyes. She took it all, even the opened bottle of vinegar.

She slid open drawers and removed rubber-tipped spoons, bibs, teething gel, baby nail clippers, sippy cups. Candles, matches, two big black flashlights heavy with batteries.

She left the bags she filled by the front door, turned around, and went back down the hallway.

The smell grew stronger as she climbed the stairs. It flooded her mouth and swam down her throat. She panted to keep it out. They were up here somewhere. The bedroom door at the end of the hall was shut. A faint humming sound came from behind the closed door. She halted, trembling. There was something familiar about it. After a moment, she placed it. Insects. Houseflies filling the air and bumping against the walls. She gagged, then blindly turned away. She wouldn't even think of entering that room.

In Jacob's room, blankets lay rumpled in the crib. A baby bottle sat on the floor beside the rocking chair. But the stench was here, too. Her eyes watered. She moved quickly, locating packages of diapers in the closet, pulling clothes from drawers. Her stomach was beginning to cramp. A shopping bag of hand-me-downs sat in the corner of the closet. Right. From Libby's sister. A size larger than Jacob was wearing now. She grabbed the bag and spun away from the closet.

She made it to the downstairs powder room just in time. She heaved into the toilet, pulled tissues from her pocket, sobbing, wiping her face.

Out in the garage, the sting of cold. She breathed greedily. Two cases of bottled water were stacked against the wall, still shrink-wrapped and dusty. Another partial case sat beside them, the few bottles ghostlike behind the shroud of torn plastic. A real find, but still less than Ann would have expected. Libby never drank soda or juice. Ann had never seen her without a plastic bottle in her hand. Maybe she and Smith had worked their way through their supply.

Ann stood considering the partial case. A big red cooler sat in the shadows by the garage door. It was the cooler Libby always heaved into her trunk when she went to coach her high school field hockey practices. She'd had a great year. Libby had been thrilled. Her team had been undefeated. Libby had had hopes of making nationals. And then there were no more games.

Ann crouched and pulled up the lid. Rows of white caps glowed in the darkness. She saw the smooth plastic shoulders. She'd found the missing water.

She made four trips, carrying the cases to the front door. The heavy weight felt welcome. All this water. A real bonanza. She'd found everything she'd been looking for, and more. She should feel nothing but gratefulness. But she still had the hollow feeling she was forgetting something. She turned and came back down the hall. She stood there and looked around the family room. What?

Her gaze fell onto the row of silver-framed photographs that lined the mantel. The center one showed Libby and Smith on their wedding day, ducking beneath the row of crossed field hockey sticks Libby's team held above their heads. Libby looked so joyful and beautiful in her white gown. Smith beamed as if he couldn't believe his good fortune.

Ann crossed the room and took it down. She pushed it into a bag, forcing it down among the folds of sleepers and sweaters. This was it. This was what she took.

She wouldn't be coming back.

# THIRTY-NINE

$P$ETER LOWERED THE DOG TO THE FLOOR AND RAPPED on the door. "Ann?"

A moment and then she was there. "Are you okay?" Her voice was hushed.

"Fine." Tired, though he didn't volunteer this. Carrying a fifty-pound animal the length of the block was wearying. "Can you get me a few things? Water, gauze, some antibacterial ointment. Nail scissors, and a blanket, if you can spare it."

"Are you hurt?"

"No. It's for the dog."

"What dog? You mean Finn's dog?"

"He hurt himself."

"Why can't Finn deal with it?"

"He's dead."

"Oh, Peter—are you sure you're all right?"

"Yeah, it's the dog I'm worried about."

"All right. Just a minute."

He removed his jacket and stood well back against the far wall. After a few minutes, she called, "Ready," and opened the door. She leaned in and looked at him, then at the dog curled, panting, on the floor, then back to him. Her gaze lingered, and he wondered what she saw. "Dinner's almost ready."

He waited until the door was shut again before retrieving the bag.

Spreading the blanket out on the floor of the minivan, he pressed on the overhead light. It wasn't much to see by, but he wouldn't be stitching up the wound. It was too late for that. He picked up Barney and placed him on the carpeted surface. The dog's rib cage rose and fell with the effort of breathing.

He clipped the fur around the wound and irrigated the site. Squeezing in a big glob of antibacterial ointment, he wound a long strip of gauze around the leg. He dripped some water into the dog's mouth and brought up the edges of the blanket to cover his body. Night was falling. He could barely see.

There was a knock on the door. "I'm opening," she called.

"Okay."

A small orange flame appeared in the darkness, flickered, grew brighter as she set the candle on the back step. The clink of china against concrete. Her voice floated to him. "You sure you're okay?"

"One hundred percent."

The door shut.

She'd left behind several things—a bowl, a spoon, a drinking glass, a bottle of water. He picked up the bowl and examined its contents by candlelight. It appeared to be a mound of pale stuff. Rice, maybe. Or oatmeal. A taste revealed it to be flavorless with a wet, grainy texture. He'd eaten this before, but when? It was sort of like couscous but lacked the nutty flavor. He took another spoonful. Then he knew. Grits. Where on earth had Ann found grits?

The glass contained apple juice. Another surprise. Where had this come from? They'd had only water these last few days. He drank it in one long draft. How could he have ever found the stuff overly sweet?

He carried the bowl and the water to the front of the garage where the door stood open and sat on the overturned bin to watch the street. The broken brick walls of the Guarnieri house rose before him in the dark. Farther down, he saw the steady gleam of firelight in Singh's family room window. The man's car had been parked in the same spot on the driveway for several days now. Had Singh gotten sick, too?

The grits went down easily enough. He ate half, then brought the remainder to where the dog lay on the floor of the minivan. Barney's eyes gleamed in the candlelight. Peter set the bowl beside him.

Barney struggled to sit up, panting a little. He lapped at the stuff.

"Good boy."

Peter poured water into the bowl. The dog waited, then lowered his head. When he'd finished, he leaned back with a sigh. Peter took the licked-clean bowl to the back step and left it there.

The evening sky was clear. Peter made out the tracery of tree branches and the sharp points of rooftops. The world had gone into slow motion. Too bad he hadn't been able to watch the sun set. He was facing the wrong direction. He sipped some water.

He'd watched plenty of sunrises and sunsets on those hunting trips with his father, though he'd never been much of a hunter. Even as a kid, he'd been too engrossed in following the wheeling motions of a hawk, mesmerized by the poetry of the birds collecting in arrows as they headed south. Often as not, it was his younger brother, Mike, who raised his gun in time. Mike, who'd grown up to become a soldier. The President had brought back the troops. Mike had to be stateside by now, reunited with his wife and son.

Barney growled. Peter glanced toward the animal. The dog had his head up.

"Dad?" A small voice came through the night. Kate's.

Peter stood hurriedly, knocking back the bin. Two forms stood on the apron of the driveway. "Don't come any closer."

"Is that a dog?" Maddie said.

Peter heard the hope in her voice. "It's Mr. Finn's dog. He got hurt, and I'm taking care of him for a little while. What are you guys doing out here?"

"Mom said we could say good night," Kate said.

"How's Jacob?"

"Cranky. Mommy made him eat green beans."

"She got them from next door," Kate said.

So that was where the grits and apple juice had come from. Good for Ann.

Maddie said, "She said Smith and Libby weren't there anymore."

Confusion colored her voice. *So Ann hadn't been specific*, Peter thought.

"That's right," he said.

"I don't get it." Kate's voice was a challenge. "Why would they leave their baby?"

Ann spoke out of the darkness. "Say good night, girls." She came up to stand behind the girls, the baby on her hip.

"Now I lay me down to sleep," Peter said.

"I pray the Lord my soul to keep," Maddie said. "May God's love be with me through the night and wake me with the morning light."

She sounded so sad. Peter longed to fold her in his arms. "Good night, you two. I love you."

"Good night, Daddy."

"Night, Dad."

He watched the girls leave, then said to Ann, "I hear you went next door."

"It was awful."

"It was smart."

"Kate knows about Libby and Smith. I hate that."

"She's still young. She's resilient, Ann."

She bit her lip and looked away. "The last thing I did was to doubt her."

She was talking about Libby. "You're taking care of her child," he reminded her gently.

She turned back to look at him. Her face was in shadow. "You're the one who rescued Jacob. I locked the door on him."

"If I hadn't brought him in, you would have."

"Would I? I don't know." Her voice was a tortured whisper.

"What's done is done," he said, and was rewarded by her sad smile.

"That's another thing your dad always said," she said, and he nodded.

The baby yawned. Absently, she jiggled him up and down in that eternal mother dance. The baby put his hand up to her neck, laid his cheek on her shoulder, and burped. They both laughed. "How's the dog?" she asked.

"I think he's in a little pain. He's going to need aspirin. I wish I had my bag." It had disappeared along with his truck.

"Would ibuprofen do?"

Peter shook his head. "I'll just keep a close eye on him."

She nodded. The baby's head lolled to one side, and she curled her hand up alongside his face. "I'd better put him down."

"Make sure you remember to lock up."

"I will."

She sounded distracted. She wasn't really listening. "Ann," he said sharply.

She stopped and looked back.

"I mean it. Make sure all the doors and windows are locked."

"All right, Peter. I'll check the locks again. I promise."

He waited until she was gone before reaching for the handle on the garage door to drag it haltingly down. Blowing out the candle, he climbed into the minivan. He heard the answering jingle of dog tags.

"Try and get some sleep, buddy."

He'd change Barney's bandage in the morning. By then, he should be able to determine whether he'd caught the infection in time. Lying back against the stiff seat, he tried to wriggle into a more comfortable position. His second and, he hoped, final night sleeping in the van. No moon tonight. The darkness was complete. He folded his arms behind his head and stared up at the ceiling hanging somewhere over his head.

*If I should die before I wake, I pray the Lord my soul to take.*

# FORTY

W HAT ABOUT THIS ONE?" MADDIE PULLED A PHOTO-
graph from the shoebox and held it up. "How old was I
here?"

Ann leaned over to take a look and smiled at little Maddie pos-
ing there in her pink push car, her chubby hand on the molded plastic door. "Two."

Jacob batted at the picture.

"No, no, Jacob. Not for you." Kate pulled back his hand and settled him more firmly in her lap. "I remember that car. I loved that
stupid thing. I used to think it was real."

"Remember your hobbyhorse? You used to pretend that was
real, too." Ann slid the picture into the sleeve of the photo album.
Kate would spend hours in the backyard, pretending to teach her
horse how to jump, her small face screwed up with fierce determination.

"Oh, yeah. Michele had one, too."

Kate's voice was matter-of-fact saying the name. Was that a
good sign or a bad one?

Maddie rummaged around in the shoebox and withdrew another find. She stared down at it. "When did Daddy have a mus-
tache?"

Ann took the photograph and studied a younger Peter standing in front of that long-ago Christmas tree. "That's when he had whooping cough. He was too sick to shave. You were just a baby, honey."

The pounds had just dropped off him then, too. Peter had lost so much weight these past few weeks. His cheeks were so lean. His two-day growth of beard only emphasized their gauntness. He said he felt fine. She'd listened hard to what lay behind the words and had discerned nothing to cause alarm. He *was* fine. Just a few more hours.

Ann realized the girls had fallen silent. She looked up at them, sitting cross-legged beside her, photo albums spread all around them. Jacob had gotten hold of an envelope and was sucking its corner. She gently removed it from his grasp. "Hey," she said. "Daddy got better, you know. He's strong."

Kate turned her head. "I hear something."

The windowpanes shivered in their frames. A truck was heading up their street. A big one, by the sound of it.

They scrambled to their feet and went to the dining room to look out. Ann heard the garage door shuddering along its tracks and knew Peter was watching, too. Across the street, Mr. and Mrs. Mitchell stood in the shadows of their porch. So they were alive. They leaned against each other, wrapped in blankets.

A large white truck eased to a stop in front of their house. It had the look of a moving truck, but the logo on its side had been spray-painted out. There were people sitting inside the cab. The driver turned his head and looked at Ann. She drew back. What did they want?

Two men came around the front of the truck, pulling on gloves.

"Do we know them, Mommy?" Maddie said.

One man was tall and lanky with a navy blue baseball cap pulled low over his forehead. The other was short and burly, with a fringe of gray hair. Strangers. They wore white protective masks and coveralls. They turned to face her house. They stepped onto the grass and headed directly for her front door.

"Girls, get back." Ann glanced at the dead bolt. Locked.

Boots clopped onto the porch. Through the narrow strips of

glass on either side of the door, she glimpsed shoulders. There was a loud knock.

"Who is it?"

"City Services. You got anybody for us?"

A man's voice, uneducated and rough.

It took her a moment to puzzle through his words, muffled by the mask. "Who are you trying to find?"

"Ma'am, you got anybody for us?"

Maybe he couldn't hear her properly, either. She put her mouth to the glass. "You have the wrong address."

"Ma'am." The second man stooped to peer at her through the peppled glass. "You have any body you need us to take?"

He paused between "any" and "body," and his meaning became clear. He was talking about a body in the literal sense.

She backed away, horrified. "No."

"There's no charge, ma'am."

"You've got the wrong house. Go away."

He turned and conferred with his partner. They both looked back at Ann, then stomped down the stairs. They climbed back into the truck and the engine rumbled to life.

"What did they want, Mom?" Kate said.

"Nothing, honey."

The truck moved down the street, but not far. She could still hear the engine throbbing nearby. She went into the den and looked out the window there. The truck now sat in front of Libby's house. The two men were walking up the front path. She heard their raised voices and the loud pounding of the doorknocker.

"They can't just go in there like that." Maddie sounded indignant.

The two men had disappeared from view. Something was about to happen, something Kate and Maddie shouldn't see. "Girls, take Jacob and go play a game. Stay away from the windows."

"But what are they *doing*?" Kate insisted.

"Now, Kate. Maddie. Please."

The two girls reluctantly turned and shuffled away.

Ann heard a shout from outside followed by a high-pitched pinging as the truck went into reverse. It bumped past Libby's SUV, still sitting askew by the mailbox, and made a wide circle onto the grass. The driver's door opened and a third man appeared, mid-sized, wearing a mask and coveralls, too. He went around to the back of the truck and swung open the doors. Now she saw activity by the front door, a man backing out with something propped on his shoulder. A few more steps and the second man appeared. They were both wearing respirators, and now she saw they carried some-thing between them, something long and rolled in a blanket. The same crimson wool blanket Smith took to Libby's field hockey games. The one Libby left draped over her sofa. The men stopped, adjusted their grip, and then came around slowly and heavily to the back of the truck. They flexed to lift the bundle to their shoulders, higher than Ann would have expected. She looked away. She couldn't bear this.

Now the driver came over. He held a clipboard. The two men paused. All three talked. The driver nodded and jotted something on the clipboard. He turned and looked at the house number, made another notation.

The Nguyens had come out to stand on the sidewalk at the cor-ner. Mr. Nguyen had his arms around his wife and mother-in-law. The younger woman was weeping. The older woman pressed a bright yellow scarf to her nose.

The two men went back into the house and reappeared a short while later. This time, it was a blue-and-gray comforter rolled up between them. A smaller burden. They moved more easily down the path. Another mighty heave, and then the driver reached up and pulled down the door. He went to the house and did something there. From this angle, Ann couldn't see what, just the swoop of his arm rising and falling. He climbed into the truck and slammed the door.

The Nguyens on the corner, the Mitchells on their porch, other neighbors standing unseen behind their windows—this was all the memorial service Libby and Smith would have.

The truck backed down to the street and turned, drove on to the next house.

Trembling, Ann put her forehead to the glass, and sent up a prayer. Was anyone listening? How many more bodies would they collect from this small neighborhood? Was there anywhere in the world this wasn't happening?

The neighbors drifted away, went back inside their houses, disappeared from behind windowpanes. Ann heard her daughters' voices from the other room teaching Jacob peekaboo, squabbling a little about how best to do it. Kate laughed and Maddie gave a whoop of triumph.

A rush of cold air struck her as she stepped outside. She came down to the bottom of the porch stairs and craned to see what the man had been doing to Libby's door before the truck had pulled away.

It was red paint, sloppily applied. She made out a circle with a number two in the middle, a line crossed through it. The paint was still dripping, glistening like blood.

KATE COUGHED.

The sound froze Ann as she rinsed the plates in the sink. She set down the dish and switched off the water. Her heart thudding, she walked over to where the girls lay sleeping by the hearth, the baby curled up nearby. She crouched. Firelight flickered over their faces. Kate had her chin resting on her stuffed owl. She cleared her throat and turned her head. She sighed. A few moments ticked by. All was silent.

False alarm.

Ann rose and turned toward the kitchen.

The back door opened and Peter stepped inside.

She halted by the table, her heart hammering. "Hey."

"Hey."

"How are you feeling?"

"Like I dodged a bullet."

They all had. The pure relief of seeing him whole and healthy, scruffy beard and all, made her dizzy. "I saved you some macaroni and cheese. The girls were so excited to have it for dinner. You'd have thought it was filet mignon. Remember how Kate used to call

it macadaw cheese?" She was babbling. She put a fork on the waiting plate and turned to him.

He smiled. "Yeah. And Maddie would only eat her peas and
corn in pairs."

"I was so sure it was a sign of serious mental illness."

"Just stubbornness. Your side of the family."

He was standing so close, staring so intently. What did he see?
She lifted a hand to her hair, long and loose, no hope of any style remaining. His eyes were dark, their color difficult to make out in the
shifting candlelight. Blue, she guessed. Navy blue. Tomorrow, they
might be green, or gray. Kate had inherited her changeable eyes
from him.

He put his hands on her shoulders and drew her toward him.

She went willingly, pressing her cheek to his shoulder. She
spread her fingers and pushed the cloth of his shirt aside, laid her
palm on his warm skin.

He kissed her eyelids, her cheeks, her throat, then her mouth.
The softness of his lips, the taste of his skin, her hand at the nape of
his neck, the curls of his hair sliding between her fingers. They
bumped against the cabinet and a dish rattled.

"Wait," she said.

He stopped, breathing hard. "Sorry."

"The girls." She took his hand, pulled him into the laundry
room, and shut the door behind them. The room was small and
dark. She stumbled back against the clothes mounded in baskets,
pulling at his shirt and yanking at the buttons. He pulled her
sweater over her head. The cold surface of the wall scraped against
her shoulder blades, then the room tilted and now the cold tiles lay
beneath her. Moonlight filtered in through the narrow window,
painting his skin in stripes of blue and white. She ran her hands
along his upper arms, rubbed the small ridged scar nestled by
his collarbone, pressed her palms against the firm smoothness of
his shoulders. He looked down at her. Tasting tears in her throat,
she reached up and brought his mouth down, opening hers so that
all the unspoken words swam from one to the other, all the questions finally answered.

# FORTY-ONE

*P*ETER SHOOK OPEN THE MAP AND SPREAD IT ACROSS the kitchen table. Columbus sat in the center of the state, highways crisscrossing it like fishing net. Lots of options, but none of them any good. If the quarantine was still in effect, and he had no reason to think it wouldn't be, they'd be stopped along any of the major roads and made to turn around. But here, snaking north, was a quiet two-lane thoroughfare that might work. The state's resources would be stretched thin. They couldn't cover every route. They'd have to be selective. They'd concentrate on 75 and 70, 80/90. They'd have to overlook a poky little road like 6.

Ann came into the room. "Jacob's finally asleep."

The road meandered past Bowling Green. From there, they had myriad options. Not a straight shot—it'd add seventy-five miles or so, but they'd pass through plenty of small towns that offered alternative routes should they need them.

"I told the girls they could use my old paints."

He glanced up at her with pleased surprise, then looked over to where the girls knelt by the table in the living room. "Nice to see them getting along."

"Maddie's making you a Welcome Back sign." Ann came closer. "What are you doing?"

"I need to talk to you about something." He saw her tense and he smiled to ease her mind. Things were still new between them. He patted the chair beside him. "Come on, sit down."

She pulled out the chair and sat. "What's with the map?"

Her hair waved softly around her face. He remembered the feel of it, silky between his fingers. She caught him looking and blushed. "Peter."

He took her hand and said with great seriousness, "It's not safe here anymore."

A small line appeared between her eyebrows. "You mean our house?"

"We're taking too many chances staying in such a big metropolitan area. It's a lucky fluke I didn't get sick. We can't count on that happening twice."

"But things are getting better. Those men said they were from City Services. That must mean things are returning to normal."

"Those men were freelancers. If anything, that's a sign that the system has failed."

"Freelancers?" She tilted her head. "How do you know that?"

He couldn't tell her they'd carted Smith and Libby's bodies to the ice rink. He couldn't bear the look in her eyes if she knew. Instead, he said, "Listen, honey. We still don't have power. 911's out. The phones don't work. There haven't been any food drops, no planes at all. No mail, no newspaper, no garbage pickup."

"But we're managing. We have food. We have water. Besides, where would we go?"

"My dad's old hunting cabin."

She bit her lower lip. She was processing this. "In Michigan?"

"It's only about four hundred miles away. We could do it in a day. Mike keeps the cabin stocked. That, plus the supplies we have here—"

She shook her head. "What if we have to go the long way? What if we run out of gas?"

"We'll figure something out."

"It's too risky. I don't want us to be stranded by the side of the road."

"The cabin's isolated. There's no one around for miles. We can boil water from the lake. We'll be surrounded by firewood. I can teach the girls to fish. We can stay there as long as we need to."

She looked around the kitchen. "What if we board up the windows? Not all of them, just the ones down here. And the sliding glass door. That's always bothered me, how open that is. Anyone could just walk right in."

She wasn't listening. She hated change. The unknown always made her apprehensive. The only time she'd taken any kind of chance had been when they'd decided to move here, and then she'd been running away from, not running toward, something. He took her other hand and held both firmly. She looked back to him.

"Ann, you need to understand. Things have changed out there. The other night, I didn't see a single police car. The Guarnieris burned alive in their home. Libby and Smith died alone in their house. So did Finn. What if that happened to us? Who would take in Kate and Maddie and Jacob?" He tightened his grasp. "Sweetheart, there's no one out there to help us. No one at all."

A look of comprehension crossed her face, chased closely by fear. "What about my parents? What if they and Beth drive out here and find us gone?"

He wrapped his arms around her and pulled her close. "We'll leave them a note." Her hair kissed his cheek. "They'll know where to find us."

"Four hundred miles . . . We could get carjacked. We could crash. We could be exposed."

He tightened his grip. "We don't have a choice."

"When do you want to leave?"

"First thing in the morning."

"SO, HOW BIG IS GRANDDAD'S PLACE?" KATE STOOD AT THE kitchen table, shaking out towels and folding them into a laundry basket. She had her stuffed owl tucked into the waistband of her jeans. Two months before, those jeans had been so tight she couldn't have fit a washcloth in there.

"It's pretty rustic, but it's got all the comforts of home." Peter knelt by the bin of camping gear and lifted out the tent. He'd have to leave it. It was too bulky to take, even with the cartop carrier he'd strapped to the roof of the minivan. Nothing was going but the absolute essentials. Even so, they'd be loaded down. "There's a stove, a fireplace, a kitchen table, bunk beds."

Kate narrowed her eyes. "What about the bathroom?"

He grinned at her. "It's got one, but you'll have to take a little hike to get to it."

"Well, that's just super. We'll be living like cavemen."

"What about a shower?" Maddie said. "Because she sure needs one."

"Oh, like you smell so great?"

"I wouldn't know. My nose is completely dead from smelling *you*."

"Just shut up."

"And your breath stinks, too."

Kate curled her hands into fists, and Ann swiftly stepped between the two girls. They'd run out of toothpaste a few days before, and Ann had been mixing up pastes with baking soda. Peter had to admit the concoctions hadn't been doing the trick. "It's all right, Katydid. I don't smell anything." He winked at her. Maddie reached into the pantry for another can of food and put it in the paper sack. "Jacob's coming, right?" she asked Peter.

"That's right."

"But what if Libby comes looking for him?"

Ann and Peter exchanged a glance. "We'll leave her a note," Ann said. "She'll be happy to know Jacob's being taken care of."

They'd have to locate Jacob's family. Libby's parents lived in Arizona, he remembered, and there was a sister somewhere. When things settled, they'd look for them.

"What about Barney?" Maddie said. "We have to take him, too."

Peter smiled at her. "Of course we do."

Ann looked up from the first-aid bin.

Peter winked at her. He was feeling much better now that he knew they were leaving. An enormous weight had been lifted.

Really, he should have thought of heading to the cabin weeks ago. "He can forage for food in the woods. He might even catch us a squirrel or two."

"That is so unnecessary, Dad," Kate said.

"Yuck," Maddie agreed.

Here was his fishing box. He snapped it open, checked the lures, closed it again, and set it beside the fishing rods. "We'd better take sunscreen and bug juice," he told Ann, and she nodded.

Maddie squealed. "Bugs?"

"Maybe a few." Peter rolled up mosquito netting. Come July, it'd be good to be able to escape the pent-up heat of the cabin and sleep mosquito-free on the front porch. "Don't worry. You guys are going to love it there. Your granddad used to take me and your uncle Mike camping there all the time."

"So, how come we've never been to this place?" Kate said.

Ann paused in the laundry room doorway and looked back at him.

"Well," Peter said, "I haven't been there in a while. Not since before you girls were born."

"Why not?" Maddie said.

Strange. It was a simple question, but Peter found he had a hard time framing a response.

Ann set the bottle of insect repellent on the table. "Well, your dad never liked hunting, so there was no reason for us to go there."

Kate looked from her to Peter, frowning. "Isn't that where Granddad had his accident?"

Ann said quietly, "That's right."

That was what the authorities had ruled it. That's what Peter wanted to believe. His brother had insisted otherwise. Their father was too experienced not to wear blaze orange that time of year, Mike had said. He thought it was too much of a coincidence that their mother had just been diagnosed with Alzheimer's. *The old guy gave up, Peter. He took the easy way out. He always did.*

Ann put a hand on Maddie's shoulder. "Looks like you're done with the pantry, honey. Why don't you girls help me pick out your clothes? One suitcase each."

"What about Jacob's car seat?" Kate said.

"Hey." Ann draped an arm around Kate's shoulders and squeezed. "Good thinking."

Kate blushed.

Peter smiled at the sight of them standing so naturally together. Finally, after so many years, this was the way they should be with one another. This was a gift, an acknowledgment that he'd made the right call in moving his family. This was a harbinger of all the good things to come.

HE LAY AWAKE LONG AFTER EVERYONE HAD FALLEN ASLEEP, watching moonlight paint shadows on the ceiling. He listened to the even rise and fall of Ann's breathing, Kate's soft snoring, Jacob's occasional squirming. Maddie lay utterly silent, the way she always slept. Maybe it was that again—listening for her breathing—that was keeping him awake, as it had all those years before. Nah. Maddie was far too old for him to be thinking about that now. There were other things to worry about. That boy Kate liked, for instance. What had she said his name was? Something weird, like Beaver. No, not an animal—an object. Scooter. That was it. Scooter.

How would Kate emerge on the other side of this? She'd been growing into a typical teenager, giggling, gossiping with her friends, worrying about her hair, and having her little crushes. But she'd been jolted out of that. Ann had told him Kate's best friend hadn't been online the other day. There was only one conclusion to draw from that. How many other friends of Kate's were gone, too? Kate would find out eventually. She probably already knew, though she hadn't said anything. Kate was like her mother that way. She kept her feelings locked inside. How much had these past few months derailed her from becoming the woman she was intended to be? They'd never know.

Of course Maddie would be affected, too, though probably in less tangible ways. She was only eight. She might ride this out, as the young sometimes did, not even straining to make the adjustment back to whatever new normal awaited them. Or she might grow up with certain phobias or behaviors that she'd never trace back to this period in her life. She might never be able to form friendships. She might shy away from making any sort of emotional commitment at all. A horrible thought. Maddie was his passionate child, always the one needing extra hugs and kisses, always the one to dash up to the car window as he pulled in for a visit.

The air in the room pressed down on him. He'd piled on too many covers. He kicked them off. Better. He flipped over onto his side.

Now he could see the front door floating there in the darkness across the expanse of hallway. It was a pretty door, with narrow rectangles of peppled glass along both sides, a broad band of glass above. One of the things he and Ann had first loved about this house was the way it seemed to be filled with light. Now all those windows represented danger. It was a good thing they were leaving. No one would bother them at the cabin. They'd have to know it was there, first. If anyone did approach, Barney would sound the alarm.

But Ann was right. Four hundred miles was a long distance. A lot could happen between here and there. For the first time since his dad died, Peter wished he still had his shotgun.

It had gotten stuffy in here. No doubt it was the residual warmth from the fireplace and too many people crowded into one small space. He pushed himself up. Maybe he'd go outside and get a breath of fresh air. He could do a perimeter check at the same time. He took a step toward the front door and saw that it was hanging wide open before him. How could this be? He'd checked the lock himself numerous times that night. He blinked. Now the door was firmly shut again. It must've been a trick of the darkness. He was probably sleepier than he'd realized.

He unlocked the door and stepped out onto the porch. The chill felt good. His days and nights were all turned around. He'd sit out here for a little while and watch the street. That truck and the three men carting off the dead had troubled him all evening. He knew they'd been hired for the job, but he wondered if they were also scouting houses for easy trespass. Work for the city by day. Work for yourself at night.

He settled himself onto the bench and leaned back against the wooden slats.

He didn't realize he'd fallen asleep until he felt something wet and cold press into his palm. He opened his eyes and saw Barney sitting there with his head in Peter's lap. The sun was up. It washed across his legs in a tide of yellow.

"How did you get out here?" Peter rubbed his eyes and stood.

Ann smiled at him from the kitchen sink. "Hey, sleepyhead. Why did you go outside last night?" She dried her hands on a dishtowel. The flip-flopping of the towel made his head squeeze painfully.

Kate looked up from where she sat at the table. "Mom says I can't take my laptop."

"There isn't any electricity," Ann said.

"Is that true?" Kate looked accusingly at Peter.

He couldn't remember. He tried to piece it together. Were there lights? An outlet to plug in a fan?

Maddie was talking now. He turned his head to her and saw that she was spooning something into Jacob's waiting mouth. Another wave of pain bounced against his temples.

"We'll have Daddy's computer," she said. "Don't be such a baby, Kate."

"Oh my God. Do you have any idea how stupid you are?" Kate sneered at her sister. "Dad's computer won't work, either."

"You think you know everything."

"Compared to you, I do." Kate dropped her spoon into her bowl with a clatter.

Peter winced. "What was Barney doing on the front porch?"

"I don't know," Ann said. "I thought you left him in the garage last night. Are you hungry?" She picked up a dish. "Peter?"

He blinked. The motion made his eyes ache.

Ann was looking at him oddly. "Girls." She sounded as though she was talking from a far distance. "I want you both to go outside. Take Jacob with you, okay?"

He blinked, another blindingly painful process, and saw he was alone with Ann.

"Honey, are you all right?" she asked.

He was fine. Of course he was. He lifted his arms to her. Why didn't she come to him? She wasn't stepping forward and placing her head against his chest. He looked down and saw that his arms had not moved but lay stiffly by his sides.

# FORTY-TWO

A NN STOOD TREMBLING BY THE KITCHEN SINK, RUN-
ning icy water over her wrists and splashing it over her face, as
if she could wash away the facts. One look at Peter standing there in
the kitchen doorway and she'd felt uneasy. There was something
worrisome about the color in his cheeks. Then he'd leaned against
the doorjamb, looking confusedly from Kate to Maddie, and she'd
known with a terrible certainty. My God. The monster was in Peter.

It had lurked inside him, biding its time, just like that alien that
had coiled hidden until everyone's guard was down before bursting
free from that fellow's abdomen while everyone backed away in
horror.

Now the monster had slithered in without their knowing and
crept around unchecked for hours. Their children had breathed it
in, spent all night with it. She and Peter had made love; he'd held
her until dawn. Could the monster be inside her, too? Then what?
Who would take care of the girls and Jacob, then?

She had to keep her head clear. She sluiced another wave of
water over her face and let it run dripping down the front of her
shirt. She was no good to anyone if she didn't get moving. She
reached for a dishtowel, then slowly uncurled her fingers. Nothing
was safe—the counters, the dishes, the pillows, the doorknobs,

everything they'd packed into the minivan. How could she possibly clean it all?

She had to focus. Peter needed her. He'd barely been able to make it up the stairs. She'd hurried the girls out the door as he trudged toward the guest room. She saw the effort it took for him not to touch the banister or the wall. The sight of it had brought tears to her eyes. Her eyes were moist again, remembering, and she pressed her fingertips to her temples.

He'd been terribly sick before. Once he'd fainted in the doctor's office. He'd had whooping cough. Sometimes he got such a bad cold that the bed shook with his fever tremors. Yet he'd always made a full recovery. He was a strong man. He wasn't in the high-risk age group.

The girls were, though, and Peter had spent the night on the porch. Somehow, deep down, he must have known. He must have known and taken himself out into the cold away from them.

Two tiny shards of hope.

She pulled out a pair of latex gloves and snapped them over her wrists. There'd been a box of masks in that old toolbox Peter lugged to his research sites, but of course it was gone, along with his truck. But he might have tucked some spares on his workbench in the garage. So much of his stuff had lain untouched this past year.

She stepped out into the garage and quickly closed the door behind her. How many germs rushed at her? Surely the freezing temperatures had killed them all. She stepped around things and went to the garage door, bent and grasped the handle. She pulled it up high enough to get her shoulder beneath the wood and gave a mighty shove. The door rolled up and banged against the back of the ceiling. She waited to see if it would slide back down. It rocked but stayed. She'd leave it open and let things air out.

There was enough light to see by now. A gray cardboard carton sat on the shelf above the workbench. When she brought it down, she found it had some heft to it, enough to make her think she'd gotten lucky. She unfastened the lid and discovered the tidy row of molded white objects nestled together. A pair of safety goggles hung by their rubber strap from the Peg-Board. She'd need those, too. She reached out for them and knocked over a tool that clattered to the floor.

Behind her she heard something, a surreptitious clicking noise. Someone was in here with her. She whirled around: Barney, standing on the blanket in the corner. His lips were curled back and his teeth were bared. The ruff of his neck stood straight up. He growled, ominous sounds that echoed around the small space.

"What's Barney doing on the porch?" Peter had said, swaying there in the kitchen and looking at her, bewildered. But the dog hadn't been on the porch. He'd been in here the whole time.

She eyed him. He no longer resembled that friendly, panting dog at the end of Finn's leash. He'd taken on some wolf. Ann dropped her gaze and backed away, stepped across the threshold, and slammed the door between them. She half expected to hear the animal hurl himself against the wood, but the door remained still.

Maybe Barney was sick, too. He'd slept in the van with Peter for two nights. Could dogs carry the flu? Why hadn't she asked Peter about that? She prayed that he'd wander away through the open garage door. If not, at least he'd keep the rats away.

In the kitchen, she set the box on the counter and withdrew a mask. Slipping it over her head, she pressed the thin strip of metal against the bridge of her nose. The paper hugged her cheeks and cupped her chin. It felt like a tight fit, but she had better make sure. Opening a cabinet, she removed the pale yellow box that sat there beside all the other spices they'd decided not to take with them and opened it to remove a slim packet of artificial sweetener. She shook the package, tore open one corner, and dumped the powder into a glass of water. On the laundry room shelf was a spray container. She poured the sugar solution into the plastic bottle, screwed on the cap, spritzed some into the air, and inhaled deeply.

There was no answering flood of sweetness in her mouth. The mask fit. There was no way to gauge when a mask would be too clogged to be effective, so she'd have to remember to swap them out regularly. If she was careful, she might get a day's use from each.

She needed enough for eight days.

Pulling out a tray, she assembled the ibuprofen, decongestant, and a bottle of saline spray. She poured a glass of apple juice with a shaking hand and set some crackers on a plate. Peter hadn't finished his meal the night before. At the time, she'd thought it was because the sauce was so salty. Now she knew. Loss of appetite was the first symptom.

She glanced at the window. The girls were still outside on the trampoline, playing some sort of game with Jacob that had him rocking back and forth on his hands and knees, grinning and drooling.

Beneath the bathroom sink upstairs, she found an old shower cap, one of those disposable ones from a long-ago hotel stay. She put on one of Peter's shirts, worn backward like a smock, picked up the bucket of cleaning supplies, wedged a box of tissues beneath her arm, and lifted the tray.

A rush of freezing air drew her down to the guest room. Stepping inside the room, she found the windows wide open, the curtains billowing in the cold air.

Peter lay in the bed, comforters heaped on top of him. He turned his face toward her. "Don't come in."

His voice was a croak. Fever had imprinted itself across his features, brightening his eyes, blooming in red circles high on his cheeks. She crossed to the window and her foot bumped something. Glancing down, she saw a pillow lying on the floor. She bent to retrieve it.

"Don't touch that. I've got it blocking the vent. Leave the windows alone."

Air flow. Of course. He was trying to keep the virus in here with him and not circulating. The furnace was off, so germs couldn't rush through the vents. But still. Even the smallest air current would be enough to send the virus swirling through the entire house. She straightened. "I'll get you some more blankets." There were some in the chest in her room. She'd pick the lightest, warmest ones, nothing that reeked of chimney smoke.

He turned his face and coughed, caught his breath. "I was contagious yesterday."

"I know." She made her voice soothing, wiped clean of the terror she felt hearing what she already knew. She came over to look down at him. "How, Peter? How could this happen?"

"It must have mutated." He struggled to keep his gaze on her. "Keep an eye on the girls."

"Of course." *Fight, Peter. Show your stubborn side. I need you. We all need you.* "How's your headache?"

"Pretty bad." Another cough rumbled in his chest.

"I brought you some ibuprofen. Can you manage something to eat or drink?"

"I'll drink something."

"Okay." She shook two pills from the bottle and placed them in his palm, handed him the glass of juice. He lifted his head from the pillow and swallowed, accepted the cracker she held out. He handed her back the glass, and she set it on the nightstand.

"Do you need help getting to the bathroom?"

His eyes were closed and his breathing had taken on a wheezing rasp. "I'm okay."

He was falling asleep. A good thing. The more rest he got, the sooner he'd recover. Sleep had always been the magic pill for him. She stood there for a long moment, watching him, hearing the children laugh and shout below, still giddy, no doubt, with the prospect of their upcoming trip. She yearned to bend and kiss his cheek, scruff and all, place her hand on his chest and feel its reassuring rise and fall. Her fingers reached out, and she shook her head. She couldn't. She didn't dare.

"Check on Barney, will you?" he mumbled.

"Don't worry about the dog."

"Ann, you have to."

"Oh, Peter. I can't deal with that." She had to focus all her energy on him, on keeping watch over their children. The dog would have to fend for himself.

But he wasn't listening. She watched him for a moment. His breathing evened out. He was asleep.

In the hall, she pulled off her mask and gloves, oversized shirt and hairnet, and left them heaped in the bucket outside the door. Maybe she did have some room inside her to care for that darned dog. How hard could it be to fill one bowl with water and another with a few scraps of food? And she'd keep the minivan packed. The minute Peter was well enough—providing no one else got sick—they'd leave. Peter had been right. They were on their own.

# FORTY-THREE

W AS IT THE THIRD DAY OR THE FOURTH? PETER couldn't be sure. He shifted in bed, trying to find a way to lie against the pillows and blankets that didn't make his limbs ache. The ibuprofen was wearing off.

Shadows slanted across the walls. He squinted at the windows, tried to make out whether early-morning rays were creeping over the sill or late-afternoon sunshine was taking its leave. The door creaked open, and he turned his head. Ann was coming into the room. She was wearing that ridiculous costume again, the white mask and big plastic goggles, her hair pulled up into a flowered shower cap, and a pair of pink rubber gloves and one of his shirts turned backward.

"You'll never get a man in that getup."

She smiled at that, her cheeks bunching up and moving the mask a little. "Good thing you're stuck with me." She brought the chair from the corner and sat. "You didn't finish your juice."

He licked his lips. His mouth was dry. She brought the glass to him. It was good. He swallowed.

"Do you think you can manage these pills?" She held out her hand.

He fumbled for the small white tablets. He couldn't seem to get a grasp on them. She lifted one to his lips, and he opened his mouth so she could place it on his tongue. He tried to swallow it down, but he gagged and spat it instead into her palm.

"Hold on," she said.

She crushed the pills with the bottom of the glass, then brought the glass down level and swept the white powder with her gloved fingers to float lazily down into the juice.

"How are the girls?"

"Playing poker. Maddie's winning. Kate's determined to eradicate her from the face of the earth. They've been fighting all morning."

"No. How are they?"

She looked at him. "Fine."

"Good."

She dipped the straw into the juice, covered the top with a finger, and carried it to his mouth. Obediently he opened his mouth, and she dripped the sweet stuff onto his tongue.

"What day is it?"

"Five days."

"Good," he croaked out.

Another strawful of juice. She looked at him expectantly. She wanted something. What did she want? She was holding out a tissue.

He coughed, and she pressed the tissue to his mouth.

"You look worried," he said. "What's wrong?"

"It's the water. It smells funny."

"Don't drink it. The water company might have . . . put something in there so you'll know it's bad."

"Can't I boil it?"

"That'll take care of the bacteria . . . but not if the chemicals are off." The effort of saying this squeezed his lungs and he lay back, panting.

She dropped the tissue away, out of sight. How many tissues was that? Where were they all going? A flood of crumpled white must stretch across the carpet. They would rise and carry his bed off.

"The baby seems fine, too," she told him. "Maybe he's immune."

The baby was fine? How could that be? They'd lost him, so long ago. He remembered the feel and heft of him in his arms, the rounded shape of his head, the steady blue of his eyes. Time couldn't erase these impressions, even though the day itself had grown cloudy. He recalled pushing past firefighters and EMTs and finding Ann sitting on the step. She was white-faced and holding little Kate in her arms, refusing to set her down. William was gone. After that, nothing had ever been the same again.

She dripped more juice onto his tongue. "Barney seems to be getting better. Though he won't let me near him to change his dressing."

He struggled to follow this. Was Barney a friend or a neighbor, a cousin of hers?

There were two of her bending toward him, then one again as she sat back.

"I think he doesn't like me. You're the one who has the way with animals."

Now he remembered. The mutt. The poor animal slinking back to the house he considered home and the man he considered his master, whom he could see through the plate glass but couldn't reach.

Now Ann was holding up a stuffed owl. He blinked, trying to see it. She wanted him to fix it, make it better. Its pale brown body drooped before him, its huge black eyes unflinching. But his specialty was migratory birds. Ann should know that.

"Kate wanted you to have this." She propped the toy up on the nightstand.

He hadn't seen her bring it into the room. Was this another visit? Had she gone out of the room and returned? He tried to focus on the stripes of the shirt Ann wore. Had she been wearing that one before?

"I gave that to her."

Ann drew her eyebrows down. He'd made her unhappy. Then she smoothed them back out again and smiled at him. The unhappiness was gone. He was relieved.

"That's right, sweetheart," she said. "You told her owls were nocturnal."

And would keep her safe at night while she slept. Kate had had so many fears. It was the only way he could think of to get her to sleep those nights long ago. He remembered the sultry heat of those July evenings, the three of them lying on top of the sheets beneath the ceiling fan as it stirred the air above them, Kate gripping his hand tightly with her small fingers, wanting to be told that the stars couldn't fall on top of them, that ghosts weren't watching them from the closet.

He heard the girls playing somewhere. One of them was singing. It reminded him of Ann singing as she painted, off-key, the same song over and over. He missed that sound.

Now she had a bowl. Steam rose from it. The room was darker. Time had passed again. He struggled to a seated position.

"Hungry?" she was saying, dipping a spoon into the bowl and carrying it to his mouth.

He wanted her to move. He threw back the covers, and she was standing now, reaching out for his arm. He shook her off. The motion tightened a band of pain around his head and jabbed knife tips behind his eyes. He had to get to the bathroom. His legs were stiff. The room spun around him. He careened into the wall, hand out for the doorknob.

"No, honey," Ann was saying. "This one."

A door yawned before him. He made it to the toilet and heaved up the contents of his stomach. He dropped to his knees and clasped the cold porcelain. He was coughing again and vomiting.

Ann helped him back to bed. She swept the covers up into the air and let them settle against his skin. She put a hand to the back of his neck and helped him suck the straw. He closed his eyes. He loved her so much. He had never loved her more. He wondered if she knew this.

"Oh, Peter," she said. She patted his forehead with a cool cloth. "Me too, darling."

# FORTY-FOUR

---

$P$ETER HAD BEEN TALKING ABOUT WILLIAM FOR DAYS. After years of silence, he'd finally opened up. "Remember him sucking his thumb on the ultrasound?" he'd say. Or "His eyes were your color, remember?"

He'd tried to get up by himself yesterday. Ann had come into the room just in time to catch him as he stumbled. "Where are you going?" she asked him, and he frowned. "I have to check on those samples—"

"Oh, Peter, those samples are long gone."

"They are?"

He looked so distressed that she quickly added, "But they were benign. Every single one of them."

"That's good." He nodded and allowed her to settle him into bed and pull up the comforters.

The girls were worried. Maddie stopped whatever she was doing to track Ann as she came down the stairs. Kate had said nothing, but on Ann's last trip up to check on Peter, she'd pushed Owl onto the tray. "Give this to Daddy."

*Daddy, not Dad.* Ann had blinked back tears, hearing that. "You won't get it back, honey."

Kate shrugged. "I don't care."

Ann put her hand on Kate's shoulder, then took the worn, limp creature. It had worked miracles before. Maybe it would again.

She had to keep moving. If she stopped, even for a moment, she'd fall asleep. She'd doze right here standing against the wall. She closed the bedroom door behind her and heard the sound of crying coming from downstairs. The baby again. There was a high-pitched urgency to it. Ann shook the shirt from her arms and stepped out of it. She left everything in the hallway, a puddle of infection.

Kate was holding Jacob and pacing the family room.

Maddie stood there, chewing her lower lip, hands on her hips, watching. She looked over as Ann ran down the stairs. "He won't stop, Mommy."

"You tried the bottle?" Ann came over and took the baby. He was red-faced and hiccuping. "Hey, you."

"It's not his diaper," Kate said. "I checked."

Jacob screwed up his face and shrieked, a bloodcurdling sound that rang in her ears.

"Shh. Shh, sweetheart."

Jacob squirmed in her grasp, refusing to be comforted. Ann lifted him more firmly to her shoulder and patted his back. He was sweaty and hot.

"Is he sick?" Kate asked.

Would that always be the fear? Would they never feel safe? Ann laid him down. She pressed his belly, but it was soft, checked his diaper, and went over his entire writhing body. Everything seemed normal. So why was he still crying? He wasn't running a fever. He didn't have a runny nose.

"I don't know." She lifted him to her shoulder again. Jacob balled his tiny fists against her and mouthed her shirt. Drool collected wetly on the cotton of her collar. She patted his back and he burped. Was that the source of all of this, a little gas? Jacob let loose a long belch.

Maddie giggled.

"There, there." Ann patted Jacob's back and smiled at Maddie. "All better."

Jacob gummed her shirt, then bit down hard.

That hurt. "Ouch!"

Surprised, Jacob began to wail again. Ann pulled the baby away and peered inside his mouth. "Guess what?" She ran her finger along his lower gum, then pulled it out hastily when he started to close his mouth. "Jacob's got his first tooth."

The girls had never labored like this for a tooth. One day they'd be all gums. The next day, they'd produce a pearly tip of tooth. William hadn't lived long enough to teethe. Blinking back tears, she pressed Jacob to her and hugged him. How normal. A first tooth. How utterly normal.

"Let me see," Maddie said.

"I'll tell you what," Ann said. "Why don't you two get him dressed while I wet a washcloth for him to chew?" Better than her shoulder.

"He can wear one of his new things," Kate said. "Now that he's a big boy."

"I'll pick it out," Maddie said, already running from the room.

"Nothing stupid," Kate said, following. "Nothing with short sleeves."

"I'm not that dumb."

"Oh, yes, you are."

Ann paused before the bathroom mirror and pulled down the neck of her shirt. Sure enough, there was a telltale angry imprint on her skin. She unscrewed a bottle of water and dripped a few precious drops onto the corner of a washcloth.

Peter had vomited for two days now. She couldn't keep up with the fluid he was losing. She'd set a bowl of water outside among all her water collection bowls and cups, in hopes of freezing it into chips she could slide between his lips, but all she'd gotten was cold, dirty water. It was above freezing now.

At least he was asleep. She couldn't tell how high his fever had gone. She'd held her gloved fingers to his forehead, and the heat of his skin had burned through the latex. She couldn't get a more accurate reading than that. He was shivering so much that she was afraid he'd bite the tip right off the thermometer. All she had to go on was the brightness in his eyes and the lucidity of his words.

Which had come and gone. Like what he'd said the other day

about his giving Kate the stuffed owl. Ann had been the one who'd found it in the shop and brought it to Kate, a welcome-home gift when at last Social Services had finished their investigation and had let them take Kate back. Peter had smiled up at her, remembering the imagined memory.

"Mommy?"

Ann looked up to see Kate standing in the doorway. She looked frightened. "Mom, it's Maddie."

Ann raced up the stairs.

Maddie sat on the floor of her bedroom. Her head had fallen forward. Her breaths came in short bursts. She held her hand to her throat.

Ann rushed to her side. "What happened?"

Maddie's face was flushed.

"We weren't doing anything," Kate said. "Honest."

Ann could see large red hives forming along Maddie's neck. "You're having a reaction." To what, though? "Kate, stay with your sister."

She had to get the EpiPen.

*Five minutes.* The nurse had been specific. Five minutes: that was all the time she had from the very first onset of symptoms. After that, there could be brain damage.

Ann ran downstairs and flung open the coat closet. Her purse hung from its usual hook. She grabbed it and dumped it on the floor. *Four.* Things went rolling every which way, and she stopped them with her hands. Kneeling, she shoved aside lipstick, wallet, key ring. It must have skidded away. She stared blankly. It had to be here.

She looked all around, checked under the sofa, and moved the chairs. Certainly she would have heard it roll away. She yanked coats from hangers and checked pockets. Things had been so chaotic. Maybe she'd moved it for some reason, stowed it somewhere else, and forgotten the thought processes that had led her to do so. She ran to the pantry and brought out the first-aid supplies. It wasn't there, either.

Had Peter found it and moved it? He'd never do such a thing without saying so. It was no use asking him now. He'd just look at her with confusion.

She was almost panting. Five minutes. How long had it already been? *Slow down. Go back in time. Think.*

"Mom?" Kate's voice was high and panicky.

*Think.*

She had filled the prescriptions right away. One had gone to school to be stored with the nurse. The other had gone in her purse. When was the last time she'd used her purse? At the grocery store with Libby. No, wait. She hadn't taken it. She'd taken it out of her purse and left it at home. She'd known that they had only the one shot now and that shot had to be kept with Maddie. She'd been in a hurry. Where had she put it? She wheeled around. Her gaze skittered across the room and came to rest on the junk drawer.

She raced back upstairs. The nurse had shown her how to do it. She had watched the video. She came into the bedroom and found Maddie motionless on the floor. Kate knelt beside her, the baby in the crook of her arm. Ann removed the cap and upended the tube. Don't touch the tip, the nurse had said. That's where the needle is.

"Okay, baby. It's okay. I'm here."

*How long had it been?*

She gripped the pen in her right hand and jabbed the tip into Maddie's thigh. Maddie didn't even jerk away. My God, was it too late? The needle was designed to penetrate clothing, but there wasn't any way to see if it had done so successfully. She clenched the pen and willed Maddie to breathe. *Come on, sweetheart.* She wanted to withdraw the device and see if the needle tip was showing, but she had to hold the pen in place for ten seconds. She counted them off.

"Mom?" Kate said.

Maddie was breathing in shallow gasps.

Ann withdrew the pen and held it up. There was something she was supposed to look at on the pen to see if it had worked. She couldn't recall what. She glanced to Maddie. Thirty minutes. That was how long she had to get her daughter to the hospital.

# FORTY-FIVE

THE ICICLES WERE MELTING, TINY SILVER DROPS POISED on the rounded tips. The ground below was reflected in them, an entire town of miniaturized people going about their business. Amazing. The sun sparkled and the drips extended, glided down the lengths of ice, collected in soft, beautiful shapes. They stretched until all that connected them were thin gossamer strands that finally snapped. *Plop.*

Peter opened his eyes. He was in a bed. His tongue was sealed to the roof of his mouth. He pulled it free and rasped it across his lips.

"Ann?"

Had he made any sound? He tried again.

"Ann?"

She was busy with the kids. She'd be up soon.

He turned his head. A glass stood there with a bright green straw. It was full of clear brown liquid. He stared at it. Tea, perhaps. Not ginger ale. It was too dark for that. He coughed. Juice of some sort. Yes.

He blinked. Drums pounded a warning against his temples. He couldn't do that again. He had to move more slowly. He closed his eyes and opened them again. Much better. Now that he had that mastered, he could pull his arm up from beneath the covers. Yes, here it came with a sly rustling noise, more reptile than human. He held up his hand and was relieved to find fingers on the ends, instead of a pink forked tongue or tiny curved claws. He flexed his hand. He turned and extended his arm across his body toward the glass.

The glass felt soft. Soft? He had to be careful not to grip too tightly and squeeze out all the juice. Up it came, the green straw bobbing in the motion.

Now it was gone. He blinked. Drumbeats. He'd forgotten to do that with more care. He hoisted himself on one elbow and looked over the edge of the mattress. There the glass lay on the carpet in a pool of brown liquid.

Coughing almost sent him over the edge of the bed. He rolled back, panting, sank against his pillows.

What was this? Someone had brought grapefruit sections in a bowl. Exactly what he wanted. He reached his spoon in, brought up a pale oblong slice, and slid it between his lips. Each particle burst on his tongue. Now a slushy chunk of watermelon, pushed between his teeth and dripping down his chin.

When he opened his eyes again, he saw time had passed. He didn't know how he knew this, but the sensation in the room was different. It felt like it was later in the day.

He coughed. His hand came away red. His lips were cracked and bleeding.

Ann was too busy. He shouldn't expect her to figure out when he was thirsty. He could at least get his own glass of water. It was a simple thing, and he felt up to it.

He pushed back the covers and dropped his feet to the floor. His breath came in harsh gasps and he waited a moment to let things settle. He picked up the glass from the floor. He'd refill it himself.

He stood. He was a little wobbly, but if he went slowly, he'd be fine.

He shuffled along the carpeted floor. His socks were unpleasantly damp for some reason. He sagged against the wall and pulled them off. Much better.

A pile of stuff sat outside his door. It looked to be a bucket and some rags. He stepped around them and moved down the hallway. It felt good to be out of bed. It would be nice to see Kate and Maddie. His two beautiful girls. They would be busy doing something, and one of them would turn and see him. They'd stop whatever it was they were doing and come running.

Why was he standing here? He was on some sort of errand. A painful swallow brought it back to him. Water. He was fetching himself a glass of water. Ann was talking about water the other day. He couldn't recall what. No matter. He'd ask her when he saw her. He smiled, imagining the relief lighting her face when she saw him enter the room.

"Oh, Peter," she'd say, coming forward. "You're feeling better."

What did you know? He *was* feeling better.

# FORTY-SIX

ANN GLANCED INTO THE REARVIEW MIRROR. MADDIE looked back at her, barely recognizable with her puffy cheeks and her eyes swollen almost shut. The epinephrine must be wearing off. It had lent them thirty minutes and they'd used ten. Why had she wasted five of them racing through the house, grabbing things? Another minute opening the garage door, a few precious seconds to fumble with the lock on the back door. She hadn't taken the time to close the garage door or to heave the suitcases out of the backseat. She hadn't even run upstairs to knock on Peter's door and let him know she was leaving for the hospital. It'd be okay. He wouldn't even realize they were gone. He'd been sleeping most of the day.

"Hold on," she told Maddie. "We're almost there."

She took the highway. A blue sedan appeared in the distance. Someone else was out, too. Surely this meant the hospital would be open. The car soared around the bend toward her. There was something wrong about it. What was it? An instant later she knew. It was on her side of the road and it was zooming straight at her.

"Mom!" Kate yelled.

Ann swerved into the far right lane. The car shot past, the man looking over and grinning.

Kate turned to watch it disappear behind them. "Why did he do that?"

"I don't know." *Because he could.* Her hands were shaking. She wiped one palm on her jeans, then the other. Peter was right. The world had changed.

Up ahead, the tall gray building came into view. She accelerated onto the ramp, looking over as she swept around the curve and saw cars scattered across the parking lot, a welcome sight that could signify nothing. To come all this way and use up their precious minutes . . .

"Mom, look," Kate said.

*Thank God.* "I see them."

People clustered around the emergency room entrance. She pulled farther down the curb, well away from the crowd.

"Can we park here?" Kate said.

"It'll be fine." She got out and came around to the back door to pull it open. Three children stared at her. "Let's go, Maddie."

Maddie climbed down from her seat. Ann could hear the whispery sounds of her breathing. Ann pulled a mask down around her daughter's head. It hung below her chin. Peter had only adult-sized masks. Ann pressed the metal strip across Maddie's nose. She peeled off a strip of the duct tape and worked the scissors through it. Maddie shook her head. Ann grabbed her hand. "We have to do this. It won't hurt, honey. When we get home, I'll Vaseline it off. Just like I do with your Band-Aids."

She pressed the tape along one side of the mask, cut off another strip, and did the other side. "Let me know if it gets hard to breathe."

Maddie's eyes were frightened above the curve of her mask.

"Hold out your hands."

Maddie extended her hands, and Ann pulled a pair of latex gloves over them. The gloves drooped from her fingers. Ann rolled up the wristbands to tighten the fit. At least Maddie's palms and fingers were covered. "Don't touch anything."

She quickly pulled on her own mask and gloves and reached for the door handle.

"Can't I come, too?" Kate said.

"I don't want you and Jacob going in with us. There are sick people in there. You're safer out here. Just stay in the car. Don't unlock the doors for anybody. Honk the horn if someone bothers you."

"But—"

"Honey, I don't have time for this." Ann slammed the door shut, pressed the button on the remote, and heard the tiny beep. She couldn't look back at her daughter's white face.

She scooped Maddie into her arms and walked as fast as she was able toward the emergency room sign. Maddie's head bumped against her shoulder.

A man stood there, arms crossed. He wore a heavy-duty respirator with circular vents. A gun rested in the holster at his hip. A woman stood beside him with a clipboard, wearing a white paper mask like the one Ann wore. Hand-lettered signs were taped to the doors.

## FLU PATIENTS TO THE LEFT.
## PLEASE USE OTHER DOOR.

Ann pushed through the crowd, trying not to jostle Maddie.

"Hey," a man said.

"Sorry." Ann kept going. Her heart thumped in her chest.

The woman wearing a mask and holding a clipboard had to be a nurse. She was talking to someone and taking notes.

"Excuse me. I need help. My daughter's had an allergy attack."

The nurse looked over. "No fever?"

"It's not the flu."

The nurse came over, glanced at Maddie's face, and then beckoned. "Come this way."

The guard reached back to open the door.

"Hey, what about me?" A woman pushed around Ann, trying to get to the door ahead of her.

The guard stepped out in front of her, his arms crossed.

"But I've been waiting." There was some scuffling as the door closed.

Ann followed the nurse down a short hallway into the waiting room. It was warm and well lit. Wheeled screens had been brought in and set up along the periphery. People were behind them. Ann could hear them moaning, could see feet beneath the curtains. People lay on stretchers and slumped in chairs. Here was where the city was. It had emptied into this room.

The nurse pulled a stretcher out from where it stood along the wall. "Put her down here."

Ann set Maddie down on the sheet. Her daughter tried to sit up and look around. Ann patted Maddie's shoulder. "Lie down, honey."

The nurse took the rail along the side and started to pull the stretcher along. Ann grabbed the other railing.

"Doctor." The nurse stopped the stretcher beside a cart on wheels. "I've got a kid in anaphylaxis."

A man detached himself from where he'd been crouching beside an elderly woman in a wheelchair and came right over. He wore a mask, and his brown eyes looked kind. "What happened?"

A doctor, just like that. After weeks of everything failing, at last something was working the way it should at the time she needed it the most. She let out a shaky breath. "She had an allergy attack. I gave her an EpiPen."

"When?" He reached for a bottle from the cart beside them and squirted a dollop of antibacterial gel onto his palms, rubbing briskly.

"Thirty minutes ago maybe."

"Get the dexamethasone," he told the nurse, then to Ann, "Has she ever had an attack before?"

"Once. She was hospitalized for two nights."

He parted Maddie's coat and leaned over her with a stethoscope.

"No gloves?" Ann said with alarm.

"Ran out weeks ago." To Maddie, "Can you say your name?"

"Maddie."

"And how old are you, Maddie?"

"Eight and a half."

He lifted her sweater. Maddie's eyes went round, and she pushed his hand away.

"She's shy," Ann said.

"Sorry, honey. I just want to take a quick look." He pulled Maddie's sweater back down and patted her shoulder. "We'll need to give her some medicine."

"The nebulizer treatment?"

"Yeah, I would if I had any, but I don't. But the shot will help."

Maddie's eyes were huge above her mask, and she shook her head.

Ann took her hand. "It's okay, sweetheart."

The nurse appeared with a syringe.

The doctor had told her to get something Ann had never heard of. "What kind of medicine are you giving her?"

"It's called dexamethasone. It's an anti-inflammatory. It takes a little while to work, but it lasts a long time."

"How long?"

"Two weeks."

Two weeks was good. Two weeks was a miracle. But should Ann allow this? Nothing about this visit resembled that first hospital trip, but the doctor seemed so confident. Really, what were her options? Maddie was watching with worried eyes.

"It's all right, honey." Ann pulled off Maddie's coat, pushed up the sleeves of the two cardigans she wore, and bared her upper arm. "It'll be over in just a second."

The nurse swabbed Maddie's skin with a pad and uncapped the needle. "Here we go. Just a small pinch."

Maddie squealed. "Ouch." She looked at Ann accusingly.

"All done," the nurse said, pulling out the needle.

"You know what triggered it?" the doctor said.

"The reaction she had before was to a cat. But we don't have a cat and we've been inside the house for months."

"Home's the best place for her right now. But you'd better figure this out, or it'll recur."

How could Maddie have developed a reaction to something in her own room? It was the middle of winter. Nothing was growing outside that either girl could have brought inside on their clothes or hair.

The doctor patted Maddie's shoulder. "You should start to feel better pretty soon." He looked to the nurse. "Keep an eye on her. Let me know if there's no relief in fifteen minutes."

The nurse nodded. "Be right back," she told Maddie, and went off.

Ann pulled over a chair and sat down beside the stretcher. It was so warm in here. She unzipped her coat and took Maddie's gloved hand in hers and squeezed. Kate and Jacob had been alone now for thirty minutes. Kate would be getting anxious, but she'd keep the car doors locked. She'd pound the horn if she had to. She was probably singing to Jacob, and rocking him. It was well past his afternoon naptime. He might fall asleep, curled up in Kate's arms. "Why don't you close your eyes, Maddie, and see if you can get a little rest?"

She hoped Peter was still sleeping, the sun falling into his room and giving the illusion of warmth. He kept kicking off the covers. She kept pulling them back up.

The waiting room was bright and surprisingly quiet. People occupied wheelchairs, folding chairs, stretchers. The nurse had gone over to talk to a young black man who leaned against the wall, cradling his elbow in one hand. A little girl sat cross-legged beside him, rose when he motioned. All three of them disappeared into a curtained alcove. An old man sat in the corner beneath the TV, gesturing and nodding to himself. IV tubing snaked out from beneath one sleeve. Someone lay softly moaning on a stretcher nearby. Ann couldn't tell if it was a woman or a man. There was a whimper from behind one screen. Booted feet thudded to the floor. Urgent murmuring, then a young woman put her head around the screen. "Doctor, he's awake."

These were the people who didn't have the flu. These were the diabetics, the heart attacks, the broken bones. What did they do if someone needed surgery? What about the women going into labor?

The nurse came over with the clipboard. "Mind filling this out?"

Ann looked down at the page and saw that it was handwritten. She glanced at the nurse, who shrugged.

"We ran out of forms a long time ago. This is the best we can do. At least we can keep up with the flow here."

Unlike the other side, where the flu patients were. Ann took the pen the nurse extended and began filling in the blanks. Name of patient, age, address. "What's it like over there?"

"You don't want to know." She put her hands on her hips and looked around the room. "Sometimes I think most everyone's died."

"My husband's sick."

The nurse looked back at Ann. She was a short woman, plain-faced, her black hair scraped back into a stubby ponytail. Her brown eyes looked gentle. "I'm sorry."

"He's had it for seven days. When should I expect him to get better?"

"It usually peaks at five days, so you're probably over the worst of it now. Make sure to keep him hydrated. But no tap water. You do know about that, right?"

"We guessed."

"Have you been giving him anything for fever?"

"Ibuprofen, when he can keep it down."

"If he's made it this long, he'll be okay. The important thing is you kept him home. Good for you. You did the right thing."

It hadn't been heroic at all. She hadn't wanted him anywhere else. "When I first drove up, I was afraid you'd be shut down. All of this is such a relief to see."

"We've had some bad patches. The generator died a couple weeks ago." The nurse picked up Maddie's wrist. "Fortunately, one of our patients was able to get it back up and running. We've gotten some supplies through, but there was a while where we were all living on vending machine candy. We've lost a lot of staff. Some of them just can't get in." She released Maddie's hand and patted it. "And some of them . . ." She shrugged her shoulders again.

Ann handed the clipboard back to the nurse. "How are you getting to and from work?"

"Carpooling. There's a gas station with a generator that only fills up for emergency vehicles. Sometimes I'm here for days before I can get a ride home." The nurse clicked the pen and jotted something down, then handed Ann a sheet of paper. "Send this in to your insurance company. Whenever."

Whenever mail service resumed. Whenever there was someone

there to receive the receipt. Whenever. Ann folded the paper and tucked it into her purse.

The nurse nodded toward Maddie. "She's looking much better." Maddie was asleep, her eyes closed, her skin losing some of that awful ruddy color. The swelling was definitely going down. "But you'd better find out what caused her reaction. Next time we might be out of everything."

"Thank you."

*For pulling us out of the crowd, for getting the doctor so quickly, for coming back to check on my daughter. For giving me some hope.*

"Sure."

Ann rose and hooked the strap of her purse over her shoulder. She put a hand on Maddie's arm and gently shook her awake.

In the parking lot, they passed a woman leaning against a car, sobbing helplessly, her hands pressed to her face. Ann put a hand on Maddie's shoulder and steered her down the sidewalk. Maddie was going to be okay. They were all okay, and Peter was getting better. By tomorrow, or maybe by the next day, he'd be well enough to get in the van.

She wondered where that gas station was the nurse had been talking about.

# FORTY-SEVEN

---

*B*LUE WALLS PRESSED AGAINST HIS HEAD AND SHOUL-
ders, then rolled back. Somehow the hallway had become an
ocean. Peter could hardly breathe. Coughing seized him and bent
him in two. He sat down heavily on the step and grabbed the railing
to keep from being swept away by the flood of carpet. His heart
pounded a warning. He placed his palm there to calm it and felt the
viruses teeming beneath his touch.

Now Ann was there, bending down. "You'd better drink this."

He blinked and he was alone again. Right. He'd been getting a
glass of water. He pushed himself to a standing position. The stair-
well shrank to a pinpoint, then expanded. He shuffled across the
cold kitchen floor. Grit rolled beneath the soles of his feet.

He reached for the faucet and curled his fingers around the
handle. Nothing moved. He wasn't pushing hard enough. A sudden
splash of water into the sink.

He looked down. He'd given Kate her first bath in a steel sink
just like this one. She'd blinked up at him with surprise as he ladled
warm water across her belly. He'd bent to kiss her forehead and Ann
had snapped the picture. She'd framed it and put it on her nightstand for a while.

William's first few baths had been quiet, the water lapping the sides of the tub, the baby lying there cocooned on his bath sponge, his tiny thumb in his mouth. Peter would work the suds around his little bald head and William's eyes would drift shut. Peter would lift him up and wrap him in a towel and carry him, sleeping, into the bedroom, where Ann would be combing Kate's hair. They would look at each other over the heads of their children. They'd had no idea how closely sadness would follow on the heels of such simple happiness.

Peter held his hand beneath the silvery stream of water. It felt as cold as lake water. He thought of Canada geese flapping in perfect V's across the golden water. A tight synchrony, but every so often a bird would veer away and head off in the wrong direction. The rest of the birds would continue on. Not one would pull out of the V to retrieve the lost comrade.

No geese this season. This year, they'd all pulled out of formation.

He brought his fingers up and patted his forehead and his cheeks, let the water drip down his neck.

Ann had almost drowned on their honeymoon in an ocean as warm as bathwater. She had waded out behind him, pulling up her knees and laughing. Then she was gone, snatched under and rolled away by the riptide. He'd plunged after her, caught her by one elbow, and yanked her free. She'd put her arms around his neck and kissed him. "My hero," she said, laughing.

He heard drums. He turned his head. The room tilted. He placed a palm on the counter to steady himself. There was muffled barking, too. He didn't remember a dog at the hotel they'd stayed at. Cats, yes, two of them slinking from room to room. But no dogs.

The walls trembled with each resounding thud. Where were they, these impatient drummers? He moved across the floor, letting the sound draw him through the dining room. His feet caught on the fringe of the rug. He lifted them free. He brushed past chairs, the hard corner of the table. *I'm coming, I'm coming.*

He was getting close. He could feel their presence in his bones. The light was brighter here, too, flooding in through panes of glass, glowing on the floor and shining up to the ceiling. The wall held him up. He saw dark shapes moving behind the glass. People were out there. He put his eye to the glass and peered out. He didn't know them. They were strangers and they wanted to get in.

He squinted. They moved into the light. He couldn't believe it.

It was his father standing there. Ann's sister, too. They'd made the journey together. Pleased, he reached for the doorknob.

# FORTY-EIGHT

W HAT TOOK SO LONG?" KATE DEMANDED AS ANN SLID
open the back door. The baby reached over to bat Kate's
chin, and she grabbed his hand and held it. "Is Maddie okay?"

"I got a shot." Maddie pushed past Ann and scrambled into the
car. She'd torn the mask from her face and gripped it in one hand.
"And the doctor pulled up my shirt in front of everybody." She fumbled for the seatbelt with fat fingers, and Ann reached to help her.

Kate sat back. "So, everything's okay now?"

"We still don't know what caused Maddie's reaction," Ann said.

"I thought she was just allergic to cats."

"She must have developed a reaction to something new." Ann
got behind the wheel and slammed the door. She looked in the
rearview mirror at Kate. "I need you to help me figure out what it
was."

Kate looked worriedly at Maddie, who was staring out the window. "How do we do that?"

"I don't know." Two weeks, the doctor had said. "Tell me what
you two were doing when Maddie got sick."

"Nothing. We were getting Jacob dressed."

Ann turned the key in the ignition and pulled away from the
curb. "You didn't go outside?"

"No."

"Maybe it's dust." How would she know? She wouldn't. "When we get home, I'll wipe everything down. Stay out of your rooms until then. Maddie, you'd better stay downstairs."

They exited onto the highway. Heat poured in from the vents. They drove past a hardware store, a cellular phone store, and a string of restaurants. All closed. The clock on the dashboard read four-fifteen. They'd been gone an hour. As soon as they got home, she'd go upstairs and check on Peter. With any luck, he'd have been asleep the whole time. They'd gone through the worst, the nurse had said. Tomorrow would be better.

Kate said, "Was that there before?"

A fire engine sat in the middle of a vacant parking lot, parked at an angle as though it had slid to a hasty stop. One door hung ajar. Ann couldn't recall whether it had been there. She'd been focused on getting to the hospital.

"It's got something written on it."

Ann glanced over. Maddie looked, too. A black circle was scrawled across the side of the engine, with a bold line crossed through it.

"I've seen that before," Kate said. "It's like that thing on Smith and Libby's door."

A huge vehicle like that had to have a big gas tank. Ann wondered if anyone else had thought of that.

"Only that one says three."

A three here, a two on Libby's door—small numbers that added up to too many.

Ann glanced into the rearview mirror and saw Kate staring out the window. Then a look of horror flashed across her face. She'd figured it out. She clapped a hand to her mouth. Jacob squirmed in her lap. After a moment, Kate allowed him to grab her hand back.

Ann tightened her grip on the steering wheel. She needed to get everyone home before they saw anything else.

Here was the grocery store, the clothing shop, the office supply store. Nothing but a row of blank windows and dark doors.

"Wait," Maddie said suddenly. "There's Heyjin."

"Who?" Kate said.

"A girl in my class from Korea. She's right there on that bus. I think she sees me." Maddie waved.

Ann glanced over to the big blue-and-silver bus that was pulling past them. She glimpsed windows filled with children's faces.

"Where's she going, Mom?"

"I don't know."

"I don't see her mom."

"I don't see anybody's mom," Kate said. "Or dad, either."

How had the children been rounded up? How long had they gone without anyone taking care of them? This was what Peter was afraid would happen. He'd been right to worry. As soon as they got home, she'd bundle him up and they'd leave. They wouldn't wait even one more hour. He could sleep just as well in the van as he could in the house, and he was past the contagious point. Better, too, to get Maddie out of the house and whatever it was that had caused her reaction.

Ann turned in to their neighborhood. She felt a heavy curtain drawing around them, close and familiar and suffocating. The road swept along the brick and stucco and columned houses, wound past the blackened husk where the Guarnieris' house once stood. She'd been to parties in some of these houses. She'd walked the girls past them on their way to the park. Now they all felt like strangers to her, soulless buildings instead of homes. It would be good to break free and head north.

"Barney's back," Kate said.

Sure enough, there he was, trotting around the back of the house. These past few days he kept disappearing, raising Ann's hopes that he'd found another family to take him in, but then he'd reappear, nosing around the patio or scratching at the garage door.

Ann bumped the van into the garage and shut off the engine. "Maddie, go straight into the laundry room. Take everything off and put it into the sink. I'm sorry, honey, but I'll have to scrub you down and wash your hair."

"In cold water?"

"I'll be quick, I promise." She bent and looked at Kate through the open car door. Whatever it was might be clinging to them, too.

"You wait here with Jacob. I'll bring you something to change into when I'm done with Maddie."

Kate nodded, looking distracted. "Why is Barney barking like that?"

"I don't know." The dog wasn't a barker. The hollow sounds reverberated around the small cul-de-sac. If Peter hadn't been awake before, he'd be awake now.

Ann prodded Maddie before her into the house. "Leave everything turned inside out. I'll go get a towel and clean clothes."

"Okay." Maddie went into the laundry room and shut the door.

There was a steady splashing sound. Strange. Ann stepped into the kitchen and saw the faucet was running. She was sure she hadn't left the water on. She hadn't been anywhere near the sink. Well, she must have. There was no other explanation. She switched it off. A peculiar silence settled around her. It was nerves, the adrenaline of rushing Maddie to the hospital and being out of the house for the first time in almost two months. No wonder coming home felt strange.

Clothes first, then she'd check on Peter. He needed to drink something, and maybe he could keep down some ibuprofen. His appetite might be returning, too. She should try and get some nourishment in him before they left. Soup, maybe. The hot liquid would soothe his throat.

She couldn't wait to go check on Peter and see for herself if his fever had finally broken. She went to the stairs and halted, hand on the railing. Something had caught her eye. Something was out of place. She turned her head. Not something but someone lying in the front hall. She glimpsed green pajamas, long, narrow feet. Whoever it was wasn't moving.

*Peter.*

Then she was beside him. She dropped to her knees and grasped his shoulders. She could feel the sinew of his arms through the flannel. He was so thin. "Honey, you shouldn't have gotten up."

He sagged against her. "Come on, sweetheart. Let me help you."

His head lolled to one side. He looked at her through half-open eyes.

She went cold. Something pushed itself into her throat. She laid her hand to his bare cheek. His skin was waxy. It had an unusual yellow color to it. His eyes had gone opaque and sightless.

"Peter?" she whispered, but she knew he wouldn't respond. Wherever Peter was, he wasn't here in this body. He was gone.

The world plummeted away from her. She began to shake.

*No.*

She pressed both hands against his cheeks. "Come back."

His mouth sagged open.

"Peter! Don't you dare leave me! Peter!"

She patted his chest, slapped his cheeks, shook him so that his head fell back.

"Peter!"

Sobbing, she wrapped her arms around him and held him as close as she could, willing her heart to beat for both of them. "Please, please." It had been like this before. It had been too late, then, for William, too.

Outside, Barney let out a howl.

# FORTY-NINE

"WHY WAS HE DOWNSTAIRS?" MADDIE STOOD BESIDE Kate at the top of the stairs. Peter lay at the bottom. This was as close as she'd let them go. Ann had covered him with the blanket she'd pulled from the bed. He'd looked so cold and miserable. So alone. She couldn't bear it. From the bedroom behind them, Jacob wailed in feeble protest.

"Maybe he was looking for us," Kate said. "Mom, we left him all by himself."

"I know."

He'd been all alone. Had he suffered? Had he been frightened? The girls pressed against her.

At last, she ushered her daughters back from the stairs and into the bedroom. They wouldn't sleep in the family room anymore. Too many memories crowded that confined space. Jacob had fallen asleep on his makeshift pallet on the floor. Ann checked him, then went to the bed and lifted up the covers. The girls slid in, one on either side of her, and lay close. Maddie was weeping. Ann held their cold hands in hers, their fingertips grazing her palms. Shadows collected along the ceiling.

Kate said, "I'm never going to love anybody ever again."

"Oh, honey." Ann rubbed her thumb against her daughter's palm.

"How could he leave us?"

"He didn't mean to."

"How come you didn't get sick?" Maddie said. "How come we didn't?"

"I don't know."

"Are you going to die?" Maddie's breath was soft against Ann's cheek.

"No." The truth? She already felt dead.

Maddie said in a small voice, "What about us, Mommy? Are we going to die, too?"

"Everyone dies." Kate tugged her hand free and rolled over onto her side, away from them.

*Yes.* Ann looked at the ceiling. *Everyone dies.* She lay there in the dark, listening to her children breathe. She filled her heart with it.

THE MOON RODE LOW AMONG THIN CLOUDS.

Ann knelt, studied the ground in the gray light, looking for tree roots. Too close to the birch and the sun would be obscured. Too far and the effect of sun through the branches would be lost. She had to frame the sunset just right. She ran a mittened hand across the surface, checking for rocky outcroppings, then stood. Wedging the tip of the blade into the hard earth, she stepped up to balance on its end the way she'd seen Peter do it. She let her body sag and bear down with all its puny weight. The shovel skidded sideways.

She wriggled the blade to get a better purchase on the soil. Still, the shovel tilted as she stepped on it. Peter had made it look so easy, one foot pushing, both hands lifting. She grasped the handle, lifted up the shovel, and drove it down. A ping as the metal struck something. Rock, perhaps. She retrieved the flashlight from where she'd set it on the ground and shone the beam across the dirt. She saw the tiny chip she'd made. It was a start.

She fell into a rhythm. Lift the shovel and let it drop. Scrape away the bits of earth. Lift, drop, scrape. After a while, she'd carved a narrow trough. It didn't have to be wide, just deep.

Peter, looking at her over the tops of his reading glasses. Reaching over to fill her coffee cup. Sitting down beside her on the couch and stretching his legs out beside hers.

The moon rose as she worked, releasing a feeble wash of light. After a while, she found she no longer needed the help of the flashlight, so she switched it off to save the batteries. Every so often, she stopped and looked around. No one was there. The street was empty, the houses dark.

Those men with the truck would return. They'd been polite the first time, but they wouldn't be so tolerant the second time. They'd hear the quality of her voice and would know she was lying to them. She couldn't leave anything for them to find. She drove the shovel down, again and again.

*It's always been like this for us,* she'd said to him on the patio that night. She'd felt so alone, all her mistakes crowded around her. He'd answered, *No, it hasn't. Don't you remember?*

Yes, she remembered.

Peter, loping behind the girls as they wheeled unsteadily on their bikes. Setting up the sprinkler on the first day of warm weather. Pointing out the flight pattern of a particular bird, parting the grass to reveal a burrow. Sitting between them on the porch and watching thunderclouds roil in the distance. All those lessons couldn't go unlearned. Somewhere in Kate and Maddie, Peter lived on.

Ann crouched on the hard earth and reached down; the hole went all the way to her elbow. Twelve inches, maybe more. Nowhere near deep enough. She climbed into the hole and went from there.

The shovel rang against something. The handle vibrated, the motion thrumming up the bones of her arms. She knelt and felt around. Through the wool of her mittens, she felt a sharp edge. She dug around with both hands and levered up a heavy chunk of limestone. This old farmland was full of it. She heaved it aside.

The digging became easier, the compacted soil giving way to softer clay. It clung in thick clumps to the shovel blade. She was up to mid-thigh now. Here was another slice of rock. She spaded away a shovelful of dirt and tried to pry the limestone free. The muscles between her shoulder blades and all along her rib cage felt tight and sore. Her fingertips throbbed and blisters were forming all around the web between thumb and forefinger. Was it her imagination or could she see her hands more clearly now?

She looked up. The sun was coming. She had to go faster. She had to be done before the girls got up. She had to erase all activity before the truck showed up. She'd left Peter alone in the end, but she wouldn't abandon him now.

CROUCHING IN THE FOYER, ANN DREW THE MATERIAL UP AND over, wrapping Peter and the top sheet together in a cocoon of cotton. Kate's owl went, too. She brought the corners up and tied them, the material bunching in her grasp. Up and down the length of the sheet, she moved, tying knots until he lay contained in a weave of cloth.

She shook open the comforter and spread it on the floor, lifted his legs, and put them on one end. She put her hands against his shoulders and pushed hard. This was the man she loved. She blinked away hot tears.

His body rocked, then settled. She picked up the corner of the comforter and dragged him across the threshold. Peter's voice as they tried to maneuver Maddie's old dresser down the stairs. *Grab it by the end, Ann.* His laughter when he realized she was pinned to the wall.

A rock snagged the fabric. She leaned and pulled, stopped to rest. Her cheeks were wet. She swiped at them with her sleeve. A jangling noise made her whirl around to see Barney slinking toward her in the half-light.

"Go away."

The dog halted.

"I mean it, damn it! Get out of here!"

Barney whirled and disappeared down the street.

BY THAT AFTERNOON, A FRIGID WIND HAD TAKEN OVER. A cold front was moving in. The three of them stood shivering beneath the empty branches of the birch. It gave no cover. Maddie huddled on one side, Kate on the other, the baby in her arms. The sun sank behind the rooftops. Ann had waited for it and the clouds had obliged, thinning themselves into frothy strands that amplified the red and orange rays of the setting sun.

She opened the Bible and thumbed through the pages, looking for the right passages. There were several options. Everything was clearly marked and italicized, when to stand, what to say. Her eyes burned. The tiny black type swam before her. A hard, painful knot was lodged in her throat. The words refused to crawl past her lips. She shut the Bible and stood there, looking at the mounded yellow earth, feeling utterly helpless to guide her husband and children through this narrow tunnel.

Maddie's cold hand crept into hers.

Wind buffeted them.

So much lost.

"Now I lay me down to sleep," Ann said.

Maddie sniffed, then lifted her voice. "I pray the Lord my soul to keep. May God's love be with me through the night..."

Kate came in at the last line, her voice tremulous and low.

"And wake me with the morning light."

# FIFTY

———

ANN STOOD BY THE BEDROOM WINDOW AND LOOKED OUT over the backyard. The moon hadn't yet risen. Everything out there was shifting black and gray, ground and house and sky. The night took on a different quality when there was no artificial light and noise to compete with it. It was longer and fuller and much more present. Getting through it required effort. She remembered this from before. She'd stood on the edge of a canyon and, for a long time, looked deep into the abyss. She'd finally stepped back. She didn't think that she could do it again.

A gust of wind rattled the panes and plucked at the eaves. What was it bringing this time? The wind could be fierce here. Once it had lifted the table from the patio and sent it spinning into Libby's backyard. Smith had come out to help her carry it back, and they'd laughed at how ferocious the wind could be.

The wind howled louder. It roared across the yard straight at the house.

Peter lay beneath it all, alone.

A shadow moved across the grass and disappeared beneath the spiky branches of the birch tree. She strained, trying to see, but the shape didn't reemerge on the other side.

She had to lean on the front door to open it. The wind wrenched it from her grasp and slammed it against the house. The blanket around her shoulders sailed up. She grabbed at its ends and knotted them around her neck. She had to work to get down the stairs, curling her body protectively around the things she carried. Objects rattled down the street. Trash cans, probably, and whatever else had been left lying around.

Now the wind was at her back, propelling her around the corner of the house. She stumbled across the uneven pitch of the ground. She stopped by the birch and stood looking a long time into the darkness. What was he doing there? The clouds parted and nascent moonlight picked out the small shape huddled at the base of the tree.

"Barney."

His eyes gleamed. He was staring at her.

"Here, boy."

She took a few steps, then stooped to set down the bowl. She didn't see him move, but there he was, hunched and lapping voraciously at the food. Reaching into her pocket, she pulled out the stiff stick of beef. It was their last stick of jerky. She peeled back the wrapper and broke off a piece. The dog came close and took it from her fingers with surprising tenderness. She gave him another bit. Another polite nibble and she fed him the final third.

He sniffed her fingers. He wasn't limping anymore. Peter had done a good job of treating his injury.

She unscrewed the jar of water and poured its contents into the bowl. He drank, pushing the bowl around on the ground, sneezed. He looked up at her, then padded back to the tree. She untied the blanket from around her shoulders and lowered it to the ground. He pawed it, nosed up a corner, turned in a circle. He collapsed with a sigh and closed his eyes.

She sat down beside him and leaned her head back against the trunk.

"Peter planted this tree."

The moon glided into view, huge and yellow and full.

"It was in memory of our son, William."

The name felt full in her mouth. The dog moved closer and rested his head on her lap. She put her hand on the scruff of his neck, the fur cold and springy beneath her fingers. She felt grateful for his simple devotion.

Peter wasn't alone anymore.

# FIFTY-ONE

ANN PRESSED A CLEAN WASHCLOTH ALONG THE PORCE-
lain interior of the bathtub, brought it up, and squeezed out a
few drops over the measuring cup. She lifted the cup and eyed the
level. She'd collected a whopping nine ounces. So now they were
down to bottled water. She'd lined the plastic bottles on the kitchen
counter. There were fifty-three of them. Fifty-three bottles wouldn't
go far among four people, even if one of them was a baby and two of
them were children. Plus, there was now Barney to think about.

She stood, swayed. Dizzy, putting a hand against the wall, she
waited for the bright spots before her eyes to dance away.

She carried the cup down the stairs. A brown haze hung in the
room. All the fires had been smoking recently. Maybe the chimney
was blocked. "Kate, open a window, please, honey."

Kate pushed herself up from where she'd been lying on the sofa.
She'd been doing a lot of lying around lately. So had Maddie. It
wasn't just grief, Ann thought, feeling a pinch of fear. Their bodies
were conserving.

Maddie said, "Would you rather have a hot fudge sundae or
pizza?"

Kate unlatched the window. "Pizza."

"What if it was a Graeter's Shamrock Surprise Sundae?"

"Doesn't matter." Kate sprawled back on the sofa. "I never want to eat anything cold again."

A persistent mist rolled against the windowpanes. Ann had waited, hopeful, all day, but it hadn't turned to rain. Still, the bowls she'd left out on the patio might hold some moisture. It was time to rotate them out, anyway.

Kate said, "Would you rather have electricity or the phone?"

It was as though they were living in some undeveloped country. Stay here and wait for help or chance the risk of exposure and go out looking? No. She wouldn't leave Peter. She pulled down the plastic bowls from the cabinet.

"If I say electricity, would that mean TV, too?" Maddie asked.

"Uh-huh."

"What about the radio?"

"Yes. I think so."

"Okay. The electricity."

Ann filled the sink with water and poured in the last of the bleach. The sharp smell of it made her eyes tear.

"You sure?" Kate asked. "If you had the phone, you could call Grandma."

Sooner or later, she would have to risk it. Leave the children alone and go look for food. How many trips would she have to make before she found an open store? Peter had said there were no police around. He'd said there'd been a scuffle in line that no one had stepped in to break up. That had been weeks ago. Tempers would be even more dangerous now. She set the containers on a dishtowel to drip-dry and glanced at the girls. Jacob scooted along the floor toward her. He was growing so fast, he was practically crawling. And Libby would miss it all.

She had seventy-four dollars in cash. She'd load up on whatever she could find, the basics, like rice and powdered milk. It might be enough to last another week. She couldn't think beyond that. Bending, she picked up the baby and pressed her lips to his warm, downy head. Something glinted on the sleeve of his shirt. She turned him around in her arms and plucked it free.

Maddie said, "Kate? Do you think the TV's working some-where?"

"I don't know."

Ann held up the golden filament. A long hair curved between her fingers. Dread curled in her belly. It looked like . . . a cat hair. But how was that possible? "Kate," she said, "where did you get this shirt Jacob's wearing?"

"From his new bag of clothes."

"The clothes I got from next door?"

"I guess."

She meant the bag of hand-me-downs Ann had retrieved from the closet in Jacob's bedroom. Libby's sister must have had a cat. So this was the source of Maddie's allergy attack: cat hair, their old enemy. Dread evaporated away into pure relief. "Look, girls," she said. "Cat hair."

They glanced over.

"I'm going to change Jacob," Ann said. "Don't put him in any more of his new things until I wash them."

Kate shrugged and flopped over on her belly. "Okay."

Ann paused in the doorway and regarded her daughters. There was no way to deliver this but directly. "Listen, girls. If anything happens, I want you to take the baby and go to Dr. Singh's." She'd glimpsed him the day before, balanced on a stepladder and doing something to one of his gutters. She'd watched him for a while. He never once coughed or wiped his nose.

"Why?" Maddie raised herself up onto an elbow. "We don't even know him."

"What do you mean, 'if anything happens'?" Kate swung her feet to the floor. "Are you sick, too?"

"I'm fine. I'm not sick." She jiggled the baby on her hip. "I just want you to be prepared. That's all. Dr. Singh's a medical doctor. He'll take care of you. He'll help you find Grandma and Aunt Beth."

"Whatever." Kate lay back down and drew up the blankets.

"Honey. You have to listen."

But Kate merely rolled onto her side and faced the sofa cush-ions.

She reminded her of Shazia, the way she was lying there, so still and distant. Where was Shazia? Had she safely reunited with her lover? A tide of loneliness washed over her.

Maddie was watching her. "I heard you, Mommy."

Ann smiled down at her compassionate child. "I know you did, darling."

Peter had been right. All the neighbors should have banded together. They should have taken turns hauling the trash to the dump and going to the market. But everyone had been terrified. No one had trusted anyone. She hadn't even trusted Libby.

*What goes around comes around.* That's what Peter's father used to say. He'd been right. She was getting what she deserved, and now there was no one there to help her.

She glanced through the window at Barney, lying there beneath the birch. The thought crept in.

Almost no one.

THE FOG MUFFLED HER FOOTSTEPS DOWN THE PAVEMENT. SHE halted at the end of the curving road and stood looking at the brick ranch house.

It had been different when she'd gone into Libby's house. Then, it had been for the baby. It hadn't felt like trespassing. She'd been inside it a million times before. She knew how the sunlight patterned the floor in the morning. She knew that the floor beneath the dining room table creaked, but only in the summer, and that if you stood at the bottom of the stairs, you could hear televisions going in three different rooms.

This house, however, was a stranger to her. She'd never been welcome here. She'd never once been invited in. The closest she'd ever come was walking past on the sidewalk when the front door hung open. Even then, she'd never really caught more than a glimpse of lamplight or wood floor before the door shut again.

The front door was securely latched. She considered the narrow window beside the door. Even if she managed to crack it open, she wouldn't be able to reach in far enough to unlatch the door. And what if it had a key lock? Her heart sank.

The side gate creaked open easily under her hand, and she found herself in a secret garden. Tall bushy shapes loomed at her. Ivy crawled across the fence. There was a pool sheeted with weathered green material, chairs stacked to one side, a shed at the back. She turned to the house. A set of French doors was centered between two large picture windows. She walked over and jiggled the door handle, but it refused to turn. She chewed her lip in frustration.

Cupping her gloved hands around her eyes, she peered in. Pale green walls. A beige curve of countertop. A small table and chairs set to one side. Below the legs of one chair lay a bedroom slipper, wrong side up. Beneath it spread a puddle of something brown. She let her focus go soft and stepped back.

All right, all right. She'd have to be quick, before she lost her nerve. She scanned the patio. The metal chairs were a possibility. She picked one up and hefted it. The French doors would be tricky, their panes close-set and bracketed by thick strips of wood. She'd have to try one of the picture windows.

Holding the chair by its arms, she swung the pointed legs at the glass. The impact rattled up her arms. The glass shook and reflected her image back at her. She hadn't even scratched it. Stepping back, she whirled in a circle and smacked the chair at the glass. The blow wrenched the chair from her grasp. Surely that had done something. But when she checked, she saw no blemish, not the tiniest crack. In disbelief, she ran her gloved fingers over the cold, perfectly smooth surface. What was this stuff, bulletproof? She clenched her hands into fists. Of course it wasn't. It was ordinary window glass. The fault lay in the chair. It wasn't heavy enough. And she wasn't strong enough.

Peter could have done this. It would have taken him one swing.

She ran her gaze over the yard. Finn had lined his gardens with bricks, pushing them into the earth so they stood at angles. Maybe she'd have better luck with a smaller weapon. Crouching, she dug her fingers into the dirt and pried a brick free.

She leaned back. With all her might, she hurled the brick at the window. The glass crazed but held. *Yes!* Scooping up the brick, she threw it again. A tiny hole opened. She bashed the brick over and over at this soft, malleable spot, watching with glee as the cobweb of cracks spread outward. When the brick crumbled beneath her grasp, she ran to dig up another.

On her third brick, her hand punched through. With a shocked gasp, she stopped herself. *My God.* What if she sliced her arm on the jagged edges? She was no better than that stranger on TV, the one she saw hammering the Watergate windows. Now she understood what drove him. Not fear, not rage. Desperation. She released the brick to fall unseen on the other side of the glass and closed her fingers into a narrow point. Slowly, inch by inch, she withdrew her arm until she stood at last whole and uninjured.

No more bricks. She used the chair instead to chip at the broken edges, widening the hole until it was big enough. She dropped the chair and climbed through.

The smell slammed into her, nauseating and thick. The mentholated Vaseline she'd spread along her upper lip did nothing to keep it at bay. The room was in shadow. She made a wide circle around the leaking thing on the linoleum, stepped to the cabinets, and banged one open. Glasses. She went from door to door, finding dishes, cups, blender, thermos, waffle iron, everything tidily put away, all of it useless.

She spun around to the pantry. Empty. So was the refrigerator. She reached into the murky interior and patted the shelves to make sure. She lowered the oven door. She checked the microwave. Peter had seen towers of cans. There'd been gallons of water. Where was it all?

She stood there.

Without meaning to, she found herself focusing on the thing lying at the end of the room. It was a black-and-yellow pool of fat and bone and sinew, covered in dark greasy material that had once been clothing. *Walter Finn, damn it, what have you done with the things you hoarded?*

The bathtubs and sinks were dusty and bare. She tracked through rooms, scanned closets, checked under beds, and unzipped suitcases. Coming to the end of the long hallway, she switched on her flashlight and pulled down the attic ladder. Standing on its top-most rung, she swept her light around the rafters. Pink insulation puffed between wooden beams. A crumpled beer can lay on its side. A magnificent spiderweb stretched across a far corner.

The basement was damp with the odor of mildew. The windows were shrouded by black plastic. One corner drooped, letting in a faint stripe of light. Weather insulation? Then no. Finn had light-proofed the basement. The furnace crouched sullenly along one wall. She spied two wooden chairs, a rolled-up rug, a dozen or so paint cans. She came around the corner and saw a long folding table with a chair positioned before it. A computer sat there. She pushed the buttons and tried the keyboard. It was dead. Same for the radio beside it. A portable heater sat beneath the table. She thought about taking it, then decided against it. It was useless without power.

The garage was empty, too. She opened car doors, shone her flashlight across the seats and footwells, raised the trunk and pushed aside the tarp and bottles of motor oil he kept there.

Back to the kitchen, gagging at the foul odor, she searched every cabinet again. Nothing. Someone else had beaten her to it. They'd come in and taken everything, leaving behind not so much as a salt-shaker or a tea bag.

But did that make sense? Trespassers would have left some evidence of their presence, either in cabinet doors hanging ajar or—she glanced at the gaping hole in the window—broken glass.

The room had grown cold and moist with fog. She looked down again to the form on the floor. "You win." *You old bastard.*

Stepping back through the jagged hole, she looked around the yard. The sun, having never made a real appearance all day, was sliding below the treetops. Night was coming. Her gaze lit on the shed tucked in the far corner.

The door was locked. Keys hung inside the front hall closet. She'd seen them dangling there. Surely one of them belonged to this door. It turned out to be the third key she tried.

She found herself in a musty space. Here, too, Finn was obses-sively tidy. Terra-cotta planters were stacked on the shelves beside containers of plant food. Garden tools hung from hooks. Bags of soil and grass seed stood upright along one wall. But she saw almost none of it. Her focus was on the long row of soup cans and the big plastic jugs of water. She let the beam of her flashlight linger on the long, narrow canvas bag.

Tomorrow they would head north.

# FIFTY-TWO

A NN SAT UP, INSTANTLY ALERT. HER HEART THUDDED inside her chest, painfully hard. It was the dream she'd been having. She remembered snatches of it, Peter smiling and beckoning to her. *Come on, honey; the water's great.* She kept sloshing through the waves toward him, only to have him reappear, farther away each time. Then the tide grabbed her and slammed her under, and there he was, his hand gripping her arm, pulling her sputtering sunward.

But it had been a dream of frustration and loss, not one to send her heart hammering.

The girls lay sleeping soundly beside her, two narrow lumps, their hair spread across their pillows. What had awakened her? The baby. Quickly, she slid out of bed and padded over to where Jacob sprawled on his back, one tiny thumb in his mouth. Kneeling, she put a hand to his chest. It was an agonizingly long moment before she felt the gentle rise of his breath. Sagging with relief, she rocked back on her heels.

"Why can't Jake sleep with us?" Maddie had said.

"Because," Ann had replied, and Maddie had glanced up at her, surprised at her tone.

Pulling a sweatshirt over her head, she went to the bank of windows. The street lay blue with moonlight. Nothing moved that would have startled her awake. It must have been her own peculiar alarm clock once again chiming for no good reason, as if waking her every night now could compensate for the single time she'd let her attention wander.

She rested her forehead on the cool glass. Back in the corner of the yard stood Peter's tree, the small shape of his guardian constant beneath it. How would she persuade Barney to come with them in the morning? Maybe she'd bring along an old shirt of Peter's and let him adopt it as his own bed.

Then she heard it. Stealthy crunching steps from the floor below. She straightened, listening hard. Silence stretched all around her.

The slow creak of a door opening. Her heart leaped into her throat.

But then she was in the hallway, crouching down and peering through the slats of the railing. A beam of light played across the floor below, glinting off a thousand sparkling diamonds. Broken glass. That was how they'd gotten in.

The bright orb of a flashlight throbbed, a bulk of shadow passing behind it. She pressed back against the wall.

No way to call 911 for help. Even if she somehow managed to get outside, there'd be no neighbors to run to. She couldn't possibly leave the children alone with strangers in the house, not even for a moment. She was defenseless. No, not defenseless. But she couldn't do it. The thought terrified her.

They might stay downstairs. They might be content to steal her food and water and leave. All their supplies sat there, temptingly, in the bags she'd packed. They could just pick them up and sneak back out into the night. But what if they ventured up the stairs to look around?

The lock on the bedroom door was useless, not intended to withstand force.

Downstairs, floorboards creaked. There was the soft scuffle of furniture being moved. What were they doing? Why didn't they hurry and leave? She stood, indecisive. A kitchen cabinet banged open. There was no way out except past them. How many of them were there? It sounded like more than one. She was outnumbered. But not helpless.

She glanced over her shoulder into the shadowy bedroom.

Edging back, she quietly drew the door shut and pressed the metal button. The click sounded like thunder in the stillness, but there was no answering shout from below. It was almost worse to be in here, where she couldn't hear where they were. She had to be quick.

Backing up, gaze steady on the doorknob, she retreated to the closet. She tore her gaze away from the door and turned. Standing on the stool, she shoved aside the sweaters and reached for the long, slim object in the back. Food and water hadn't been the only things she'd found in Finn's storage building. She unzipped the canvas and slowly removed the gun.

Peter had once shown her how.

*This is a Remington 870 classic twelve-gauge shotgun. The gauge refers to barrel size and shell type. It's a pump-action.*

She had no idea what gauge this gun was, but she was pretty sure it was a shotgun. The same principles had to apply. She lifted the hamper lid and pulled the fabric liner away from its Velcro strips, cringing at the loud ripping noise. She felt around at the bottom for the heavy cardboard box.

*You slide the shells into the magazine. There's a little catch to prevent shells from sliding back out. You try it, Ann.*

She tilted the barrel up and looked down. Here was the opening where the shells went in. Here was the handle she pulled to insert them. There was an audible *ka-chuck* sound. Her heart leaped. She stopped and looked over her shoulder. All was silent.

Her palms were slippery with sweat. She wiped them on her sweatshirt. Now what? She wouldn't go downstairs after them. She wouldn't leave three sleeping children to go down and confront them. She'd stay up here. She'd wait for them to leave. Maybe they already had.

A sound floated up through the heat register. Laughter. They were still here, in the room below her, her kitchen, relaxed and happy as they went through her house and stole her children's food and water. There was another muffled laugh. They were growing brazen.

These were the very same kind of people who had killed Peter.

The door sprang open and she was in the hall, walking toward the head of the stairs. There was only one stairway. They wouldn't be able to get by her to the children upstairs.

Drawers opening. More footsteps. A low chuckle.

A man came out of the dining room, plastic bottle tipped to his mouth.

He spotted her at the same instant and froze. Then he lowered the bottle, water dripping down his bearded chin. He was dressed in bulky layers and wore a knit hat pulled low over his forehead.

"Get out of my house." Her voice sounded like a stranger's to her, low and uncertain. She could barely hear it over the hammering of her heart.

He swiped a forearm across his mouth. "Sorry, lady. Didn't know anyone was home."

"Get out."

Her arms trembled. She was terrified she was going to drop the shotgun. Her hands were so sweaty. She heard the clatter behind him, the rattle of dishes, cabinets banging open and closed.

"All right, all right. Calm down." He set the bottle on the dining room table behind him. It toppled over, dribbling three, maybe four, ounces' worth. What she measured for each child at mealtime.

Fury boiled up in her. She lifted the gun and braced it against her shoulder. "You think you can push us around?" Her voice was a growl. "Fuck you people."

"Come on." He patted the air. "Calm down. No one needs to get hurt."

*See the bead. That's how you aim. Come on, Ann, pay attention. It's not the most accurate. You have to hold the gun slightly below your target.*

She went down the stairs. He backed away and stumbled into the kitchen.

She glimpsed another shape turning behind him. She had the impression of height and skinniness. Just the two men, then. She stopped in the doorway. Any farther and she couldn't keep an eye on both of them. "Get out. Both of you."

His gaze shifted to a point behind Ann. "Hey, cutie. What's your name?"

"Mom?"

*Oh my God.*

"Kate, get back into bed," Ann said. "Right now."

Where was the second man? He was no longer standing there by the cabinets. She swung her gun and the bearded man thrust his hands up.

"You're not going to shoot me in front of Kate here, are you? You don't want your little girl seeing that."

"Where's your friend?" she hissed.

"Mom." Kate's voice trembled.

"I told you to go back to bed." *Where the hell was that other guy?*

"Mom, there's someone else here." Kate's voice, high with fear.

Footsteps shuffled in the front hall. They were coming at her from two directions.

"Kate, get behind me."

She turned so that her back and Kate were against the wall. The shadowy shape of a man slid across the dining room toward them. One in the kitchen, one in the dining room. The one in the kitchen was closer. And there was nothing standing between him and her, nothing to impede her aim.

*Shotgun barrels come in three sizes. Thirty-inch, twenty-eight-inch, twenty-six-inch, going from tighter to wider spread. This is a twenty-eight. Pretty good for hunting, but up close, it doesn't matter. Up close, you'll get your target.*

"You're shaking," he said. "Bet you've never shot someone before."

She gripped the barrel with her left hand and squinted at the little rectangular chip protruding from the barrel's tip. She lowered the muzzle to the man's crotch.

He took a step toward her. "Think you can do it?" he challenged softly. "Kill someone at close range?"

She heard Kate's panicked breath behind her.

She would shoot him. She would.

"I'm not even carrying a knife." He opened his jacket and showed her the empty pockets. "See?"

He was unarmed. Could she shoot an unarmed man?

Then he lunged. Kate shrieked.

Ann depressed the trigger and heard the empty click. *What?* She pressed the trigger again. Her heart dropped. Nothing.

Laughing, he reached over and grabbed the barrel. "Works better if you have the safety off."

Ann stared at him. Now he had both hands on the barrel and he was close. She could smell the perspiration and staleness of him. He grinned at her.

She leaned back, the metal biting into the flesh of her palm. If she could just reach the safety.

"Bill," said the other guy.

Dog tags jangled.

The bearded guy looked sideways. A brown furry blur leaped toward him, and he flung up an arm.

A deafening blast.

For Immediate Release

## FLU VACCINE
## TO BE DISTRIBUTED

---

Department of Health and Human Services Secretary Andrew Ward announced today the distribution of a vaccine for H5N1 influenza. The vaccine will be distributed to all fifty states and U.S. territories and possessions in doses according to individual population. Two doses per individual will be necessary.

Persons receiving the first innoculations will be those involved in the production, distribution, and administration of the vaccine; hospital staff, police officers, and emergency response personnel; key government officials; utility and communication workers; and those involved in food manufacturing and distribution. These persons are asked to report to their places of employment with proof of identification.

The second group to be vaccinated will be healthy individuals aged two to sixty-four years with no associated risk factors. These vaccinations will be given in hospital clinics. People are asked to bring photo identification.

*HHS Press Office*

# EPILOGUE

*D*AD ALWAYS SAID, THE MORE THINGS CHANGE, THE more they stay the same. As I get older, I begin to see the truth of that.

The phone rang as I was going out the door. I punched the button on the wall. "Mom?" At eight in the morning, smack-dab in the middle of her studio time? Something was up.

Her voice floated to me from the speaker. "Hi, honey."

I pictured her walking through the kitchen, speaking into that hopelessly ancient cordless phone. I had no idea how she even managed to get batteries for it. Maddie and I had tried to talk her into updating, but Mom said it was foolish to rely on electronics.

"I know you're on your way to work, Kate, but I wanted to make sure you haven't forgotten about Friday."

Like that would ever happen. I knew what Friday was—the one day we all made sure to get together, besides the holidays. "I'll be there. Frank's coming, too."

"Wonderful. We'll have a full house. Six o'clock okay?"

Mom lived an hour away. I'd have to leave the lab early. "Fine. Does Jacob need a ride?"

"Your uncle Mike's picking him up."

I felt a prick of alarm. "Are you sure that's a good idea?"

"Yes, of course. It's only a two-hour drive to campus, and it's early in the day."

"Still." The strangest things could set my uncle off. A song on the radio, the smell of sugar cookies baking.

"I know," Mom said. "But Mike will be careful. And he needs that time alone with Jake."

"All right." I had to stop the oldest-sister routine. Mom wouldn't take unnecessary risks. That was one thing you could say about her. That was one thing that never changed, no matter how everything else went topsy-turvy.

"Oh, and Kate. I've got a surprise for you."

I could hear the smile in her voice. "What kind of surprise?" She was selling the house, getting remarried? Moving away? But not all surprises were bad ones. I had to remember that.

"Oh, you'll find out." Her tone was playful.

Surprises meant change. I wasn't good with that. I thought of it as upheaval. I hoped this surprise was a minor one, one that would barely register on my Richter scale.

WE DIDN'T STAY AT THE CABIN LONG, ONLY TWO YEARS, LONG enough for Mom to be certain things had returned as much as they ever would to normal. But I always had the same reaction pulling into the driveway now as I'd had back then when we finally returned home. Trepidation.

The Guarnieris' old house was gone now, toppled timber by timber, brick by brick, into ruins. People had come and salvaged the bits. Nature reclaimed what little the scavengers left behind. Maddie and her friends called it the haunted house, and though I ridiculed them, I never liked to walk past it at night. I was always sure I glimpsed Jodi's ghost flitting between the tangled grass and gnarled tree trunks.

Other neighborhoods had their haunted houses, too, the surprising gaps where a house had once stood and been lost when the owners had gone. You'd be driving down a street or walking along the sidewalk and there before you would rise a mailbox to a house that no longer existed, or a front path that wandered nowhere.

Frank smiled encouragingly at me and swung open the car door. "Ready?"

Maddie was already there. I saw her blue car pulled off to one side, heard the whoops of laughter coming from the fenced yard. Barney the Third came bounding around the corner, barking and wagging his tail. Black-and-white where Barney the First had been cream and milk chocolate, but Mom had picked him out of all the others at the animal shelter, and she was right. He had the same spirit.

I bent down to rub his ears. He licked my face. Good old Barney was in there, somewhere.

Uncle Mike swung open the front door. "Katydid! Thought I heard your car pull in."

He stood there, the light shining behind him. The shape of his shoulders and the way he cocked his head . . . It all came flooding back, sucking my breath away with it. Dad. Mom saw it, too. I'd noticed her looking at him with an odd expression, the sudden sadness collapsing her face.

"Uncle Mike, you remember Frank."

"Sure, sure." He grinned at Frank with genuine affection and pounded him on the shoulder. Frank had that effect on people. He was quiet, but his constancy shone through. Frank was a person you knew instantly that you could rely on, a person you could trust, as much as you could trust anyone. "You're the fellow who's going to save the world."

"I hope to, sir. With your niece's help."

"Well, we sure need saving." Uncle Mike put his hand on my arm and drew me forward. "Don't just stand there, Katy. Come on in." He shut the door behind us and I felt a little dizzy.

I could never step into the front hall of this house without remembering walking in as a fifteen-year-old, smelling wet soot and ash, seeing the spray of black bullet holes across one wall, hearing the crunch of broken glass beneath my shoes.

Mom had sucked in her breath and Maddie had crowded in be-

hind me that day, an impossibly bright sunny morning. We'd followed Mom from room to room, our footsteps echoing across the
empty spaces. In the two years we'd been gone, people had broken
into our house, stolen things, burned furniture, ripped curtains
from the windows. Mom stood there for a silent moment, taking it
in. Her gaze alit on the wisp of a bird's nest dangling in the spokes
of the chandelier above. "Well, girls," she'd said. "It looks like we had
a few visitors while we were out."

Mom held the shotgun by her side. We'd grown used to seeing
her with it. We slept in the same room with it, and when we ventured into town, we always kept it hidden between the front seats.
But she'd needed it only that one time, that last night when I
thought she'd killed that man, and, worse, killed Barney.

Barney had been fine. The stranger hadn't fared as well.

He'd lain there groaning on the floor. Barney growled and
barked, snapping at him every time he rolled. I stood there pressed
against the wall, horrified by the sight of so much blood. In the
moonlight, it gleamed like black paint.

Mom had aimed the shotgun at the other man. "Take him and
get out," she'd said in the coldest voice I'd ever heard her use. The
sound of it frightened me. The tall skinny man had darted forward
out of the shadows and bent to drag his buddy away. The injured
man had howled with pain as his body bumped down the porch
stairs. I hated to admit it, but it'd felt good hearing him scream.

We never did find out what happened to either of them. Mom
stood there watching for long after they disappeared into the darkness, holding the gun, and then she turned to me.

"Kate," she said. "I need you to start loading the car."

Her voice had gone back to normal, but she had changed.

It took a while to rebuild, but Uncle Mike helped. He showed
up one day, scaring the daylights out of me when he loomed across
the threshold, but it turned out Mom had been in touch with him
over email. She'd come running down the stairs and threw her arms
around him. "I was hoping you'd come." She'd wept tears of joy and
kissed both his cheeks. "We're a family now," she'd told him. At the
time, I'd bristled, thinking she meant he completed our family.
Now, of course, I know that we completed his. His wife was gone,

and his son, Mikey, whom I only sort of remembered. He'd liked toy cars and playing in the sprinkler. Or maybe it was Jacob I was remembering. Memory could be funny that way.

"Everyone's out back," Uncle Mike said. "Jake went out for ice, but he'll be back any minute."

We walked through the kitchen. Here was where the biggest changes were. Mom had torn out all the wood flooring, installed heated pipes, and laid down terra-cotta tile. The old furniture was gone, replaced by leather and iron filigree pieces that one of her artist-colony friends had made. Brightly colored serapes hung alongside the windows. A fire blazed in the fireplace though it was a warm October evening. There were other changes, too, that were less visible—the huge generator in the garage, the solar panels on the roof.

Bowls of food sat on the kitchen table. A leafy salad, red and yellow apples, bunches of grapes. There was more food still on the counter. A platter of cheeses, a bowl of avocados, a bristling pineapple. I knew without looking that the pantry was filled top to bottom with boxes and cans. The refrigerator was stocked with milk and vegetables, the freezer neatly packed with meat.

My brother-in-law was pulling something from the oven. One of Mom's old pots, battered and black-bottomed. Maddie and I had bought her a new set a few Christmases ago, but we'd never seen her use it.

"Always amazes me that this thing still works." Alan shut the oven door with a bent knee. He came around the kitchen island and gave me a bear hug. His shirt was bright red, and his tie was yellow.

Exuberant as ever. And had he lost a little weight? Maddie was always after him to exercise. "Smells wonderful, Alan."

He pumped Frank's hand. "I'm trying out something new. Let me know what you think."

Uncle Mike lifted a glass from the counter. "How 'bout I get you two something to drink." He put a hand on the counter to steady himself. He'd already started, then.

Mom had told me he didn't used to drink. I hoped he'd been sober when he'd gone to pick up Jacob.

"Maybe later," I said, and Frank nodded.

Maddie was back by the swings with her kids. She waved, and I waved back. Mom was sitting on the patio, looking over at where the birch tree once stood. Lightning had taken it down a few years back. I showed up one afternoon to find Mom in the backyard, struggling to lift a burlapped sapling into its place. It had taken both of us and old Dr. Singh from across the street to manage to get it situated. Mom rose as we stepped out. Her embrace was full-on, the way it always was. She smelled the same, too—sun-baked cotton and roses.

I held her a moment longer than necessary. The gate creaked behind us.

"Katie!"

I stepped back and turned to see my little brother standing there, tall and tan and . . . beardless. "You got rid of that thing."

He rubbed his chin ruefully. "Yeah. It wasn't the girl magnet I figured it'd be." He dumped the bag of ice into the cooler by the table and came over to wrap his long arms around me. I stood on my tiptoes to hug him back.

Of course he wasn't William. He couldn't ever be William. He was blond, for one thing, and his eyes were brown. He had dimples that Maddie and I would kill for and a devilish streak that landed him in predicaments only a studious application of his charm could wrestle him from, but he shared our history and loved our mom just as much as we did. If that wasn't family, what was?

"Hey, Mom," he said. "I ran into Connie Nguyen at the store. She said to say hi."

Mom smiled. "She's a nice girl."

Jake rolled his eyes. "Yeah, yeah."

Mom was always trying to set him up.

"Mom says you've been behaving yourself this semester," I said. His grin widened. "Okay."

I groaned and punched him lightly on the biceps. "If Mom gets another call from the dean . . ."

Laughing, he shook Frank's hand. "Good to see you."

"Likewise." Frank smiled. "So, how's that film-editing course coming along?"

"Man, you should see the setup they've got." He pulled out a chair, and Frank sat down beside him, both of them immediately immersed in terms the rest of us had no prayer of following.

I rolled my eyes and Mom smiled. "Go say hi to your sister. I'll stay here and visit with my boys."

*My boys*, including Frank. See? Everyone liked him. That didn't seem to make it any easier.

Maddie perched on the rim of the sandbox, watching little Petey smack a shovel up and down. Kayla crouched by the swings, poking at something on the ground. She saw me and squealed. "Aunt Kate! Aunt Kate!"

"Hi, pumpkin." I waved and sat down beside my sister.

Maddie looked up at me and grinned. "She's made you a picture."

"Great." I kept a collection of Kayla's drawings. I teased her that they were my retirement plan. Kayla had recently graduated to oil pastel, Mom had told me, adding that it was an early medium for a five-year-old. The art genes had clearly passed down through the maternal line. Except for me. I could barely draw a stick figure.

"How's your gallery exhibit coming?" I said.

"We've got a critic from Chicago coming for the opening." Maddie dug her bare toes into the sand. Petey reached over and bashed her foot with the plastic shovel. "Ouch." She yanked her foot back and rubbed her ankle.

"Wow, he's gotten big."

"The doctor says he's ninety-fifth percentile in height."

"Takes after Alan, then. He sure didn't get it from our side of the family." We shared a smile.

Kayla called from the swings, "Give me a push, Aunt Kate!"

"Okay," I called back. "I'll be there in a minute."

She nodded and wriggled her bottom onto the wooden seat.

"Mom say anything about a surprise to you?" I asked Maddie.

She nodded. "I have a feeling it's more for you than for me or Jacob."

I groaned. "Not another big fat hint about setting a wedding date."

Maddie looked across the yard to the patio where Mom and Uncle Mike sat, laughing at something Jacob had just said. Frank was leaning back, arms crossed, looking pleased. "How are things between you two?" she asked.

"Good, I guess." Push and pull. I teetered on the wall, Humpty Dumpty–like. Sometimes it seemed so simple, like when Frank and I sat reading before a fire or when I watched him sleep. *Why not?* Then when I caught him looking at me that way, his heart so open and bare, I clenched deep inside and knew I'd gone as far as I could.

"He won't wait forever." My sister's voice was gentle.

I shrugged and looked down at the baby, trickling sand into a bucket, his plump face crinkled into a ferocious frown.

"Oh." Maddie's voice changed, and I looked up to see her wearing a puzzled expression.

"What?" I turned to follow her gaze back to the house.

"Kate! Maddie!" my mom called. "Someone's here to see you."

A figure stood beside her. I lifted my hand to shield my eyes and saw that it was a tall, slim woman.

"Who's that?" Maddie asked me in a low voice.

"Haven't a clue." But there was something familiar about her. Mom was walking toward us now, the woman striding alongside her. Seeing them together like that tore back the years and suddenly I was thirteen again and it was winter. I stood, disbelieving.

Gleaming black hair smoothed back, almond-shaped eyes, the hesitant smile. "You've grown up," she told us. Her vowels were soft, the consonants precise. That, too, was familiar. Her gaze lingered on me, moved to Maddie, returned to me. "You look so much like your father."

"Shazia," I said.

We were both astonished, I thought, when we threw out our arms. She smelled of patchouli, and her grip was strong. With a cry of delight, Maddie stepped into our embrace, too.

I finally pulled back. "Where have you been? Mom, how on earth did you find her?"

Mom smiled. "How else?"

Her nonprofit business, Family Finders.

The donations associated with that had saved us those early years while we waited for the university and the insurance company to come through. I'd been bemused at the sight of my technologically handicapped mother sitting for hours before the computer, helping people locate lost loved ones. But the real change had come later, when Mom started painting again. Turned out there was a pent-up demand for post-Pandemic art. I'd wandered down to the kitchen one morning to find Mom on the patio, standing before an easel I'd never seen before. The way she stood there holding her palette and leaning forward to dab paintbrush to canvas, re-creating the landscape before her in unbelievable beauty, made me realize I didn't really know her. Maybe that was when things changed between us. Like I'd said, not all surprises were bad.

"I have a son," Shazia said. "Ali." She glanced at Jacob, who was standing there beside my mom, watching us with curiosity. "He's about your age," she told him, then shook her head. "I still can't believe it. You're a man now."

"At least that's what he wants us to think," I said, teasing, and Jake grinned at me.

Mom put her hand on Shazia's arm. "I'd love to meet Ali."

Shazia nodded. "I'd like that, too. He's at the University of Cairo now. I brought pictures."

Later, Alan brought out skewers of shrimp and peppers, paella, butternut squash soup. Jacob and Uncle Mike wandered around lighting the torches. I watched Uncle Mike, but Jacob was taking care to make sure he held the flame steady. Candles were everywhere, flickering and bright, releasing the aromas of flowers and sandalwood, vanilla and spice.

The trees played hide-and-seek with the setting sun. Now a long ray of golden light, now a glimpse of magenta.

I went into the kitchen to help Mom with the cake. It was always the same kind, carrot with cream-cheese frosting. I used to protest.

"Why can't we have a real cake?" I would pout.

Wouldn't you know? Carrot cake was now my favorite, too.

"Has Shazia said anything to you about where she went that night?" I whispered, though there was no one in the room but us.

Mom shook her head. "She won't talk about it." She bumped the drawer closed with her hip and turned around with a stack of plates. "It's not that unusual."

I nodded. There were things we didn't talk about from that time, either.

"But I don't think she ever found him."

"Ali's father?"

"Maybe sometime she'll talk about it. We're just beginning to know each other again."

"Still, she should've written or called to let you know she was okay. She had to know you and Dad would be worried."

"I think she felt guilty."

"About what?"

"It was something your father mentioned. He'd gone into the lab to analyze the samples from that second die-off, and when he came home, he was puzzled about something. The number of samples from that first die-off didn't match. There was one missing. He wouldn't say, but I figured it out later, after he died."

Dad had found high-pathogenic H5. The university had kept his records. Years later, they'd granted me access. He'd been a thorough, careful scientist. "A missing sample? That doesn't sound like him."

"It wasn't. It was Shazia." Mom lifted her head and glanced out the window to the patio, where everyone sat ranged around the table. Then she looked back at me. "She must have dropped it or something. She came into our home knowing she'd been exposed."

"Really." I felt breathless with the news. I leaned against the counter and stared at her, sickened at the possibilities of what we had escaped.

"Thank God she didn't get sick. I actually hated her for a while. Then I realized she'd made the best choice she could. Infect our family of four or put an entire dorm full of people at risk? Your father would have done the same thing."

"She should have said something."

"Think how terrified she must have been, Kate. Twenty-six years old, thousands of miles from her family. She didn't know me. She didn't know what I'd do."

*What she'd done.* I remembered how Mom had stood planted against the door while Dad had slipped around and brought Jake in. I didn't say it aloud, but Mom nodded at me, her eyes shadowed, as though she knew exactly what I'd been thinking. On the whole, she seemed at peace with it now.

She poked candles into a colorful ring, gripping each one carefully between thumb and forefinger. She stirred her iced tea in the same way, as though she was gripping a stylus. Small constancies like this comforted me. Her love for me had never wavered. It was what pulled me through those years. I didn't know if I could ever become the woman she was.

"Frank asked me to marry him," I found myself saying.

She looked up at me. "And?"

I shook my head.

"Sweetheart—"

Tears clogged my throat. "Mom. I just can't."

My niece slid the door open. "Hurry, Grandma. The sun's setting."

It was time.

I carried the cake outside. Kayla climbed onto a box to blow out the candles. Alan ruffled her hair. Petey was asleep, curled in Maddie's arms. I set Uncle Mike's plate down before him, though it was no use. His chin had sunk into his chest and he was snoring a little. Later, Jacob and Frank could help carry him to the guest room.

THE NEXT MORNING, MY MOTHER PULLED ME INTO HER STUdio. The garage was gone, the space opened up and skylights installed. More change. My mom, whom I had fixed in my mind as one way, kept surprising me. Her earlier paintings were soft watercolors stacked in the closet behind us. Someday they would be Maddie's and Jacob's and mine, she'd told us, if we wanted them.

I did. But I loved the work she did now, big canvases of bright acrylic colors. In their whorls and lines and shapes, I saw courage, determination. Hope.

She reached into that closet now and drew down a wooden box. Setting it on her drafting table, she motioned me over. "I think you should look at this."

I'd never seen this box before. She lifted the lid, and I came closer.

Papers, dozens of them, brown-edged and lying neatly stacked. A luxury of paper. Interesting how people used to write everything down like that. But more precious still was the handwriting on them—a narrow slanted penmanship that crowded the margins and went off on arrowed tangents.

"What is this?"

"It's that book your father was working on. Some other things."

She had such tenderness in her voice. I'm glad Mom and Dad made up before he died. I remember waking that morning and finding them standing close together in the kitchen. I knew instantly that something had altered between them. Was it my teenage imagination that makes me think they'd never stopped loving each other, even during that awful year they were apart? I lifted the top sheet and tried to decipher the words.

The rise and fall of virus in feral birds and their water source has been going on for centuries, a complicated and beautiful process undulating with the fluid exchange of virus between feral and domestic birds.

And then it had flooded mankind and killed almost half the world's population. Estimates later set the American death toll at almost forty percent. One hundred and twenty million people. Some of them had been my friends. Many had been our neighbors. The world seemed much smaller afterward. The survivors moved more hesitantly. I remember how cars used to zoom past us on the freeway. I remember talking fast in that impatient, speedy teenage language. That fell away. Now people drive the speed limit. Now I pause before I speak. We all do.

I set that sheet aside, looked at the one below. *Sparrow Lake*, I read. I frowned, thinking. "That's where Dad found that first die-off."

"Yes, but I don't think of it like that. Your father loved that lake. It wasn't just a research site for him."

I recognized the handwriting on the next page. "I wrote this," I exclaimed. "Dad had me and Maddie write letters to all the neighbors. I was so bored, I didn't even complain about it."

Here was a piece of white paper folded into a square.

"I found that in your father's pants pocket."

I opened it and read the typed words. *Ann. Sorry to write out of the blue like this given how we left things, but I just had to. We made it to Virginia and I was online searching databases this morning. I'm so sorry to see that your mom and sister died. I know you were close to them. Maybe when this is all over, we can reconnect. We all miss you. Rachel*

I looked up at Mom. "Who's Rachel?" The name sounded vaguely familiar.

"The mother of one of Maddie's friends."

That's right. Hannah, Maddie's best friend when she was little.

"This is how you found out about Grandma and Aunt Beth?" I asked, and Mom nodded.

We never did learn what happened to my grandfather. My mother tried to find out, but he'd vanished, along with so many others. But Mom wouldn't give up looking. Just like with Shazia. Twenty years had passed, but she'd never stopped looking, not for one day.

I reached deeper into the box and found a yellowed newspaper clipping. I stared at my long-ago brother's face. William. "God, he looks like Petey!"

"I see it, too."

I stared down at the thin paper. My hand was shaking.

Mom put her hand on my arm. "You never let me talk to you about this."

"I barely remember him."

"You were three. You were a baby yourself."

I should have remembered. But I didn't. I didn't remember taking my pillow and climbing into my baby brother's crib. I had no memory at all of my mom coming into the room and grabbing William from beneath the pillow I'd accidentally pushed over him.

I didn't remember his still, silent little body. I didn't remember the social worker taking me away from my parents while the authorities sorted things out. My memory didn't start until two years later with a vague image of my kindergarten teacher and the way she wore her light-colored hair pulled back in a bun. But some part of me must have remembered. I'd never slept with a pillow since. When Jacob came along, I had a chance to do it differently. I had a chance to make up for what I'd done.

"Honey, Frank is a wonderful man," my mother said softly.

So, this was what this was about. I started to give her back the box, and Mom shook her head.

"I've held on to this stuff for so long. I don't need it to remember your father."

That night, I read everything twice through to brand it into my memory. Then I burned it, stirring the pile until there was nothing left but ash.

I BUMPED MY PICKUP DOWN THE NARROW RUTTED ROAD. RED pines pressed in close on both sides, filling the truck with their scent, then fell away to reveal a sandy beach and the calm gray water beyond. I pulled into the narrow clearing and turned off the engine. No sign of anyone or anything. I got out and slammed the cab door. A hawk wheeled overhead. I walked to the shore. The lake lapped the toes of my boots. Shadowy shapes nudged the leather, then darted away. Fish. They'd come back, too.

The boat slid easily into the water. When I was far enough from shore, I opened up the motor and went bouncing across the hard surface. My hair whipped my face. The hawk followed me, soaring out of sight, then reappearing. Dad taught me how to distinguish the owl from the gull, the eagle from the hawk. It was more than their profiles. Sometimes they were too far away to see. You had to watch their flight pattern. I'd learned that applied to people, too.

I turned the tiller and skipped along the shoreline to the right, imagining how this must have looked twenty years before. I bet there were more houses and at least one other boat on the water. Now there was just me and the hawk and the ghost of that old duck blind rising up on broken stilts, its body long gone, collapsed to the water below and sunk out of sight.

The lake curved around a finger of land spiky with fir trees. Slowing the boat, I turned to follow the shore and puttered into a small cove. This was where Dad came upon the teal. There was nothing remarkable to mark the site. It was just another puddle of water, a quiet shore, a fringe of trees. But Dad would have recognized this spot instantly. He'd been transformed by the experience. I remembered hearing him talking to Shazia in the den. I'd been coming in to ask for help with my homework and they sat there, their backs to me. *They'd gone there to die.* His words had stopped me in the doorway, made me take a cautious step back to listen unobserved.

*They must have flown around, looking for a secluded spot. Then they settled on the water and, one by one, rolled over.*

*Do you think it's high-path?* she asked.

The kind that spread rapidly and usually killed its victims.

He replied, *I hope not.*

I pictured it now, hundreds of the small, pretty birds with their little feet curled against their feathered bellies, their heads submerged, their beaks opened. Their bodies would have touched the shores and bumped against the sides of the boat.

I almost expected to see their ghosts hovering above the lake now, but there was nothing, just softly moving water and the reflection of the drifting clouds above. Dad would have had to come up close, bend over the side of the boat and haul in the first little body. I saw him capping tubes, returning the bird to the water, and retrieving the next one. There had been two fishermen with him that dawn. They would have assisted, bringing the boat around the bobbing mass, leaning over and fishing out the next corpse. They would have been troubled. They would have asked questions. Dad would have shaken his head and replied noncommittally, but he must have known right then.

It would have taken him a day to confirm his suspicions. Now all it took was one drop and a shake and Frank and I could know instantly what we'd found. Dad would be amazed. Would he be surprised, too, to learn that I'd taken up where he left off?

Switching off the ignition, I reached for the box I'd set on the bow and raised the lid. The breeze stirred the contents. I leaned over the gunwale and upended the box. The ashes flew out, caught by the wind and carried.

I thought I'd say yes to Frank. People changed. They grew up. They took chances.

In the distance, the hawk spun in languid circles above the tree tips. Fall was settling in. The days were growing cooler, and the trees were turning the colors of flame. In a week or two, the ducks would start their annual migration. *The more things change, the more they stay the same.* Dad used to say that. Like the things that keep us here.

Soon, it would be flu season again.

# ACKNOWLEDGMENTS

*I*T HAS BEEN A LONG JOURNEY. I AM MOST GRATEFUL TO those who hiked alongside me. My agent, Pam Ahearn, whose step never faltered, despite 9/11 and Hurricane Katrina, and everything in between. Thank you for finding my path. My sister, Liese, who nudged me back on course whenever I sat down to rub my feet and complain that I was going home. You could not have been more generous with your time, energy, and talent. My editor, Kate Miciak, who welcomed me at the end of the road, handed me a cool drink, and threw open the doors to dreams. Thank you for the many ways in which you breathed life into this novel. And those writers I am fortunate enough to consider friends: Nancy Gotter Gates, Loree Lough, and Robert Broomall. Thank you for believing in me.

As I climbed the steep banks of research, I stumbled across some boulders. Thanks to those who lifted aside these obstacles and cleared my way: Armando Hoet, DVM, PhD, who described the science behind an avian influenza pandemic and showed me how the virus would be handled in the lab; Richard Slemons, DVM, PhD, who explained why we should be watching the migratory bird population so closely; Frank Holtzhauer, PhD, who helped me understand how communities are preparing for a pandemic; Jay Schwarz, who gave me a glimpse into how the food industry is gearing up; and William Buckley, who took me on a virtual duck-hunting trip.

And whenever I stopped to check my bearings, my husband and children were right there to hold the compass and point to the stars. Tim, Jillian, Jonathon, and Jocelyn—without you, I would never have dared to dream.

# ABOUT THE AUTHOR

CARLA BUCKLEY was born in Washington, DC, and has called many places home since then. She currently resides in Ohio with her husband and three children. *The Things That Keep Us Here* is her first novel.

Visit the author's website at www.CarlaBuckley.com.

# ABOUT THE TYPE

The text of this book was set in Miller Text, designed by Matthew Carter. It is a "Scotch Roman" typeface, of a class of sturdy general-purpose types of Scottish origin widely popular in the United States in the last century. Released in 1997, Carter's Miller Text takes its inspiration from typefaces cut in the early nineteenth century by Richard Austin in London for use by foundries in Glasgow. Among the first typefaces designed specifically with newspapers in mind, Miller Text was immediately popular with modern newspapers and was chosen for the redesigned *Boston Globe* and, in the United Kingdom, *The Guardian*.